Praise for *Fire in the Stars*, book one of the Amanda Doucette Mysteries

★ Fradkin, a retired psychologist, creates well-drawn, complex characters, and she knows how to build tension and drama that hold readers to the end.
— *Publishers Weekly* (starred review)

Masterly … it's the wilderness that provides the story's passion.
— *Toronto Star*

The book also leaves one wishing to know more about Amanda Doucette. She is a plucky, adventurous, smart, caring person with an exciting, globetrotting career, and the potential for many great stories.
— *Ottawa Citizen*

If you want to get a real feel (and fear) of the woods, this is the book for you.
— *Globe and Mail*

A terrific read.
— *Winnipeg Free Press*

Believable, nuanced characters, and unpredictable plots.
— *Atlantic Books Today*

A simply riveting read from first page to last by a master of the genre.
— *Midwest Book Review*

Other Amanda Doucette Mysteries

Fire in the Stars

THE TRICKSTER'S LULLABY

An Amanda Doucette Mystery

Barbara
Fradkin

DUNDURN
TORONTO

Cover image: TREES: istock.com/Andrew_Mayovskyy; WOLF: 123RF.com/Eros Erika
Printer: Webcom

Library and Archives Canada Cataloguing in Publication

Fradkin, Barbara Fraser, 1947-, author
The trickster's lullaby / Barbara Fradkin.

(An Amanda Doucette mystery)
Issued in print and electronic formats.
ISBN 978-1-4597-3540-8 (softcover).--ISBN 978-1-4597-3541-5 (PDF).--
ISBN 978-1-4597-3542-2 (EPUB)

I. Title. II. Series: Fradkin, Barbara Fraser, 1947- . Amanda Doucette mystery.

PS8561.R233T75 2017 C813'.6 C2017-900031-4
C2017-900032-2

1 2 3 4 5 21 20 19 18 17

Conseil des Arts du Canada
Canada Council for the Arts

ONTARIO ARTS COUNCIL
CONSEIL DES ARTS DE L'ONTARIO
an Ontario government agency
un organisme du gouvernement de l'Ontario

We acknowledge the support of the **Canada Council for the Arts**, which last year invested $153 million to bring the arts to Canadians throughout the country, and the **Ontario Arts Council** for our publishing program. We also acknowledge the financial support of the **Government of Ontario**, through the **Ontario Book Publishing Tax Credit** and the **Ontario Media Development Corporation**, and the **Government of Canada.**

Nous remercions le **Conseil des arts du Canada** de son soutien. L'an dernier, le Conseil a investi 153 millions de dollars pour mettre de l'art dans la vie des Canadiennes et des Canadiens de tout le pays.

Printed and bound in Canada.

VISIT US AT

dundurn.com | @dundurnpress | dundurnpress | dundurnpress

Dundurn
3 Church Street, Suite 500
Toronto, Ontario, Canada
M5E 1M2

In memory of my mother,
Katharine Mary Gurd Currie

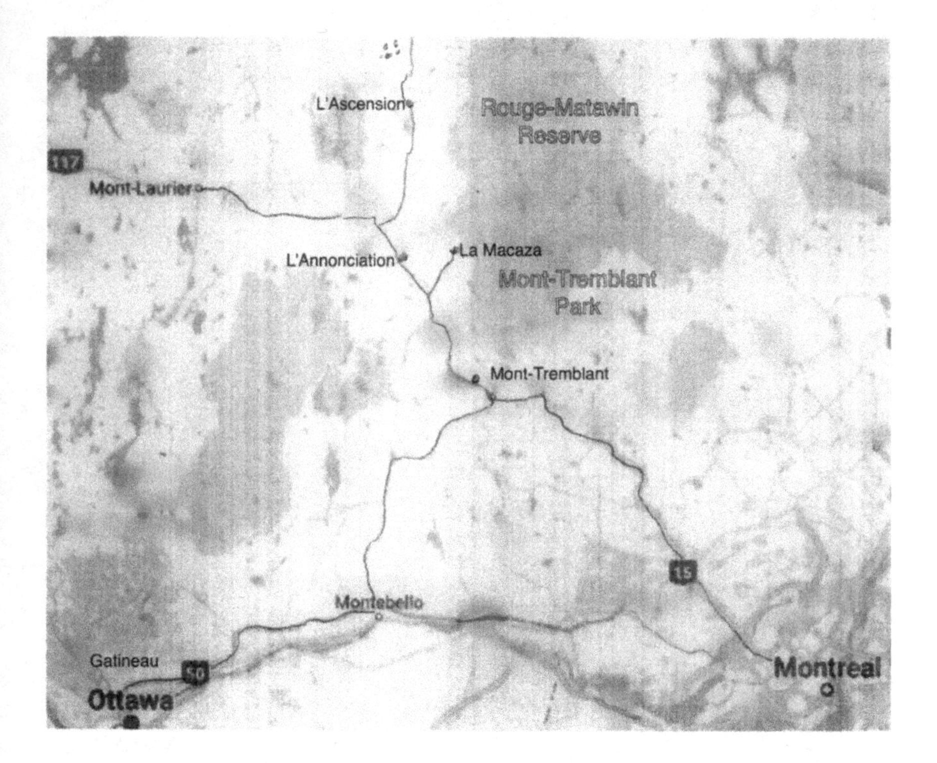
L'Ascension
Rouge-Matawin
Reserve
117
Mont-Laurier
L'Annonciation
La Macaza
Mont-Tremblant
Park
Mont-Tremblant
15
Montebello
Gatineau
50
Ottawa
Montreal

CHAPTER ONE

The stranger who hammered on the door made no apologies or introduction. She stood in the doorway, braced against the cold, her breath swirling in the frosty air.

"Amanda Doucette?" she demanded.

At her tone, Amanda stepped back warily. Dressed in a frayed navy parka with a red cloche hat and matching mittens, the woman looked harmless enough, but her tone held an edge of desperation. From her years in international aid work, Amanda knew desperation could make people dangerous. She was alone, and even in this quiet country cottage in the backwoods of Quebec, trouble could still find her.

"Are you Amanda Doucette?" the woman repeated, even more sharply this time. A faint Québécois inflection was now audible in her speech.

Amanda glanced at the small Honda parked in the snowy drive. The car had once been white, but layers of salt and rust gave it a mottled look. One headlight was broken and the fender was dented. Like its owner, it looked battered by time. She softened.

"Yes," she replied. "May I help you?" Kaylee had raced up to greet the visitor, and she held the dog back. She should have invited the woman in, but even after a year and a half, trust was still a fragile ally for her, fleeing at the first hint of threat. This cottage was her private sanctuary, hidden and unpublicized in order to keep curiosity-seekers at bay. Almost no one knew where it was.

"I want you to take my son on your trip."

Amanda's heart sank. This was a pressure she had not anticipated when Matthew Goderich persuaded her to launch her Fun for Families charity tour last September. The idea had been inspired: to take disadvantaged youth on adventure trips that provided a brief escape from the daily struggle of their lives. And Matthew, the consummate salesman, had promised her, "You plan the fun, I'll find the families." But the demand for the adventures had been huge and the selection of participants agonizing. So many needy children, so few spaces on her trips.

"Is he on the list?" she asked, hearing the echo of a thousand bureaucrats in her words.

"He should have been, but the college said he was unsuitable because of his past. An eighteen-year-old isn't allowed to make mistakes? To take a bad path?" Her fingers dug into Amanda's arm. "He's a good boy, but he needs encouragement to find his way. Please."

Amanda wrapped her baggy fleece tighter against the cold air blowing through the open doorway. She had two choices: either to turn the woman away with that dreaded bureaucratic sleight of hand — *I don't make the lists* — or to invite her in to tell her side of the story. Amanda had fought arbitrary bureaucratic obfuscation in the international aid world for too many years to have any stomach for it herself.

A smile of gratitude brightened the woman's face when Amanda invited her in. As she tugged off her boots, she apologized for the snow on the pine floorboards. "*Merci mille fois*," she said. "Just to have someone listen and not reject my son as a bad apple."

"What's his name?"

She looked up, her blonde curls falling across her eyes. The blonde was out of a bottle, and an inch of grey showed at the roots, but she'd done her best to style it. "I'm so sorry. I'm Ghyslaine Prevost, and he's Luc Prevost. Well, technically he's Luc Prevost-MacLean, but he doesn't like the MacLean part. Ever since his father left us. I don't like to upset him by insisting."

Amanda had seen the list of twelve youths who were enrolled in her Laurentian Extreme Adventure, and the son's name had not been on it. Nor had it been on the longer list of thirty submitted for consideration to Matthew Goderich by the youth counsellor working on the project.

International aid had been Amanda's life passion for more than ten years, and she had never planned to give it up, but Boko Haram's murderous rampage in the Nigerian village where she worked had changed all that. Nearly two hundred school children abducted or killed, their parents slaughtered, and their village torched. Two years later, the memories of that night and her own terrifying escape were still so vivid that she doubted she could ever go back overseas.

When, while in search of a new way forward last fall, she had conceived of Fun for Families, the premise had been simple: a charity fundraising tour centred around adventures in iconic settings across Canada. The adventures would nurture joy, a sense of belonging, but most of all hope for the future, for her as well as the families and youth involved.

However, the logistics of the projects were proving a whole lot more complicated than she'd imagined. Choosing the venues and the adventures had been easy — this one was six days of snowshoeing, cross-country skiing, and winter camping near the world-renowned Mont Tremblant National Park north of Montreal — but selecting the participants had not been. Ever since her fundraising idea had hit the news, partly because of Matthew's hyperactive talent for galvanizing social media, she had been flooded with suggestions for needy groups and pleas from parents to include their own children.

It had been Matthew's idea to insulate her from the crush — and the resulting resentments — by assuming that job. Although he claimed it allowed her to face the groups unencumbered by a history, she suspected he also saw her mental strength wavering. Matthew knew her better than anyone; since he was an overseas journalist, their paths had often crossed in remote trouble spots in the world. He had been in West Africa covering Boko Haram; he had seen her in the aftermath of the massacre, and again after her terrifying ordeal in the Newfoundland wilderness last fall. He knew her stress points, perhaps even better than she did.

When she ushered Ghyslaine into the main room, the woman perched on the edge of the sofa near the door like a bird poised for flight. Kaylee jumped up to nestle next to her, instinctively responding to the woman's distress. Amanda was about to call the dog away when the woman sank her fingers into Kaylee's silky red fur and smiled as if the dog had already performed her magic.

"What a cute little Golden Retriever," she said. "What's his name?"

"Kaylee," Amanda replied, warming immediately to the woman. At the mention of her name, the dog perked up. "It means party. She's actually a Nova Scotia Duck Tolling Retriever. They're sometimes called little Goldens with attitude."

The woman looked around the spartan cabin, furnished by Amanda's aunt from yard sales and flea markets. Aunt Jean had the good sense to spend the winter in Florida, which left her cottage and her car free for Amanda's use. The woman had no aesthetic sense, so the only criterion had been comfort, which suited Amanda just fine. It was to this simple, remote Laurentian refuge that she came to recover from Nigeria and later from Newfoundland. The only nods to modernity were the phone and the laptop open on the desk by the front window. From there, Amanda could see the road and always knew who was coming. A small measure of reassurance.

Her guest seemed to register the lack of opulence, for she lowered her head. "I'm sorry to disturb you. I know you are busy preparing for the trip, but Monsieur Zidane is not returning my calls. He says the decision is made. A violent criminal record, he said. That wasn't Luc, I told him, that was the drugs. Yes, Luc was angry and confused, but it was the drugs that made him desperate."

Drugs and violence, Amanda thought with dismay. "Has he done jail time?"

Perhaps the woman saw the door swinging shut, for her eyes hardened. "Yes, but—"

"How many times?"

"Only once—"

"How many convictions?"

"Why do you people only pay attention to the bad? Why did Luc take drugs? To feel happier, to forget his father's rejection. That's what's important. Luc needs some hope, some light to shine on his world."

"But the drugs, Madame Prevost—"

"Please. Ghyslaine. He's clean now. It is Monsieur Zidane himself who counselled him and said he's better. Then suddenly he turns his back on him, just when Luc was finally beginning to trust him. What kind of counsellor does that? It was like a rejection all over again!"

"How long has he been clean?"

"This time, three months."

This time. Not a promising sign. Amanda's heart felt heavy as she steeled herself to face the woman. "You understand that we cannot have any risk of drug use or violence on the trip? We will be five days in the wilderness, living together in tents, without Internet and out of touch with help. That's part of the experience."

"There are satellite phones," Ghyslaine said.

"Only for extreme emergencies. The group is fragile, Ghyslaine. I have to protect all of them, some recently arrived from violent homelands. There are other groups more suited to teens with your son's problems."

"Sure. Throw him in with a bunch of druggies and gangsters. That will help him find the path!"

At the woman's sharp tone, Kaylee raised her head and edged away. Amanda couldn't argue with the mother's logic, so she searched for a more positive answer. The woman, and her son, needed help, and Amanda hated to turn her back. Had always hated to turn her back on need.

Ghyslaine took her silence as refusal, for she stood up and reached for her parka. "Monsieur Zidane only cares about the Muslims. That's his loyalty. Luc is a spoiled little Canadian brat who doesn't know what real suffering is."

Amanda mentally reviewed the list of the twelve candidates. A small niggle of doubt took hold. Had Zidane deliberately turned his back on a needy young man, simply because the boy was Canadian? Amanda had found the counsellor guarded and inscrutable, but the college had been effusive in its praise of his work. It was true there were several Middle Eastern and North African names, but then the college Zidane worked at was in a largely immigrant area. That was one of the reasons she'd chosen it. Immigrant children struggled to feel at home in Canada and often had no chance to experience the rugged charms of their chosen land, which was so removed from the hot, crowded countries they had left behind.

Almost as if reading her mind, Ghyslaine glared at her. "And don't tell me that nonsense about exposing them to Canada. We live in the same shitty neighbourhood they do, see the same drug deals in the parks, the same girls selling themselves on the corner. We hear the same crying babies and smell the stench of their cooking. You need to care about Canadian kids, too. Does Luc have less right just because he was born here? Will you punish my son because his father cheated us and left us with nothing but black eyes and a mountain of debts?"

The images flashed before Amanda's eyes as she followed Ghyslaine to the door. Unknowingly, the woman had articulated the exact reasons Amanda had conceived of Fun for Families in the first place — to give beleaguered children a glimpse at hope.

"I'll talk to Mr. Goderich," she found herself saying. "I won't promise anything, but I'll see what he says."

Matthew Goderich tipped his chair and pushed his fedora back in frustration. His little office was housed in the minuscule bedroom of his third-floor walk-up in Lower Westmount, and it was overflowing its space. Three laptop computers sat on the desk, open to different news websites; books and papers threatened to explode from the bookcases lining the walls, and more papers were spread out on the unmade single bed. It looked like utter chaos, but Amanda suspected he knew the location and contents of every scrap of paper.

Matthew was a seasoned journalist used to setting up shop and reporting from the most inhospitable corners of the world. He was accustomed to travelling with only the essentials he could fit into a backpack, and this cluttered apartment, rented on a short-term sublet, was testament to how much he'd settled down since his return to Canada.

"Luc Prevost is a heap of trouble," he said.

She smiled indulgently at him. She loved Matthew, every crag and bulge in his rumpled, middle-aged body, but sometimes he tried too hard to run her life. All in the interests of protecting her, but that in itself was annoying. If he continued to treat her as broken, how would she ever feel whole? How often she wished that she'd never confided in him about her harrowing escape through the Nigerian countryside.

"Hear me out," she countered and went on to sketch out Ghyslaine's plea. Before she was even halfway through, Matthew snorted.

"Mothers! Their precious babies' bottoms are always as pink as the day they were born."

"But she has a point. If ever there was a young man in need of a glimpse beyond his walls, it's him."

"Him and hundreds of other punks running around our inner cities. Amanda, even you can't save the world, so we have to pick our battles. Zidane doesn't trust this kid. He says he's a misfit — surly and defensive when he's sober, explosive and paranoid when he's high. His drug of choice is cocaine, which makes him feel powerful and on top of the world. Putting him in with this group would be like tossing a match into a pile of kindling."

"Zidane dumped him as a client."

"And what does that tell you?"

"His mother says he's been clean for three months."

"And you and I know that's not nearly long enough. First hint of trouble — and there will be that, guaranteed — he'll be looking to score some coke on the slopes of Mont Tremblant itself." He leaned in, softening. "We've got twelve really nice kids who are all eager to do this. Why would Luc Prevost even want to? There's no fun in spending a week cut off from all his buddies, his music and Internet, and his evening hangouts, all to freeze his ass off in a tent listening to the wolves howl. No, this is his mother's agenda. Why drag a surly, antisocial kid into the middle of this trip?"

She twirled her coffee cup, steeling herself to take a sip. Matthew's coffee could power a jet engine, and she always wondered how he could consume ten cups of it without taking off into the ether. "Maybe precisely because he *is* surly and antisocial? And his mother says he does want to go."

"Like I said, mothers."

"The mother also says Zidane is favouring Muslims. You know I want a mixed group so people can learn about each other."

"And it is. Haitians, Asians, Africans. It's true it's about half Muslim, but that's the demographic Zidane works with, and I'd say the mother's comment gives us a glimpse at the subtext here. And where Luc gets the great big chip on his shoulder from."

To buy herself time, she ventured a cautious sip of her coffee, and her pulse thrummed even as the rich, smoky flavour hit her tongue. She knew Matthew was right on all points. The trip could be ruined for everyone if a disruptive, possibly criminal element was introduced. Yet she had embarked on this odyssey to help young people caught in the world of their adults' making. To help change the course of their lives.

"Let me talk to him. I'm not going to promise him anything, but I want to see for myself what kind of kid he is before I toss him aside as unsalvageable."

Amanda had been prepared for just about any version of Angry Young Man. A Goth rebel dressed in black, complete with clanking chains and black eye makeup. A burly, bearded gorilla covered in snake tattoos. Or a wisp of pale skin, sunken eyes, and trembling limbs. But the young man who hesitated at the entrance to the restaurant was none of these. Beneath the parka, he was impeccably dressed in black jeans and a turtleneck sweater that matched his eyes. His mother's eyes, sky-blue and fringed with dark lashes. He sported a neatly trimmed hipster beard and looked like someone from exclusive Lower Canada College, not some east-end tenement.

His gaze settled on her, and he smiled — an eager smile with a hint of shyness. She was dressed in her usual understated fashion of jeans and fleece, and with her soft, honey-coloured hair pulled into a ponytail and no makeup to mask her freckles, she suspected she looked more like a petite college co-ed than a burned-out thirty-something woman of the world. But he clearly knew what she looked like.

He hurried across the room and held out his hand. "Madame Doucette? Hi, I'm Luc." His fingers were chilled from the cold, but the handshake was firm. He pulled out the chair, slipped his parka over the back, and folded his gangly six-foot frame into it. Amanda wondered how much his mother had coached him and how long the façade would last. Or had he titrated his drugs just right?

"Nice to meet you, Luc. I hope you like Vietnamese." The restaurant had been a careful choice. She had considered a Lebanese place but decided the Muslim reference might be too obvious. Besides being ethnic, this place had excellent food and enough privacy to talk in confidence, but sufficient crowds to provide safety if he proved difficult.

"Never had it." He glanced around at the neighbouring tables, where most patrons were eating large bowls of soup. "Take-out pizza and St. Hubert barbequed chicken are my mother's go-to choices."

His English was flawless, reminding her of the neglected MacLean part of his heritage. Beneath his amiable manner thrummed an undercurrent of nerves. "Where do you live?" she asked to put him at ease.

He named a street she'd never heard of. "East end. It's tiny but my mother has made it nice. She's an artist, and she has an eye for that stuff."

"And how long have you been at Collège de La Salle?"

He hesitated. "I'm in my second year, with some … interruption. If I can get my grades up, I want to go to university next year."

"Studying what?"

"Not sure yet. The way my grades are right now, I'll probably just squeak into a general arts program at Concordia, but I like political science and history."

At least he was astute enough not to say Global Development, she thought wryly. Naming her own field of study would have been too obvious. "Quebec history?"

He shook his head. "Everybody wants to study that. It's kinda weird, but after all the stuff on TV — *The Tudors*, *Wolf Hall*, *Borgia* — sixteenth-century Europe seems really cool."

"The Renaissance?" She masked her surprise with an effort. Luc was proving to be nothing like the sullen misfit she'd been expecting.

His eyes crinkled. "Yeah, right. Rebirth. Seems more like hatred, murder plots, and religious wars, pretty much like today. That's what's so cool about history. We really haven't changed."

"Maybe that's just human nature. Goodness is hard to sustain."

"The world's not looking good right now, for sure. Well, you know that better than anybody."

Again she worked to hide her surprise. How much had this young man unearthed about her, and, more importantly, why? Deftly, she avoided the obvious attempt to dig up more and tossed the ball back into his court. "So how are your grades?"

His face fell. "I won't lie — they suck. I spent the last year — well, the last couple of years — AWOL from school and studies."

"How?"

He shifted in his chair. "Should we order?"

"I already have, their signature pho for both of us." She kept her eyes on him. "How?"

He looked nonplussed, affording a glimpse of the eighteen-year-old she'd been expecting. "You read my file?"

"Yes, but I want to hear your version."

He sighed. "Okay. When I got to CEGEP last year, I started hanging with the wrong crowd. None of my high school friends were going there, so I didn't know anybody. I admit it was stupid. I was pissed off. My father had just ditched us, sold the house out from under us, buried his money in offshore companies, and moved into Westmount with his new wife. So I was in a new home, new neighbourhood, new college, a bitter kid ripped from his roots. Some kids showed me how to make it all go away. First weed and E, but cocaine worked way better."

"How did you pay for the cocaine?"

He quivered, but his blue eyes met hers. "How do you think?"

"I can think of several ways."

"And I did them all." He looked away. "I don't like to think about it. It's like a black hole I'm trying hard not to fall back into."

"How did you turn things around?"

"Counselling."

"Zidane?"

He nodded. "First rehab in the group home, but when I went back to school, yeah, Zidane. The college had brought him in to try to help because they had quite a few kids struggling. CEGEP is like junior college, but it has one big problem. Throw a whole bunch of seventeen- and eighteen-year-olds together in a new place, and they're all going to be trying to find their place. There are lots of temptations to go wrong."

"So how did Zidane help you?"

"We talked about my father, who he was, who I wanted to be. We talked about respecting myself and taking care of my body ..." He flushed and lowered his lashes. "It's personal."

She debating asking him about his falling out with Zidane but chose to go to the heart of the issue. She threw the question casually into his embarrassment. "Are you clean?"

"Yes."

"How long?"

"Three months."

"A drop of sand in the life of a cocaine addict."

"I know, but I'm working on it. That's all I can do."

"How?" Out of the corner of her eye, she saw the waiter approaching with their pho. She gave him a barely perceptible shake of the head.

Luc was oblivious. He leaned in as if eager to convince her. "I don't take anything that might harm me. No alcohol, no drugs, no smoking, not even caffeine or sugar. I go to the gym every day. I'm trying to restore my body, and through it, my mind."

Amanda kept her expression impassive with an effort. Luc was following the same regime she had to expunge the horrors of Africa and to reassert control. As if by building her power and strength, she could vanquish the memory of helplessness. "Is that difficult?"

"Yes. But I also feel way better, and my grades are starting to improve. I've got five months to turn things around so I can get into Concordia. Or maybe even McGill."

"Is that why you want to go on this trip? So it looks good on your application?"

His nostrils flared, as if a foul odour had wafted through the room. He sat back. "I don't know what to say to that. I'm not playing a game. Yeah, I admit, going on this trip would look good. But really, my final grades are all that matter, and I know

I can get them up if I apply myself. But I want to..." He faltered and looked down at his hands, which were shaking slightly now. Emotion or addiction, she wondered.

"You want to what?"

"I want to prove I can do it. To myself. I know I've been weak and have failed just about every test of character thrown at me. I want to know ... do I have the guts to pass this one? Belief builds belief. I need that."

CHAPTER TWO

Fresh snow was falling, cloaking the trees in white. The road and ditches blurred together, so Amanda gripped the steering wheel tightly as she squinted ahead. Kaylee rode shotgun, turning her head constantly in eager anticipation. She didn't know where they were going, but Amanda knew she recognized the endless trees, frozen lakes, and rolling mountains. Country meant running free, off leash and snuffling the animal trails. Country meant adventure.

Amanda ruffled her ears. "Yes, it's an adventure, princess, but not today. We've got a big problem I need to fix. I promise a little walk, maybe even a short ski, but first I have to talk to some friends."

"Friends" was a bit of an exaggeration, since she'd only met Sebastien and Sylvie a few times, but that distinction was irrelevant to the dog. For Kaylee, friendship was easily earned; anyone who threw a ball for her was her friend for life. Other subtleties of character were unimportant.

Amanda's Laurentian Extreme Adventure was scheduled to launch in a week from a trailhead in the nature reserve just north of Mont Tremblant National Park. All the plans had been falling smoothly into place until two days ago, when the tour guides had phoned to say they were pulling out of the deal. It was the wife, Sylvie, who made the call, but she quickly became too incoherent with rage to explain, even in French. Her husband took over, calmer but firm.

"Nothing personal, Amanda. You know how much we admire what you're trying to do. It's a noble cause. But politics should have no part in it, especially repressive politics that insult women. We will not be part of that, and I will not turn my back while Sylvie is discriminated against."

Amanda had been in her aunt's cottage, finalizing her activities. "What are you talking about? What happened?"

"Monsieur Zidane phoned to ask if I could find a male guide to accompany us on the trip instead of Sylvie. When I asked the reason, he said that certain of the students were very conservative and would be uncomfortable sharing the camp and the group activities with a woman."

Amanda was astonished. "That makes no sense! There are boys and girls on the trip. In any case, Sylvie is a guide, not a chaperone. We already agreed she won't be sharing a tent with the boys."

"No, but they would be sharing lavatories—"

"There are no lavatories!"

"All the worse. And there is no privacy. They will need to seek Sylvie's help for teaching, for equipment."

"We have four adult leaders, Sebastien. Two male and two female. I'm female. Is he suddenly objecting to me, too?"

"I'm only telling you what he told me. Students have expressed concerns—"

"Students? Or their parents?"

"He said students," Sebastien said. "Under the circumstances, you understand my objections. If these students find it unacceptable to interact with a woman ..."

"Leave it with me, Sebastien. Don't quit just yet."

"The insult is already done, Amanda."

"I'll fix it."

Within five seconds she'd been on the phone to Matthew Goderich. "Matthew, what the hell? Who does Zidane think he is, telling our guides they can't send a woman? First he tries to veto Luc Prevost, and now he's going all fundamentalist?"

"Some of the parents threatened to pull their kids."

"Their kids are seventeen and eighteen years old! And the parents don't run the zoo. Neither does Zidane. You know me better than that. You know how hard I've always fought for tolerance and women's rights. Do you think I'd countenance this on one of my own trips? It goes against everything I'm trying to accomplish — to bring people together, to build respect, to lift children above their everyday constraints." She scowled out the cottage window. Flakes had begun to swirl down through the trees. "Why didn't you tell me about this?"

"There's been some big money donated—"

"Oh, no you don't!" She gripped the phone, forcing calm. "Fun for Families is not about raising money. Yes, I'm really happy I'm raising money for children's charities — and given the present jihadi mess, Roméo Dallaire's Child Soldier Initiative couldn't be a more perfect choice — but my first goal is to give young people an experience that will bring joy, hope, and with any luck a broader perspective on their future. This trip is supposed to bring immigrant youth from different parts of the world together."

"And it does," Matthew said. "But with that comes some old-fashioned cultural views. If we want to draw these kids in, we can't just run roughshod over those."

She rolled her eyes. The snow was falling more heavily, dancing in the porch light and promising fabulous snow conditions for their skiing adventure. "Including a woman on the trip is hardly running roughshod, Matthew. I'm being as respectful as I can, but we do comprise fifty percent of the population, and if any of the students are uncomfortable interacting with us, then perhaps this is not the trip for them."

"So you're saying you'd rather exclude the students?"

She sighed. She hated to exclude anyone who was eager to go, but she needed some basic level of mutual respect for the experience to be a success. She had seen too much embedded prejudice and tribalism in her years overseas to underestimate its destructive power. Not everyone could be reached, or turned, at least not in a week.

"Yes," she said. "Put it to Zidane. I'm sure he has some kids on the waiting list. Meanwhile I'll try to salvage our deal with Sylvie and Sebastien."

On the way up to the outfitter's chalet, Amanda ran through the various arguments in her mind. As she drove, the mountains grew taller and the little Laurentian towns fewer, tucked into hills criss-crossed with ski runs. Named after saints and dominated by tall, silver church spires, the towns reflected the powerful stranglehold the Catholic Church had once exerted over Quebec life. No more. Sylvie exemplified the modern Quebecker, defiantly and protectively secular. Amanda knew she couldn't ask her to be anything less.

The Laurentians were Montreal's playground. Part of the ancient ridge of the Appalachian range that twisted like a granite spine down the eastern side of North America, it was a lush paradise of sparkling mountain lakes in the summer and world-class ski resorts in the winter.

Mont Tremblant was the jewel in the crown, a legendary, almost three-thousand-foot-high monolith that loomed over lakes and rivers below. The Algonquin had named it Mountain of the Spirits, and it was believed whenever the spirits were disturbed, the mountain trembled. *The spirits should see it now*, Amanda thought wryly. In recent years it had been developed into an alpine-style resort with ninety-six downhill runs as well as cross-country trails, restaurants, and lavish mountain lodges. Condos, time-shares, golf courses, and boutiques had sprouted up, dwarfing the bucolic little Quebec village that had nestled in the valley for centuries.

After years spent working in crowded, hot countries, Amanda had come to cherish the wide-open spaces, clean rivers, and lush green of her native land, and when she went searching for the perfect location for her next charity adventure, she had been dismayed by the clutter and traffic of the Laurentians.

Until she got to know Sylvie and Sebastien Laroque. They had introduced themselves back in November on a ferry in the middle of the St. Lawrence River. She had been on a promotional motorcycle tour, crossing the river into Quebec from New Brunswick in search of her next adventure location. The first had been a modest, experimental affair, a weekend in Nova Scotia's Cape Breton Highlands with some children of unemployed local coal miners. The success of that weekend — and Matthew's incessant badgering — had encouraged her to plan the next one while she was still in the public eye.

She was standing on the deck of the ferry, considering the stunning geography of the Gaspé at the mouth of the St. Lawrence, when a young couple rushed up to her.

"Amanda Doucette!" they exclaimed. "Your green motorcycle and your red dog — we'd know you anywhere! Let us buy you a drink when we land in Godbout."

The drink had become dinner, with the wine and the jumbled bilingual conversation flowing freely. When Amanda mentioned she was thinking of a winter adventure based in the Gaspé, their eyes widened.

"*Ben non!* In Quebec it must be Mont Tremblant. Nothing is as spectacular, as vast, as challenging. It offers any winter activity you wish. And only a hundred kilometres from Montreal. Sebastien and I run a private tour company near there, and we would be honoured!"

Amanda was dubious. Her Aunt Jean had told her horror stories of the resort's development. "But it's full of tourists, golf courses, and luxury condos," she replied.

"Not everywhere," Sylvie said. Her English, only lightly accented, was better than her husband's, so she did most of the talking. "The national park is huge, and most of the northern part is wild. And there's a big wildlife reserve beside it. I promise you will never see a BMW or a spa where we take you. We can offer winter camping, cross-country skiing, dog sledding, and as a bonus, Sebastien and I are both gourmet cooks on a camp stove."

And so the partnership had begun. Amanda had visited their outfitter's store outside the little village of La Macaza and had hiked some of the wilderness just as the first snow was falling. She was instantly in love. The area was a delicate lace of lakes and creeks that wove their way around forested hills and tumbled over rocky outcrops. Matthew was skeptical of Sylvie and Sebastien's motives, suspecting they saw her as a goldmine of publicity for their fledgling business. But they insisted they were committed to the ideals of her project.

Until now Amanda had harboured her own lingering doubts, but their abrupt cancelling of the deal had dispelled all doubt. Sebastien and Sylvie had far more to lose from pulling out than she did, no matter how righteous a spin they put on it.

Sylvie and Sebastien's home business was in a century-old farmhouse that had once been a modest hotel. They had bought the old building for a song two years earlier, after it had been shuttered for several years by the larger, more modern lodges surrounding Mont Tremblant resort. Away from the throngs of the tourist hub, Sylvie and Sebastien had rebuilt it as an intimate eco-tour company for private, customized adventures.

"We can do anything!" Sylvie had assured her on that first visit as she ladled out a divine venison stew that was testament to her gourmet skills. The walls of the cosy farm kitchen were covered with Montreal Canadiens hockey paraphernalia, from signed hockey jerseys to old skates and hockey sticks. Sylvie's eyes were dancing with the confidence of her youth. "Sebastien and I grew up in these mountains. We know every river and trail. Snowshoe, ski nordique, and even we can do dog sledding!"

"I am taking inner city Montreal kids into the wilderness," Amanda had said. "They want to try everything, but they are novices. I want them to feel the joy and accomplishment of new experiences, but safely. They don't need to cover thirty kilometres a day on skis; I just want them to discover the thrill of gliding like a feather over snow. And some of them are from cultures that are afraid of dogs, so we should avoid dog sledding. I am bringing Kaylee, but any more than that might be too stressful. I want them to bond together, laugh, share, and fall a little bit in love with this land."

"*Pas d'problème*. We can do three kilometres a day if you wish. Leave the idea with me, and I will make it perfect."

And she had. She had designed a five-day excursion into the backcountry of the Rouge-Matawin wildlife reserve north of Mont Tremblant that included a four-kilometre snowshoe trek in and four nights at a base camp nestled in the woods on the edge of a small frozen lake. She had pulled strings and cajoled officials to obtain special permits for camping and ice fishing, she had worked out an exquisite menu of local cuisine, all to be cooked on the woodstove, and she had even agreed to forego her signature homemade French Canadian farmer's pork sausage and tourtière out of respect for Muslim food restrictions. She'd been brimming with ideas and excitement about the trip.

But this time, when she opened the shop door to let Amanda and Kaylee in, there was no smile and no light in her eyes. "Thank you for supporting me," she said.

"Zidane has agreed to your coming," Amanda said. "Most of the students have agreed or persuaded their parents."

"It should not have been necessary."

Amanda tried for a middle road. "There are a lot of complexities facing new Canadians, who are not just new to this land, but to our culture and our way of doing things. It can be scary for the kids and their parents."

"I know that. But these are Canadian values. They are my values. The clients don't get to negotiate them." She turned to lead Amanda through the store to the alcove office at the back, where her husband was working on the computer. He stopped to ruffle Kaylee's ears.

"At least we sorted it out," Amanda said. "The families are fine as long as both of you are coming. The girls will stay with you in one tent and the boys in two tents with Sebastien and Zidane."

When Sebastien gave her a sad smile, she realized it was not sorted out. Sylvie crossed her arms over her chest in defiance. "I've thought a lot about it, and I don't believe I can work with that man."

"Zidane?"

"*Oui.* That he would ask me such a thing shows his prejudices and how little he understands equality."

"Believe me, he is light years ahead of much of the world," Amanda replied. "We have come to our equality and our tolerance of differences through centuries of adjustment. Less than a hundred years ago, our own Protestant and Catholic ancestors brawled in the village streets all across Ontario and Quebec. We are not so far removed. Bigotry is still alive and well today, even with our privileged Canadian values."

"All the more reason to stand up for them," Sylvie replied. "It's so fragile — this equality and respect — that we must protect it. Probably I would kill the guy before the second day."

"She would," Sebastien piped up, bringing welcome laughter.

"But quitting now means those prejudices have won," Amanda said. "Standing up to him, showing him who you are and what you believe — that's the way to protect that equality." Uncertainly flitted across Sylvie's face, and Amanda pressed her point. "You've worked so hard, Sylvie. You have designed a wonderful program. And the menu! Don't throw it all away over … over …"

"A principle?"

Amanda laughed. "I was going to say a man."

Sylvie looked at her, her lips twitching in spite of herself. In the background, Sebastien chuckled. Finally Sylvie threw up her hands.

"*Bon!* The food is already ordered. We go. But I will not keep my mouth shut. Don't expect me to be a — a mouse to keep the peace. I will teach that man a thing or two about a woman's place!"

CHAPTER THREE

What have I got myself into? Amanda wondered as she watched the wide-eyed group tumble out of the van, wrestling duffel bags and clutching impossibly large parkas against the sudden cold. They looked like a mini United Nations — from the Congo, Somalia, Vietnam, Syria, Iraq, Iran, and Haiti — all eager to share an adventure. Their boots were still shiny new, and some of their mitts still had price tags attached. Most of the gear had been rented or bought with donations, far warmer than they would ever need as they dashed between the subway and the college buildings in Montreal.

Luc brought up the rear, descending the steps as if uncertain of his welcome. He had ditched his Lower Canada College look for backcountry bumpkin, wearing a rumpled parka, Montreal Canadiens toque, and rough woollen scarf. *Trying to fit in?* she wondered. Or trying to be inconspicuous?

The youth all spoke little as they took in the scene: the wide, windswept Lac Macaza, the brooding, snow-laden spruce, the jumble of rough-hewn log outbuildings, and cradled in the middle, Sylvie and Sebastien's two-storey farmhouse with its antique dogsled propped by the door and the snowshoes hanging on the whitewashed clapboard wall. As if belying the studied pioneer look, a satellite protruded from the stovepipes on the roof and a collection of snowmobiles was lined up at the side of the house. Amanda saw a flicker of relief cross the faces of her young charges as they spotted the satellite. Civilization after all.

Last off the van was the youth counsellor, Zidane, who'd been collecting the forgotten scarves and mittens the students left on the seats. Amanda brushed away a niggle of dislike. According to Matthew's background check, the man had his own personal story of hardship and was passionately devoted to his students.

He was a small, slight man of Algerian origin who spoke French impeccably and English with only a trace of an accent. After spending several unsettling years in a refugee camp in the Sahara Desert, he'd immigrated in his early teens to Montreal, where he'd studied anthropology and psychology. His facility with several languages, including Arabic and Somali, as well as his experience in both new and old worlds, made him an excellent choice for youth counsellor in Montreal's eclectic inner city. Having never married or had children of his own, his students were his life. His bearing was unfailingly polite and dignified, but reserved, as if he held his true nature in check.

Now his face was inscrutable as Sylvie approached and acknowledged him with a curt nod before turning on the enthusiasm for the students. As she welcomed each in turn, there was a glint of challenge in her gaze, but to Amanda's relief, she did not offer to shake their hands, opting instead to place her hand on her heart in a more modest greeting. Amanda studied the faces of the students. Some hesitated, perhaps shy or uncertain about proper etiquette, but all returned the gesture.

Amanda had met them all the week before during an orientation session in Montreal, and she'd been impressed with their questions and excitement. In that familiar campus meeting room, they had been outgoing and ready to explore. Here, the reality of endless snow, unrelenting cold, and the challenge of campfires, snow shelters, and primitive bucket latrines seemed to overwhelm them. Several looked ready to climb back into the van and retreat to the city.

As Sylvie led them all inside, Amanda counted heads. Nine. Six boys and three girls. She frowned as she mentally reviewed the list. Two girls and one boy were missing.

She walked over to Zidane as he unloaded gear from the van. "Who's missing?"

He climbed down from the van and locked it. "The two Nigerian girls and the Tunisian boy. They got cold feet." A flicker of humour crossed his impassive face. "And Faisel al-Karim withdrew at the last minute."

Amanda conjured up a blurry memory of dark, serious eyes and a baby face with a wisp of black beard. "I'm sorry to hear that. He seemed eager to come. Parental concern?"

Zidane shrugged. "I didn't speak to him. I received his email two days ago. But I was able to find one replacement." He gestured to a shivering young man who was struggling to zip up his unfamiliar parka against the cold. "Hassan is from Syria. We will be in three tents, two male and one female."

To recreate the traditional winter camping experience, Sylvie and Sebastien had wanted a communal tent heated by a woodstove in the centre, but even they quickly conceded that mixing the sexes would be ill-advised. The compromise had been smaller tents segregated by gender, as well as an individual tent for Amanda and Kaylee. Earlier in the week, Sylvie and Sebastien had transported most of the heavy gear, including tents and stoves, to the base camp by snowmobile. When the group embarked on their adventure the next morning, they would only be hauling lightweight toboggans with their personal gear and food.

The rest of the day was spent fitting the students with traditional handmade moccasins and snowshoes. Laughter and wails of frustration filled the yard as they all learned the rudiments of technique. By nightfall, everyone was grateful to crawl into warm sleeping bags in the rough-plank bedrooms of the farmhouse. A soft snow dusted the night, but the next morning dawned bright and cold.

Sylvie and Sebastien had their own snowmobiles, but they'd enlisted additional help from local villagers to get the group to the trailhead. While the gear was being loaded into the snowmobile trailers, Amanda made one last check of the weather on her cellphone. The forecast for the Mont Tremblant region over the next five days was crisp and mostly sunny, with a few flurries. In short, perfect. But in February, anything was possible.

Sylvie and Sebastien would carry a satellite phone for emergencies, but beyond that they would all be out of cellphone range for most of the trip. Unplugging the students from their global electronic tether was to be part of the experience.

Once everything was lashed on and ready to go, Sebastien squinted into the blue sky. "*Parfait.* Maybe some snow will come tomorrow, but the condition are good, and I just make a new trail two days ago."

Soon the air was filled with the roar of engines and the smell of gasoline as the convoy of snowmobiles set off single-file down the trail. After nearly half an hour of snaking through the bush, they arrived at the drop-off point, where they dumped the gear in the snow beside the toboggans. Within minutes the whine of retreating snowmobiles faded into the forest, leaving thirteen trekkers standing in a silent circle, aware for the first time of how alone they were. The morning sun sparkled on the snowy spruce boughs, casting a magical, crystalline light. Up ahead stretched a wide expanse of snow-covered lake.

"Are there bears?" asked one of the girls in a hushed voice, as if the very sound might rouse their interest. Over her traditional dress of long skirt and hijab she was swaddled in parka and toque, with only her large almond eyes showing, but Amanda recognized her as Yasmina, who had argued fiercely with her protective parents for the right to come on the trip. Over roast chicken the night before, Yasmina had announced that she wanted to be a human rights lawyer and was waiting for acceptance to McGill University. Both her English and French were almost perfect. A bright, spirited girl who no doubt presented a constant challenge for her parents.

Sylvie smiled at her now. "The bears are hibernating. Probably the only animals we will see are more scared of us than we are of them. Deer, moose, foxes ..."

"Wolves?" Yasmina countered.

"Possibly. But wolves will stay in the distance."

Around the group, eyes widened. "In any case," Amanda interjected cheerfully, "Kaylee will warn us if anything comes near."

Kaylee was romping through the nearby woods, snuffling the animal tracks. The group eyed her dubiously. A few of them had come up to pat her, and Jean-Charles, a gentle giant from Haiti, was tossing sticks for her, but most kept a wary distance. In many parts of the world, dogs are viewed with fear or distaste, but Amanda hoped that over the week, Kaylee's exuberance would win most of their hearts.

The soft blanket of snow was already criss-crossed with fresh animal tracks. Sebastien paused to point out the large, deep impressions. "Deer," he said.

Sylvie shot him a look. "No, that's—"

"Deer," he repeated, and she took the hint. *Was she about to say wolf?* Amanda wondered.

Two days earlier, Sylvie and Sebastien had come out to check the thickness of the ice on the lake for safety. The area around the test hole was trampled with snowshoes and animal tracks, but farther out, the snow was pristine. It took over an hour to get all the toboggans loaded and the snowshoes strapped on. In the preceding weeks, Zidane had taken most of the students to Mount Royal Park in the heart of Montreal to teach them some snowshoeing basics, but the packed, icy trails of Mont Royal bore little resemblance to the deep, fluffy snow that now enveloped them at each step.

The group floundered and laughed as Sylvie and Sebastien eased the toboggans down the short hill onto the lake, where Sebastien paused for a lesson on ice safety. He carried a pole, which he used to test the feel of the ice.

"Ice on the lake should be at least thirty centimetres thick by February, but if the water is near a creek or an underwater spring, it can be much thinner. It looks safe but suddenly, poof, you are in the water."

The students stepped warily off the lake.

"If you fall through, lie with your arms and legs flat out to spread your weight, and pull yourself forward onto the ice. Don't panic or kick. Who can swim?"

A couple of tentative hands went up.

"If the water is deep, try to take your parka and your boots off. In this water, your muscle coordination disappears within five minutes, so breathe slowly and head to shore."

Amanda watched as Hassan and the Vietnamese girl, Kim-ly, backed even farther from the lake. "That's why Sebastien is testing the ice before we walk," she said gaily. "And if you do fall through, we will all be here to help you."

Eventually, after reviewing a few more safety features, the caravan set off single file across the lake, with Sebastien breaking trail in the lead and Sylvie bringing up the rear to keep an eye on the stragglers. The trek across the lake was only two kilometres, but it felt like ten as the students tripped and thrashed about in the deep snow. By the time they reached the far end of the lake and hauled the toboggans up the slope onto a sheltered point for lunch, they collapsed in a panting, sweaty heap. Only Kaylee seemed to have energy to spare, eagerly bringing sticks to anyone willing to throw them.

Sebastien's announcement that they still had another lake to cross was met with moans of protest. But Kaylee's entertaining antics, along with hot soup and sandwiches, revived them enough to get them back on the trail.

As the afternoon wore on, Amanda's toboggan felt heavier and heavier, and even Kaylee abandoned her forays into the deep snow and fell into line on the packed trail behind her. Sun slipped toward the distant treetops behind them and their long shadows danced on the lake ahead. Amanda was grateful that Sebastien and Sylvie had planned for a base camp only four kilometres into the bush, from which daily excursions and activities would be run. Four kilometres was just far enough away from the snowmobile trail to give the illusion of true wilderness.

By the time they dragged the toboggans up the final steep hill and down into the natural, protected valley where the rest of the gear awaited them, the sun was deep in the trees and even Amanda had barely an ounce of strength left. The students kicked off their snowshoes, peeled off sweaty toques and mitts, and sank down on their packs, too tired even for complaint.

"No rest yet!" Sylvie cried, dragging a large bundle into the middle of the clearing. "We need to set up camp!"

Muted groans greeted her, and no one moved. "Unless you want to sleep under the stars and go without dinner, we need to get the tents up and the stoves going."

Only two youths struggled to their feet — Luc and Kalifa, who as a competitive basketball player was the tallest and strongest of the girls.

Sylvie frowned and continued to snap orders. "We need teams of two students and one adult." She signalled to the students and ticked off items on her fingers. "You cut firewood, you collect fir boughs for the floors of the tents, you go with Sebastien to dig a hole to bring water from the lake, and you stay with me to put up the tents. Then I can cook!"

A few more dragged themselves to their feet, but Hassan and Jean-Charles merely plunged their faces into their hands. Sebastien smiled as he handed out snacks and hot tea. "She's the slave driver, I'm the nice guy. Take five minutes and then we'll get started. If we all pitch in, we can do it fast."

The rest of the group reluctantly joined in, following Sylvie's lead to prepare the campsite. As they worked, their fatigue and shyness melted away, and by the time the tents were up and warmth from the stoves was seeping into the corners, they were laughing and chatting again. Darkness had set in by the time Sylvie finally had a huge pot of chili bubbling on the stove in the girls' tent. Afterward, they all clustered around the woodstove with their jackets, mitts, and moccasins hanging from the ceiling to dry, while Sylvie taught them French Canadian folk songs, accompanied by Sebastien on the mouth organ.

"You don't want to hear me sing," he quipped with a broad grin.

Soon they all crawled away to their tents. In the darkness of the tent she shared only with Kaylee, Amanda could hear them whispering and giggling. The three girls, Somali, Vietnamese, and Iraqi, shared the cook tent with Sylvie and spoke French because it was the most comfortable language between them, but in one of the boys' tents she heard snatches of Arabic. The three Arab youths had joined together with Zidane in one tent, leaving Luc Prevost with the Haitian and Congolese in the other with Sebastien. They appeared to be speaking some compromise of French dialects, of which she could barely decipher a word.

Not too happy about the division of the students, Amanda resolved to discuss the issue with Zidane in the morning. Perhaps the boys should rotate sleeping arrangements to encourage bonding. Surely here, more than in the hustle and pressure of the city, these kids would find common ground, transcending race and religion and history.

Finally the whispering stopped, and the deep silence of the night settled in, punctuated only by soft snoring. Amanda pulled her toque down tight and huddled in her thick down sleeping bag with Kaylee, feeling the dog's slow, deep breathing. Her tent had a tiny woodstove, but she had let the fire go out. Even the smallest flicker of flame still evoked frightening memories, and although her rational mind told her she was in the peaceful Quebec wilderness, not in a burning Nigerian village, she couldn't have slowed the racing of her heart and the panicked flutter of her thoughts. With this thick down sleeping bag and her dog's warmth, she should be warm enough.

She awoke with a start in the pitch black. Kaylee was growling. Struggling to extricate herself from her sleeping bag, which she had drawn up to her nose, Amanda peered into the darkness. Only the softest glimmer of moonlight penetrated the tent, enough to reveal the faint smudge of Kaylee pawing at the front flap of the tent.

Amanda grabbed her collar and clamped her hand over her muzzle so as not to wake and frighten the others. She sifted the night silence for the howl of wolves or the snuffle of smaller animals. To be safe from animals, Sylvie and Sebastien had secured all the food in airtight barrels, but the curious forest creatures could be checking them out.

She heard nothing. Kaylee growled again, her body rigid as she fought to free herself from Amanda's grip. From the tents next door came the deep rhythmic snores of the men, oblivious to the disturbance, no doubt used to sleeping without one ear tuned for the sounds of threat. *Will I ever be free of Africa?* Amanda wondered.

She thought she heard the faint crunch of snow. Kaylee managed one short bark. The crunching stopped. Amanda held her breath and listened. Silence, then more soft crunches, fading away, leaving nothing but the sibilant whisper of wind. *Just someone going to the latrine*, she thought, shaking her head at her own fear. At worst an animal hoping for a snack. *We're in their world here; we're the threat.*

But the fear lingered, and in the morning Amanda walked around the edge of the campsite, looking for fresh animal tracks in the snow. There were several, but all too small to have made that much noise. But in the forest just beyond their makeshift latrine, she found another set of prints — huge oval imprints through the snow and up the steep hill. Not a bear, not a cougar, not a moose.

Snowshoes.

The first shafts of sun were barely peeking through the trees when the students began to stumble from their tents. Zidane led a small group to the edge of the compound, where Amanda could hear the soft chant of morning prayers. They scurried back within minutes, stiff and shivering. Amanda estimated the temperature to be about minus fifteen degrees Celsius — hardly conducive to the pious cleansing and prayer the Qur'an had in mind.

Sylvie had stoked the fire in the girls' tent and had a large pot of sweet, hot coffee brewing on the stove. She stirred oatmeal in another pot. The students all huddled gratefully around the woodstove, wrapping their cups in chilled hands and speaking little as they slowly came awake. Amanda studied their faces for clues to the nocturnal wanderer. Averted eyes, fidgety hands. Had one of them strapped on snowshoes and gone for a midnight tramp?

The three girls were leaning against each other for warmth, with the Vietnamese girl in the middle. Kim-ly barely topped five feet and ninety pounds, so Kalifa, the Somali girl, had put an arm around her. Yasmina sat slightly apart, watching Sylvie stir dried apple and maple syrup into the oatmeal.

Luc Prevost was with his two tent mates, but they were all staring groggily into their coffees as if trying to revive. So far Luc had not proved the disruptive force Zidane had warned her of. He had managed the four-kilometre trek with ease, displaying a facility on snowshoes that the others had not, and he'd pitched in to set up camp the night before, even volunteering to forage the woods for extra firewood. This morning he had helped his tent mate Jean-Charles apply ointment to a blister on his heel.

The three Arab boys were hunched together at one side of the tent with Zidane, who was muttering the occasional instruction in Arabic. Amanda bristled. The leaders had all agreed that only English and French were to be spoken during the adventure, in order to give everyone an equal chance to participate. Was Zidane going to prove useless as a leader? she wondered irritably. Perhaps even a liability.

The night before, he had lagged back while the others pitched the tents and Sylvie prepared dinner. Amanda had noticed him eying Yasmina obliquely. Yasmina was the most beautiful of the girls. Kim-ly was a delicate porcelain doll, and the Somali girl, Kalifa, had the tall, slender grace of a sapling and skin like ebony silk. But Yasmina had the large, soulful eyes and rich olive skin of a classic Mediterranean beauty. The black hijab that framed her face lent her an unintentionally seductive air. If she was aware of Zidane's eyes on her, she'd studiously ignored him. Perhaps she was used to it. No doubt she turned heads wherever she went.

Amanda raised her voice. "Monsieur Zidane, may I talk to you a moment?" Without waiting for his answer, she walked toward the door of the tent. She caught his fleeting frown before he stood up. He said something to his three companions, which drew a laugh from them, before he joined her at the edge of the camp.

"I want to change the tent assignments for tonight. Move Hassan into the other tent."

Zidane frowned. "But the boys are comfortable with each other. And their English is not good."

"I don't want them just comfortable. I want them expanding their horizons."

"They are expanding their horizons just by being here."

"You know what I mean. This is a bridge-building experience to meet new people with different outlooks."

"We have five days for that. They will all know each other by the end."

"Or they will have settled into little cliques. It's best to establish this routine right at the beginning. We can't mix the girls up, but we can rotate the boys every night."

Zidane pressed his lips tight as if to stifle his protest. He had small, hooded eyes and a thin, bloodless mouth that seemed set in a perpetual slash of disapproval. Why had she not noticed this prissy side of him before? When he'd first put his group forward for the trip, he'd professed enthusiasm for the wilderness experience and support for its multicultural intent. *These kids need to get out of their ghettos,* he'd said. *They need to discover the vast pleasures and opportunities that Canada presents.* Had that all been for show?

"Very well," he said finally. "But please don't move Hassan yet. He's a new refugee and still insecure. Move Jalil."

Amanda said nothing for a moment. Although Hassan didn't appear thrilled by the cold and the hard work, he hadn't struck her as insecure. The Syrian refugee was a survivor, having fled the city of Homs with his mother and sister when Bashir al-Assad began bombing rebel enclaves, and having travelled on foot to Lebanon before being accepted into Canada last year. The family was educated and urbane; his father had been a schoolteacher in Syria and one of the first protesters killed by Assad's cluster bombs at the start of the uprising. Hassan had picked up both English and French quickly and was on track for acceptance into engineering at the University of Waterloo. War and death, it seemed, had served to strengthen rather than crush him.

Zidane seemed to read disagreement into her silence, for he set his jaw. "I know these young people, I know their hearts and their limits."

She knew she needed his continuing co-operation; five days was a long time to have an antagonist in the ranks, but co-operation did not mean dominance. "I understand," she said as amiably as she could. "But I think Hassan can manage some change."

While the others lingered over coffee, Amanda surreptitiously checked out the snowshoes stuck in the snow outside the tents. She could see no sign that they had been moved or disturbed. Traces of snow and ice from yesterday still clung to them, but nothing seemed fresh. She pondered the mystery. Because the path to the latrine was well travelled, no one needed snowshoes, and she doubted any of them, other than Sylvie and

Sebastien, would have ventured beyond the safety of the camp at night.

Sebastien approached her as she was bent over a pair of snowshoes. "*Problème?*" he asked.

She was aware of heads turning, of Zidane and a couple of students watching. She leaned in and lowered her voice. "Did you go out beyond the camp on snowshoes last night?"

His eyebrows shot up. "No, why?"

"There are snowshoe tracks up the hill behind the latrine."

"Probably one of them collects firewood."

"They went straight up the hill, like they knew where they were going."

He straightened. "Show me."

When he set off toward the latrine, she hesitated and he raised his voice. "Amanda, maybe you can help me with the latrine. Always a popular job."

Together they trudged the fifty metres to the makeshift latrine, no more than a lidded bucket in the snow and another lined with a paper bag for refuse. The site was screened from the camp by lacy pine trees but close enough for safety. Sebastien studied the tracks with a puzzled frown. Now that Amanda took a good look at them, she realized they went in and out of the bush using the same imprints. To save effort or to camouflage the trail?

Sebastien raised his head to study the woods. "Our farmhouse is twenty kilometres west, and in the south is the border of the Mont Tremblant National Park. People do backcountry camping in the park, but not often this far north."

"In any case, this trail seems to be heading north, away from the park."

"There's nothing up there. Just the wildlife reserve for miles."

"Could it be one of our group?" She told him about Kaylee's warning growl.

He shrugged. “It’s our handmade snowshoes, but we also sell them at our store. But who would go? In the dark, with the wolves? What time did Kaylee wake you?”

“I don’t know, it was dark.” She tried to picture the light in the tent. Faintly grey, which she’d attributed to the moon. “It might have been early morning, I suppose.”

He shook his head again. “Bizarre. Do you want to ask the others?”

She could think of only two reasons anyone outside the group would have ventured so close without actually coming into camp. Either they were spying, or they were having a secret rendezvous with one of the members. She didn’t like either explanation.

“Let’s not say anything yet. Let’s wait to see whether it happens again. But meanwhile, I suggest we keep a close eye on the group for anyone acting strange.”

CHAPTER FOUR

The morning was occupied with camp chores such as collecting firewood, preparing a portable lunch, and drawing fresh water from the lake for dishes and cooking. Sebastien showed the group how to chop a hole in the ice to collect water. As the sun climbed in the sky and spread its warmth through the protected campsite, everyone's spirits rose.

Amanda kept a close eye on the students, but although she could detect nothing suspicious, she noticed that small cliques were already forming. Kim-ly and Kalifa, the Somali girl, joined forces to wash dishes, their disparate sizes making a comical study in contrasts. Yasmina seemed to be holding herself aloof, tending to the clothes drying in the tents. Among the boys, Luc seemed to be the loner, while the Arab boys stayed together on water detail and the Haitian and Congolese boys sawed wood. Although those divisions seemed natural, Amanda was uneasy about the apparently deliberate exclusion of Luc. He wandered the site, dabbling in one task after another with a distracted air.

Once the chores were done, Sebastien announced it was time for a good, old-fashioned cross-country ski adventure. He and Sylvie had brought the ski equipment in along with the camp gear earlier in the week. By the time everyone had sorted out their sizes, fumbled to attach their skis, and mastered a rudimentary stride and kick motion, it was almost lunchtime. Instead, Sebastien pointed to a distant bluff across the bay.

"We will ski over there and stop for lunch in the shelter of the rock," he said. When a chorus of groans greeted him, he laughed. "We have not even started! *C'est bien fun*, I promise you. There's a great hill just on the other side of the rocks. We will climb, and we will come down!"

True to his promise, it was a glorious afternoon. The kids spent much of it trying to master the herringbone and the snow-plough, but they were enthralled. The cold wind rushed in their faces as they picked up speed, and they shrieked with terrified joy as they landed in a snowy heap somewhere along the descent. They cheered each other on, boys and girls, Vietnamese and Syrian alike, just as Amanda had hoped. She took dozens of photos.

By the time the sun slipped low across the bay, they were bruised, exhausted, and covered in snow. Wordlessly they straggled back into camp to be greeted by the aroma of woodsmoke and sautéed garlic. They were too tired and hungry to muster any more than mild surprise when they were told of the new sleeping arrangements and directed to their new tents. By the time they had peeled off and hung up their wet clothes, Sebastien was searing a huge pot of venison meat on the woodstove.

Sylvie watched as one by one they filed into the cook tent. Keeping her voice carefully nonchalant, she signalled to Hassan and Yasmina. "You two will help Sebastien cook the stew, and Kim-ly and Jalil will wash up after."

Both men looked shocked, and Luc laughed. "That will teach you, Hassan."

Hassan scowled, and out of the corner of her eye, Amanda saw Zidane rising to intervene. "Great idea!" she exclaimed. "You'll all get a turn. Learning to handle all aspects of the camping experience is essential."

Sebastien was quick to join in. "We men are very disadvantaged if we don't know how to cook."

By the time the venison stew was tender, it was late and eyelids were heavy. Hassan had scorched the bottom of the pan, and Luc spat out a mouthful.

"Good one, Hassan!" he crowed. "You burned the bottom, and now the whole thing tastes smoky."

Hassan flushed darkly. "If you are hungry, you will eat it."

"Barely," Luc muttered.

Hassan clenched his fists. Amanda noticed he hadn't touched his own food.

"It was my fault," Yasmina said. "I wasn't watching the fire. The stove was too hot."

"It wasn't your fault either, Yasmina," Sebastien said. "You are all learning. You will all get better."

The rest of the dinner passed in testy silence, and afterward Jalil complained that the burned pot was impossible to clean. Yasmina moved to take over.

"Oh, for fuck's sake!" Luc exclaimed. "Give it a rest, dudes." He snatched the pot from Jalil and leaned into the task. "All it takes is a bit of strength."

He joined Yasmina and washed the dishes with a triumphant flourish. Afterward, he prepared her a cup of tea, and as he handed it to her, their touch lingered for an instant before she pulled away. During that instant, a smile twitched on his lips, fleeting but long enough to elicit a frown from Hassan. *What's that about?* Amanda wondered.

By the time all the food was safely stored away, the group was stumbling toward their tents. Some, like Yasmina, were so exhausted they could barely walk straight. Amanda watched Luc and Hassan trying to avoid each other as they both headed for the same tent. She called Luc aside.

"Listen, I agreed to take you on this trip, so don't be a jerk."

He arched his eyebrows innocently. Instead of elaborating, she waited him out until the innocence grew sullen. "They're such wusses; they'd crumble on the first day of real roughing it."

The sneering words carried through the quiet of the campsite. *No wonder the group has ostracized him,* Amanda thought. Was he being deliberately obnoxious, or was this his natural style? She gripped his arm and lowered her voice. "They're trying. We don't all start from the same circumstances, and trust me, they've endured a lot more hardship than you have. You're the only native-born Canadian, so show some leadership!"

"You think they respect me?" he said, still too loud. "They're spoiled rotten by their families. Look at how Hassan whines about the cold."

"Hassan is new from Syria. This is a huge adjustment. In fact, they're all from the tropics or the desert. You wouldn't fare too well there either, and you'd appreciate a little understanding."

He seemed to be trying to think up a rebuttal, so she turned away. "Just try walking in their shoes, will you?" she snapped. "That skill will stand you in good stead wherever you go in life."

As she watched him slouch away toward the tent, she wasn't sure her words had had any impact. Luc was a puzzle, professing eagerness to improve himself and yet descending into petty provocation. The whole interaction felt slightly staged, like a bad actor going for an effect. But what effect? And why?

Once again Kaylee woke her in the night with a low, bubbling growl. In the darkness, Amanda reached to quiet her and felt the dog's tension beneath her hand. She lay sifting the sounds of the night. Wind rustled through the trees, masking the lonely howl of a wolf. Closer by, the murmur of snores. And closer still, the soft squeak of footsteps on snow. Another camper going to the latrine? A raccoon or fox searching for scraps?

She crawled out of her sleeping bag, gasping in the frigid air, and peered out the front flap of her tent. A soft snow was falling, but the faint grey of the moon illuminated the outlines of the camp and the ring of trees beyond. In the distance, she saw a hint of shadow moving up the hill. She stared into the darkness for a while, shivering, but there was nothing more. Just tree boughs swaying in the wind, she decided.

She dragged the dog back into the warmth of her sleeping bag. "Kaylee," she whispered, "you've got to stop freaking out about every little noise."

They both lay awake, listening to the distant wolves and the rising wind, until gradually Amanda felt the dog relax. Even then, she slept fitfully, waking to listen for new footsteps. Unwanted sounds filled the quiet. The thunder of fire, the wails of children, voices raised in panic, hatred, and rage …

She willed the morning to arrive. At first light, she crawled out of her tent with relief and made her way to the cook tent, where she found the girls still curled in their sleeping bags but Sylvie awake and stoking the woodstove. Soon she had a hearty blaze going and a pot of water heating on the stovetop for coffee. The girls stretched languidly and slid out of their cocoons to dress for the day before the boys arrived. Amanda went back to feed Kaylee and then watched as one by one the tent flaps drew back and campers emerged, swaddled in toques, scarves, and mitts against the cold. That morning, only a couple of them straggled off for morning prayers. Neither Yasmina nor Hassan was among them.

Eventually there were eight youths huddled close to the woodstove, cradling cups of coffee. Amanda did silent inventory.

"Where's Luc?" she asked Hassan.

"Still asleep."

Amanda glanced at Zidane, whose expression seemed to say *I told you so.* "Thanks for the support, dickhead," she muttered to herself as she walked over to the tent. "Luc! Time to get up. *Lève-toi!*"

No sound from within. Not even the soft curse of protest she'd expected. She knew it was difficult to leave the warm cocoon of a sleeping bag in the morning, but at least he had a warm stove and a hot cup of coffee waiting for him.

Back in the cook tent, she gestured to Hassan. "Can you go wake him up?"

"Not me!" Hassan exclaimed. "He will knock my head off." He was huddled by the fire with his knees drawn to his chest and the hood of his parka pulled so tight that his eyes were barely visible through the fur trim.

She turned to Luc's other tent mate, who was helping Sebastien stoke the fire. Before she could even ask, Jean-Charles nodded, put down a log, and set off toward the tent. He was back within seconds.

"He is gone."

Yasmina lifted her head. She looked a little unfocused, as if still trying to wake up. "*What?*" She struggled to her feet, but Zidane, quick as a cat, blocked her path. He spoke to her in Arabic, and Amanda watched the girl reluctantly sink back down.

As Zidane turned back, Amanda felt a twinge of alarm. Something in that exchange had seemed furtive. "All of you, stay here," she said.

She marched over to Luc's tent and flung open the flap. The four sleeping bags were lined up in a row, three of them empty but the fourth piled up high over a mound in the middle. She pulled back the cover to reveal the pillow bunched beneath. The oldest deception in the book, practised by cheating spouses and grounded teenagers everywhere.

She looked around the tent. Clothes spilled from duffel bags, moccasins lay in twisted heaps, and mitts and hats hung from a cord along the roof. Before she could make sense of the possessions, Jean-Charles appeared at her shoulder. "His backpack is gone with most of his things."

She rushed out to check the skis and snowshoes, colliding with Yasmina, who had obviously escaped Zidane's clutches. "Is he really gone?" the girl demanded.

"I'm not sure." The area around the skis had been well trampled the night before. Quickly Amanda counted. Thirteen pairs of skis and poles. None missing. If Luc had sneaked away in the night, he had not taken his skis.

Sylvie appeared through the trees. "He's not at the latrine," she said. "But there are new tracks up the hill."

Amanda caught sight of Sebastien examining the snowshoes, which stood like sentinels in the snow outside the tents. He looked over grimly. "This time a pair of snowshoes is missing."

Amanda had little time to waste on outrage. The little bastard had been reprimanded. Had he reacted by running off in a fit of pique? With little heed to the fact that he was miles from the nearest road and without shelter, food, or means of defence?

Snowflakes were beginning to sift through the trees again, falling soft and soundless on the tracks. She called a quick conference with Sylvie, Sebastien, and Zidane.

"If the snow keeps up, we only have a few hours before it completely obscures his tracks. Should we involve the kids in the search?"

Zidane scowled. "He left; he can find his own way back. I won't put the rest of the students at risk. They don't know the wilderness and the winter. Luc does."

"But in this snow, all the terrain begins to look the same," Sebastien said. "He may get lost and not realize it."

"Then he's a fool. I know this kid. I bet he's watching right now from just beyond those trees, laughing at our worry."

Amanda studied him in puzzlement. Zidane had come to her weeks ago, passionate and persuasive in his commitment to his students. He had seemed like a man who cared about struggling youth, yet his antipathy to Luc was almost visceral. "Am I missing something? When I met him, he was all about turning his life around so he could go to university."

Zidane grunted. "He's a drug addict. His priorities change from one hour to the next."

Then they will change again, one hour from now, when he's lost in the bush, she wanted to retort. Her protective instincts rose up. "He said he was clean," she said. Even as the words left her lips, she heard their feeble ring. Predictably, even Sebastien snorted. "Anyway, there are no drugs out here in the wilds, for God's sake!"

"We're only four kilometres from the trailhead," Sebastien said. "He just has to retrace his steps to there, and some yahoo from Mont Tremblant will come along on a snowmobile. Mont Tremblant is a party town; it's full of drugs if you know who to ask. High-end drugs."

She thought about the first set of tracks in the snow the night before last. Had that been a rendezvous? Had Luc arranged some kind of pick-up? She clenched her fists, trying to hide her rising fear and outrage from the young campers, who were probably listening intently. What did they know? She sensed Luc had few allies among them, but would they be willing to rat on him?

Snatches of an argument in Arabic caught her ear, and she turned just as the flap to Luc's tent flung back and Yasmina emerged, looking more angry than worried. Hassan appeared in the doorway behind her, frowning as he watched her stalk across the camp, her black skirt swirling over the snow. Amanda remembered the subtle touch that had passed between Luc and her the evening before, which had caught Hassan's disapproving eye. Did these two know something, and was it somehow connected to Luc's disappearance?

"This is all speculation," she said to Sebastien. "Unless I'm a worse judge of character than I thought, Luc seemed sincere. Maybe he just needs some space this morning. Maybe his tent mates have been giving him a hard time."

Zidane gave a curt shake of his head. "He lies as easily as he breathes. I think he's up to something."

"I should at least notify his mother. She was so committed."

"The boy is eighteen. Under the law, he's an adult. If he wants to take off to sulk or get high, that's not for Mother to know."

What was with this guy? He looked as if he believed every nonsense syllable he uttered. "Oh come on, Zidane. The law is an ass. You don't stop being a parent just because your brainless kid turns eighteen."

"He could sue us."

That made her mind up. "I've faced far worse than lawyers." Through the half-open door of the cook tent, she could make out Hassan just inside, still watching Yasmina closely. "I'm going to talk to Hassan."

The youth blinked with alarm when she pulled back the tent flap. He tightened his hood around his head as if struck by a sudden chill, but she suspected it was to conceal himself further. Thanks to the woodstove, the tent was nearly a sauna.

He launched the first volley. "I didn't see anything."

"But he had to climb over you and Jean-Charles to get out the tent door."

His eyes narrowed, as if he were focusing inward. "Yes," he said finally. "I remember he stepped on my foot."

"What time?"

Hassan raised his thin shoulders. "It was dark."

"Did he come back?"

"I don't know. I fell asleep."

"Did you three talk at all before bed?"

"We argued. He wanted to sleep in front of the door. I like the middle because it's warm, and Jean-Charles likes the door. Monsieur Zidane was at the stove. Luc tried to make Jean-Charles to move, but I wouldn't allow it. After, Luc turned his back and didn't say a word more." Hassan gave her a sidelong glance through his long black lashes. "I don't think he wanted to be in our tent either."

Amanda bit back a retort. The kid was probably right. She still had a lot to learn about this family fun business. She thanked him and moved on to his tent mate, who was helping Sebastien replenish the firewood inside the tents. Amanda led him to a quiet corner of the campsite, where he faced her with apprehension. Jean-Charles had the massive frame of a linebacker but the eyes of a small boy afraid of the dark.

"Yes, I heard him," Jean-Charles said in his soft Haitian French. "He was moving around, putting things in his bag."

"Did you speak to him?"

Jean-Charles shook his head. "I thought he was putting on his clothes to go to the latrine."

"Did you hear him come back?"

"No. But maybe Hassan knows. They were talking."

Amanda hid her surprise. "In the tent?"

"Outside."

"What did they say?"

"I couldn't hear. They were whispering in English." He paused as if casting his thoughts back. "Hassan asked him a question. He seemed angry. Luc said don't worry."

"You're sure it was Hassan?"

"Oh, yes." Jean-Charles's face clouded with doubt. "I think so. I think I heard him come back inside. But I was very sleepy. Maybe ... I am mistaken."

Amanda glanced across the campsite and saw Hassan leave the cook tent to go back to his own tent. Part of her wanted to strangle him. Luc was in potentially serious trouble wandering around in the bush in the dead of winter, and Hassan's misplaced loyalty was not helping him. Unless the kid wanted Luc to freeze to death.

She brushed the idea aside. The group clearly did not like Luc, and he had done nothing to win them over, but she doubted any of them would actively wish him dead. While she deliberated, Hassan re-emerged from the tent, picked up the bear horn and toilet paper, and headed for the latrine.

Was it her overactive imagination, or did he have a secretive air?

She waited until he had disappeared into the trees before circling around to approach the latrine from the back. All around her, the snow was woven with animal tracks. Hassan was indeed sitting on the latrine, but he was fully clothed and thumbing his cellphone as if searching for a signal. Her anger spiked. Part of the agreement was that all the students hand over their devices to Sebastien at the beginning of the trip. There was no cellphone signal in the camp area, but she wanted to prevent them from playing games or listening to music as well. She should have known, however, that this generation was far too attached to their electronic tether to sever it completely.

After staring at his phone awhile, Hassan cursed in frustration and raised his head to search the woods. Amanda ducked behind a wide, swooping fir tree. An instant later, he pocketed his phone in disgust and rose to leave. Amanda intercepted him on the path halfway back to camp, feigning surprise.

"There you are!" she exclaimed. He recoiled in shock and his nostrils flared. "Jean-Charles said he heard you and Luc talking outside the tent during the night."

Hassan looked doleful. "Jean-Charles dreams. Every night, strong dreams that he is back in Haiti. Thieves and bad people all around."

How do you know? she wondered, *since last night was your first night sharing a tent.* "He was very specific in what he heard," she said instead, stretching the truth. "You asked Luc something and he said don't worry. It sounded as if you were angry at him."

"I am not responsible for Jean-Charles's dreams." He stiffened and his voice rose, as if seeking an audience. "Are you accusing me?"

"I'm trying to find Luc. This is dangerous terrain to be lost without equipment. Unless he was meeting someone." She scrutinized his expression, but it betrayed nothing. Silently he stared her down.

She decided to let him lead, to see where he would go. "Do you think we should call the police?"

He shrugged. "That's your decision."

"But I don't know Luc. You do. What do you think has happened?"

"I think he is watching us." His arms swept wide to encompass the forest. "Watching to see what we will do. When we do nothing and he gets bored and hungry, he will come back to camp. He will tell us a story about getting lost on his way to the latrine at night."

"So you think we should do nothing?"

"My opinion is not important, because I am not responsible. I don't have to worry about his mother or the press."

The words were said without malice — indeed, on the surface with a sympathetic smile — but she wondered if they held a subtle threat.

Back at the camp, the kitchen detail was cleaning up while the rest packed their daypacks in preparation for the day's adventure. The plan was to ski to a nearby lake, where Sylvie and Sebastien would teach them ice fishing. If the fish — and the weather — co-operated, they would build a bonfire on the shore and barbeque the fish.

Amanda found Jean-Charles in his tent, rolling up his sleeping bag. "Jean-Charles, do you have bad dreams?"

The youth looked up, his liquid brown eyes wide with dismay. Unlike Hassan, he had an expressive face that betrayed his every emotion. She waited.

He bowed his head. "Sometimes," he said quietly. "I remember things in my dreams."

From reading his file, she had a good idea what those memories were. She knelt beside him. "I know. When I was in Nigeria, some rebels invaded the village one night. In my sleep, it seems so real I think I'm back there." *Hearing the screams, smelling the smoke.* Seeing the pain flit across his face, she laid her hand on his arm. "I don't mean to upset you. Does that happen to you?"

"Does it ever go away?" he asked, his voice barely more than a whisper.

"I don't know. It's only been a year and a half for me. How long for you?"

"Seven years. It is not going away." A faint shimmer of tears shone in his dark eyes.

She knew both his parents had died in the earthquake in Haiti, and he'd been buried alive in the rubble for three days. He had been brought to Montreal by his mother's sister at the age of twelve.

Amanda wanted to hug him, to hold him close as she had the frightened children in Africa, but he was twice her size and a man now. Instead, she softened her voice. "Do you talk to anyone? Your aunt?"

"My aunt says I am safe now and I must forget. She doesn't like to hear about it. My mother was dead beside me in the hole, and the flies ... the smell ..."

Impulsively Amanda grasped his hands in hers and squeezed tight. "I know. The smell."

"I could not move," he said, memories tumbling out. "I lie in the dark, and I think she was whispering to me in that hole. She tells me to be brave. I don't know if it was real."

Casting her reservations aside, Amanda slipped her arm around him. He leaned his head on hers. "You know in your heart she was speaking to you, even if the words came from you," she said. "That's what your mother would have said."

"Do you believe in spirits?"

"I believe we keep people alive in our hearts. People we love, people we need." *People we fail.* The thought rose unbidden, and she thrust it away. When would she ever be free of guilt? For the Nigerian girls and for Phil, both of whom she had tried so hard to save.

Jean-Charles must have felt her anger, for he lifted his head to face her. "I am not imagining that Hassan and Luc talk," he said firmly. "If Hassan says that, he is lying."

"Why would he lie?"

"He does not want to be in trouble. He wants to go in engineering at Waterloo University, and he does not want anything to stop that."

It seemed a weak excuse for lying about something as innocuous as a midnight chat, but Amanda didn't argue. Instead, she extricated herself and clambered out of the tent into the soft morning light. Hassan was helping Sebastien load a toboggan with fishing supplies, and he looked the picture of helpful innocence.

She knew that dreams and flashbacks could seem very real, the smells and sounds and sights of memory even more vivid than the mundane reality of the present. Had Jean-Charles hallucinated the conversation? Had he heard the words *Don't worry* from the mouth of his own dead mother?

Or was Hassan lying?

CHAPTER FIVE

As Amanda crossed the camp, Sebastien spotted her and signalled her aside. "We should go," he said. "We have two kilometres to get to the lake. What do you want to do about Luc?"

She studied the group, most of whom were dressed and ready, stamping their feet in the snow to stay warm. She approached Sylvie and Zidane.

"I've asked them all," Zidane said. "No one knows where Luc went. But they think he is safe, whatever he's doing. They want to go on."

"With all due respect," Amanda said, "none of these kids know the dangers of the Canadian wilderness. I want to follow that trail from the latrine to see where it goes. We'll leave a note for him here in case he returns. You take the kids on ahead, and I'll catch up with you. If he's not back or I don't find him by midday, I'm calling his mother."

No one argued with her. As she was packing some food and emergency supplies, Yasmina approached. "I will stay here at camp today in case he returns."

Amanda smiled. The girl seemed to be the only one showing any concern for Luc. "Thanks for offering, Yasmina, but I don't want us split up any more than we already are, and besides, you will miss the fun."

Yasmina returned the smile. "I will imagine it. And I am very sore from yesterday. I think I hurt my ankle."

Amanda gently touched her arm. "I don't want to worry about you too. If it snows or the fire goes out ..."

Yasmina continued to smile, but her eyes hardened. "I'm a big girl, not a child. I promise, if trouble occurs, I will go to meet the others."

Aware that she was losing precious time, Amanda backed off and went to explain the situation to Sylvie. "Yasmina is a proud and capable young woman, and I don't want to belittle her—"

"*Vas-y!*" Sylvie exclaimed, shaking her head in frustration. "Don't worry, we will take care of Yasmina."

With a final goodbye, Amanda shouldered her daypack and snapped on her skis, which would be faster than snowshoes. She set off up the hill with Kaylee safely on a leash behind her. The threat of wolves and even cougars was bad enough, but she also didn't want the exuberant dog to mar Luc's faint snowshoe tracks.

Within minutes the snow-laden woods had swallowed her up. Except for the squeak and swish of her skis and the rhythm of her breath, the silence was absolute. The sky was a pale pewter wash and the snow a fluffy quilt stitched with the tracks of small animals.

The group's snowshoe trail of two days earlier was almost completely obscured, leaving only a thin, wavering thread up through the trees. Luc's snowshoe trail was clearer, as if he had started his trek halfway through the snowfall, which had continued most of the night. Would Luc have been able to see the earlier snowshoe trail in the dark? His own tracks seemed to be following the same route. Admittedly, it was the straightest, easiest path through the dense underbrush, but had he chosen the route intentionally, knowing it led to the main snowmobile trail only four kilometres away?

With the trail packed down by the snowshoes, she was able to make good time once she reached the top of the hill. As she ate up the distance, her anger mounted. Luc was clearly on a mission. He was not hanging out on the periphery of the group as Hassan had suggested; he was heading directly back toward civilization, apparently unconcerned about the worry she and the others would face. Perhaps even enjoying it.

Little bugger.

At the trailhead, would he have stolen one of the tour guides' snowmobiles? Unlike the others, Luc had grown up in Quebec and might know how to drive one, perhaps even hotwire one. However, snowmobiles were not exactly stealth vehicles; the roar of their engines could be heard for miles. She had heard no sound of them during the night, but the falling snow could have muffled it. Additionally, hills did strange things to sound waves, dissipating them up into the atmosphere so that nothing would be heard even from the other side.

In less than an hour, she and Kaylee reached the trailhead. The two snowmobiles were still parked where the Sylvie and Sebastien had left them, tucked off the trail under the protection of tall pines. Their canvas covers sported a thin layer of snow. These snowmobiles had not been touched in the past two days.

She studied the snow carefully, trying to make sense of the tangle of snowshoe and vehicle tracks. She was about to take the main trial back toward civilization, but Kaylee was snuffling the trail in the opposite direction. Most of it was covered in a thick blanket of snow, suggesting no snowmobile had been along it in quite awhile. But two strange treads ran down the middle, partially obscured by last night's snow but still visible enough to betray the presence of something large. Not a snowmobile, not a moose, not even the clear indents of snowshoes, but huge tires.

What the hell was this? An all-terrain vehicle? She signalled Kaylee to go behind her as she set off along the side of the trail so as not to disturb the tracks. It followed the snowmobile trail some distance up a steep hill and skirted a rocky outcrop before veering off the snowmobile path and down across a frozen lake that was windswept into ripples of crusty snow. She had to press hard into the wind as she fought her way across to the far side of the lake, where the twin tracks disappeared again into thick woods. Amanda leaned on her poles and panted for breath as she glanced at her watch. She was on unmarked terrain, far off the official trail. The snow was heavy and fought her skis at every thrust.

She found a tree stump and pulled a sandwich from her backpack. Around her the stillness was serene, save for an eagle that arced high overhead. If anything happened to her, she might not be found for months.

She'd been travelling for over three hours and had probably covered close to twenty kilometres. It was past noon; it would be dark in four hours. If she wanted to catch up to the others before then, she had to turn back soon. Thanks to her rigorous fitness regimen, designed as much to fortify her mind as her body, she was in excellent shape, but fuelled by nothing but a sandwich and energy bars, forty kilometres of backcountry trail breaking would be close to her limit.

Besides, she needed to alert Sylvie and Sebastien to send out a search party. Something strange was going on. No matter what Luc's motivation for leaving the camp, he had linked up with someone else, and instead of taking the obvious route back to civilization, he'd headed quite deliberately in the opposite direction. Into the wilderness.

Amanda covered the twenty-odd kilometres back to camp as fast as she could, leaning forward and kicking back with each powerful thrust in a mindless rhythm that ate up the distance. Push, kick, push, kick. Anger fired her up. By the time she neared the campsite, pale twilight had descended and she could barely distinguish the ribbon of ski tracks that stretched ahead.

Finally, the scent of wood smoke wafted through the trees and she swooped down the last hill on rubber legs. Candlelight glowed in the tents, but most of the students were clustered around the fire in the cook tent, ladling boiling water from a pot into their cups for tea. They all cheered at the sight of her. Poor Kaylee had been trailing behind, her head drooping, but she managed a final burst of energy to rush into their midst.

Amanda was exhausted and wanted nothing more than to peel off her sweaty clothes and collapse by the stove, as Kaylee did. But instead she drew Sylvie, Sebastien, and Zidane outside to the edge of the camp.

"He met someone," she said, still breathless. "The little bastard knew exactly what he was doing. This was no fit of adolescent rebellion. He snowshoed out to the main trail for a pre-arranged meeting, and the two of them took off in what looked like an ATV."

Sebastien frowned. "What direction did they go?"

"The opposite way from your store. Deeper into the woods and across a lake—"

"There are a thousand lakes."

"What's farther north?" she asked. Her whole body was soaked with perspiration, and as she cooled down, she felt the clammy cold against her skin. An involuntary shiver ran through her. Sylvie was the only one to notice.

"You need to change out of your wet clothes and get some tea. We will meet in Sebastien's tent in five minutes."

Five minutes later, when Amanda entered the tent with her cup of tea, Sebastien already had a topographical map spread out on his sleeping bag. He and Sylvie were sitting cross-legged on the floor, shining a powerful flashlight and examining the map with a magnifying glass.

A moment later, Zidane opened the flap and crouched to enter. "There's not room, Monsieur Zidane," Sylvie said firmly. "We will take care of this. You and the students can start dinner."

Zidane stiffened. Amanda saw his eyes dart from Sebastien to the map and back as if looking for support from the man of the group. If Sylvie noticed — and Amanda suspected not much escaped her — she didn't react. "We're having boiled vegetables and beef sausage tonight."

"What happened to the ice fishing?" Amanda asked in surprise. "No luck?"

Sylvie softened. "Tomorrow. It was Kalifa's idea. The group wanted to wait until you could join us, and Yasmina was too sore to come with us. So we climbed up that mountain and learned about animal tracks, wolf dens, and bear caves."

Belatedly, Amanda remembered Yasmina's sore ankle. "How is Yasmina?"

Sylvie glanced at Zidane. "She seems fine now, eh? She rested today, and Zidane stayed at the camp with her." Sylvie chuckled. "She wasn't too happy about being babysat."

Amanda remembered the calculated look Zidane had given the girl, and her antennae quivered with unease. She shot him a look. "What did she do all day?"

As usual, the man's expression was unreadable. He shrugged. "Not much. She stayed in her tent."

Sylvie seemed to sense the tension, for she gestured to Zidane. "We'll be done here soon. The sausage and vegetables are in the food barrel, but you will need to get more water."

Zidane ignored her, choosing to pitch his argument to Sebastien. "This is my student. My responsibility."

"But we're familiar with the area," Sylvie countered. "And Amanda knows where Luc went. That's what's important."

Zidane hovered in the doorway a few more seconds as if waiting for Sebastien to assert control. When he didn't, Zidane turned to withdraw. But not before giving a parting shot at Amanda. "I don't think we should waste any effort on him. I didn't want him, and this proves I was right."

You're all heart, Zidane, Amanda thought. *The perfect guy to be counselling disaffected youth.*

"I can't stand that man!" Sylvie muttered. Amanda grinned in silent sympathy before taking a few moments to orient herself to the map and trace the route she had followed. On the map she could clearly see the snowmobile trail that cut across the untouched wilderness of the wildlife reserve, as well as the lake Luc had crossed. Into nowhere.

"Where the hell were they going?" she wondered aloud.

"There's nothing out there," Sylvie said. "And Luc has only energy bars and water. He didn't take any shelter or sleeping gear."

"Then something is out there."

Sebastien was bent over the map, magnifying glass in hand. He tapped a thin orange line farther north. "There's a road a few kilometres farther. Gravel. In summer, people use it to access cottages farther north."

Sylvie snorted. "That's not much of a road. In the winter, it might not even be ploughed."

Sebastien smiled his slow, patient smile. "Maybe not, but with an ATV, it would be passable."

"But why?" Amanda said. "It's entirely in the wrong direction! The nearest towns up there are way on the other side of the reserve." As she tried to make sense of what she knew about Luc, an idea struck her. "Unless there's a drug operation — a grow-op or drug lab — hidden up there. Is that possible?"

Sylvie frowned, but Sebastien merely chuckled. "You need electricity, a lot of it, and a transport system for goods in and out."

"Even one pickup truck can carry a huge quantity of weed or ecstasy," Amanda said. "As for electricity, what about generators or solar panels?"

"It's a big leap," Sebastien said. "Why would Luc have left us to travel miles through the wilderness to get to this drug lab? He has his dealers in the city. Why not go there?"

Amanda traced her finger over the squiggly orange line that led up into the hinterland at least thirty kilometres farther north. "He met someone. And it wasn't spur of the moment, because he's been without a cellphone since we left."

"Unless he had one hidden in his things."

Amanda remembered Hassan thumbing his cellphone in vain. *What was going on?* "But there's no signal in the area," she said.

"Sometimes there is a weak one at the top of the hill."

Amanda thought about the nocturnal wanderer of the night before. "The bugger set this up before — whatever this is — and left us to worry and search for him needlessly." She shoved herself stiffly to her feet. "Well, okay, Luc, you want worry? I'm calling the police to report him missing. Let them discover the grow-op."

Sylvie eyed her steadily. "And what will we tell them?"

"That one of our campers is missing and we fear for his safety."

"And once they learn that he left on his own and met up with someone, they'll drop the search. They won't get near any grow-op."

"Maybe they already know about the grow-op. Maybe they have it under surveillance."

"And maybe they're already on the payroll," Sylvie retorted. "Trust me, I know the Sûreté du Québec cops around here. They're busy with traffic accidents and rich tourists getting lost.

They are going to laugh you and your story of grow-ops right out of the office."

"Well, I have to do something. I can't just ignore this! As much as I am furious with the little prick, he might be in danger."

Sebastien had been quiet as he watched tempers rise. He must have seen a dangerous spark in his wife's eye, for he finally held up a soothing hand. "Call his mother. That's the place to start. See if she's heard from him or has any idea what he's up to."

Amanda emerged from the tent to find Zidane returning from the bush with the prayer group. Yasmina hung back while he and Hassan walked together, speaking in low tones. They broke off as Amanda appeared, but she sensed an argument hanging unresolved in the air. Hassan was flushed, but Zidane turned to Amanda with a perfect mask on his dark face.

"I told them Luc met up with someone," he said, "and they are naturally concerned. I hoped they know what he was doing, or who he met, but ..."

Hassan kicked at the snow. Unlike Zidane, he looked guilty. "Luc was a loner at school," he said. "He wanted to be our friend, but none of us ... we didn't completely trust him."

"Why not?"

"He had so many faces. He changed his views all the time. We felt like he said things just to be our friend."

Hardly a mortal sin, Amanda thought with a reluctant twinge of sympathy for the young man trying to find his way. "Did you ever see him using drugs?"

Hassan seemed to weigh his answer before shaking his head. "There was talk that before he came to our school, yes."

"Was there any talk he was a dealer?"

"He went to jail for that. But he told us he was trying to quit, to stay clean. He knew our group didn't use drugs or alcohol, and he wanted to know our reasons."

"Maybe that's why he wanted to be your friend. You were a good influence."

Hassan nodded, but discomfort showed in his evasive eyes. He cast a sidelong glance at Zidane. *Asking permission?* Amanda wondered curiously. Because he was a trusted adult, or was there more to it? How much power did this man have?

Zidane himself intervened. "Perhaps. But Luc was never what he seemed. As for where he's gone now, do you intend to call the police?"

"Probably," she said, noting the change of subject. "But first I'm going to check with his mother."

"A good idea," Zidane said. "Although I think she will be the last to know what he's up to."

"Oh?"

He shrugged indulgently. "Mothers, you know. Always wanting to believe their little boys are misunderstood angels."

Maybe just wanting to believe the best of them, as any mother should, Amanda thought, wondering whether she'd survive this whole trip without murdering the man.

Any hope she had that Luc's mother would know evaporated the moment she heard the panic in the woman's voice. She reached her at her home, using Sebastien's emergency satellite phone.

"What do you mean, he's missing!" she shrieked. "How can he be missing?"

"He got up in the middle of the night and left."

"In the dark? With the wolves and the bears?"

"He clearly knew what he was doing, Ghyslaine. He seems to have set up a meeting with someone on the main snowmobile trail."

"Oh! Oh!" The woman choked, her voice ragged with fear.

"He hasn't contacted you?"

"No, he hasn't contacted me!" she shot back. "If he did, I'd say so."

"Right. What about his father?"

"Not in a million years."

"You're sure?"

"Yes!" There was a beat. "I can't imagine ..."

"Where does his father live?"

"In Westmount."

"Does Luc have any relatives or friends in the region north of Mont Tremblant?"

"No, no. We're all from Montreal. I told you, Luc has hardly ever been to the country. He wouldn't know what to do with bears or wolves...." Panic rose in her voice again.

For someone who's hardly been in the wilds, he's managing pretty damn well, Amanda thought. "Do you have any idea who he might have met, or where he might be going?"

"No, none. *Mon Dieu!* I — I don't even know his friends."

"Would you like me to call the police? Or will you do it?"

A sharp intake of breath. "*Non!* No police." Silence descended on the line, followed by muttered curses in French. "Not yet."

"But it's been almost twenty-four hours. In this cold ..."

"Please don't call the police. Try to find him yourself."

"I can't do that, Ghyslaine. I have a group of young people here to take care of."

"But the police ..." She flailed about in search of a solution. "Please! Maybe he is just on the run. Maybe it is drugs. I thought he was clean, but he's been acting strange—"

"In what way?"

"Secretive phone calls, going out at night. He said they were counselling sessions. I don't want to think about it, but I don't know if that was the truth."

"Counselling sessions with Zidane?"

"And others. He said they were sponsors. I thought it was a good thing. He seemed excited, like he'd finally found some friends. He said he didn't want to jinx it, so I didn't ask for details. But ask Monsieur Zidane. Luc must have confided in him during their counselling. Perhaps he knows."

Amanda weighed her options. Without the support of the mother, any request for police assistance was likely to go nowhere. Yet there was an inexperienced city boy possibly in over his head in the wilds.

As if hearing Amanda's doubt, Ghyslaine barrelled ahead. "Give me until the morning. I will check around. I will check his room and his computer. It may have some clues. Kids these days, they put everything on the web."

"You have his passwords?"

"No, but I can guess."

Amanda signed off, nagged by unease. The mother's initial reaction had been one of panic and accusation, both understandable maternal responses to the news of a lost child. But halfway through the conversation, her protective instincts had kicked in. Not protection from the wild animals and brutal elements, but from discovery. As if she knew he had a secret worse than the threat of death.

Amanda sat in her tent awhile, mulling over the woman's words. Wondering what the secret late nights could be, the meetings with the unknown new friends. Could it be a criminal gang? A drug operation far larger than the street-level dealing he'd done before? Luc had been so convincing when he had persuaded her to take him on this trip. *He says what people want to hear*, Hassan had said, and she'd wanted to hear redemption.

She had fallen for his plea hook, line, and sinker. *Idiot*, she told herself. *After all these years in the quagmire of desperate societies, you should have known better.*

The tent flap parted slightly as Kaylee's pink nose shoved through. An instant later, the dog wriggled in beside her and laid her head in her lap. Absently, Amanda slipped her fingers through the dog's silky red fur and felt her frayed nerves ease.

"Yes, I know, it's dinner time. You and I have earned our dinner, haven't we? Any sign of mine out there?"

Kaylee thumped her tail at the word "dinner." Most of the other words likely went over her head.

"I wish you could talk. I know you're wise. I bet you'd never have been taken in by that little bastard. You'd have smelled a rat the first time we met. And now I'm stuck out here in the middle of nowhere, where I can't possibly find answers."

Matthew! Amanda sat up abruptly, startling the dog. She knew his number by heart. Two rings, three ... *Come on, come on! What kind of reporter are you, not answering your phone?*

"Goderich!" came Matthew's voice, brusque and on guard.

Amanda recognized the wariness of answering an unknown number. "Matthew, it's me."

"Amanda! What's wrong?"

The guy doesn't miss a beat, Amanda thought. All those years of taking calls from terrified sources in even more terrifying corners of the world. She briefly filled him in on the day. On Luc's deliberate disappearance, his secret rendezvous, his mother's panic followed by her sudden reversal of concern. Her revelations about his new, secret life and her refusal to involve the police.

Like a good reporter. Matthew listened and asked only enough questions to get the story straight in his mind.

"Ghyslaine is going to check with his friends and explore his computer," Amanda concluded. "But of course, if she finds out something bad or criminal, she's not going to tell me."

"Okay," Matthew said. "Let me get this straight. The mother doesn't want the police involved, and it sounds as if Luc has things under control. So maybe … Amanda, as much as this is not your nature, maybe you should just let this play out for a while."

She wrestled her frustration under control. "But what if he's not safe? He's eighteen years old, and you know how stupidly invincible they feel at that age. This is my trip! The first major one of my tour, and it's turning out to be a hell of a lot harder in reality than it seemed in our dreams. I can't just ignore a potential danger to one of my kids! And even if I could …" She dropped her voice, "you know I wouldn't."

Silence on the line. She hoped he wouldn't state the obvious — that they were in Quebec, not Africa, and that there were no gun-wielding jihadists after Luc. He knew her mind went places she couldn't control.

"Okay, what do you want me to do?"

Relief and affection flooded through her. "Poke around. Use that reporter's snout of yours. Find out if Luc is back on drugs and if he's dealing. If he's got a secret stash of money or dubious friends. And find out if there are any suspected drug labs or grow-ops in the bush north of here."

Matthew laughed. "Oh, sure. I'll just ask the cops. 'And why do you want to know, Mr. Goderich?' 'Just curious, Officer.'"

She chuckled. "Matthew, if you can get secrets out of African dictators and desert warlords, the Quebec police should be a piece of cake. Use your charming French."

"What French?"

"The bumbling kind. It works for you just fine."

He laughed again, and by the time they'd signed off, she was laughing too. Luc was probably fine. He was not a helpless child like the schoolgirls in Nigeria. He was big and strong, and whatever danger he was in, it was of his own choosing.

Time to eat, sleep, and get on with the ice-fishing adventure!

CHAPTER SIX

Sylvie and Sebastien had brought all the fishing equipment to the site earlier in the week and had hauled two huts out onto the lake by snowmobile. In classic Quebec style, they had equipped each with a small woodstove, cozy rugs, little stools, and a couple of cooking pots. How they had managed to wangle special permits, collect all the materials, and drag the little shacks out onto the lake in the short time they had, Amanda couldn't imagine. When she asked Sebastien if he had friends in high places, he merely smiled his slow, easy smile.

"I want them to have the real experience," he said. "They can't huddle out there over open holes, with the wind turning them to ice."

Amanda hugged him with joy. What a stroke of luck that these two had come into her life!

By the time the group had managed the short ski to the remote lake, he had both stoves fired up and two pots of coffee on. He gathered the group in one of the huts and used an ice auger to drill an eight-inch hole in the middle of the hut. Through the ice, the dark water glistened.

"Old-fashioned style!" he exclaimed, opting to give the lesson in French. "Nowadays, fishermen often use sonar to tell them what's going on down there. But in the old days, it was just their wits, patience, and a good deck of cards. So that's what we're going to do. How many of you have fished before?"

Most of them looked blank, but Jean-Charles's eyes lit up. "Back in Haiti, when I was a child, I fished with a pole off the pier."

"Once I fished from the bridge over the Lachine Canal," ventured Patrice, the Congolese youth, provoking a laugh from the others. The Lachine Canal was an old waterway running through the heart of Montreal, as urban as one could get.

"This is no different," Sebastien said cheerfully. "A fish is a fish. The lakes around here are full of trout, pike, perch, and bass, all swimming around down there looking for food. We're going to keep it simple and go for perch. Perfect for lunch." He selected a short rod from the collection of tackle in the corner. "Ice fishing is not complicated. First you drill some holes to test where the fish are, and then you pick the right rod and bait for the fish."

They all peered at the lures in the tackle box, neatly sorted by style and size. With delicate fingers, Sebastien selected one of the small, silver, spoon-shaped ones.

"The old-timers use live minnows or worms, but these shine like minnows and they don't introduce diseases to the lakes." He connected the lure to the hook and tested the line carefully before lowering the line into the hole.

"What if the ice breaks?" Hassan asked, edging nervously away from the hole.

"It won't. By February it is almost two feet thick. You can see the thickness in the fishing hole."

He reeled the line out slowly, until eventually it went slack. "Okay, we've hit the bottom, about forty feet down. That's perfect. Perch hang out near the bottom, so we'll reel it up about a foot or two, keep an eye on the tip of the rod, and gently move it up and down. Just enough to catch the fish's attention."

He talked them through the rest of the lesson and then handed his rod over to Jean-Charles so he could set up a second rod. "I'll drill a couple of holes outside, too, so some of you can fish outside if you want. Take turns so you don't get cold."

By the end of an hour, they were hovered over holes, their gaze fixed on their rods, and soon six good-sized perch glistened silver and gold in the pail. With each catch, laughter and shouts of excitement echoed across the lake. During breaks, Sebastien taught the group a traditional French Canadian card game called *Mitaines,* and competition for both fish and points became fierce. But, in the novelty, warm bonds were being forged.

Amanda moved from one dark, smoky hut to the other, offering snacks and taking photos. She smiled as she focused on Kalifa bent intently over her rod. With her huge brown eyes, long, fluid limbs, and the clash of orange and red scarves against her ebony skin, the young Somali girl was the perfect poster child for the trip.

After a couple of hours, she heard shrill voices raised on shore. She emerged from the hut and squinted against the glare of the snow to see Hassan and Yasmina facing each other on shore. The girl was stamping her foot and waving her arms, and although Amanda couldn't understand the Arabic, she could tell it was a tirade.

Hassan grabbed her arm, speaking too softly to be heard, but Yasmina abruptly broke off her rant. As Amanda strode toward them, preparing to intervene, they stepped apart.

"It's all right, Miss," Yasmina said.

"We're arguing about who gets firewood," Hassan added. Both were smiling at her, but Amanda could still see the angry flush of the girl's skin.

"Hassan doesn't want me to go into the woods alone," she said, her teasing tone belying her anger. "Well, I'm not, see?

Sylvie sent me to fill the water pail." With that, she turned and marched away, flipping her hijab over her shoulder in rebellion.

It was a small shred of interaction, but the hidden messages bothered Amanda. She returned to the fishing hut to find her crew standing in the doorway, watching.

"Hassan is afraid she is going to meet Luc," Jalil said.

Amanda looked at him in surprise. So far on the trip, the Iranian youth had spoken little and had kept slightly aloof. Unlike many of the other students, he had been in Canada for years and spoke English with barely an accent. "Does Hassan think Luc is still around?" she asked.

Jalil nodded.

Her gaze swept the group. "Do you all think he's still around?"

Nods all around.

Amanda had not told the group about the snowshoe trail she had followed for miles from the camp. "And why would Yasmina go to meet him, instead of telling me where he is?"

Jalil looked at the ground. Poked his boot in the snow. "You'll have to ask her."

"I'm asking you! If you know something, I need to know it. I'm responsible for all your safety."

When they all faced her like a wall, she tamped down her frustration with an effort. "Do any of you know? Patrice? Kalifa?"

One by one they looked away. Finally Jalil shot a wary glance at the others. "Maybe to keep him safe?"

Amanda turned and headed to shore, suspecting she'd get nothing out of him in front of the others. "Jalil, come with me."

He hesitated just long enough to show reluctance before following her. She angled down the shore, out of earshot of both the huts and the campfire. "Explain."

"I don't know anything, miss. They don't talk to me."

"But you suspect something."

"Hassan doesn't want Yasmina to see Luc."

"I got that part. But what about keeping him safe? Would Hassan hurt him?"

Jalil chewed on his lip. She knew from the files that the Persian youth was from an activist family and that his father had been a prominent journalist in Iran before being thrown in prison for criticizing the theocratic state. From the safety of Canada, his mother, a physician, had been waging a desperate war to free him. The family was smart, educated, and fearless. What was Jalil afraid of?

"Jalil? Are you afraid of Hassan?"

He looked shocked. "No! But ... he might hurt Luc. Or at least that's probably what Yasmina thinks."

"Do you think that's why Luc ran away?"

"Hassan only came on this trip because of Yasmina."

She pondered this. It didn't explain the snowshoe tracks leading miles away, but it was an important piece of evidence. A peek behind the wall of silence the group had erected. She didn't blame them. In war-torn countries, distrust and silence were crucial tools of self-preservation that had probably saved their lives more than once.

She thought back to the day before Luc's disappearance. Luc ...helping Yasmina with the dishes, making her tea, fingers touching. The smile between them.

Luc had been rubbing Hassan's nose in it all day long.

"Has Hassan done this before, with other young men?" she said. "Threatened them?"

"He doesn't have to. He just tells her he could go to her brother. It's enough."

Amanda was intimately familiar with the dance of male domination practised in much of the world. In some cultures, merely being seen in public with a man outside the family was enough to get a woman whipped. Or worse. It was the job of the male family members to control the females.

Not here, she thought. *Not on my watch.*

"What's it to Hassan?" she asked. "Is there an understanding between them? That she and he will someday—?"

"Oh, no. Hassan is her brother's friend. To let her come on this trip, he promised he'd watch her." He rolled his eyes. "We are not all like that, Miss Amanda, but I understand it is difficult for some families. The girls want to be like other Canadian girls. They want to sing and dance and go out with boys. Their families try to understand, because they are happy to be in Canada, but they are afraid too. Sometimes the girls change their clothes in the girls' washroom at school. They take off their hijab and put on makeup."

"Did Yasmina do that?"

Jalil frowned as if trying to remember. "She used to wear Western clothes and acted like other girls, yes, but I don't think her parents disapproved. But they sent her and her brother to summer school in Egypt, and now she acts more devout." He looked thoughtful. "It could be an act she puts on for the family."

It was difficult to picture Yasmina in a miniskirt and tank top instead of the black hijab and long black skirt she wore now, as traditional and modest as possible without a face covering. Amanda proceeded carefully, not wanting Jalil to become defensive. "Yes, I do understand that. All new Canadians wrestle with this clash between the old world and new, and with dating outside the group. Did Luc and Yasmina date secretly?"

He stared off into the woods where Yasmina had disappeared. It seemed a long way to go for a bucket of snow. Hassan had followed her discreetly at a distance, and now neither was in sight. Amanda felt a twinge of alarm. How far would he go to control her? Indeed, how far had he already gone?

Jalil broke the silence. "Once I was cutting through campus on my way home, and I saw Luc and her together. They were behind some bushes, sitting in a corner on the steps."

"Were they touching?"

"Just talking. But the way he looked at her ..."

"When was this?"

"Just after the Christmas break. I don't know if there was really anything going on. They have a religion class together, and maybe ..."

Amanda was only half listening. It was after the Christmas break that Luc's mother had come to her and that Luc himself had made his articulate plea. Had it all been a sham? A front, so he could be near the forbidden and untouchable girl he loved?

If so, had Zidane known? And more to the point, was that his real reason for wanting Luc excluded from the group?

As he scurried across the college campus, Matthew Goderich pulled down his fedora and turned up the collar of his leather jacket against the damp wind. Once again he cursed the country into which he'd been born. After decades pursuing stories in Asia and Africa, his body had forgotten such cold existed. To call the faux fur lining of his battered leather coat "insulation" was a joke, and if this cold kept up, he would have to relinquish his beloved fedora for a toque, for fuck's sake!

His mood was not improved by the dismal harvest of the morning's inquiries at Collège de La Salle. Because it was Saturday, the campus was almost deserted, and those few administrative and teaching staff he'd managed to find had all refused to discuss anything with him, although he could tell from their expressions that Luc was no prize. Confidentiality, they'd said. Every reporter's nightmare.

As he passed by the maintenance shed at the edge of the property, he spotted a large black man huddled on the back stoop, bundled head to toe in jackets and scarves and struggling to light a cigarette with his frozen fingers. *Ah-hah!* Probably one of the custodial staff who might be less wedded to the latest cover-your-ass privacy laws.

The custodian looked up as if alarmed to be caught smoking but relaxed when Matthew produced his own cigarette. He gave his name as Olu Yemitan from Nigeria, and since his English was on a par with his French, Matthew settled gratefully on the former. Throughout their brief conversation, Olu kept glancing nervously at the administration building, as if expecting a witch to emerge at any moment. Matthew lit them both a cigarette and chatted amiably about Canadian winter and the challenges of managing a smoke before venturing a question about marijuana smoking on campus.

"No marijuana!" Olu exclaimed. "Not here."

"What about other drugs?"

"Not here!"

Matthew sighed. "I'm not the police, okay? I'm trying to find a kid called Luc Prevost. I'm afraid he's got himself into trouble."

"What trouble?"

"He's missing." Matthew pulled a worried face. "If he's selling drugs, I'm afraid someone might have hurt him."

"Not drugs."

"You mean Luc wasn't selling drugs? Or there are no drugs here?"

The custodian shrugged and flicked his gaze toward the main building.

Matthew tried again. "Do you know who Luc Prevost is?"

The man nodded.

"Why?"

A startled look.

"Why do you know him? There must be … what … five thousand students here?"

"They ask me to watch him."

"Why?"

"For trouble."

Matthew smiled to himself. So the administrators used this underpaid, overworked immigrant to spy for them. Who better than a custodian, a jack-of-all-trades who could be fixing a light bulb in one place or trimming the shrubbery in another? An invisible cog in the workings of the school.

"What kind of trouble?"

"He meets strange people."

"Who?"

The custodian pressed his lips together, as if realizing too late he had already said more than he should. "I don't know them. Older. Luc don't have too much friends here."

"Who asked you to watch him? The director general?"

The custodian nearly choked on his cigarette. "No, no!"

"Then who?"

"Nothing bad. He cares about his students. He asks me to watch them."

"A professor?"

"No. He comes here, to help students."

"What's his name?"

The custodian had been watching the main door closely. Now he glanced at his watch, pinched his cigarette between callused fingers, and slipped the butt into his jacket pocket. A second later, the door opened and the director general strode out, her long cloak flapping in the wind. The custodian stood up to leave.

"I don't want trouble," he said, ducking his head against the chill as he disappeared, leaving Matthew in midquestion. *Who came to help students?*

It was only when he was racing across Sherbrooke Street half an hour later on his way to Luc's mother's house that a possible answer came to him.

Zidane.

CHAPTER SEVEN

By noon the sun was warm, and in the sheltered nook of the beach, the snow grew soggy underfoot. As promised, Sebastien had lit a bonfire to cook their lunch. The group clustered around the fire, laughing and licking their fingers as they barbequed the morning's catch on green balsam sticks. A few fish got singed and mangled in the process, but even so, there were more than enough to give everyone their fill. Kaylee delighted in the leftovers.

All through the meal, Amanda had watched a discreet dance between Hassan and Yasmina. It was hot by the campfire, and most of the others had shed their mitts and hats, but Yasmina was still swaddled in woollen scarves. Hassan had contrived to sit beside her during the meal, but when she got up for more fish, she had moved around the fire and squeezed herself between the two other girls, as if barricading herself against him. In turn, Zidane moved to take her spot beside Hassan, and the two of them chatted quietly in Arabic and slipped occasional sidelong glances at Yasmina.

Amanda's discomfort grew. She considered breaking into their private chat but in the end decided to wait until she could get Zidane alone before confronting him. Instead, she stood and gestured to Yasmina.

"Let's go into the woods and get more firewood."

The girl looked startled, for the fire was still blazing, and a good pile of wood sat beside it. She frowned as she followed Amanda away from the group. The pristine snow glistened white, and the sun twinkled through the lacy treetops, shooting slivers of golden light across the snow. Amanda led her into a clearing and gestured to the flawless blue sky. She began an oblique approach.

"It's so big and empty out here. Makes me feel small. A bit scared, too."

Yasmina looked alarmed. "Of wild animals?"

"No. Of the unknown. I was in Northern Africa a couple of years ago. It was mostly plains, and it felt like this, like standing on the edge of nothingness." She shivered at the memory. The threat there had been far less existential, the dusty scrub filled not with shadows on snow but with imagined ambushes and the rustle of scurrying feet.

Yasmina spoke shyly, as if groping her way forward. "I … I know what you went through."

"Who told you?"

"Monsieur Zidane. He told us you knew what it meant to be afraid. To be running away."

Amanda absorbed this with dismay. Her ordeal, and her escape, had been all over the news at the time and had been revisited last fall when she launched the Fun for Families project. She had wanted the adventure trips to be about resilience and hope, not about fear and escape, but obviously that was naïve. And perhaps misguided. If the kids could draw inspiration from her, so much the better.

She trod carefully. "He's a good guy, Monsieur Zidane?"

Yasmina quivered. A small spasm, quickly corrected. "He is very helpful."

"But do you like him? He seems to have a lot of influence."

"He gives guidance. He knows we need it. But we should get firewood."

Amanda wanted to ask more. At the beginning of the trip, Yasmina had joined Zidane's small prayer group on the outskirts of the camp, but recently she had not. Did it have anything to do with yesterday, when she'd been forced to spend the day in camp with him? Did it have to do with Luc's disappearance? Or with Hassan's control, which she clearly resented?

But the level of distrust was still too great, so Amanda smiled reassuringly and gestured to a massive fir that had fallen across the clearing. Without a word, she brandished her axe like an advancing army.

As they hacked off the boughs, Amanda cobbled together her next line of approach. "I noticed you arguing with Hassan this morning. He seems to want to protect you. That must get annoying."

Yasmina brought the axe down fiercely. "I can handle Hassan."

Amanda shot her a glance. The girl was smiling, belying the vehemence in her tone. Amanda chuckled. "I bet you can. But what a nuisance that you have to. Is that your parents' idea?"

"There are dangers. Canadian girls wear miniskirts, get drunk, dance like they're having sex. Sleep with men. This is not what the Qur'an teaches."

"But to be forced. To be spied on. Are you afraid?"

Yasmina threw the axe down. "What? You think they will lock me up? Beat me? Kill me? Like the propaganda in the Western media?"

Amanda held up her hands. "I'm not buying propaganda, Yasmina. But I have seen the worst that religious fanatics can do, so I never underestimate the dangers women face. You were upset when Hassan grabbed you today. You tried to hide it, but I saw it in your face."

"You can't help me with this. Let me handle it. I know how."

Reluctantly, Amanda backed off. Yasmina was right. Her clumsy intervention could make things worse. As with anyone being controlled, the biggest danger often came when they tried to break free. "Okay," she murmured, for the first time aware of the hushed woods and of the loud echo of their words carrying over the snow. "But I am here for you. If you ever want me to help, ever need anything, just make up an excuse to ask for help. I will be listening."

Yasmina's stance softened, and her eyes glinted in the dappled light. "You are very kind, Miss Amanda. I'm sorry I spoke harshly. You care about people. What you experienced in Africa was terrible. Does your family help you?"

Amanda was grateful for the shadows in the woods, which masked her surprise. Was this an overture? A prelude to further confidences? She picked her words carefully. "Once you've been through something that traumatic, there are few people who understand."

Yasmina nodded. "It's lonely. You have to find people who've been through it too. Does your family live in Montreal?"

"No, Ottawa." How long had it been since she'd seen them? Christmastime, for the obligatory gift exchange and turkey dinner, complete with clichéd toasts and pecks on the cheeks, during which not a single genuine feeling was shared. "They're both professors at Carleton University."

"Ah! Mine are at University of Montreal." Yasmina's eyes danced mischievously. "Are they wise?"

"Not really. Not about life."

"Mine neither." Yasmina laughed. "But at the end, it's not good to be alone. A husband, family, those are the greatest gifts." With that, she bent to gather an armload of kindling and tromped back toward the bonfire.

Amanda remained on the spot, puzzling over her cryptic words. On the surface, they sounded as if they were directed at Amanda, and God knows there was truth in them. She *was* alone. She'd built homes, only to leave them. Made friends, only to lose them. She'd been home from Africa a year and a half now, and she was still living in her aunt's cottage. And she'd drifted very far away from any hope of husband and family. She thought of Chris back in Newfoundland, of their last evening together, hand in hand, promising to stay in touch. The story of her life.

But perhaps Yasmina's cryptic words were meant instead as a reference to her own feelings? As a hint about the choices she was facing?

Possibly it was both. The girl was no fool; she was perceptive and subtle. Amanda had opened the door and offered her hand. Now she had to trust that the girl would accept the offer if she truly needed it.

Just as she arrived back at the bonfire, a muffled, incessant ringing chased that small sense of hope from her mind. The sound was coming from Sebastien's satellite phone. Was it Matthew? The police? Had something happened to Luc?

"Must be some emergency," Sebastien muttered, groping in his pocket. "Only our family has this number."

As he answered, he walked away from the questioning looks of the youth. Amanda followed, trying to be patient as a thousand concerns raced through her mind.

Sebastien was speaking French, answering in short questions. "Who? … No … A man? … Where? … What happened?" There was a long pause while the other person on the line talked. "I will discuss it, but I don't think it's a problem. Don't worry, don't worry!"

After he disconnected, he stood awhile toying with the phone. Amanda heard footsteps behind her and turned to see Sylvie at her side. "What is it?" she whispered. "His father? He's been sick."

Amanda shook her head. "Something has happened. Perhaps to do with Luc."

Sebastien reached into his supply box for his tube of maps. He gestured them over to one of the fishing huts, and only once they were inside did he speak. His voice was low. "That was my brother. He's a paramedic in L'Annonciation. He says they found a body—"

Amanda gasped. "Luc?"

Sebastien shook his head. "He doesn't know. That's all he heard. But he said it was in the bush north of here, and he wanted to warn me. He wants us to cut short the trip."

"What happened?"

"The police aren't releasing any details, but they are asking people to report any unusual activity or sightings in the area. From that, everyone is concluding the man was murdered."

Amanda clutched at straws. "But … it could be an accident, and police are just looking for witnesses."

Sebastien didn't respond. Amanda reached for more straws. "And it could have been dead for months. In this cold, there would be little decomposition."

It was Sylvie who yanked that straw out of reach. "If it was even from last week, the snowfall would have buried it."

Amanda cursed in frustration at herself. *Get a grip, Doucette. We need facts, not runaway speculation.* "Where was the body found?"

"Farther north, my brother said. Some dogs found it in the bush off a country road."

Sylvie was already unfurling the topographical map on the stool. As Sebastien turned on a flashlight, the three of them bent over the map. Sebastien found the country road and the approximate area. He studied the area, which was served by a single gravel road that ran northeast from the remote village of L'Ascension, slicing across the northern tip of the wildlife reserve. "Not much up there. A sugarbush and some back woodlots. There used to be farms, but it's too harsh a climate and too far from anywhere to keep the farms running. When the kids moved to the city, the farms were abandoned. Our own house was once part of a dairy farm."

Sylvie traced her finger back to their camp's location. "It's miles away. I don't see this as a threat. I don't think we need to change our plans."

As Amanda followed her finger, she felt a chill. It was true that the body was quite far away, but the route between it and their campsite ran right by the trail Luc and his mystery companion had followed. She suppressed her fear with an effort. "I have to tell the police about Luc," she said. "There's no fooling around now. What if it's him?" *Or almost as bad, what if he's responsible!*

Sylvie glanced at Sebastien. "Why don't you phone Danny?" She turned to Amanda. "He's a friend with the Sûreté du Québec. Sebastien has taken his son's class on wilderness trips, and Danny goes along."

"He's based out of the Mont-Laurier post," Sebastien said. "Farther west."

"But he might know who the victim is."

It took Sebastien a few phone calls to connect to the Mont-Laurier police station, only to discover that his friend was not on duty. From his end of the frustrating conversation, Amanda could tell that the clerk manning the phone was new and would not divulge a single iota of information, not even to confirm the existence of a body. She agreed to pass his message on to Danny when he came on duty, but she advised Sebastien that if he had any information related to a crime, he should report it directly to the main SQ post in Rawdon.

After jotting down the number, Sebastien hung up. "Bureaucratese," he grunted. "It's crept all the way up to Mont-Laurier. Should I wait for Danny to call me back, or should I try my luck with the Rawdon post?"

At first the clerk at the Rawdon post was no more forthcoming, even when Sebastien told her he had potential information about the death. She gave a desultory promise to pass his information on to the post commander. Only when Sebastien asked her directly whether his tour group should evacuate the area did she show any concern. She apparently asked him where they were, for he bent over the map and read out the coordinates of the campsite. A silence ensued, during which Sebastien covered the phone.

"She's checking with someone," he muttered. A moment later a male voice came on, tinny over the airwaves but loud enough for Amanda and Sylvie to hear. Sebastien held the phone away from his ear.

The man's French was clipped and formal. "I'm not at liberty to divulge any details of an ongoing investigation, sir."

"I understand," Sebastien retorted. "I only want to know whether our group is in any danger where we are."

"As I said, I—"

"I'm just asking — should we get the fuck out?"

A pause. "You're not in the immediate vicinity of the incident, so I won't advise an evacuation."

"What's the incident?"

"However, you may choose to go. And we will notify you if the situation changes."

Keeping the sarcasm out of his voice with an effort, Sebastien thanked him and hung up. He turned to Amanda with a questioning shrug. "Your call. It's your group."

Amanda looked at the map. Through her fear, she tried to be objective. "We're at least thirty kilometres away, and we're not on any route to anywhere. If there is a killer, why would he come through here? Much more likely that he got out using this gravel road up here."

"Or the snowmobile trail," Sebastien said. "But even that is four kilometres away through dense bush."

"And we have only one more day in the bush," Sylvie said. "This afternoon we are tobogganing. I know the kids are looking forward to that."

Amanda glanced out of the fishing hut. The students were toasting marshmallows around the bonfire, but there was a quiet watchfulness in their eyes.

"I wonder if we should tell them," she said, "and if so, what?"

"*Non,*" said Sylvie. "We tell them nothing. Make them scared for no reason?"

"But they have a right to know there's some danger, however small. And they may know something about Luc that they haven't told us."

"These kids have had enough of fear. They escaped from war!"

Sebastien smiled indulgently at his wife. "It's Amanda's call. Her head on the chopping block."

Amanda managed a grim smile. The obvious solution was to tell Zidane and get his input. Much as she hated to admit it, he knew these youths better than anyone. She'd just have to ignore the fact he could be an irritating, patronizing prick.

To her surprise, Zidane was neither irritating nor patronizing when she beckoned him to join them. The youth, their antennae finely tuned by a life of danger, sensed something was amiss. Their smiles faded and their solemn gazes followed Zidane's progress to the hut.

As soon as she mentioned the discovery of a body, Zidane snapped to attention. "Who?"

"We don't know. If the police know, they aren't telling us."

"Where?"

She bent over the map to point out the location of the body. Zidane studied it a long time, tracing down the road as it led south toward civilization. He swept the area surrounding the body with his finger. "And this is all farms?"

"Or bush. Sebastien says the farms are mostly abandoned."

"Who owns them?"

"I have no idea." Amanda felt a niggle of suspicion. "Zidane, do you know something?"

Zidane jerked back from the map as if he'd been stung. "No! I am trying to figure out who the dead person could be. Who lives in that area? Not many people, it seems."

"You're worried it may be Luc?"

He levelled his small, narrow eyes at her. "Aren't you?"

"Yes." *There, I've said it.* "But until we have more information from the police …"

"If someone killed him, they are probably in Montreal by now. Maybe out of—" He stopped so abruptly, he nearly choked.

"Out of what?" Amanda asked. "You mean out of the country?"

"Isn't that what killers do when they are trying to get away? They leave the country? Go to the States? Mexico?"

Suspicion still niggled at her, but she pretended to buy his excuse. Killers did escape to the United States and Mexico, especially if they had underworld connections and a safe haven there. Like drug dealers.

"I don't think we need to cancel the last day of the trip," she said, "but I have to tell the police, and I do think we should tell the kids."

Zidane was back studying the map. He seemed to have regained a sense of equilibrium, for his voice was calm. “What would we tell them? You say it’s more than thirty kilometres away. They are not in danger, and until we know more, I don’t want them worrying about Luc. This is probably some drunken snowmobiler who hit a tree.”

“The kids have a right to know about it.”

He stared her down. Her anger mounted. She debated reminding him that she was the boss, but in the end, she decided the words would sound weak. As if she were trying to convince herself.

Eventually, he himself broke the stare. “Very well. Do you want me to tell them?”

Not on your life, she thought. This time she did remind him. “It’s my expedition, my responsibility.”

As he turned to leave, a war of emotions flitted across his face. Not resentment, as she had expected, but something unreadable. Worry? Fear? Maybe even dread?

The man knows something, damn it, she thought. What the hell is he playing at, and just whose side is he on?

CHAPTER EIGHT

The duplex was a dump. The whole neighbourhood was a dump. Matthew had seen a lot of dumps in his time overseas and had learned to look for the little signs of trouble. In Montreal's east end, the old, crumbling, cold-water flats had been taken over by hipsters and yuppies eager for authentic urban cool. They'd repainted the wrought-iron railings, planted flowers in window boxes, laid expensive stone paths, and in some cases parked their shiny white Priuses in the lanes.

Ghyslaine Prevost's brick duplex had none of that. The steel staircase that spiralled up to the second and third floors probably hadn't seen fresh paint in half a century. Paint peeled from the battle-scarred front doors and the windows were grimy with the soot of passing buses. Creative window coverings had been tacked or taped in place.

There was not a Prius in sight.

Ghyslaine was on the top floor, and Matthew stood on the sidewalk for a moment, breathing deeply to shore up his reserves for the climb. Nonetheless, he was puffing by the time he hauled himself up to her little balcony. It was the middle of the day, so he'd phoned ahead to make sure she was home. He was prepared for hostility, since it had been his job to turn down her son's application on the first round, but she flung back the door the moment his boot hit the landing. She had slashed on some pink lipstick and black eyeliner, neither of which enhanced the yellow tinge of her skin, and she had curled her bleached hair into corkscrews that defied gravity. She was wearing hot pink leggings and a purple cowl sweater that plunged low over her breasts.

Good God, he thought, *she's pulling out all the stops. For me.* Immediately he wondered why.

"I made coffee," she said in English, thus sparing him the embarrassment of his French. She flashed him a coy smile. "I hope you like it strong."

He'd already had enough strong coffee that morning to power a rocket ship, but he played along. "Never turn down a cup of strong coffee."

He followed her into the flat, which was stiflingly hot, and glanced around to assess his surroundings. The furniture was worn but solid, reminding him that before her divorce there had been money in the marriage. Most of the good stuff had probably migrated to Westmount with the new wife, but clearly the new wife had not wanted the overstuffed leather sofa and the one-ton oak coffee table. A huge, yellowed print of the Eiffel Tower hung over the sofa, likely also a reject from wife number two.

In an effort at décor, however, bright pink curtains hung on the window, and amateur Montreal street scenes in garish acrylics plastered the walls. A quick glance at the signatures confirmed they had been painted by Ghyslaine herself.

"Sit down," she called over her shoulder as she disappeared down the narrow, dark hall. "I'll only be a minute."

Instead of sitting down, he prowled the room, peering at the books in the bookcases — mostly pop psychology, self-help, and bodice-ripping romances — and the CDs in teetering piles on the top. To his surprise, Ghyslaine's musical tastes ran from opera to classic Quebec folk.

Well-thumbed magazines sat in a neat stack in the corner of the coffee table, with *Elle* on the top. The only sign that a teenage male inhabited the flat was several pairs of large sneakers and a guitar in the corner.

Ghyslaine came back into the room just as he was examining the magazines. With a shy smile, she set two cups of coffee down on the oak monstrosity. "Do you have news?"

He shook his head. "Do you?"

"I've called all his friends that I know. I posted a message to his Facebook and Instagram accounts." Her chin wobbled. "Nothing."

"Did you call his father?"

She swallowed hard and looked away. "Brad doesn't care about Luc. And Luc knows it."

"Even so, fathers are important to children. Maybe Luc didn't want you to ..." Matthew hesitated in search of words. *Freak out* seemed unwise. "... worry, so he contacted his father."

She whipped her head back and forth, sending the curls leaping. "He'll get nothing from his father but a swift kick in the ass."

"What about money?"

She snorted. "Brad give him money? For nothing? No, no. 'The kid's eighteen, time to make his own money!'" She mimicked a man's scoffing tone. "Brad *says* he's putting money in a trust that Luc can't touch until he's twenty-five, but Luc gets the message loud and clear — he's a loser and his dad doesn't trust him. He'd ask me before he went begging to his father. Besides, what would he need money for?"

"Drugs."

She stiffened then slammed her cup down so hard, the coffee sloshed over the rim onto the table. She made no move to wipe it up. "Why does everyone assume the worst? He's clean!"

"Even if he's clean," Matthew said quietly, "he could owe people. Drug dealers don't forgive debts just because someone goes clean, and they have some scary ways to persuade you to pay."

Her face grew slack and she blinked rapidly.

"Has anyone unusual tried to contact him? Or you?"

"There have been some hang-ups. But there always are, eh? Luc made me get call display when he got out of jail. There are a lot of numbers I don't know. Luc says they're telemarketers and I shouldn't answer."

"Can I see your phone?"

When she brought him the phone, he scrolled through the recent call history. As she said, most looked like robocalls with area codes in the 800s, and she identified a couple as her friends.

He jotted down numbers. "Do you mind if I look at his computer?"

"I've already checked it. No clues."

"But still … fresh eyes."

She wavered. "He likes his privacy. He hates me even going in his room."

"Do you want me to help find him or not?"

She tightened her lips. After a brief battle with herself, she marched down the hall.

For a teenaged boy, Luc's room was surprisingly neat. "Jail taught him that," she said, as if seeing the incredulity on his face. "A clean room is a clean mind, he said. It helped him to feel in control."

Luc's laptop sat in the centre of his spotless desk. It was an old, clunky PC that took several minutes to boot up, and while they waited, Matthew did a cursory search of the youth's bookcase. Mostly course packs and used texts of political science and history, but a couple of books on dreams struck him as odd. Besides the classic *The Interpretation of Dreams* by Sigmund Freud, there were some promoting fanciful, new-age theories about the hidden messages in dreams. He picked one up to thumb through it. Big on spiritualism, thin on science.

Ghyslaine looked up from the computer. "That was a phase. Luc had trouble sleeping when he first got out of the group home, and he had some bizarre dreams. He was always looking for answers."

Matthew set the book back and moved on to the next shelf, which was entirely dedicated to classic French literature, including *L'Étranger* by Albert Camus, *La Porte Étroite* by André Gide, and *Huis Clos* by Jean-Paul Sartre. All three were powerful voices exploring the meaning of existence and individual morality within the strictures of colonialism and social expectations. Heady stuff for an eighteen-year-old.

Matthew remembered being enraptured himself as a student by the idea of finding one's own meaning in an essentially absurd world. It had led to his flirtation with communism, with Buddhism, and even, in his darkest moments, with nihilism before he finally stumbled upon a useful place for himself in the world — as a witness to the struggles of the masses. Was it significant that Luc was reaching back more than half a century to these classic thinkers?

"Why was he reading this stuff?" he asked. "Another phase?"

Ghyslaine frowned at the titles as if they were in Swahili. "Probably for his college course," she said without interest.

"I see he was studying history and political science, and all of these writers were philosophers and political thinkers of their time. Did he talk about their ideas?"

"I don't see what this has to do with his disappearance."

Matthew moved back over to open the desk drawers, where he found stacks of papers and notebooks. An essay about *Huis Clos* — *No Way Out*, if his memory served him right — about moral choices, and another on Camus, about the rejection of God. The papers were thin and the marks middling. Comments in red pen suggested that Luc demonstrated good potential but an inadequate grasp of the context. Matthew thumbed through other notes and assignments, which revealed similar comments about failing to live up to his potential.

Ghyslaine was watching him, her face reddening. "His father says he's not smart enough for university. Luc gets upset. But this stuff ..." She waved a dismissive hand at the classic books. "Who needs to know any of it anyway?"

"Who does he hang around with at the college?"

"He doesn't have many friends. He used to spend most of his time playing video games."

"But you told Amanda he went out late at night to meet people you didn't know."

Alarm flickered across her face, quickly replaced with impatience. "Luc was an unhappy boy, I know that. He wanted solutions. He tried all sorts of ideas, but he always got fed up with them."

"What sorts of ideas?"

"Oh, you know. Quebec separation, Idle No More, that Occupy stuff — any excuse to protest the oil pipeline, student tuition, big business." She paused. "He was angry about a lot of things, but really he was angry at his father. When you can't get your father's love and respect, no matter how hard you try, you lose faith in all people. Most of all in yourself."

Her soft words alarmed him, but before he could ask her if she was hinting at suicide, her gaze flicked to the computer. "Oh, it's ready!"

His fingers hovered over the keyboard. "What's the password?"

"I'll do it." She elbowed in front of him to shield the keyboard from his sight and tapped the keys. "For his privacy, you know?"

Matthew watched as the screen filled with icons. "How come you know the password? Did he tell you?"

She gave a sharp shake of her head. "I guessed. I have to make sure he stays okay. There was this girl … I found her name written all over his notebooks."

"Who?"

She wagged an admonishing finger at him. "There was nothing going on. She wasn't interested in him. But that's Luc, keeping his little heartbreaking dreams alive."

Matthew activated first the email page and then the social media pages, looking for themes, clues, and a recurring girl's name. For a young person, Luc didn't have many recent emails or much presence on social media. It was as if he were disconnected from the world of his peers. He had less than a hundred Facebook friends and rarely posted or commented. Most of his emails were ads from businesses or information from the college.

Ghyslaine was peering over his shoulder as he jotted down names of friends and professors. "Luc doesn't like the Internet much. He doesn't like companies spying on him and the government knowing too much about him. Once it's up on the net, you can't take it down again, he says, and ten years from now, someone might use it against you. He also thinks it makes us lonelier. *All we do is talk to a screen, Mom,* he says. *Look, I have eighty-six friends but nobody to go to a movie with.*"

After half an hour of browsing, Matthew had a sense of the boy's isolation and fears. He liked dystopian films, post-apocalyptic fantasies about unlikely heroes and the survival of the few in the face of world calamity. He worried about hurricanes and earthquakes and nature's wrath about our greedy destruction of the planet. A boy feeling lonely, powerless, and overwhelmed.

Like just about any other sensitive, thoughtful eighteen-year-old in today's world.

If Ghyslaine was aware of her son's existential despair, she didn't let on. Briefly, Matthew wondered whether he contemplated ending it all, whether wandering off into the wilderness in the dead of winter was a deliberate invitation to death. He was just debating whether to broach the subject when she turned briskly toward the door. "*Bon. C'est tout.* You have some material to investigate?"

"I'd like to do a quick search of his room," he said, opening up the second desk drawer. He hoped that somewhere in the neat pile of notebooks, there would be the name of a girl.

"No," Ghyslaine snapped. "That is too much of an invasion."

"Ghyslaine…." He didn't wait for permission as he rummaged through the drawers and knelt to peer under the bed. Nada. The room was remarkably spartan. Either the youth had never had many possessions, or he had got rid of them all when he left his father's house. Ghyslaine hovered, wringing her hands. What was she afraid he would find? A drug cache? Notes threatening to shoot up the school?

What he did find, in a cloth grocery sack hanging in the deepest corner of the closet, was another laptop. Sleek, paper-thin, and much more modern than the old clunker on his desk. Ghyslaine's eyes widened in genuine shock as he pulled it out of the bag.

"No!" she cried, trying to grab it from him.

He wrestled it out of her reach and flipped it open. His heart raced. Instinctively he knew he'd hit the jackpot. "What's the password?"

She whipped her head back and forth.

"Have you seen this before?"

"No!"

"Where did he get it? This is a top-of-the-line machine."

"It's not his! Maybe … maybe he's keeping it for a friend."

"Does he often keep things for 'a friend'?"

"Or maybe someone hid it there."

"Yes," he said. "Luc. How can he afford this?"

Tears gathered in her eyes. "I don't know. I don't understand. It can't be his!"

"What's his password? That will tell us soon enough."

She grabbed for the machine. "No! If he has this, if he has things he wants to hide from me, I can't betray him. No matter what, he is my son. He has a reason."

He sensed she was teetering at the crossroads, unwilling to follow the implications where they might lead. Unwilling to know. He held the laptop out of reach.

"Ghyslaine—" His cellphone rang. Ghyslaine jumped a foot. Recognizing the number as the one Amanda had used, he answered.

Amanda wasted no time on chit-chat. "Any word on Luc? Has he turned up in Montreal?"

He glanced at Ghyslaine. "No and no."

There was a pause. "Do you have any leads?"

"Nothing definitive, but possibly. Can I call you back?"

"Ah. You are with someone."

"Yes."

"Luc's mother?"

"Yes." He suspected he sounded like a third-rate spy. Luc's mother was frowning at him.

"Okay, just listen," Amanda said. "There's been a development, and she may hear about it on the news. A body has been found, not yet identified but in the general vicinity of where Luc went missing. I've got no details yet—"

"Fuck," he muttered.

"Well, nothing's confirmed, but since he hasn't turned up back home, I have to report him to the police. You should let her know, before the police come knocking at her door."

"Right. Can I call you back?"

After he'd signed off, he turned reluctantly to Ghyslaine. She must have read the gravity of his expression, for she sank down on the edge of Luc's bed. "News on Luc?"

There was no way to varnish the truth. "Not directly, but you need to know that police have found an unidentified body up in the area."

She gave a sharp wail, quickly stifled. "Where?"

"Amanda doesn't know any details. Near where he disappeared, that's all we know."

"But it could be anybody."

"Yes, but she has to tell the police Luc is missing now."

"No!'

"Ghyslaine, it's crucial information."

"Find out who it is! Find out the description and the age. Please! Before she tells the police."

"What the hell is going on? What are you hiding?" He brandished the laptop. "What is this hiding? The police need to know what's going on!"

"Give me that!" With demonic strength, she dived for the laptop. As he wrestled it away, tears coursed down her cheeks. "He can't be dead! Please don't give that to the police. I don't know what he's hiding, but if he's already dead, it won't matter. But if he's alive … he needs my protection. Above all else, no matter what he's done, I won't betray him."

It was a strange turn of phrase. *No matter what he's done.* She seemed more intent on keeping his secret than on finding out whether he was alive. As if she already knew something.

"All right," he said, following his instincts. "The police may visit you, and they may search his room to track his movements and contacts. Let me take this laptop away so I can see what's on it."

"No, no, no."

"I promise I'll tell you before I turn any information over to the police."

"But …" She struggled to breathe.

"We need to know, Ghyslaine. I can't find him for you if I don't know what he's up to."

She still had one hand on the bag as she searched his face. "You'll find him?"

"I'll try."

CHAPTER NINE

The three girls sailed down the hill amid shrieks of terror and joy, their toques awry and their cheeks polished red by the cold. When their toboggan hit a bump and capsized, they landed in a laughing heap in the snow. Snapping photos of them, even Amanda forgot for a moment the pall of worry hanging over them all. The kids had taken the news of the body — and its possible implications for Luc — with remarkable calm. Perhaps it meant that Luc's fate meant little to them, or perhaps death felt very far away in this vast wilderness.

By now the setting sun lit the clouds to the west in a golden wash, and shadows were settling deep in the woods. The campsite was nearly a half-hour trek from the toboggan hill, and Amanda knew they would soon have to head back. But the teens kept begging for one last run, and Amanda didn't have the heart to refuse. They were happy. Far from tropical Vietnam, drought-stricken Syria, and stifling Haiti, they were all revelling in the thrill of a classic Canadian sport. They were breathless and sweating from the climbs, red-cheeked and snowy from the descent. If they wanted to stay half an hour longer, the joy was worth it. The full moon on the snow would light the way back.

Sebastien had wanted to return to the base camp to monitor his sat phone for calls from the police, but Amanda had persuaded him that he could answer the phone just as easily from the toboggan hill. He flung himself into the spirit, but as evening approached, Amanda grew increasingly restless. She hated being out of the loop. She had made the missing persons report to the police station in Rawdon hours ago but had sensed from their doubtful questions that they suspected Luc was just sick of winter camping. There had been no follow-up call or news about the body. No call from Sebastien's police friend Danny or from the officer in charge of the death investigation. And now — damn him — no call from Matthew Goderich, who had promised to call her back with more news on Luc's mother and an update on his sleuthing.

Even while enjoying the fun, Amanda kept a watchful eye on the group. It seemed unlikely they knew anything about the mystery body, but she was less sure about their innocence when it came to Luc. Had he and Hassan really been arguing the night he disappeared? Did Zidane, who'd been so quick to dismiss any concern, know something he was keeping secret? But of all the students, it was Yasmina who seemed distracted and unpredictable, laughing wildly when the toboggan crashed and staring off into space halfway back up the hill.

They were strapping on their skis in preparation for the trip back to camp when Amanda heard the dim ringing of a phone. She snapped her head up and watched Sebastien's face as he answered. She saw his disappointment and his glance in her direction before he held out the phone to her.

It was Matthew calling her back. Finally! "You go ahead," she mouthed to Sebastien and then waited while the group shuffled off into the rich coral sunset. Then she listened while Matthew summarized his visit to Luc's home and his interview with the college custodian. She was particularly intrigued that someone at Luc's college, likely Zidane, was keeping tabs on his activities and that Luc had been meeting with older boys who were not from the college.

"The mother paints him as an unhappy, friendless kid who's looking for answers and also for someone to blame his troubles on. She's got an answer all ready; his father's rejection — the oldest blame-game in the world."

"That's handy for her. But …" She thought back over the conflicting facades Luc presented. "It's way more complicated than that. I can't get a handle on him. Sometimes he comes off as a sulky, condescending teenager and you can see why he has no friends. But I've seen another side — an articulate young man with a dream of where he wants to go and at least flashes of the intelligence needed to get there. Plus his disappearance doesn't add up. Zidane thinks it's to buy drugs, and the other kids think he's just messing with them, but I keep feeling we're missing something."

"And maybe we are. I think he has a secret, and his mother is playing both sides of the street on this one. She's terrified of getting the police involved, even though her kid is missing and may be in danger of freezing to death."

"May even be dead already."

"Right. It's as if she knows something terrible about him. I found this high-end laptop hidden in the back of his closet. His regular PC has nothing but lonely teenage trivia on it, but this laptop …"

Excitement surged through Amanda. Perhaps this held the key to Luc's contradictions! "What's on it?"

"I don't know yet. I've had no luck cracking the password, so I've got a call in to my tech geek contact. Meanwhile, I'm on my way to talk to the father. Maybe he gave it to him."

Amanda gazed off into the trees, skeletal grey sentinels against the pale snow. The full moon was rising in the indigo sky, promising a magical moonlit night. Sebastien had an after-dinner excursion of moon-gazing planned.

A niggle of fear wormed through her. "Let me know the minute you crack that laptop or talk to the father. It looks as if Luc was up to something. I don't know what that something is, but I'm getting a bad feeling. I've reported his disappearance to the police. Do you have any contacts in the SQ?"

"Sûreté du Québec? No. They're mainly in the rural areas and small towns. I do know a guy in the Montreal Police."

"He might know something. Maybe there's a BOLO out, or a bulletin about the body. Can you ask him what's going on? Sebastien's paramedic brother told him the body looked like it had been beaten. There aren't too many murders in rural Quebec, so it would be big news. Cops talk."

She was relieved when Matthew agreed without hesitation. Just as she was about to sign off, another idea struck her. "And while you're talking to your cop, can you ask him about criminal activity, like a drug lab or a grow-op, up here north of Mont Tremblant? It's pretty empty up here and the roads are terrible, so it would be easy to hide an operation in the bush."

Matthew chuckled. "Anything else you want the police to blab about?"

She laughed. It felt good to have a partner in crime who understood her so well. "Just call me if you get any information from Luc's dad."

"Will do. I'm just pulling up to his place now." He let out a long, low whistle. "Holy fuck, you should see this place. Five million if it's a buck. All that's missing are lions at the front gate."

"Ghyslaine didn't get the better end of that divorce deal, then?"

"Not by a long shot. I did a quick background check. The house is in new wifey's name, and on paper he has almost no assets. Neat trick if you can pull it off. I'm pulling up behind a Cadillac Escalade." He snorted. "And a Lexus for new wifey. No wonder Luc's nose is out of joint."

Amanda heard the car engine rattle to a stop and the door screech open. "Wish me luck, sweetheart," he said. "I'm not sure my pre-owned Toyota Corolla is going to impress."

Amanda arrived back at the base camp to find the group inside the cook tent, lolling around the stove and sipping hot tea. A hush fell over them as she pulled back the flap. Sylvie hovered over the stove, stirring a large pot. Delicious odours of molasses and tomatoes wafted from the pot. Sylvie smiled. "Old-fashioned baked beans tonight, without the pork fat. I substituted beef."

"It doesn't matter," Sebastien said. "I'm pan-frying some bass I caught this morning too." He sneaked a small, mischievous grin before turning serious. "Any news?"

Amanda glanced at the ring of attentive students. "Nothing much, but it's time to bug the police. I'll call from my tent."

She was too late to reach the police station before it closed for the day, and the clerk on call either knew nothing about the dead body or had been well trained in the art of stonewalling. No details concerning that case were being released at this time, and the clerk was aware of no new information regarding the status of the missing persons report.

"Can you at least tell me if it's been assigned?" She was speaking French in the hope of enhancing co-operation.

"That information is confidential, madame."

"But it's me who made the report!" Amanda exclaimed. "I'm concerned it may have something to do with the body found up north."

"That incident is being handled by a team from regional headquarters, madame. All inquiries or information should be passed on to them."

Amanda sighed. Perhaps she should try a softer approach and appeal to the woman's maternal side. "I will, but it's late and I'm out in the bush with nothing but a satellite phone and a bunch of scared kids whose friend has gone missing. I just need to reassure them that their friend is not dead and that every effort is being made to find him. He has ..." She hesitated. It was a shot in the dark. "He has a drug problem, you see, that we've all been trying to help him with. I'm concerned he may have gone looking for drugs or hooked up with a dealer operating somewhere up here. Do you know if there are much drugs up here in the Rouge-Matawin area?"

"It's not like the city," the woman said, "but you don't need a dealer. You can order almost anything on the Internet. You just need a post-office box."

Amanda's heart sank. Of course you could. But would Luc have had the time or forethought to set up a post-office box? "Oh dear," she replied. "How scary. Can you pass that information on to the investigating officer? It may be irrelevant, but he should know about Luc's possible drug involvement, in case that turns out to be relevant to the dead man too."

The clerk muttered a non-committal reassurance before signing off. Afterward, when Amanda relayed the conversation to Sylvie, Sebastien, and Zidane, Sebastien nodded grimly. "The Internet is the great equalizer. Even guns can be delivered by Canada Post right under the eyes of the police."

"Maybe so," Amanda said, "but to get his shipment of drugs, Luc would still need a post-office box or a mailing address, and he seemed to be heading in the wrong direction for either. I hope the cops are astute enough to see that subtlety."

"Oh, they're not the bumbling fools we often think they are," Sebastien said. "Drugs are big business in Quebec. We have a long, proud history of criminal corruption and trafficking in drugs, alcohol, and guns. Our biker gangs rank with the best, and they keep our cops on their toes. The SQ will play their cards really close to the vest, and we might think they're paying no attention to Luc, but they'll be investigating. Don't doubt it for a minute. With his criminal record, and the dead man, he'll be under a microscope."

Luc's mother couldn't have been more wrong, Matthew thought, as he watched Bradford MacLean turn several shades of crimson and purple before hitting his stride. Luc's father did care.

"What the fuck do you mean, *missing*?" he erupted. "Where? How long?"

"Well, it's not clear he's actually missing, Mr. MacLean." Matthew hadn't expected such emotion, and he lounged back in the sofa, hoping to model calm. Not difficult, since the white leather pillows enveloped him like whipped butter. It wasn't often he regretted his nomadic, penniless lifestyle, but a week in this mansion might be worth selling out a principle or two. "Your son sneaked away from the campsite, apparently met up with a companion, and headed north. Clearly on a mission."

"When?"

"Two nights ago."

Bradford MacLean grew a dangerously pre-apoplectic colour. It wouldn't take much to push this man over, Matthew thought. Heavy-jowled, overweight, and florid, he looked as if he lived life at full speed, bursting out of the gate at sunrise and going flat out until bed at 2:00 a.m. Matthew had known journalists like that, men who couldn't dial it down without a couple of strong Scotches by the bedside. Men who chased money, stories, and women, and who never seemed to get enough of any.

Men used to getting their way.

"And I'm just hearing about this now? Goddamn brainless bitch!" Bradford reached for his phone and snapped an order at it. "Google, call Ghyslaine."

"Hold on, Mr. MacLean. There's no point getting on her case. She's just as much in the dark as you are."

"But this was her stupid idea. Find himself winter camping, for fuck's sake! The kid's not going to find himself out there freezing his ass off. He's going to do it here in the city, by getting a part-time job slinging burgers, studying hard, laying off those stupid video games, and staying away from his loser friends." He cancelled the call and, as an alternative, leaped up to pace. "He's got brains but no staying power. He flits, always looking for the easiest way forward."

"When was the last time you saw him, Mr. MacLean?"

"What are you, the cops? Why the hell are you mixed up in this anyway? A journalist. Now that you've milked the Doucette story dry, is this your next big score? Pampered trucking tycoon's son caves under the pressures of modern life? I can see it now — portrait of a modern-day lost soul. Mother forgives him everything, father nothing. I do that to counter her, you know. Because if she had her way, he'd never let go of her teat."

Bradford picked up his phone again and dialled three digits.

"What are you doing?" Matthew exclaimed in surprise.

"Calling 911."

"Don't do that. They won't know anything down here. The SQ up north are handling it."

"Fuck the SQ. This is my *son!* You think I'm interested in the bureaucratic run-around? I'm taking the short cut. Hello? Yes, I want to report my son missing … Yes … No, he's eighteen … He *has* been missing forty-eight hours."

Matthew listened as Bradford talked his way through the labyrinth of questions. In the effortless assumption of privilege, he spoke in English, and although he was forced sometimes to repeat or rephrase, he never once raised his voice, lost his patience, or uttered a single swear word.

Within five minutes he was speaking to an officer in the missing persons' section, who appeared to be taking down the information Bradford supplied. Bradford played a little loose with the facts, claiming that his son had no experience in the wilderness and had stumbled away from the camp by accident in the dark. Local police had been notified, but everyone knew how short-staffed they were.

Matters only became tense when Bradford demanded to know when he would hear a report back. "I understand it's not your jurisdiction, but I have no access to the local Sûreté up there. You said the alert would be province-wide and all the jurisdictions co-operate, so I expect to hear everything that you do."

Matthew had to smile in admiration. It was an impressive show worthy of the best journalist, and when Bradford hung up, he grunted in satisfaction.

"Well, at least that lit a fire under their asses. He said the SQ would probably get local search-and-rescue involved. Everybody up there has a snowmobile and a 4x4. Somebody will find the little idiot."

Matthew winced at the casual contempt. "You told the officer you speak to your son often and saw him just last week. Is that true?"

Bradford sank into the matching white leather loveseat and picked up a glass of amber liquid from the glass side table. He had not offered Matthew anything, and now he swirled the ice around in a taunting way. "As it happens, I did speak to him last week.

Not for months before that, but he did show up on my doorstep one dark night — nearly midnight, in fact — looking like shit. Like he wasn't eating, wasn't sleeping, hadn't shaved in weeks."

"What did he want?"

"Money. He sat right on that couch where you're sitting and asked me for five grand."

Matthew hid his surprise with an effort. "Did he say why?"

"He said he was in a jam. I asked what's her name and he said it wasn't like that. I said no one ever solved a jam by throwing money at it. You solve it by facing it, so what's the jam, I said. He wouldn't tell me. Said he *couldn't* tell me. But if I loved him and I ever wanted to see him again, I'd give him the money."

"Did you take that as a threat, or—"

"A threat. Worthy of his mother. Just a loan, he assured me. He promised he'd pay me back when he was on his feet. Oh, like that five hundred bucks I gave you last year, that went straight up your nose? I was trying to make him mad. I want this kid to fight, to stand for something. And standing up to his tough-love old man was a good place to start. But you know what he did?" Bradford broke off, took a deep breath, and stared into his drink. "He started bawling and ran out of the house. Fucking bawling."

Matthew let the silence lengthen. The man had a weight on his shoulders. He'd refused his son's desperate plea, and now that son was missing. Maybe dead.

If you ever want to see me again could have meant far more than a petulant threat. "What's your guess?" he asked finally.

"Oh, it's not a guess. He's in over his head with some bad guys. Way, way over his head. If you don't pay your drug debts, you're in trouble really fast."

"So you think he needed the money to pay off a debt?"

"Either that or to get out of town. As far away as he could."

From his car, Matthew arranged to have a drink with Rolly Gendron, his contact in the Montreal Police, an investigator currently assigned to the bulging organized crime file. *Good luck with that,* Matthew thought, *and I hope you have a bulletproof vest and eyes in the back of your head.*

The file touched on most of the criminal activity in Montreal and reached its tentacles into drugs, border security, and the international cartels. Gendron had earned his stripes working undercover in a Quebec biker gang, but now after three wives and a stint in rehab, he did most of his intelligence work behind a desk on a computer. The Montreal Police Service seemed to view a small, mostly contained Scotch habit as an acceptable trade-off for his continued insights and skill.

Matthew arrived nearly half an hour late for his meeting with Gendron and found the cop seated in a dark corner with his back to the wall. What looked like a single-malt glowed amber in a tumbler beside a small glass of water. Matthew winced. He had no expense account and no news service prepared to pick up the tab, just his own paltry freelance earnings and Amanda's charitable fundraising account for Fun for Families. Even his flexible ethical standards did not stretch that far.

He waited until they had both ordered dinner — Gendron a sixteen-ounce rib steak with a third Scotch and himself a beer and burger — before he broached the reasons he'd asked for the meeting. His first priority was to find out what the police knew about the dead man in Mont Tremblant.

Gendron blinked in surprise, and Matthew could see him trying to make sense of the possible implications. "Why do you want to know?"

"Because Amanda Doucette is up in the area camping with a group of young people."

Gendron asked for her location and then grunted. "Probably she's in more danger from wolves than from the killer."

Matthew felt a chill race through him. "So he was murdered?"

Gendron grew still. "I didn't say that."

"Yes, you did."

"Fine. Yes, preliminary analysis at the scene suggests possible foul play. Hit on the head until there was not much left of it."

"Who's the dead guy?"

"It's not our jurisdiction."

Matthew rolled his eyes. "Come on, you guys get alerts all the time. Who is it?"

"He is not ID'd yet. There was nothing on the body, and like I said, the face is hamburger. There's a theory, but it's going to take dental work to confirm."

"What theory?"

"Come on, Goderich! That's way out of line. What's going on?"

Matthew sighed. The third Scotch was helping, but not enough. Time to broach his second question. "One of the kids went missing from the camping group two nights ago. He met up with someone and they disappeared into the bush." He paused. "Heading north toward the scene of that murder."

Gendron grew alert, all cop, as if the third Scotch hadn't touched him. "Does the SQ know this?"

"Yes. Amanda reported it, and so did the kid's father."

"Then they'll follow up."

"Have you heard anything? Anything I can reassure Amanda with?"

Gendron shook his head. "But we wouldn't. Not details. It's not our jurisdiction."

Their food arrived and Matthew signalled for another round of drinks, stalling while he formulated his next line of approach. "There may be a drug connection. The kid who's missing has

— or at least had — a drug habit and has done time as a young offender for dealing."

Gendron shovelled a chunk of steak into his mouth, showing more interest in his meal than in Matthew's piece of news. Matthew wondered whether he already knew.

"Not my jurisdiction," was all he said.

"Come on, Rolly! You don't get three Scotches and a one-pound steak for nothing!"

"I got nothing to trade. It's the first I heard of it."

"Okay, but is there any drug activity up there? Clandestine labs, grow-ops? And don't tell me it's not your jurisdiction. Anything that's grown or made up there is going to come through Montreal, and one of the organizations is going to be involved. Sooner or later, the intel will cross your desk."

"You think I have time for every two-bit drug lab or grow-op in the province? They're all over the place, and we don't even see half of them because the stuff goes straight online. Delivered in a nice pretty parcel by Canada Post. We've got more than our hands full just keeping up with all the biker gang and Mafia games in Montreal and down across the border. In case you haven't noticed, the Mafia have been bumping each other off in the past few years, and the Hells Angels are back in the game in a big way. All those guys I helped put away a couple of years ago? Back in business, and smarter this time around."

Matthew made a sympathetic face. No wonder the man had a three-Scotch habit. "Okay, can you find out if the SQ knows about any drug labs in the boonies of the Rouge-Matawin? And if they don't know, maybe they'd like to check it out."

"Northern part of Rouge-Matawin?" Gendron looked skeptical. "Transportation and postal services up there aren't world class, and you're getting into First Nations territory.

They usually like to run their own operations without using some two-bit white college kid from Montreal."

"But you can ask. Come on, Rolly, you've got your contacts in the SQ. You guys work together all the time."

Gendron carved up the last of his steak and used it to mop up the grease and gravy on his plate. He sighed. "I can ask. They might not tell me. The corruption inquiry has us all looking over our shoulders. When police chiefs and mayors are in the pocket of the mob, you have to watch who you confide in."

It was precious little to move forward on, more like a goddamn waste of an evening and two hundred bucks, Matthew thought as he paid the bill and steered Gendron into a cab. A light snow was falling, turning to slush on the salted streets. The lights made haloes of red and yellow in the darkness. Grumbling, he cleared off his car and climbed into its frozen interior. It was only ten o'clock, and in his world of journalism, the night was still young. His empty apartment held no appeal, and the nagging mystery of drug operations in the Quebec hinterland beckoned. Damn it. He'd been out of the country so long, he'd lost all his contacts. Did he know anybody who knew anybody in the SQ? Did he know anybody else in law enforcement?

As his little car shuddered reluctantly to life, a brilliant idea came to him. Because drugs involved organized crime with national, even international connections, police forces often worked together on joint task forces to coordinate raids, surveillance, and intelligence gathering. That meant that even in fiercely independent Quebec, in addition to municipal and provincial police services, sometimes the RCMP meddled.

And he did have the perfect contact in the RCMP. A cop not afraid to bend the rules, to charge into danger, to refuse to take no. A cop, moreover, who probably loved Amanda

Doucette as much as he did. Which was a problem he'd face another time.

RCMP Corporal Chris Tymko.

CHAPTER TEN

It was still pitch black when Amanda woke to the distant ringing of a satellite phone. She bolted upright and groped for her headlamp to read the time: 6:31 a.m.

Fear spiked through her. A call at that hour meant bad news. *Luc!* She scrambled to the front of her tent and fumbled with the zipper. Before she could grab Kaylee, the dog shot out of the tent, eager to investigate. As Amanda pulled on her parka, she registered a male voice. Initially the voice was just a muffled murmur emanating from a distant tent across the compound, but it grew louder with each response. Sharp and argumentative.

And more alarming still, in Arabic.

Amanda clambered out of the tent and played the beam of her flashlight across the snow until it picked up a figure walking away from the tents, his head bent as if cradling a phone. The figure whirled around to glare at the unexpected light. Zidane. He waved her away with an impatient chop of his hand and continued to distance himself from the camp.

One by one, flashlights lit up inside tents and murmurs arose. Sebastien and Sylvie emerged from their tents, hastily pulling on parkas against the breath-stopping predawn cold. Slowly the students too began to appear, wide-eyed and worried. Amanda heard Luc's name tossed about in alarm. Zidane was now out of sight, and his angry words were muffled.

Amanda approached Sebastien. "Is that your sat phone?"

He shook his head. "He must have brought his own."

Amanda stifled her irritation. The agreement had been a full wilderness experience, with all emergency communication channelled through Sebastien. Even she had not brought a sat phone. But her annoyance was quickly overpowered by worry, for Zidane sounded both angry and alarmed. She approached Hassan, who was standing outside his tent shivering in parka and moccasins. The whites of his eyes shone in the shifting light.

"Who's he talking to, Hassan?"

The youth looked evasive. "I'm not sure. A parent."

"What's it about? What's he saying?"

"Just arguing. Monsieur Zidane is telling him everything is fine."

More students clustered around. Those who spoke Arabic were nodding. "Monsieur Zidane says don't come. They want to come."

"No," Jalil corrected. "They *are* coming."

"Who?"

As one, they shrugged. Around the compound, Sebastien lit torches and Sylvie gathered an armload of firewood for the cook tent. "We're up," she muttered. "It's almost time anyway."

In the distance, Kaylee began to bark, and as Amanda set off to investigate, Zidane reappeared, having finished his phone conversation. As the camp torches played over his features, Amanda could see the tight set of his jaw. "I am sorry I woke everyone."

"What was that about?"

"A worried parent. They heard about the death, and they are sending their son to get the daughter."

"Sending him here?" Amanda was incredulous. "How?"

"The son has hired two men from the village."

"That's ridiculous. There are no roads near here."

"Snowmobiles. The men know where we are. The whole village knows."

Amanda was at a loss for words. The trip was unravelling before her eyes. First the demand that Sylvie be excluded, then the disappearance of Luc and the petty squabbling among the students. And now, a panicked, overreacting parent was descending into the middle of their pristine wilderness camp in a noisy, smelly snowmobile.

She made one last-ditch attempt to rescue her vision. "Let me speak to them," she said, holding out her hand for the phone.

He shook his head. "Too late. The brother has already left the village, so he won't hear the phone."

She made a rough calculation. Their base camp was probably twenty kilometres from the village, on a reasonably fast snowmobile less than an hour's ride. Her ears sifted the silence for the whine of an engine. Nothing. Not yet.

She gritted her teeth. "Who is the student? Before her brother arrives, I want to ask her what she wants to do."

"It won't matter. The family has decided."

"Who, Zidane?"

"Yasmina."

Amanda's heart sank. So much potential, so little power. "I still want to ask her," she said. "This is Canada and she is eighteen. What she wants *does* matter. And if she can't tell them that, I will."

He glared at her. "What do you think? That she's an oppressed, controlled woman who has no rights and no voice? Take away the hijab and the Muslim background, and they are parents, no more, no less. They want to keep her safe, that's all."

Amanda softened. They were standing at the edge of the camp, speaking in hoarse whispers to avoid being overheard by the students, who were now milling around the tents. Sparks from the smokestack in the cook tent shot high into the indigo sky as Sylvie stoked the fire, and to the east, pale peach smudged the horizon through the trees. "I do know that, Mr. Zidane. I'm not going to throw my values in their faces; I'm just going to try to persuade them to let her finish the trip with the group. We go back to the farmhouse today anyway. Let her enjoy these last two days with her new friends."

"You've got it all wrong," Zidane said. "They want this life for her. They are both university professors. They came to Canada to give her this life. Your life — an educated woman who chooses her own path, instead of being married at eighteen and controlled first by her father and then her husband."

"But they wouldn't let her come on this trip unless Hassan promised to look out for her."

"Because he's a family friend, and because it's a big, dangerous wilderness out here, that is all. They come from war. They ran to save their children from murderers and rapists, and now there is a man murdered right here in the area. That is why they are afraid." He paused, and his dark eyes took on a haunted look. "When you have experienced war, you never feel safe."

His words hit home, and yet something niggled at her. "She wears a hijab, yet she fights against her tradition."

"How many young people do you know who struggle with their identity? Who don't know who they are and where they belong? And when you come from another land, where the traditions are so different and you want to know how much of them you should honour, that is even harder. Her parents don't insist on the hijab — Yasmina does. It is Yasmina who insists on prayers and purity."

"She mentioned a husband, as if it was the most important gift she could have."

"Did she?" He pushed past her. "I need to talk to her. To give her time to pack and prepare herself. She can be a fighter, little Yasmina, and in this situation, that would not be a good idea."

When they reached the cook tent, they found the group clustered around the morning coffee pot. They were accosted with questions, but Zidane ignored them all as he scanned the group in search of Yasmina. There was no sign of her.

Outside, the campsite was deserted, the tents empty. It was Hassan who raised the alarm. He came rushing back from the direction of the latrine.

"She's gone," he cried, strident with panic. "She has packed her backpack and she has gone!"

After three days, the campsite was so trampled with footprints and toboggan tracks that it was impossible to tell in which direction Yasmina had gone. The students had several theories. Maybe she had gone to meet Luc, maybe she was afraid of her brother, or maybe she was trying to escape an arranged marriage.

Or maybe all three, Amanda thought.

Unlike Luc's disappearance, Yasmina's worried them. It was clear that even those who weren't her close friends admired her spirit and feared the brutal threat of winter. She didn't have warm enough boots and mitts, Jean-Charles said. She doesn't know how to snowshoe well enough, Kim-ly said. Only Kalifa was silent, her eyes round and dark with fear.

Amanda drew her aside. "When did she leave?" she asked quietly.

Kalifa shook her head in bewilderment. "When the argument woke us, she was here. She sat up and asked what was going on. When we all went outside, I thought she was with us. I didn't notice until Hassan said she was missing."

Amanda reviewed the sequence of events. Zidane's phone conversation, her questions to the students, her discussion with

Zidane, and their quick search of the grounds. It could not have taken much more than fifteen minutes. "Then she can't have gone far. Think, Kalifa. Did you see her at all in the crowd? Did you see her sneaking away?"

"I didn't see anything. At first she was behind me, and then she was gone!"

"What about her bag? Did you notice whether it was packed?"

"She always kept her bag packed." Kalifa allowed herself a shy smile. "Yasmina shared her bedroom with three younger sisters, so she was very private. Younger sisters are nosy and talk too much."

Amanda had never had a sister, much to her regret, although she had often imagined the mischief they would have created together. But she'd seen enough large, crowded families in Africa and Cambodia to know that siblings could be a curse as well as a blessing.

She thanked the girl and moved to join Sebastien and Sylvie, who were snapping on their skis. "We're going to check the perimeter of the camp to see if we can pick up her trail," Sebastien said.

"She doesn't have much of a head start," Amanda said. "She seems to have run away when she heard Zidane arguing on the phone. Maybe it was a spur of the moment decision because she heard her brother was coming."

Sylvie looked up, a lock of dark hair falling over her eyes. "That poor girl. What a life. Caught between the threat of her family and the threat of nature. But if we don't find her, she won't stand a chance out there."

Two snowmobiles, ancient, battered beasts, barrelled into the camp in a swirl of noise and gasoline fumes. Before they had even stopped, the passenger on the back of the first jumped down and yanked off his helmet, revealing a delicate young man with a tangle of black curls and the same striking good looks as his sister. Dark almond eyes fringed with long lashes, chiselled cheekbones, and flawless olive skin. His eyes darted anxiously over the crowd.

"Where is she?" he demanded in lightly accented French.

A few people shook their heads.

"She's *gone?*"

Zidane moved toward him. "Abdul …"

Ignoring him, Abdul whirled on Hassan. "You were supposed to keep her safe!"

Hassan took a defensive step backward, beginning a muttered protest in Arabic, but Abdul was not finished. He shouted at him, waving his arms, and although Amanda couldn't understand a word, the panic in his voice rang through. Zidane murmured for calm as he laid his hand on Abdul's arm, but the young man shook it off and shouted at both of them. *Why the freakout?* Amanda wondered. *The girl has been missing barely an hour.*

Zidane continued to be soothing as step by step he led the man away from the crowd. The argument drifted out of earshot, until only an occasional angry outburst from Abdul could be heard above the murmur. The other students stood in uneasy silence, their routine suspended. Although everyone sensed the gravity of the crisis, those who spoke Arabic looked wide-eyed with shock.

Amanda glanced at Jalil. "What's going on?"

He shook his head. "It's bad."

"What is?"

"If she dies, the family will sue you all, the brother says. You, and Sebastien, and Sylvie."

"She's not going to die!" Amanda snapped. "She has only been gone an hour or so. Sebastien and Sylvie will find her."

At that moment Abdul and Zidane emerged from the woods, and Amanda stepped forward to introduce herself.

Abdul barely looked at her. "Forgive me, but I have no time to waste—"

"Don't worry, we'll find her," she said. "Sebastien and Sylvie know these woods very well."

Abdul climbed back on the snowmobile and nodded to the driver. "So do these men. I'd rather put my trust in them than in those who lost her in the first place."

The snowmobiles sputtered to life, drowning out Amanda's attempt at a reply. From the corner of her eye, she saw Zidane draw Hassan inside his tent.

"When I find her," Abdul shouted, "I will not be bringing her back here!" He touched the driver, and the man gunned the throttle, leaving nothing but a haze of gas as the snowmobile disappeared into the trees.

Amanda fought back a surge of emotions. *Arrogant little twat* was her instinctive reaction, superseded by an effort at a more tempered compassion. The young man was afraid and looking for someone to blame. Yet she sensed something more than fear, something more primitive. Dread. Surely on this gentle February morning, which was dawning sunny and serene, there was little immediate danger from the wilderness.

She singled out Jalil again. "What was that argument about? What are we dealing with here?"

The Persian youth was the least loyal of the group, but even he looked uncomfortable about betraying a confidence. "The brother is afraid she has run away."

"Where?" Amanda demanded. "To Luc?"

Jalil shrugged. The other Arabic-speaking students studied their feet intently.

"What will he do to her if she has gone to Luc?"

Silence. A chill tickled her spine. "But Zidane says the family is progressive."

"They think Luc is a bad influence. Drugs, jail, broken home ... and he's not one of ... them."

Amanda replayed Yasmina's behaviour of the past few days — her anger at finding Luc gone, her secretive attempts to slip away from Hassan's overbearing vigilance, her claim to injury in order to stay behind at the campsite on the day Luc disappeared.

"Jalil, you're a good observer. Did Yasmina fake that ankle injury so she could sneak after Luc?"

Jalil didn't flinch, as if the idea was not new to him.

"And Zidane suspected it, didn't he? That's why he insisted on staying with her."

He raised his hands in a gesture of equivocation. "I know nothing for sure. But Yasmina was very angry that Luc left."

Amanda caught a glimpse of movement through the trees, and seconds later Sebastien and Sylvie skied into camp. In response to the questioning looks, they shook their heads. "We couldn't find her trail, but her brother will find her. They can cover a lot of ground on the snowmobile much faster than she can."

Not if she hides from them, Amanda thought, overcome by a sudden need to escape, to find a few moments to herself. To refocus and calm her growing fear. "I'll just have a quick look around myself. The rest of you should start breakfast. We've got a heavy day ahead."

As she leaned down to snap on her skis, her heart was racing. *What a mess!* Two children missing, gone God knows where, and families up in arms. This was supposed to be a happy escape from the pressures of growing up in a new country. An escape from danger, from their war-torn past and their confusing, conflicted present.

What a deluded fool I was to think I could inspire them and give them a taste of hope. To think I could counter all the fears and prejudices that had shaped their lives.

She was so busy berating herself that she didn't hear Kalifa approach until the Somali girl touched her on the shoulder. Amanda recoiled in surprise and ducked her head to hide the tears in her eyes.

Kalifa was not fooled. "I'm sorry," she said, her voice soft and deferential.

"Don't be." Amanda reached out to hug her. "I'm on edge, worried about Yasmina and Luc."

Kalifa nodded. "There's more. I heard some words when the brother was arguing with Hassan and Monsieur Zidane. It is not about Luc."

"What is it about?"

Kalifa hesitated and lowered her voice even further. "The family found a plane ticket on her computer. Yasmina had deleted it, but it was in the trash."

"She was running away with Luc?"

"The plane ticket is to Istanbul. And her passport is missing."

"Istanbul!" Amanda's thoughts cartwheeled. Of all the places in the world! "Does she know anyone in Istanbul?"

"There were emails on her computer. She is going to meet a man the family doesn't know. Abu Osama. They are very, very scared." Kalifa paused. "Zidane knows of him."

"Zidane!" *What the hell!* Amanda glanced around the camp. There was no sign of Hassan or Zidane. "Who is Abu Osama? An online boyfriend?"

Kalifa took a deep breath. "Maybe. I couldn't hear everything. Just the word *marriage*, and the word *Iraq*."

Jesus Christ, Amanda thought. From Turkey to Iraq. ISIS?

CHAPTER ELEVEN

Amanda skied around the perimeter of the camp, looking for Zidane and trying to pick up Yasmina's trail. It was no use. Snowmobile tracks swept in and out, and the whole group had trampled trails through the woods in the past four days in search of firewood.

The silence hung overhead, breathless and airy, broken only by the occasional whine of engines. When the snowmobiles finally faded from earshot, Amanda returned to camp to find breakfast over and the students packing up camp. Expressions were glum. Gone was the mixture of exhilaration and apprehension that had animated them in the previous days. They looked as though they were plodding through the motions, their thoughts already returning to school, friends, family, and their beloved cellphones.

She walked from group to group, offering assurances that Yasmina had likely already been rescued and was on her way back to Montreal with her family. Zidane was nowhere in sight, but she found Hassan in their tent, rolling up his sleeping bag. Zidane's sleeping spot was empty.

"He's gone," Hassan muttered, avoiding her gaze. His voice was subdued, and he looked close to tears.

"Where?"

The youth knelt on his hands and knees, wrestling the bag into submission. "Hassan, gone where?"

"Back to Montreal. To deal with this."

"How the hell is he getting back to Montreal?"

"I don't know. The other snowmobile took him back to the village."

"And what is he going to do once he gets to Montreal?"

"He said he was going to meet with some people."

"Who?"

Hassan shrugged.

Amanda knelt in front of him, forcing him to look at her. "Abu Osama?"

Hassan's eyes widened. "I don't know anything about him."

"Then what do you know? Is Yasmina running away to Iraq?"

A long silence. A deep swallow.

"Hassan, you realize this could be a serious national security matter. The police may be involved."

"That's what the family wants to avoid. That's why they want to stop her. So there are no police."

"Okay, but I can't help if I'm in the dark. Talk to me! Are you involved with this disappearance too?"

He whipped his head back and forth. "Abdul is my friend. Their family and mine are friends. They are nice people, but they are worrying about Yasmina. She was dropping her friends. She was asking her family to be more strict — no TV, no music — and she was refusing their food and reading only the Qur'an and religious poetry. She put on the hijab and asked her sisters to respect their modesty too. Her parents thought she was just questioning her place and exploring her roots. But they worried about how much time she spent on the Internet and the secrets she had. They asked me to watch her at school."

"To report to them?"

He flinched. "To tell them who she was meeting. When she wanted to come on this trip, they were very happy. But they worry when they learn Luc was coming too. They think he is a bad influence."

She thought about Hassan's last-minute enrolment in the trip. "So they asked you to go along?"

He shrugged. "To please Abdul and my parents, I said yes. But this cold and snow ..."

"I could tell it wasn't really your idea of fun."

He managed a thin smile. "That's all I know. I was to watch out for her and Luc. Monsieur Zidane told me to watch her too. He has been advising the family."

"How?"

"That's all I know. Maybe to tell them how they are handling her new ways. They aren't traditional, and Canadian life has been good to them. I think he told them she should explore. If they try to stop her, they push her more away."

Amanda considered the implications. If that were true, then Zidane's advice had backfired and now he would be in deep trouble with the family. No wonder he'd hurried back to the city to deal with it.

She stood up to let the youth continue packing. He looked shattered. He too had failed in his assignment and would be censured when he faced his family and hers again. But Amanda wondered whether there was more to his distress. She had seen the yearning glances he'd given Yasmina and scowls he'd directed at Luc. Had this also been, deep down, an affair of the heart? A love triangle that had been blown apart by an interloper?

She headed outside. She had to call Matthew. He needed to know the latest developments, and she needed him to start digging into the interloper's identity.

Abu Osama. The seducer from Iraq.

Matthew's finger hovered over the keypad of his cellphone. He was plagued by second thoughts. After his meeting with his police contact the night before, he'd been all fired up about enlisting Chris Tymko's help with the case of the mysterious drug lab, but in the sober morning light, he balked.

Chris Tymko was a hero — the sort of upright, straight-as-an-arrow Mountie that the force dreamed of. If he wasn't your matinee-idol, perfect-looks type of guy, he made up for it in heart and folksy charm. Furthermore, he was six inches taller than Matthew and fifteen years younger. With Chris in the room, Amanda wouldn't give Matthew a second thought. Not that he harboured any illusions about his chances anyway, but it didn't help his ego to be cast into the shadow by the shine of Tymko's halo.

In the end, however, it was the thought of Amanda that forced his finger to dial. She'd asked him for help, and as if that weren't reason enough, she might even be in danger up there in the wilds if there was a criminal enterprise nearby.

He was half hoping the call would go to voicemail so he could ease into the contact slowly, but Chris picked up on the second ring. His hearty voice burst over the speaker, full of surprise and delight. "God! Wow, I was just thinking about you."

Matthew grinned at the nickname, which was a Tymko trademark, usually intended with irony. "Not a freckle-faced, five-foot-two ball of fire?"

Chis laughed. "Her too. I just arrived in Quebec, and I wondered if we could all meet up, or if Amanda had started her winter adventure trip."

"Where in Quebec?"

"Montreal. Just grabbing a rental at the airport."

"Leaving the beloved Rock already?"

Chris laughed again. He had always laughed often and easily, and Matthew could picture his whole face crinkling in delight.

"No, I'm still in Newfoundland, but a buddy and I signed up for a French language training course. I'm going to try to turn this Saskatchewan farm boy into a bilingual asset. But you called. What's up?"

"Have you had breakfast yet?"

"The best Air Canada has to offer."

"So, no. Set your GPS to Café Joe on Rue St. Antoine. It's a bit artsy, but the food's great. You're in Montreal, the centre of the culinary universe."

"You springing for it?"

"Hah! You're the one earning a living."

When Matthew hung up, he was smiling. It felt good to hear Chris's voice. Memories of Newfoundland flooded in. Newfoundland had brought the three of them together as they tried desperately to rescue a friend who had lost his way. The effort, and the outcome, had been powerful and life-changing for all of them.

Matthew barely had time to scurry down Greene Avenue and along St. Antoine to the café before he spotted a shiny new pickup truck trying to squeeze into a spot across the street.

The tall Mountie jackknifed himself out the door, bumping his head on the doorframe as he unfolded himself. At well over six feet, he was like an oversized marionette controlled by an inexpert puppeteer. Arms and legs seemed to go every which way, and the fur flaps of his Mountie's hat slid over his eyes.

The two men shook hands before Chris shoved his hat out of his eyes and stood wide-eyed for a moment, drinking in the clamour and clutter of the old street. "Wow, that's some crazy driving getting here! And there are more cars on this street than in all of Newfoundland!"

"This is an old part of the city," Matthew said. "It's been to hell and back, first settled by the poor Irish and black working class, now hip and artistic. I like how it has always thumbed its nose at snooty Westmount just up the hill."

They walked to the homey little café on the corner and lucked into a table in the front window. Plants and paintings overflowed the space, and soft jazz washed the air. Chris was still grinning ear to ear like a kid let loose in Disney World.

"Their crepes are a weekend specialty," Matthew said.

"I'm more a bacon and eggs guy." Chris looked around at the other tables, where young patrons sporting beards and trailing scarves sipped cappuccinos. He wrinkled his brow. "They do that, don't they?"

Matthew laughed. He was thirty years older than most of the crowd, but at least he looked suitably rumpled. Chris, spit-polished and ramrod-straight, was all cop.

Matthew waited until Chris had ordered two eggs sunny side up with bacon and home fries and had downed half a cup of fabulous coffee before broaching the subject at hand.

"There have been some complications in Amanda's trip."

Chris's smile faded, replaced by classic cop focus. "Is she all right?"

Matthew shrugged. "She's camping in the middle of freezing nowhere, if anybody can be okay with that."

"So what are the complications?"

Matthew filled him in on the disappearance of Luc, his drug history, and his plea for five thousand dollars from his father. "It looks as if the kid was deliberately heading north, further into the boonies, so we're wondering if there's a clan lab — meth, ecstasy, marijuana grow-op — up there. Whether there's anything on the cops' radar."

Chris had been piling egg onto his toast and paused with a forkful halfway to his mouth. He eyed it longingly before laying it down. "And you want me to work my cop magic and find out?"

Matthew spread his hands sheepishly.

"I can't just willy-nilly hand over confidential police information, God, even if I could dig it up."

"You don't have to hand it over. Just look into it, and let me know if there's any reason for concern. One word, Chris. Yes or no. To ease her mind."

If any hook was going to work, that should. Chris shovelled the toast into his mouth and chewed thoughtfully. "There's an awful lot of confidential information contained in that simple yes or no. And it would probably be an SQ operation. A lowly, unilingual Mountie from a Newfoundland outpost isn't going to pry much out of them."

Matthew grinned. "Since when has that stopped you before? Anyway, there's another complication."

Chris stopped chewing. Waited. Matthew told him about the dead body found not far from Amanda's camp. For dramatic purposes, he exaggerated the proximity a little. Now Chris looked alarmed. He asked the name of the police post handling the case and jotted down the information.

"The cops there say Amanda's group isn't in danger," Matthew said, "but my contact in the Montreal Police says the man was beaten around the head, making identification difficult. We're worried it might be Luc. Can you—"

"Absolutely. I'll find out who he is, at least get a general description like age and size, so you can rule out Luc." Chris paused. "Or not."

"And can you find out what the cops think is going on? If there's a connection to drugs, or …"

Chris wrote a few notes and then sat twirling his pen over his notebook. After a moment, he sighed. "I get it. Drugs, clan labs …" He gave Matthew a big smile. "All part of my cop magic."

In the interests of encouraging French practice, the training course participants were being housed in a small, budget apartment hotel in Montreal's east end, far from the city's eclectic, multilingual core. The course had been Liam McIntyre's idea, but Chris had jumped at the chance. Liam was a friend from their rookie days together in Alberta, and friends were hard enough to come by, let alone keep. Moreover, it was a chance to see Montreal. Not that he didn't love his posting in Deer Lake, Newfoundland. He was a country boy at heart, fond of open spaces, blue skies, hiking, and fishing. But Montreal meant the possibility of seeing Amanda again.

Liam's motives for taking the course were more direct. Although most of his postings had been in Western Canada, he was originally from rural Outaouais in the western corner of Quebec. Settled by the Irish in the 1800s, the Outaouais had retained its stubborn Irish blue-collar identity, and Liam McIntyre had managed to spend the first eighteen years of his life in a French province without learning more than a few French swear words. Now, ten years later and gazing up the promotional ladder of his chosen profession, he regretted that pig-headed pride.

Chris doubted stubbornness was an asset in the promotional game either, but Liam had other useful qualities. Gregarious and fun-loving, he made friends wherever he went. As it turned out, one of those friends was a childhood pal posted to an SQ detachment right smack in the middle of the Laurentian District.

Chris had already decided that to find the answers Matthew needed, informal networks would be safer and more effective than any attempt to breach the walls of the SQ or the RCMP head on. He didn't want some police bureaucrat somewhere wondering why a patrol corporal from rural Newfoundland wanted to know about dead bodies and clan labs in northern Quebec.

Chris broached the subject of the dead body as soon as they reached their room. He didn't beat around the bush. Liam was a joker, but he wasn't a fool. Chris gave him a version of the truth that emphasized his concern for the safety of a friend in the area.

Liam's eyes twinkled. "Friend, eh? Female? Finally?"

Chris felt a flush creep up his neck. He could never think of Amanda without a rush of emotion. She'd been a lost and broken soul when he'd met her back in Newfoundland, and he'd planned to let her heal back home with her family for a couple of months before renewing the contact. But that couple of months had stretched to six with only sporadic emails from her, and the dream of connection had faded. The rush of emotion had not.

His red face was his Achilles heel, betraying him at the worst times. "A friend, for now," he said sheepishly. "She's been through a couple of tough years, and she doesn't need more danger."

"You want me to ask my friend Butch what the investigation has revealed?"

Chris nodded and Liam studied him in silence. Slowly the twinkle faded from his eyes. Liam wasn't a tall man, but his barrel chest rippled with muscle. He'd already insisted Chris come to the local gym with him to add some weight to his reedy frame. Chicks love that stuff, he'd said. Chris had once tried to bulk up by weightlifting, but it had been useless. Maybe it was worth another try.

He put on a crooked grin. "Even if you just introduce me to him, I'd owe you big-time. Maybe even a few sessions at the gym."

"To see that, it would be worth it. But I'll have to butter him up first. He's not the sharpest knife in the drawer, but he's a straight-up guy. We were high school friends, played in a band together, but it's been years."

"Fair enough." Chris waited a beat. "Can you put it on speakerphone?"

"Sure, but it might take me a while to reach him. It's Sunday." Liam pulled out his cellphone and settled into the armchair in the corner of the room. After a series of calls and inquiries, his face lit up and he switched to speakerphone.

"Butchie! You old sonofabitch! It's Mac. How the hell are you?"

A brief silence ensued, followed by "Mac? McIntyre? Shawville Rockers?"

"The one and only."

"Where are you? Alberta?" Butch, whose real name was Boucher, spoke English with a light French-Canadian accent.

"Montreal. French language training."

Boucher laughed, a long, hearty roar that rippled through the room. "How's that going?"

"Starts tomorrow. But I've been practising up on my swear words. *Tabernac*, we have to get together while I'm here, catch up on news."

"Are you going to visit the old place while you're out east?"

A flicker passed over Liam's face before he spoke. "Nobody left there except those in the ground. How's the SQ been treating you? You doing anything besides breaking up bar fights and handing out speeding tickets?"

"It's a living. It's pretty busy, actually. We got a murder inquiry."

Liam paused, and Chris could see him calculating how to play it. In the end he opted to drop the pretence. "Yeah, I heard. That's one reason I called. I mean, it's great to talk to you, and we have to get together while I'm here, but right now I need a favour for a buddy. A fellow officer."

Boucher breathed a soft curse. "*Câline.* What's going on, McIntyre?"

Liam related what Chris had told him about Amanda and the missing student. "I don't want to put you on the spot, Butchie. It's just it would really ease this guy's mind if he knew whether you'd ID'd the victim. And who killed him."

"It's not our investigation. It's being handled by the regional crime unit."

"Is there anything you can tell me? How about the identity of the victim?"

"Can't say until next of kin is notified."

"But you've identified him."

Pause. "Yeah."

"Is he a white male, medium height and build?"

"Yeah."

"Age about eighteen to twenty?"

"He's not the missing kid."

Hearing this, Chris felt a surge of relief. He mouthed *Who?* to Liam. "Who is he, then?" Liam asked obligingly. "Not his name, but generally. A tourist?"

"A local. That's all I can say. His son is on his way to Montreal to identify the remains."

"And how did he die?"

"Looks like severe blows to the head. The post-mortem is scheduled for tomorrow."

"Any suspects? Motives?

"Not a clue. He was a quiet guy, lived alone on his farm. Well, he didn't farm it any more, he just did some construction jobs."

"So … no suggestion this missing kid was involved?"

Boucher seemed to remember, a bit late, that he wasn't supposed to discuss the case. "I can't say, Mac. That's out of bounds."

Chris gestured to Liam to let him talk. After a bit of mimed disagreement, Liam returned to the conversation. "Listen, Butchie, do you mind talking to my friend directly? His name is Chris Tymko. He's got a bit of information, so it might be worth your while to talk to him. Can't hurt your career, you know?"

Chris crackled the line before speaking, as if they were exchanging phones. "Thanks for easing my mind that it's not my friend's student who's dead."

"I can't tell you any more."

"I know. This isn't official, but I want—"

"Mac says you got information."

"The missing student has a drug problem and a history of dealing — coke, ecstasy, as well as marijuana. He was last seen in the area near the body. Maybe there's a drug operation up there?"

"Not that I know of."

"Are the detectives pursuing it?"

"Yeah, they are."

"Looking at sat photos, hydro records, increased or unusual traffic? Should be easy to spot if there's nothing but empty bush up there."

"So far there's been no unusual activity. Some construction vehicles have been spotted, and some parked trailers, but the dead man worked construction, and he let hunters on his property in the fall, and fishermen in the spring. Makes a few bucks any way he can, I guess."

"Okay, but meth and ecstasy are really cheap and easy to move, so even small increases in traffic might mean something. Trailers especially — they make great portable labs."

"Well, I don't know if there's anything like that."

"Worth mentioning it to your superior anyway, so he can pass it on."

There was a silence. Then a frosty tone. "Do you know something you're not telling me?"

Maybe not the sharpest knife, Chris thought, but not the dullest either. "I'm just trying to put the pieces together."

"What force are you with?"

"RCMP."

"Then you can ask your own bosses, because you guys are running the show now anyways."

"What do you mean?"

"They've muscled in and taken over the investigation. They won't tell the local SQ a damn thing. So you're not getting a damn thing more out of me either."

CHAPTER TWELVE

Matthew lingered at Café Joe after Chris left, enjoying the funky ambience and reluctant to go back out into the cold. The rest of the breakfast crowd had thinned, so he ordered a third cup of coffee and took over an extra table for his notes and laptop. He was still deeply immersed in the machinations of Quebec's underworld when Chris phoned with an update on his conversation with his SQ contacts. With a deep sigh of relief, Matthew was preparing to pass on the good news to Amanda when his phone rang again.

"Amanda! Good news," he cried when he heard her voice.

She sounded breathless and strained. "Thank God. You've found Luc?'

"No, but I put Chris Tymko on it to find out what he could about your dead man and any drug connection."

"Chris! Oh!" To his chagrin, she sounded as if a light had shone into her darkness. "Where is he?"

"Here in Montreal, on French language training."

She laughed. "And he's already looking for an escape? What did he find out?"

"The dead man is not Luc." When he filled her in on the highlights of Chris's report, her relief was palpable but short-lived. "But this whole adventure has gone from bad to worse. It's a mess! Now we've had a second kid run away, and this one may be heading for Montreal airport."

"Who?"

"The young Iraqi woman named Yasmina. She and Luc have a history — I'm not sure what — so it's even possible he's making his way to the airport too. Did you find any airline tickets on his computer?"

"No, but—" He drew a sharp breath. He'd been so caught up in talking to the police that he'd all but forgotten the other computer. "There's a second computer, a secret one hidden in his closet."

"Can you check it?"

"Yeah, but it's at my apartment." He slammed the laptop shut and started to pack his notes into his bag. "I'll get on it."

"You need to get to the airport. I don't know when Yasmina's flight is, but she ran away early this morning, so if she manages to reach Mont Tremblant's tiny airport and catches a flight, she might arrive in Montreal in a couple of hours. That's all the time you have."

"Have the police been notified?"

"I don't know, but judging from the family's frantic reaction, I think they're trying to stop her themselves."

"Why?"

"Because she's flying to Istanbul, and she's run away to meet a man called Abu Osama."

"An online boyfriend?"

"I don't think so." Her voice grew hushed. "That's why the family's freaked. I think he may be an ISIS recruiter."

Jesus! He thrust back his chair and threw on his parka. "I'm on my way!"

"Please! Keep me informed. I don't know what Luc's involvement is, but if he was trying to stop her or ..."

She left the possibilities unspoken, but he was one step ahead of her. As he flagged down a passing cab, his mind was already racing ahead to the implications. Luc had begged his father for five thousand dollars and wept when he was refused. Was that money to help Yasmina or to make his own travel plans to go with her? The password to the secret computer had stymied him, but now the obvious answer was right before him. *A girl's name,* his mother had said.

Reaching his apartment in barely five minutes, he flung his coat and bag on the bed and snatched up the small, ultra-thin computer. His fingers flew over the keyboard.

Bingo!

The desktop opened up into an array of documents and applications, including the encryption software used to access the cyber underworld popular with terrorists, criminals, and others wanting to leave no digital trace. Nervously, Matthew opened it and slipped into the anonymous ether of the Dark Web. Some of the documents were still encrypted, but the social media program opened without effort, flooding the screen with messages dating back to the fall and ending the day before the camping trip. Many of the messages were strung together in an online, running conversation between two people. One was a man named al-Kanadi, whom, after reading a number of his emails, Matthew came to recognize as Luc.

The other man called himself Imam Mahmoud.

Matthew felt that rush of adrenaline that always happened when a story broke wide open. Quivering with anticipation, he settled down to read. The conversation led him to Facebook and Twitter pages, YouTube videos, and even to the glossy, violence-laced *Dabiq* magazine, which he knew to be the propaganda outlet of the jihadi movement. Propaganda was as crucial a weapon of global jihad as actual warfare, and the jihadi groups competed fiercely with each other to put out the slickest, most outrageous propaganda in an effort to lure fresh new foreign recruits to their team. Bold and defiant, ISIS was winning the propaganda war by a landslide, ensuring a steady stream of new cannon fodder.

It appeared that Luc's connection had begun on the regular Internet months earlier when he'd done a Google search on the interpretation of dreams. He was trying to understand a recurring disturbing dream in which a man with a long white beard, a black mask, and a falcon on his arm appeared, urging him to follow him out of the desert. One website host responded by asking if his life felt empty and bleak, like a desert, and suggesting there might be a deeper meaning to the invitation. Very subtly and slowly, the host, who finally identified himself as an imam, began to talk about the prophetic power of dreams in Islam. At first, Luc had demanded to know how a religion of peace could condone the bombing of cafés and concert halls. The imam seemed to sense Luc was struggling with a loss of meaning and purpose and looking for a toehold of hope. Dreams can show us the path, he replied, and help us hear the word of God.

Over the weeks, the lost, vulnerable boy began to open up. First about his confusion, anger, and bitterness — over his father's marital betrayal, his failure in his father's eyes, and the hypocrisy of his father's demands. Later, the two explored Luc's longing for meaning, his loneliness and emptiness, his struggle against the blissful relief of drugs. And in his darkest moments, his thoughts of suicide.

In a carefully choreographed dance, the imam led him down the path to personal jihad. The greatest struggle, the imam said, is for your own soul. Your culture has lost its soul. It worships superficial pleasures like going to the movies, getting drunk at parties, and buying bigger and better gadgets, while the rest of the world starves and dies. And once you have all these things, is it enough? Does it bring fulfillment? No, just a craving for more. Western culture is the biggest drug of all. Your personal jihad is against that drug and all its empty promises, in favour of purity within yourself. Faith and practice will lead you there. Islam provides not just hope and belief, but a path to follow.

When Luc was deeply enmeshed in this dance, the imam introduced him to another man known simply as Abu Osama. At the name, Matthew sat back in shock. He glanced at his watch, which revealed that it was over an hour since Amanda had told him to go to the airport. He slipped the computer into his bag, threw on his coat again, and ran outside to his car.

At nearly noon on a Sunday, Montreal's Pierre Elliott Trudeau airport was awash in travellers. A constant, honking stream of cabs and private cars dropped people off at the departure level, and overloaded travellers wrestled bags through doors and into ticket lines.

Matthew elbowed his way around families of crying children and squabbling parents on his way to the check-ins for international flights. He quickly discovered that there were no direct flights to Istanbul; Yasmina would have to travel either through Toronto or more likely through a European hub, and her trail would be hidden in a maze of international transfers.

Frustrated, he phoned Amanda back. "News?" he asked.

"Where are you?"

"At the airport, but it's a zoo. What airline is she travelling, and through what transfer point?"

"Oh God, I don't know! Her brother never came back, and Zidane has gone back to Montreal, so there's no one here to ask. But ... maybe you can just watch for her?"

Matthew looked around at the sea of faces. At all the fresh-faced young women waiting in lines, some wearing colourful wraps and saris, others in hijabs, still others with ponytails and ripped jeans.

"We need the police, Amanda. I cracked Luc's computer, and this Abu Osama contacted him, too. They may both be headed to Iraq."

"What!" Amanda bit the word off in midshriek. He waited while she absorbed the news. "Why would he do that?"

"Why do they ever do that? Looking for a place to fit in? Looking for a cause to believe in or a way to hit back? He's not the first non-Muslim Canadian kid to get drawn in. After the attack on Parliament Hill, local mosques said they got a big surge in young men wanting to convert, probably for the chance to join the fight."

"Of all the stupid, stupid—!" She dropped her voice. "I can't talk here. We're on the trail back to the outfitters' place, and the kids are all ears. Let me ask Hassan if he knows anything. I don't want those two kids getting caught in the police antiterrorism net."

"But I don't want them dead in Iraq either," Matthew retorted.

"I know, I know. Give me half an hour. Meanwhile, just try to keep an eye open for Yasmina. Unless she has new clothes, she's likely to be wearing a black hijab, a black skirt, and a bright pink parka. She'll be alone. Or … Jesus, with Luc."

When Matthew signed off, he turned his attention back to the crowds that jostled and poured through the corridor. His mind blurred and his eyes burned with fatigue as he watched dozens of olive-skinned, hijab-wearing girls check in and disappear toward security.

"Fuck this," he muttered eventually. "I can at least call Chris."

The group was trudging single-file across the lake, their heads down and their spirits deflated as they leaned into the tow straps of their toboggans. Even Amanda's toboggan felt heavier now than when they'd set out so full of excitement four days earlier.

Before Matthew phoned, she'd been wracking her brains trying to come up with an activity for the final evening that would salvage at least some of that excitement and some of the bridge-building goals of the trip. She didn't want them to return to the inner city with nothing but the memory of two vanished friends. Those friends had chosen to leave on their own, indeed had clearly used the trip as a cover for a more sinister agenda. They might be lost, frightened souls, but they were also calculating, ruthless manipulators.

Goddamn them, she thought. These remaining kids didn't deserve to have their own fun hijacked. These were the kids she needed to focus on. By the time Matthew phoned, she was almost angry enough to bring in the police and let them handle the whole sorry mess. If Yasmina ended up facing terrorism charges, so be it.

But when Matthew told her Luc had also been recruited, a million images tumbled through her head. The two kids were eighteen years old, but while Yasmina had had the privilege of a good family, Luc had lost part of his childhood to drugs. As a drug addict, he'd slipped into the dark underworld of the desperate, selling his body, betraying his morals, and sinking to shameful lows that he'd probably found difficult to forgive. The lifelines that adolescents usually reach for when they are sinking — school, friends, parents, the familiar safety of community — all these had been taken from him by the upheaval of his parents.

She'd seen lost teenagers in Africa, orphaned by AIDS or war, forced to flee their homes. Disposable, loveless, and purposeless, they'd hung around the fringes of refugee camps. They had been naturally drawn to each other for protection, belonging, and power, and some of them had ended up riding the streets in Jeeps with their Kalashnikovs on proud display. They'd been easy prey for charismatic rebel leaders. It didn't matter the cause.

All that mattered was they were somebodies now, with a place to belong and something to fight for.

The streets of Montreal did not compare to the violence and terror of Africa, but in the mind of an impressionable teen caught in free fall, the pain could feel just as real.

She didn't know Yasmina nearly as well, but she sensed they were both victims, expertly played by a master seducer who'd known just what pressure points to massage. What sweet nothings to whisper in their ears.

Now she stepped aside out of line and waited for Hassan to catch up with her. He was bringing up the rear, buried deep in his parka and looking even more disconsolate and defeated than the others. She signalled to him to drop back, and the two of them plodded on side by side. In the chilly sunlight, puffs of breath swirled around them.

Amanda leaned in, lowering her voice but pulling no punches. Time was racing by. "Hassan, are Luc and Yasmina going to join ISIS?"

He tripped over his snowshoes and steadied himself. "What are you talking about?"

"Don't play coy. This is important."

"I don't know. Lots of kids admire ISIS, but it doesn't mean anything."

"You mean among your friends? The kids at college?"

"The more the West bombs Iraq and Syria, the more kids want to protect them."

Including you? Amanda wanted to ask, but she held her tongue. She knew that some Western kids who'd never known bombs or terror from either side felt sympathy for their beleaguered Muslim brothers in their native lands. They viewed ISIS as freedom fighters defending their land, their faith, and their way of life from Western domination. For some, ISIS was the only group supporting the overthrow of corrupt foreign invaders and their domestic lackeys. They were the new revolutionaries.

Heady stuff to an idealistic teen.

"But have Luc and Yasmina taken it one step further?"

He shrugged. "Possibly."

"What do you know about this man Abu Osama?"

Hassan stopped in his tracks. He stared at the ground, his lips pressed together as if censoring himself.

"Look," she said, "if Yasmina goes over there, it won't be to fight, no matter what they've promised her. You realize that, Hassan. I've been in rebel war zones; I've seen how women are treated. If she's lucky, she'll be married off to a warrior to bear children for the cause. If what I've read is true, maybe several warriors in a row as they die in martyrdom. If she's unlucky, she'll be little more than a sex slave. A warrior's reward for a battle well fought."

"That's American propaganda," he countered.

She suppressed a flash of impatience. "Maybe, but I'm not sure she knows what it's like over there, and clearly her family doesn't want her there. And Luc — why is he even in this fight? Are he and Yasmina in love?"

He blew out a dismissive puff of air. "Maybe Luc thought so. He converted to Islam."

"When?"

"A few months ago. A little while after he came to the college."

A thought chilled her. "Had he started counselling with Monsieur Zidane?"

"No. Well, yes … but this is not Monsieur Zidane's fault. He was trying to stop them."

"Stop them from what? From going to Iraq?"

Burrowing his face into his scarf, he nodded. "And from … their radical beliefs."

"But did he encourage Luc to convert in the first place?"

Hassan was silent for so long that she wondered if he had heard her. They were trudging steadily across the lake toward a distant fringe of trees, but the gap between them and the group ahead was widening. "Possibly," Hassan said suddenly. "He mixed Islam into his counselling. Islam preaches purity of the body. No alcohol or drugs or bad habits. But I think Luc converted because of Yasmina."

Amanda glanced at him sharply. His face was red from exertion and his eyes watered. "You mean — to be allowed to date her?"

"Yasmina did not mean to encourage him."

Amanda took a stab in the dark. "She was more interested in this Abu Osama? Had she met him?"

Hassan said nothing. *Jesus*, Amanda thought, *it's as if he's being asked to betray his own brother!* "Who is this guy, Hassan?"

"I only hear rumours. No one knows for sure."

"What are the rumours?"

"That he's Canadian. Was Canadian. He burned his passport when he went back to Egypt."

"So he's originally from Egypt?"

"He came over as a child. The rumour is his family lives in Montreal. That's all I know."

"Does he still have connections and contacts here?"

"I don't know who they are." Hassan's response was too quick, meant to shut her off.

"But there are rumours he does. Did he go to Collège de La Salle?"

"All the students from the area go to the college."

He would need an accomplice, she thought. Eyes on the inside to spot kids who might be ripe for recruitment. "Any younger siblings at the college now?"

"I'm not repeating rumours," Hassan said, shaking his head. "I have heard different stories about his identity. Students are fascinated. He's like … almost a hero. Doing brave, dangerous things to protect our people while the rest of them sit in math class, feeling guilty." He shrugged. "I'm not one of them, but I understand that."

So do I, Amanda thought wearily. From the beginning of time, young people had been caught up in the romance of battling for a cause, and they always believed their cause to be noble. People want to devote themselves to an ideal greater than themselves.

"Thank you, Hassan," she said. "I know this is difficult. I've worked all my life to help people improve their lives, and I know how hard it is. How important hope is. All I care about is that Luc and Yasmina are safe. We may be running out of time to stop them from leaving the country."

"But why should we stop them if they want to go? How does that hurt Canada?"

She reached across to touch him lightly on the arm. "You know it's not as simple as that. They are young and idealistic. They don't know the realities of war. They will be forced to do beheadings, maybe even suicide bombings."

He snorted. "That's more Western propaganda."

"Oh, come on, Hassan! ISIS makes videos of it. They're proud of it! The more they can horrify us and push us to react, the better for them." Seeing his stubborn pout, she tried another tack. "You love Yasmina, don't you? As a sister, maybe? Do you want this for her?"

"No, but it's what she wants."

Amanda glanced at her watch. To her dismay, nearly six hours had passed since Yasmina's disappearance. "What do you know about the airline ticket? What airline? What time?"

"They will find her. If not her family, then Monsieur Zidane."

"Okay, but the more eyes, the better. Mr. Goderich is already at the airport looking for her."

He looked startled. "It's not today. The ticket is for next week. February twentieth. They will find her."

It was Amanda's turn to be startled. That made no sense! In a week's time, the group, including Luc and Yasmina, would all be safely back at their desks at the college. Why would the pair have come on this trip in the first place, and why would they have risked their safety by setting off alone into the wilderness, if their departure was eight days away?

And more importantly, what would they be up to during those mysterious eight days?

CHAPTER THIRTEEN

After an hour spent keeping one eye on the security clearance line and the other browsing the web for tidbits on Abu Osama, Matthew was beginning to suspect he'd been sent on a fool's errand. Even if Luc and Yasmina were taking an overseas flight, they'd be nearly impossible to spot in the swirls of international travellers pushing through Trudeau Airport.

He'd had more luck with Abu Osama. After the group Anonymous hacked into jihadi websites two years earlier, much of the recruitment, planning, and coordination among terrorists had moved underground to the encrypted Dark Web. Even on the open web, however, he found the name Abu Osama sprinkled all over the Internet in connection with jihadi movements. There seemed to be no shortage of Abu Osamas linked to the Islamic State, all with differing full names that reflected where they came from, or where they had done their terrorism training, or where they were fighting. Thus there was Abu Osama al-Masri, Abu Osama al-Faranci, Abu Osama al-Amriki, and so on. Among them were Americans, Brits, and Frenchmen, and at least some of them were influential recruiters and propagandists. The more ground ISIS lost in Iraq and the Middle East, the more fiercely they stepped up their foreign recruitment campaign.

A quick look at their online opinions and activities, still openly displayed on Twitter and Facebook, revealed how passionately they all believed in the global jihad they were waging, as defenders of their faith and way of life against attack by the West. Without knowing the full name or at least the origin of the Abu Osama he wanted, narrowing down the search was next to impossible.

Besides, Abu Osama was almost certainly a warrior name rather than the man's real name, and many of these jihadi fighters had several aliases to allow them to fade into anonymity and re-emerge on another front. Osama, meaning lion, was a good warrior name, earning special reverence since the execution of Osama bin Laden.

Matthew was about to phone Amanda back to cancel the airport vigil when his cellphone rang. "Speak of the devil," he said when he heard her voice.

"Where are you?" she asked. The sound of her laboured breathing and the rustle of the wind nearly drowned her out.

"Just about to leave the airport. No sign of our jihadi lovers."

"They're not there, that's why I'm calling."

He listened while she gave him the highlights of her conversation with Hassan. "Eight days? Maybe this disappearance is a romantic hook-up after all." The frozen north would not be his first choice for romance, but maybe he was missing something. He'd not had the best track record in the romance department.

"That would explain the family's panic and her brother's determination to find her," Amanda replied, her thoughts obviously more focused than his. "Otherwise, if they knew the time and date of her flight, why not just lay in wait for her then? On the other hand, one of the girls here got the impression from the argument she overheard this morning that Yasmina was sneaking away to meet this Abu Osama."

"The two ideas don't have to be mutually exclusive. I think Abu Osama is a recruiter, and he may be facilitating both their travel arrangements to Iraq."

"Matthew, see if you can find out exactly what Yasmina's family has uncovered. And talk to Luc's mother again. If the two really have sneaked off for a quickie before Iraq, there is still time to head them off."

"This is too big for us, Amanda. You know that, don't you? We're talking about possible terrorist recruitment here."

Her voice dropped. "I know, I know. And I will report it, once I get back from this trip. But now that I know they're not about to leave the country, it buys us a little time to get them out of harm's way before all the antiterrorist apparatus descends on them. Terrorism charges, arrest and detention, security certificates, watch lists and no-fly lists. They're barely eighteen years old, and this could haunt them forever."

Matthew considered his next move. He could reassure and placate her, at least until she'd got her group safely back home. That should be her first priority. But he knew the time for silence had passed. They were grappling with an enemy far too devious and brutal to be managed on their own.

Before he could think of a reply, Amanda broke into his thoughts. "Oh, and one more thing? I don't think this Abu Osama is just a foreign recruiter trying to get them into Iraq. I think he wants Yasmina. I think he knows her. Apparently he's a Canadian, born in Egypt but raised in Montreal. He may even have attended the same college as the rest of the group. If you want something else to do, grill Zidane about him when he gets back to Montreal. That man could use some grilling!"

That does it, Matthew thought as he hung up. This was way, way too big for him and Amanda to handle on their own. Despite his worries, his heart began to beat with that old familiar excitement. It had been months since he'd had a story big enough to grab international headlines. If he was careful, he could inform the cops and still keep his hand in the game.

He punched in another number and was grateful to hear the familiar, cheerful voice.

"We need to meet. ASAP," he said.

Chris tipped the flimsy chair and squeezed his legs under the bed in a futile attempt to get more space. Goderich's apartment, even without the printer, the extra computers, and the piles of files and books, would have been barely large enough for the short, pudgy journalist, let alone a lanky, six-foot-two cop, especially when the journalist kept hopping up from one computer to another.

The temperature in the third-floor walk-up was sweltering due to an aging radiator you could fry an egg on, and Chris had unpeeled layers down to his T-shirt without much relief. Goderich was sweating freely, making him look even more dishevelled than usual. Chris liked the rumpled bastard and knew his heart was in the right place when it came to Amanda, but old habits died hard, and Chris wasn't about to forget the man was a headline junkie above all else.

While Matthew filled him in on Luc's secret computer, his Internet search on Abu Osama, and Amanda's conversation with Hassan, he managed to keep his cop poker face in place, but his heart raced. This was, as Matthew said, really big. Not clan labs or illicit teenage hook-ups, but national security! Possible terrorists were running around the countryside, and Amanda was stuck right in the middle.

Matthew poured them both a fresh cup of rocket fuel espresso. "Amanda didn't want me calling the cops just yet. She figures we have two weeks to find these kids and stop them from making the worst mistake of their lives."

Chris thought about the RCMP takeover of the investigation into the farmer's murder, but he held back. "It's possible the RCMP already knows," he said. "Or at least CSIS. They may have had these kids under surveillance for months, especially if this Abu Osama creep is a Canadian gone overseas. And with Luc Prevost's missing persons report, the alert level will have gone up."

"Are you going to report what I told you?"

"You know I have to."

Matthew sighed. "Yeah, I know. And it's probably the right thing to do. Better Amanda is pissed off at you than me. You have more brownie points in the bank."

Chris laughed, once again cursing the heat that spread over his cheeks. "Maybe one or two. But she still doesn't have much use for cops."

"Except you, dufus," Matthew muttered, so quietly that Chris wasn't sure he'd heard right. Then Matthew cleared his throat and reached for his coffee. "Well, in her experience overseas, cops were often on the wrong side."

"I get that. And in this case, the law may come down hard on these kids, depending on what terrorism offences they've already committed. Conspiracy, financial support, incitement. But I'll let the spooks do their own investigating. I'll tell them about Yasmina's ticket to Istanbul." He nodded to Luc's computer. "Is there a record of Luc buying a ticket to Istanbul as well?"

"Not that I found."

"They'll want to look for themselves. For that, and other things."

Matthew laid a protective hand on the computer. "You'll need a search warrant."

"They have their ways."

"You know, I didn't have to tell you anything."

"But you did. Because you're worried."

"But I want something in return."

Chris rolled his eyes. "Matthew, this is way beyond me. I'm just a grunt cop from Newfoundland. I can't go handing national security secrets over to the press."

Matthew set the computer aside and gathered his notes together in a pile out of Chris's reach. "I'm not going to jeopardize the country's security, for fuck's sake. I'm not asking for secrets. But I know some things, and if I get the feeling the system is dicking those kids around, don't expect me to play good little boy."

What the hell does that mean? Chris thought. He was out on a flimsy limb as it was without Matthew sawing away at it from the sidelines.

"Goderich, if you want my co-operation, now or later, don't threaten me."

"And if you want me to go where you can't, and uncover information that you can't through your official channels, you will work with me. I'm not reckless, but I retain the right to call it if the spooks go too far."

"Don't jeopardize the investigation. I don't want to, either. So I'm not going anywhere near this case."

"So you say."

Chris stood up. "We're done here."

"But you'll keep me in the loop?"

"I might just strangle you with it."

Chris got outside the building before he allowed himself to shake. What the hell was he sitting on? It didn't seem like much — a couple of misguided eighteen-year-olds with stars in their eyes and shit for brains had been seduced by a radical ideology and booked themselves tickets to Istanbul. Left to their own devices, chances were that a few beheadings and rapes in the war zone would have them rethinking the nobility of their cause and scurrying back to Canada within a year. If they lived that long.

But it was the same misguided youths with distorted ideals and shit for brains who had blown up bystanders in the Boston marathon and shot dead a soldier on the steps of Canada's war memorial. It was impossible to know the risk, and the risk of doing nothing was even higher.

He wasn't worried about his own career. Goderich was just pushing his buttons, hoping for an inside track on the story, but Chris doubted the journalist would do anything rash. Even if the man didn't take the national security angle seriously, he was too wily and experienced to burn useful bridges.

As Chris walked toward his truck, enjoying the sunny February afternoon, he started putting the pieces together. The clandestine lab scenario looked like a dead end. Luc was not trying to connect with a dealer to feed his habit; he was going off to war. Second, the mysterious dead body discovered nearby was now an RCMP concern, with a shroud of silence dropped over it. Did the RCMP suspect Luc of killing him? Did they know something about his jihadi sympathies? And who was Luc's accomplice? Another terrorist? Where was Luc going when Amanda tracked him into the bush?

Nothing but questions! He held such small pieces of the puzzle in his hands, and without more pieces, he was guessing in the dark. But the guesses, no matter how cautious, all pointed toward some scary possibilities; that there was at least one killer, but very likely more than one, who harboured some twisted theories about who the enemy was and how to put the world right, and that these killers were, for reasons unknown, last seen in the middle of the Quebec wilderness.

As was Amanda, who saw them as bewildered, hurting teenagers rather than violent fanatics.

He had to report what he knew. As he drove back to his hotel, he tried to figure out whom to report it to. In the normal chain of command, the information should be reported to his superior, who would take it up the line. But what use would it be to report to a detachment commander in rural Newfoundland, two thousand kilometres away from the heart of things?

He could try to track down the liaison officer within the security division or within INSET, the multi-agency Integrated National Security Enforcement Team responsible for all aspects of antiterrorism. But even the thought of trying to negotiate the labyrinthine channels of communication within that secretive organization gave him a headache. And God only knew what they'd do with the information.

He was just walking back into his hotel when a much better solution came to him. Quite literally, as a woman stepped off the elevator into the lobby. She was dressed in a black and silver jogging outfit, ready to take on the sunny February afternoon, but Liam had told him she was a sergeant assigned to some obscure security section in National Headquarters in Ottawa. For all Chris knew, she worked in HR, but since all national security activities were run out of headquarters, she might know who to pass his information on to.

Unlike him, Sergeant Sandy Sechrest was taking French language training as part of an attempt to go from sergeant to staff sergeant in her obscure section. Liam, having far more astute sexual radar than Chris, had pointed out the way she'd cozied up to him during lunch. Your move, buddy, he'd said with a wink.

To Chris's chagrin, she looked pleased, although somewhat startled, when he approached her by the front desk. The afternoon orientation session was in full swing, so it seemed they were both playing hooky.

Her smile broadened when he asked for a few words with her, and she quickly scanned the lobby. "Where?" She hesitated as if reading his face. "There's a Tim Hortons down the street."

He suspected lots of fellow truants found their way to Tim's, but he didn't argue. Despite her trim figure and her jogging attire, she bought a Boston cream doughnut to go with her double double and led the way to a booth against the wall in the back corner. Her hair was pulled back in a youthful ponytail, but in the bright lights of the shop, he could see the crow's feet and the hard angles of her face. She was no rookie.

"Aren't we bad," she said, licking chocolate icing from her lip with a long, curling tongue.

He stared into his coffee and blundered ahead. "I need your advice," he said and launched into his story, beginning with an explanation of his role in it — as a friend of Amanda Doucette, who was up in the Laurentians with a group of immigrant students from Montreal. As she listened, she dropped her attempt at flirtation and sat up straight in her chair, all business. To his surprise, not only did she know who Amanda was, but she'd even heard of him. It seemed his heroic search-and-rescue exploits with Amanda in Newfoundland had made it into the general gossip lore of the force.

"You play pretty loose with the rules," she said.

He eyed her warily. How much of a stickler for rules was she, and what would she do with his information? Blowing off the orientation session was one thing, bending security protocol quite another.

"Being on your own out in the bush, you learn to make judgment calls," he replied.

"And this Doucette woman has got herself into trouble again?"

"Not directly, no." Bristling at the veiled disdain, he explained about the disappearance of Luc and then Yasmina, as well as the discovery of a body not far away. "The body turned out to be a local farmer, but I'm concerned not only for the young people's safety, but also for Amanda's."

"Have MisPers reports been filed?"

"On the young man, yes."

"Who've you been dealing with? The Sûreté?"

"And the Montreal Police. But apparently the RCMP has taken over."

"Who told you that?"

"Some information has come to my attention, and I want to make sure it—"

"Stop pussyfooting around. What information?"

This woman is not a pencil-pusher in HR, he thought. *More likely a full-speed-ahead, blast-open-the-door frontline cop.* But it was too late to pull back now. "Concerns from the girl's family that the two may be together. The girl bought a one-way ticket to Istanbul."

"For when?"

"February twentieth. So our counterterrorism people will have time to look into it, but I just want to put these two kids on their radar."

"Why aren't you going through official channels?"

He ventured a smile. "I like the personal touch."

When she didn't smile back, he felt a flush beginning. "There's more," he said, "but I've only heard hints of it, third-hand."

"Who's the third hand?"

He skirted that. "We'd need official search warrants and phone requisitions. I just want to expedite it to make sure this lands in the right hands."

"Riddles, Tymko. Goddamn, you're like getting blood from a stone! What are we looking for?"

"Computers — hers and a secret one he has hidden." He

hesitated. Matthew had Luc's secret computer. Should he give her his name? "And a connection to a Canadian called Abu Osama."

At the mention of the recruiter's name, she shoved her doughnut away and thrust her chair back. "Right. Someone will be in touch with you, Tymko. If your third hand tells you anything else, pass it on to me ASAP. Don't go AWOL like you did last time in Newfoundland."

He watched her stalk out of Tim Hortons and jog back across the street toward the hotel. *Well, it's done,* he thought. *I've dropped myself in it. Why is that small comfort?* Sechrest's reaction unnerved him. Was she always this poker-faced, or did she already know much of what he'd told her? Why had she not asked more about Luc, and why did she freak out when he mentioned Abu Osama's name? Did that mean the man was already on their radar?

Just who the hell was Sechrest, and why had she really turned up in his French course in Montreal? *Paranoid, Tymko*, he chastised himself. That's way too devious, even for the spooks.

CHAPTER FOURTEEN

Darkness had fallen. One by one, cars had pulled into the nearby drives, and lights had turned on behind the leaded glass windows of the stately houses. Matthew had been sitting in his cramped Toyota for nearly three hours. He had parked discreetly down the block and across the street, positioned so the house was in clear view, but he was aware that on this elegant Outremont side street, his car stuck out. Most of the Beemers and Audis were tucked into private drives behind snowbanks, and the subdued lighting from the homes cast everything into shadow.

At least his aging Corolla didn't look like anyone's idea of a police surveillance car, although he wouldn't put it past the spooks at CSIS to use the most common car on the road.

Yasmina's parents had been away all day, probably still searching for their daughter, and Matthew was just about to give up the vigil. He was cold and starving and he needed a piss. From the background checks he'd done in preparation for the camping trip, he knew that the mother taught linguistics and the father software engineering at the University of Montreal. Part of the educated elite in Iraq, they'd fled to Canada with their young family fifteen years ago during Saddam Hussein's brutal regime. They'd managed to get some of their money out of the country, but it was mainly through further study and hard work that they'd clawed their way back up the academic ladder and attained the pinnacle of the Canadian dream: an extravagant house in a desirable neighbourhood and two BMWs to go with it.

Matthew wondered how Yasmina and her brother felt about being uprooted from the eclectic immigrant neighbourhood they had grown up in west of Côte-des-Neiges and transplanted into the thin, alien soil of this old-money French neighbourhood. As a small concession, the parents had let Yasmina finish out her year at the Collège de La Salle with her friends, but her brother was already attending engineering at nearby University of Montreal.

Since it was Sunday, few of their colleagues were at work, but those Matthew spoke to knew nothing about Yasmina's disappearance. He wondered whether the parents had chosen to avoid the shame and suspicion the news might evoke.

A sleek black BMW roared up the street past him and slewed into the drive. The doors flew open, illuminating three figures as they climbed out: mother, father, and a young man Matthew recognized from earlier meetings as the older brother. He must have made good time from the country, but obviously he had not found Yasmina.

The three trudged up the stone steps in silence. Like much of upper Outremont, the street clung to the side of the mountain, and the steps up to the house were steep. Matthew gave them two minutes inside, just long enough to take off their boots and coats, before he left his car and huffed up the steps himself. He could hear arguing, which stopped the instant he rang the bell. The door flung open and he found himself face to face with the brother Abdul. Hope died on the young man's delicate face.

"News?" he demanded, as if Matthew were personally to blame. Perhaps they thought he was, because he'd approved her application to go on the trip.

"Not directly," he said, "but perhaps I can help."

The father elbowed forward. "No police or media!"

Matthew shook his head. "I'm not here for that. But I have connections, and I can find out things. Believe me, I want her found too."

Father and son stood rooted to the spot in indecision. Behind them, Matthew could see a lushly decorated hall with gleaming wood trim, Persian carpets, and an ornate chandelier. From the back of the house came the sound of a television, mingled with the chatter of young girls. The mother, Leila, appeared from the back, silencing the chatter with a few words in Arabic before turning gravely to Matthew.

"Please come in, Mr. Goderich. I will prepare some tea."

She disappeared again, leaving the men to settle him into a loveseat piled high with cushions. The chatter from the back resumed. The room was hot, crammed with heavy furniture and knickknacks, and vibrant with colour. So much more welcoming than the current Western love affair with black and steel.

"How did your search go?" Matthew asked as he sank amid the cushions.

Abdul shook his head. "Too many tracks, and when we came to the snowmobile trail, my driver said it was futile."

The parents spoke English with a slight accent, but Abdul, like Yasmina, had none. Matthew suspected his French was equally good.

"They said a snowmobile probably picked her up," he added. "Tomorrow we may hire an airplane. There is a small airport up there, and I've made inquiries about local bush pilots."

"A good idea," Matthew said. He knew how difficult it was to spot anyone from the air, particularly if they kept to the cover of dense trees, but the family needed to try. Equally important, he needed to keep them on his side. "Do you have any idea who she was meeting?"

They exchanged glances and said nothing.

"Could it be Luc Prevost?"

Abdul snorted. "She's not interested in him."

"But they were friends at one time. Close friends, I'm told."

"Perhaps Luc thought so, but not Yasmina."

"So who was she close to? Who might have got her into this?"

"I think she got herself into it," Leila said as she entered the room bearing a large tray with a teapot, cups, and platters of food. Tomatoes, olives, cucumbers, pita, and hummus. She set it down on the coffee table. "I'm sorry, there is not much," she said in what Matthew thought was the most wildly inaccurate statement imaginable. The platter had more food than the contents of his fridge ever did. He scooped some hummus onto a triangle of pita, reduced to silence.

"She was exploring her roots," the mother said. "It started with a religion class at school, comparing the great religions. The teacher was not ..." She pursed her lips together as if to censor her choice of words. "Not generous to Islam."

"He was a racist," the father said.

Leila inclined her head. "I believe his sources were mostly from the Roman Catholic perspective. Yasmina was offended, as were most of the Muslim students, and she began to read on her own. She joined the Muslim Students' Association—"

"We blame them," the father interjected. "Anti-Western radicals. Talk is easy in this country that gave them safety."

"You cannot blame them," Leila said patiently. "Yasmina is an intelligent girl, but she is sensitive. She reads the newspapers and hears what people say. There is a lot of prejudice in Quebec, and it's not so hidden. First there was the Charter of Values, which even though it never made it into law, still had a lot of support among Quebeckers. And now, every time there is a bombing, strangers accost her in the street and on the bus, they call her a terrorist and tell her to take off her hijab. Twice people spat on her. That is not just hurtful, it's scary. She doesn't always feel … wanted here."

Matthew was familiar with some of Quebec's prejudices and more flagrant assaults on religious diversity, including the previous government's infamous Charter of Values, which would have banned public servants from wearing visible religious symbols and clothing. Quebec was struggling to maintain its distinct culture and identity in an increasingly diverse and global country, but its tactics often felt like intolerance to others. "So she started thinking about leaving?"

"Looking back now, yes, but we didn't realize.… We thought she was just asking questions and seeking her own path. Along that path, she explored traditional practices like modest dress, daily prayer, and more devout friends, but we didn't think that was all bad. College culture can be destructive. There is a worship of the trivial — celebrities, silly movies, offensive music, superficial relationships — at the expense of solid values and true fulfillment. We thought this critiquing was healthy, so we didn't …" She broke off with a helpless gesture. "We didn't see this coming."

"We should have," the father said, "when she started with that boy."

"Dad!" Abdul warned, but Matthew was all ears.

"What boy?"

"There is a young man at school. His family is very devout, and he taught Yasmina a great deal about Islam. But he was very polite, very respectful. There was never any …" The father's English wasn't as fluent as his wife's, and he groped for a word.

"Hassan?" Matthew asked.

The mother looked astonished. "Oh no. It was—"

Abdul gave a short reprimand in Arabic, but Leila ignored him. "Faisel al-Karim."

"The young man who dropped out of the trip?" Matthew asked in surprise.

She nodded. "We were surprised he dropped out, because it was he who persuaded her to apply in the first place. There was never any impropriety, because there would always be plenty of other people around, but I suppose his family must have decided it was too liberal."

"Do you know them?"

"Well, his older brother …" Leila glanced at Abdul as if asking permission to elaborate. When he scowled, she dropped it. "The family keep to themselves, or at least to their own community. My husband and I don't agree with that. They have been here almost ten years, but they still wear the old-fashioned clothes. They don't mix. I was happy that Faisel wanted to go on this trip, because I thought perhaps he was opening up. We hoped also that the trip would change Yasmina's views too, so that she could see the beautiful freedoms of Canada, not only its prejudices. But …" She trembled now as she busied herself pouring more tea. "It seems it was all a trick."

"What do you know about Abu Osama?"

Abdul recoiled as if slapped, but his parents showed no such shock. The father shrugged. "Nothing."

"I understand he's Canadian," Matthew said.

"Who told you that?" Abdul demanded. He was on the edge of his chair, vibrating as if about to levitate.

Matthew ignored him. "He's Egyptian-born, but he grew up right here in Montreal and attended Collège de La Salle."

Now the parents looked shocked. Matthew pressed on. "Is it possible Yasmina knew him there?"

"Impossible," Abdul said. "We've never heard of this man."

"I can ask at the college, if you like. Perhaps Zidane has heard of him."

"No!" Abdul cast about. "Surely he would be too old for her."

The mother stirred. "But Faisel al-Karim—"

"Mum! Don't!"

A sharp exchange in Arabic followed. The mother was outraged, the father was quietly rational, and the son adamantly shook his head. *Oh, to have an automatic Google Translate option*, Matthew thought as he tried to read the nonverbal cues. After a few minutes of arguing, the mother stood up.

"I am sorry, this is very impolite of us. We have differing views about revealing information that is not ours to reveal. It is gossip and rumour only, and we have no wish to harm reputations. Thank you for telling us about Abu Osama, which is more than we knew." She shot a glare at her son, who was watching her tensely. "If I learn more that will help you find Yasmina, I will contact you."

And with those velvet gloves, she ushered him out the door.

Matthew was lost in thought as he descended the stone steps. There had clearly been tension in the family, notably between the son and his mother. The father was a bit of a dark horse, less fluent in English and content to criticize from the sidelines, but overall both parents seemed reasonable. They were elite professionals who probably placed a high value on knowledge and achievement. The house was full of books and art, and Matthew suspected the academic expectations placed on Abdul, Yasmina, and the younger sisters were high. Abdul was already attending university, and Matthew recalled that Yasmina had aspirations to study international law.

What would lure such a well-grounded, competent young woman from a liberal family into the arms of ISIS? He knew there were many reasons why the jihadi movement appealed. For some, it was a chance to fight back and lash out against oppression, for others a chance for adventure and glory or an outlet for bitterness. For still others, it was the only global revolutionary movement prepared to overthrow the evil, soulless, exploitive nature of capitalism. But whatever noble ideals it claimed to promote, its answers, like those of the Marxist utopians of yesteryear, were simplistic. Even if Yasmina had concerns for the oppressed people of the world, surely such a sophisticated and informed young woman could find a more nuanced, less destructive answer.

He was aware that, like those Marxist ideologues, the leaders of ISIS and many of its foreign fighters were drawn not from the oppressed and uneducated masses but from the ranks of engineers, doctors, and scientists. They had witnessed the decay in Western society and the rape of the world that corporate greed had wrought, and they had turned away in search of a more meaningful path.

Had this been Yasmina's journey? Had she given up as untenable her dream of international human rights law and chosen a more direct path toward a just and ideal world? Had she been yearning for a deeper spiritual meaning and been seduced by the promise of the perfect path to God? Or had she been seduced by Abu Osama himself, whispering promises of love, glory, and paradise in his arms?

She was, despite her intelligence and her aspirations, still an eighteen-year-old girl trying to figure out not just her place in the world but her feelings as a woman.

Luc Prevost's radicalization was easier to grasp. He was a lost soul struggling to find a toehold above the abyss of drugs and suicide. He needed an unambiguous answer that gave him a home, an outlet for his anger, and a cause to hang on to.

Abu Osama had been his lifeline.

Who *was* the man? Matthew felt he could almost reach out and touch him, yet the answer danced just beyond his grasp. Egyptian-born, raised in Montreal, attended Collège de La Salle.

Abdul knew who he was. Despite his denials, he had shut his mother up when she tried to speculate. And when she mentioned Faisel al-Karim, he had raised his alert level to red.

Yet Faisel was clearly too young to be Abu Osama. He was still in college, whereas the jihadist was reportedly back in Iraq. Yet there must be a connection. It was there in his memory, just out of reach.

Matthew threw his car into gear and headed back to his apartment. Half an hour later, he had unearthed all the original application forms for the winter camping adventure and spread them out on the bed. He found Faisel al-Karim's near the bottom and scanned it quickly. The youth was the middle of nine children, six of them boys. His mother was a homemaker and his father drove a taxi, worked construction, and managed a few rental properties in a dubious slum district in Montreal East, where Matthew knew gangs and drugs were rampant. The boys all worked part-time in the business once they were old enough, and between them all, the family cobbled together an adequate living to send the older boys to university.

The family had come to Canada ten years earlier as refugees from Hosni Mubarak's Egypt.

Bingo.

Matthew was just picking up his phone to alert Chris Tymko when it rang in his hand. He barely managed a hello.

"Goderich, what the fucking hell is going on!"

Matthew jerked the phone away from his ear. No need to ask who it was. "Mr. MacLean."

"What the fuck is this crap about Luc joining Looney Tunes ISIS? Who the hell told the cops that?"

"Back up, Mr. MacLean. What's happened?"

"I just slammed the door on the backsides of two RCMP storm troopers who came here asking all sorts of questions about Luc. National security, they said, acting on information they'd received." He parroted an officious bureaucratic voice. "They even had a search warrant to look for a computer. My lawyer said I should co-operate, so they tore my house apart. Didn't find a fucking thing. I told them they wouldn't. Luc's never stayed here, I said, he doesn't even have a room here. But did he ever visit, they asked, and I said just the once. So they tore the place apart."

Matthew looked at the sleek little computer sitting on his desk. Chris had obviously spilled the news to his bosses, but he hadn't betrayed Matthew's role. "Did they say how they knew about him?"

"Acting on information was all they said. That he was planning on going to Iraq. Ridiculous! I told them Luc wouldn't go to Iraq in a million years. Luc doesn't give a fuck about religion. His mother is some kind of half-assed Catholic who goes to mass twice a year and to confession when she's feeling extra bad. Easter bunnies and Santa Claus were about as far as religion went in our family, and most of the time Easter and Christmas dinners ended up in drunken fights."

"Did the cops say what evidence they had that he'd joined ISIS?"

"Their lips were tighter than a Jew's purse strings. Pardon my French. But it makes no fucking sense. If he did join ISIS, he did it for the attention — or maybe somebody told him about the seventy-two virgins crap — but I can't picture him in the desert waving a rifle around. The first beheading he sees, he'll be on the phone begging me for a ticket back home."

"Did you mention me to the Mounties?"

"No, I wasn't going to give them an inch. I didn't tell them about the five thousand bucks he wanted either. He's just a kid — a dumb, mixed-up kid — but he's my kid."

Matthew breathed easier. "Did they say what they're going to do next?"

"Like I said, their lips were tighter ... but I'm betting they're on their way over to his mother's. Ghyslaine will have a fucking fit. She'll be on the phone to me the minute they arrive."

Brad MacLean was right about one thing, Matthew thought as he hung up. Luc's mother would have a fit. But she wouldn't be surprised. She knew Luc had a secret, although perhaps not exactly what it was, but a secret so dreadful that she hadn't wanted the police involved when he went missing, even when he was possibly dead. A secret so frightening, she hadn't wanted Matthew to take his computer.

She hadn't known of the computer's existence, because her shock at its discovery had seemed genuine. But she'd immediately realized it was the key to his secret. Matthew wasn't worried that she'd tell the police he had the computer; in fact, he doubted they would learn a thing from her, even about his visit. But now she'd be on the loose, panicked and in full protective mode. God knows what she'd do.

CHAPTER FIFTEEN

Amanda was just rolling up her sleeping bag when she heard the rumble of an engine outside. The room she'd been given for the final night was tucked under the eaves on the third floor of Sebastien and Sylvie's farmhouse, and it was chilly. She peered out the tiny attic window, hoping to see the van arriving from Montreal to transport the students back home. Instead, a black pickup crunched to a stop on the icy drive, the driver's door opened, and a lanky, parka-clad man unfolded himself.

Kaylee, who had joined her at the window, barked and wagged her tail. Amanda took a little longer to recognize Chris Tymko. A thousand butterflies took flight inside her, warming her to the tips of her fingers and paralyzing her for a moment before she raced down the two flights of stairs and out the front door.

Kaylee beat her to it, hurling herself at Chris and whirling around his legs in a frenzy of red silk. He crouched to pet her, smiling his big, crinkly grin as she covered his face in licks. When he straightened to face Amanda, the grin wavered a little at the edges.

They had not seen each other since her last night in Newfoundland six months ago. At that time, their harrowing ordeal had ignited a spark between them, and they had committed to staying in touch, but Amanda had said goodbye to too many good friends during her foreign service years, and she wasn't sure she had the stomach for prolonging the pain. For the ache of loss and the promises of reunions that never came.

Over time, she had walled herself in.

Now, however, the six months dissolved in a rush of affection. She walked up and took his gloved hands in hers. "Hello, you," she murmured.

His grin widened as he enveloped her in a hug. She inhaled his scent — wool, leather, and musky aftershave — and allowed herself to revel in his arms, remembering how they had soothed and stirred her all those months ago. Finally, reluctant but embarrassed, she pulled back to peer up at him. Same merry blue eyes and ski jump nose, same cropped dark curls barely visible beneath his hat. In deference to his prairie farm roots, a Winnipeg Jets toque.

She tugged it down over his eyes teasingly. "Them's fighting words around here. You might want to get yourself a Montreal Canadiens one."

"And have my grandmother haunting my dreams? But if you've got any hot coffee in there, I might be persuaded."

She turned to see a small contingent of curious students in the doorway. "Absolutely. We've just finished breakfast but for you, I'll make a fresh pot."

As they made their way through the throng, she paused to introduce him as '*mon ami Chris,*' evoking knowing smiles from some of them. She laughed. "If you can get your minds out of the gutter, the bus will be here any minute. So when you finish packing, put your bags by the front door."

In the large farm kitchen, they found Sylvie washing up the breakfast dishes. They kept conversation light while Amanda brewed the coffee. "Chris and I will go upstairs to talk, but let me know when the bus arrives."

Another knowing smile, this one from Sylvie. Chris had to duck as they made their way up the narrow stairs to the attic. They sat side by side on the bed, and both laughed as Kaylee jumped up to snuggle between them. The air seemed to thrum with tension.

Amanda tried for nonchalance. "I thought you were supposed to be taking French classes."

"Voluntary, on my own time. And hey, here I am in the middle of rural Quebec — the best immersion of all. I even ordered my coffee in French." He paused. "Matthew filled me in. You've got yourself in the middle of quite a mess."

She laughed. "Don't I always?"

His eyes met hers, and they grinned at the shared memory. "National security this time, no less."

"I'm not getting involved with that," she said. "I'm only worried about my two kids. They could be in huge trouble out there." Doubt flickered through her. "Are you here as a cop?"

"I told the RCMP enough to set them on the trail, but I'm here unofficially, hoping I can help you by digging up some answers."

"And if you find them, will you be passing them on to your bosses?"

"Amanda, I can't withhold information. But I can help." He paused and lowered his voice as if the walls of the 150-year-old farmhouse had ears. "Off the record, I can tell you things you need to know."

"I'm very worried about Luc. He was in the vicinity of where that farmer was killed. What if he ...?"

He voiced her fear. "Is the killer? Then he has to face whatever is coming to him. He's an adult, Amanda. Misguided and stupid, but those aren't excuses."

"I know, but I brought them up here."

He reached out and curled his little finger around hers. "And they both betrayed your trust."

She dropped her gaze. That was an anger she'd kept at bay these past couple of days, but it bubbled up now. She'd been betrayed before, in Nigeria, by opportunistic young men with their own agendas. That betrayal had cost lives, very nearly including her own.

It had also left her never quite trusting her own instincts about people again.

"I want to go with you," she said. "I want to see for myself what's happened."

"But you've got the rest of the group. They're your responsibility too."

She knew he was right, doubly so now that Dickhead Zidane had gone back to Montreal and left her without a second chaperone. But the frustration of conflicting wishes tied her in knots. "But I know this area, and I can show you where I tracked Luc to."

"I'll get more out of the local cops and investigators on my own."

"With that hat and your French?"

He yanked off his Jets toque. "I've been brushing up. That and my prairie charm ought to do the trick."

She sneaked him an oblique glance. "Don't you want me along?"

His hesitation was answer enough. She felt a flash of hurt defiance. "I won't get in your way. I promise to hide in the truck when you talk to the cops."

"Until you don't."

"I can't just sit on the sidelines. You know that."

"Is that right?" His laughter died as he shook his head. "No, you need to take the kids back. Don't forget, they're worried too. Let me check with the local SQ to find out how the search for Luc is going and what they know about the farmer's murder. I'll keep you in the loop. I've got a cellphone and a sat phone."

She glared at him, hating that he was right. She saw his soft, crinkly smile steal across his face. "And if all else fails," he said, "there's smoke signals."

Chris had to backtrack through the village of La Macaza in order to reach the nearest Sûreté du Québec post. Before leaving Montreal, he'd done a little homework and had determined that, depending on the exact location of the body and of the search for Luc, the investigation might span two separate police districts, complicating channels of communication and command. Chris assumed the homicide investigation itself would be handled by detectives and crime scene experts from a centralized unit, but much of the grunt work would still fall to locals, and they'd be much more likely to talk than hot-shot detectives would be. He knew small-town policing. After endless days of writing speeding tickets, breaking up bar fights, and responding to noise complaints, a real live murder would be the talk of the station.

The name La Macaza intrigued him. Most of the villages in the Laurentians were named after saints, and the strong Roman Catholic heritage was evident in the silver-spired churches that dominated them. La Macaza, despite its name, was no different; a church and adjacent graveyard held pride of place on the main — and possibly only — street, but as Chris cruised by, he was startled to see Polish names on the tombstones.

He pulled into the café cum gas station across the road, hoping to find a few locals with time on their hands and an intimate knowledge of the area. With any luck, a passing command of English as well. For the occasion he had borrowed a Montreal Canadiens toque from Sebastien's collection and made sure he kept it on as he approached the counter.

Two old-timers were sitting at a table, chatting with the waitress in a rapid-fire language that might as well have been Swahili. One of them, marginally younger and with a fuller head of grey hair, was sporting a Canadiens jersey. Uttering a silent thank-you to Amanda, Chris took the table beside them and ordered a coffee and a piece of homemade sugar pie, knowing that his teeth would ache for a week. Then, with an exaggerated flourish, he unrolled a topographical map on the table and leaned over it with a magnifying glass, muttering with dismay.

Within seconds the two men stopped their banter and craned their necks to see the map. When he figured he'd set the hook well enough, he tried his hand at mangled French, augmented by pantomime.

"*Excusez. Connaissez-vous….* Do you know this part up here — *le Rouge-Matawin*?"

Nods all around. "Are you lost?" the Canadiens fan asked, mercifully switching to English.

"*Merci,*" Chris said, extending his hand. "*Oui.* I'm Chris."

Introductions all around. The Canadiens fan was Gaetan, the waitress Jeanne Marie. Gaetan pulled his chair over and asked what Chris was looking for.

"I want to talk to the police about the man who was killed up here," Chris said. "They tell me I have to go to Mont-Laurier, but that's way up west of here, and the body was found over here somewhere, right?" He gestured to a portion of the map.

"There is an SQ trailer parked up there," Gaetan said.

"It left this morning," the waitress interjected. She was young, making her own fashion statement with a multicoloured cape, turquoise hair and eye shadow, and large hoop earrings. She leaned over the map and pointed to a vast, empty area on the border of the wildlife reserve. "The body was here."

Chris peered at it. There appeared to be nothing but lakes and creeks. He allowed a hint of incredulity to creep into his voice. "Wow. He had a farm up there?"

Gaetan snorted. "Not much. His father had some cows and a *sucrerie*. Sugarbush. And they did some ..." He muttered something incomprehensible.

"Logging," Jeanne Marie translated. "But mostly he hunted and trapped, rented hunt camps, did all kind of jobs to earn money. He even built a hunting lodge up at his farm for the rich Americans." She shook her head ruefully.

"He give up on that," said Gaetan. He appeared to be the only one of the two men who spoke English. "He complain too much regulation, and you need all this Internet stuff — email, website, Facebook. He lose patience. So last summer he go to work in Montreal. Roofing, construction. I didn't know he come back."

"Did you know him well?"

The man shrugged. "He stay to hisself. Not very friendly with us. But more bad this year. He don't even let hunters on his land no more."

"But was he local? Grew up here?"

"*Eh ben,* twenty mile from here? We go to school together. He was an okay guy back then."

The waitress shook her head impatiently. "My dad said it was the fire. He never recover." Her eyes filled with pity. "The barn burned down, all their animals died, and the father and two brothers died when they try to save them. They lost the house, too. Only Yves and his mother survive."

Remembering his small farming community in Saskatchewan, Chris felt a twinge of sorrow. Barn fires had been a constant threat, caused by grass fires, lightning strikes, an overturned lantern, or even a woodstove too close to the hay. Far from help and a water supply, often the family could only watch helplessly as the flames took it all.

"What was Yves's last name?"

"Stremski." Seeing Chris's surprise, the man shrugged. "Years ago, Polish people settled here, but we are all mixed together now. Yves was as Québécois as me and Jean. He even try to run for the Parti Québécois years ago. That was before the fire. After the fire, *ben …*" Gaetan blew out a puff of air. "Pfftt."

"Poor man," Chris murmured. "Any idea who killed him?"

"Some stranger probably. Maybe on his land illegally."

"No disagreements? Fights over property?"

"No. Except he don't let us pass on it no more."

"What about the missing kids from the camping group? Do you think one of then could have killed him?"

The man's expression grew hard. "*Musulmans?*"

Even Chris understood that, and the hostile tone. "Some of them are Muslims, yes."

"It's possible," Gaetan said. "The police aren't talking, and they don't let us search. Me and Jean, we are member of the search-and-rescue team here, but the police say too dangerous for us."

"So no one is looking for these kids?"

"Well, not us. And even the local SQ, the one who patrol here, they don't know anything. Maybe in Mont-Laurier, you will have luck."

Mont-Laurier was a good hour's drive to the northwest of La Macaza, up through rolling Laurentian hills. As he drove, he phoned Amanda to update her on what he had learned. She sounded rushed, as if she were trying to get out the door. "That's ridiculous that they won't let the local SARs search," she said. "Meet me back at Sebastien and Sylvie's this evening. I'll drive back up once I deliver the kids to Montreal, and we can poke around some more tomorrow. I'm not going to leave this unsettled."

He hung up, flushed by the prospect of an evening with her, drinking wine, catching up, and maybe rekindling that little bit of magic they'd left behind in Newfoundland. He'd felt it as a physical tug that morning.

Mont-Laurier was a midsized town on the banks of the meandering Rivière du Lièvre. Although it proclaimed itself the Capital of the Upper Laurentians, it had the feel of an unadorned industrial town. He found the Sûreté du Québec post on the outskirts, a sprawling white building surrounded by parking lots and windswept grounds. Chris parked his truck in the visitors' section and fished out his RCMP ID, prepared to run the gauntlet of security and suspicion.

The young clerk at the front wicket greeted him with carefully studied neutrality, but her eyes widened at the sight of his badge. Once again he dragged out his high school French, and this time she did not switch to English.

She had to repeat her question three times, but he finally gleaned that she thought he was the liaison officer.

"Liaison for what?" he asked.

She blinked and checked herself. "Not important. Who do you want to see?"

He floundered on. "The officer in charge of the missing person case. Luc Prevost." Because Yasmina's disappearance hadn't been officially reported, he kept it simple.

"Oh!" she exclaimed. "That case is terminated."

"He is found?"

"No, but Ottawa has taken charge." She frowned. "You should know that."

The door behind her opened and an SQ officer strode out. The bars on his epaulettes identified him as a captain, probably the post commander. He was built like a sumo wrestler, and his uniform strained across his bulging stomach. Although Chris was taller, he suspected the man could knock him over with a flick of his wrist.

"*Qu'est-ce qu'y a*?" he demanded, causing the young woman to shrink back. Chris managed to decipher enough of the exchange to determine that his presence wasn't welcome. The captain glowered at him and switched to English. "You are not part of the team who is managing this?"

"No, I'm looking for the missing students. Student," he corrected himself hastily. "A man has been killed, and there is an innocent group of young people nearby. If they are in any danger—"

"They are not."

"But Luc Prevost is one of those young people, and he's gone missing."

"His disappearance has nothing to do with the homicide."

"How can you know that?"

"The victim is local."

Chris didn't see how that made any difference, but the captain obviously knew more than he was letting on. He slipped his question in casually. "So a suspect has been apprehended?"

"I know nothing about it," he snapped. "Ask your own people. Or INSET."

So the Integrated National Security Enforcement Team is involved, Chris thought. *Fast work on the part of Sergeant Sechrest.*

"I just received an order from my chief inspector. Pull your men out, he said." The captain turned on his heel without giving Chris a backward glance. "Your problem now."

CHAPTER SIXTEEN

The al-Karim family lived in a typical three-storey red-brick walk-up linked to half a dozen identical rowhouses on the crowded side street off Côte-des-Neiges Boulevard. The area had once been an immigrant Jewish neighbourhood, but it was now one of the most eclectic and densely populated in the city, with a colourful mix of families from all over the world living alongside students attending nearby University of Montreal. Most of the houses were probably rental units, but Matthew had done some homework before heading out to tackle the al-Karims that morning. He knew that although the family lived frugally, al-Karim Senior owned his whole house, as well as several more on the block. From modest beginnings, he had begun to realize the immigrant dream.

Blinds covered all the windows, as if signalling the family's isolation from the community. Having finally wedged his Corolla into the only parking spot left on the street, Matthew sat in his car a moment, gathering his thoughts. He couldn't simply ask the family outright about their ties to terrorism or even their sympathies toward the rebel movements in the Middle East. Several hours spent last night calling up sources and badgering overseas colleagues had netted him very little information on al-Karim Senior, other than that, according to his refugee claim, he'd feared imprisonment and torture under the Mubarak regime. A claim the Canadian government had obviously found credible.

Matthew suspected he'd probably been a member of Egypt's Muslim Brotherhood, a powerful Islamic movement banned by Mubarak as a terrorist group. If al-Karim had stayed true to those roots, he had likely brought those fundamentalist sympathies to Canada and raised his family in their values. Breaking that allegiance would be no easy task.

While he was still debating his opening move, the front door opened and a young man lurched down the steps, struggling under the weight of two large duffel bags. He paused to glance up and down the street before loading the bags into the back of a late-model black SUV. The windows were tinted, preventing Matthew from seeing inside, but the young man did not appear to speak to anyone. He climbed back upstairs and reappeared with two more duffel bags. As Matthew watched, he repeated this three times before slamming the back hatch and climbing into the driver's seat.

Faisel al-Karim was on the move.

Matthew allowed another car to get between them before nosing his car out into the traffic. He followed at a discreet distance as the black Ford Explorer navigated the maze of narrow one-way streets on its way east. A few minutes later it turned into the parking garage of Plaza Côte-des-Neiges, a big, modern mall that sprawled over an entire city block in the heart of the district. Matthew accelerated, concerned about losing Faisel among the rows and rows of cars.

The Explorer drove around and around the parking lot, passing numerous empty spaces before choosing one in a remote dark corner. Faisel climbed out, and with another nervous glance headed straight for him. Killing his engine and lights, Matthew dove down out of sight, *Tinted windows,* he thought. *There's an idea if I'm going to play spy again.*

In his rear-view mirror he watched Faisel walk up the ramp to the mall entrance before he drove by the Explorer and snapped several quick cellphone photos of it and adjacent cars. James Bond would be proud, he thought. Then he parked his own car and made a dash for the mall. His footsteps rang loud on the concrete as he tried to catch up. Luck was with him; as he reached the entrance, he caught sight of Faisel through the glass, halfway up the escalator to the upper level. He slipped into the bustling mall and was immediately engulfed by the feeling of an Asian street market. Colourful wares from India, China, and Vietnam spilled out into the corridors, and strains of Indian music filled the air. It was midmorning, and people of all nationalities and dress were milling through the racks.

A warm nostalgia washed over him as he climbed onto the escalator.

When he reached the upper floor, he spotted Faisel standing in line at a coffee shop directly ahead. Pulling his toque lower and wrapping his scarf high on his neck, he hid behind a bubble tea wagon until Faisel had chosen a seat before ordering his own coffee. The coffee smelled and looked like old engine oil, but that wasn't the point. Choosing an inconspicuous table with a clear view of Faisel, he settled down to watch. He was curious to know what the young man was up to, for he had a tense, purposeful air, not like someone just grabbing a coffee before heading off to school.

Ignoring his coffee, Faisel alternated between fiddling with his cellphone and scanning the mall as if he were looking for someone. Matthew shrank back in his chair. It was difficult to be inconspicuous while sitting in a sweltering mall swaddled to the ears in a scarf and toque. To add realism, Matthew pretended to text on his own phone as he sneaked the occasional photo. Sweat prickled his neck beneath the scarf.

He was about to give up the pretence and head over to join Faisel when another man strode rapidly up the escalator. Matthew caught his breath. The man was older than Faisel by a few years, heavier set and with a full beard, thinning black hair pulled up into a man-bun, and a pair of black-rimmed glasses. He was dressed in a nondescript navy parka and black jeans, yet despite the everyman outfit, he radiated power. His hawk-like eyes flitted restlessly as he paused to scan the mall before seizing the chair opposite Faisel.

Despite the differences in age and size, the resemblance between the two was unmistakeable. Matthew's heart beat faster. As he watched, the two brothers talked, texted, and compared notes on their phones. They acted like two friends sharing a coffee, yet beneath the calm, the older man's eyes never stopped scanning. Around them other customers chatted and laughed.

All normal as hell. But was a terror plot being coordinated right under his nose?

Faisel didn't touch his coffee, but the older man drank not only his own but his brother's. When he had drained the second cup, he received what looked like another text. A brief frown flickered across his face as he glanced at it. He said a word or two to Faisel, who took a set of keys from his pocket and laid them on the table.

By then, Matthew felt as if he were in a sauna. Everything itched. Mesmerized by the man's powerful gaze, he didn't dare move. He watched as Faisel stood up and without a backward glance headed back toward the escalator. Only once the youth had disappeared from view did his older brother pocket the keys and prepare to leave. Matthew lifted his own phone from the table and, pretending to type a text, he aimed the camera.

As he snapped the photo — an unobtrusive little click that shouldn't have been audible more than ten feet away — the man looked across the café directly at him. His expression was blank, but his gaze held. Matthew felt the strength drain from his limbs. Ducking his head, he thrust his phone into his pocket, stood up, picked up his coffee cup, and, as calmly and slowly as he could manage, walked away.

Only when he was back in the parking garage did he risk looking behind him. Was it his imagination, or were there footsteps running on concrete? He scurried to his car and peeled past the Explorer that still sat where Faisel had left it. With the tinted windows, he couldn't tell whether Faisel was waiting inside or not.

Out on the street, he kept one eye on the rear-view mirror and the other on the traffic honking all around him. He could see nothing suspicious and no car taking an undue interest, but with instant messaging, either brother could have set up a tail within minutes. As a precaution he took the long way back downtown, leading his possible tracker on a merry tour of the elegant crescents of the Town of Mount Royal and the crowded duplexes of Park Extension before heading back south and west toward Greene Avenue.

His heart was pounding, and to his horror, his hands shook so badly he could barely steer. He'd been in war zones, dodged bullets. Was he losing his nerve, growing soft on the gentler soil of home? What had he just witnessed? Two brothers innocently passing the keys to the family car from one to the other? He didn't believe that for a minute. For not only had the vehicle been put in the older brother's charge, but perhaps more importantly, the half-dozen duffel bags in the back. Duffel bags that could contain enough clothes for a long trip.

Or something far worse.

The sun was high and the icicles were dripping off the steeply pitched farmhouse roof by the time Amanda completed her final check of the gear with Sebastien and climbed onto the minibus. The students were already on board, their heads bent eagerly over their cellphones as they devoured all the social media chatter they had missed.

She almost didn't hear her own cellphone ringing in her pocket and snatched it out at the last minute. It was Chris, sounding frustrated. "I'm in Mont-Laurier. They called off the goddamn search!"

"Who?"

"The SQ. On orders from the RCMP, it seems. The guys here are not too forthcoming because they blame me. Like I have any control over the security brass!"

He was shouting to be heard over the trucks rumbling in the background. She glanced at the expectant faces and climbed off the bus in search of privacy. "So what next?"

"We could wait to see how this plays out," he said. "I don't think INSET is sitting on their hands, I think they're actively but secretly looking for Luc and the girl. And don't forget, these kids made their own beds."

Amanda was silent a minute as she analyzed her own feelings. On the one hand, she was angry that the two were rejecting the country that she knew from bitter experience was one of the most welcoming in the world. She felt betrayed that they had used her adventure trip as a launching pad for that escape. Part of her thought that they were adults — young, reckless, and ill-informed, but possessed of a brain and the ability to make choices — and therefore should endure the consequences of those choices.

She thought of the Toronto 18, a group of young Muslims

and Muslim converts who'd been arrested for their plans to blow up Parliament and behead the prime minister. Bungling and hapless, in the words of the informants who had helped bring them down. They had been dealt with by the courts and most had been given jail time. A proper response by a civilized nation.

On the other hand, Luc and Yasmina were running around the frigid countryside, probably unarmed, ill-equipped and poorly trained, tracked by all the forces the state could marshal against them. Hundreds of police and security officers had been involved in the Toronto 18 case. How many officers, armed with assault rifles and expert surveillance capability, would be gunning for Luc and Yasmina, especially if they were suspected of murdering the farmer? Their level of risk assessment would be so high that they might be shot dead on sight.

That didn't bear thinking about. "Or?" she asked Chris.

"Or I go look for them myself."

She felt a rush of warmth. "*We* go looking for them."

"No, you don't."

"Oh, for god's sake, Chris! You can either take me with you or I'll just follow you."

"This is too dangerous. Even for me, it's dangerous, and I'm trained."

"Don't forget who you're talking to. Who travelled four hundred miles through hostile territory in the dead of night to get to safety?"

There was a silence. She wondered whether he was thinking, as she was — *And look what it did to you.*

"At least if I'm with you, you can keep an eye on me," she said before he could put the thought into words.

"Right now you have to take the kids back to Montreal, so I'll poke around some more," he countered. "We'll discuss it tonight, back at the farmhouse."

It wasn't a complete capitulation, but as she hung up, she knew she was pushing her luck to get that far. Chris was right; even he was venturing deeper into the case than he should, and all for her sake. It was like Newfoundland all over again. When her phone rang a few seconds later, she thought it was him, having changed his mind.

"What?" she snapped.

A brief silence. Ragged breathing. Then "Miss Amanda?"

It was a young voice, cracking with fear. "Luc?" she gasped. She stared at the number on her phone. No caller ID.

"You have to help us," he said.

"What's going on?"

"I'm in so much trouble, I don't know who else to call."

Visions of AK-47s, index fingers raised in the air, and traitors executed raced through her mind. "Are you in danger?"

"No. Not me."

"Yasmina?"

"Yes."

"Is she with you?"

"Not exactly."

"Luc, talk to me! What's going on?"

"I can't tell you. It's not important. I just want you to get Yasmina out."

"Where are you?"

Silence. Was there a gun to his head? "Are you being threatened? Forced against your will? Yes or no."

"Don't worry about me. It's Yasmina you need to help."

Anger welled up. "Luc, I can't help you if you won't even tell me where you are or what danger you both face!"

"I'm sorry, I'm sorry. This is all my fault. I don't care about me, but Yasmina is in way over her head! I just need her out of danger." He broke off, as if wrestling for control. "But you have to hurry. There's an old stone church somewhere off the road that runs along the edge of the nature reserve. It's deserted and the road is bad. You will need a four-wheel drive or a snowmobile."

"I can get one. My friend Chris has a truck, and we can—"

"Chris?" Luc's voice rose an octave. "Your friend from Newfoundland? The cop?"

Amanda paused only briefly to wonder how he knew that. "Yes, but—"

"Is he with you?"

"No, but he'll be here soon. He's a friend."

"No! No, no!"

"I'm not walking into this blind!" she snapped and then realized she was talking to empty air.

She rushed back inside and found Sebastien on his computer in his little back office. He looked up in surprise. "I thought you'd left already."

"Can you get me the topographical map of the area north of here?"

He shoved back from his computer. "Why?"

"Something has come up." She debated how much to tell him. Unlike his intense, volatile wife — or perhaps because of it — Sebastien took most things in stride. He'd be a steadying hand in a crisis, and more importantly, he ought to know every deserted church and backcountry road in the whole area.

On the other hand, he'd probably never let her go if he thought she was heading into danger. He'd be right, of course.

She stalled. "Let me see the map first. I'll explain."

He fetched the tube of maps and unrolled them on his large equipment table. They shuffled through them until they found the one she needed. Amanda traced a road that led north through the bush from the village of L'Ascension.

"Is there a deserted stone church somewhere along this road?"

"Churches are usually in villages, and there's nothing up there for miles."

Sylvie poked her head through the doorway. "The kids are getting restless." She frowned at the sight of the map. "What's going on?"

"Amanda is being a mystery," Sebastien said and explained about the church. Sylvie bent her head over the map and tapped a squiggly line branching off from the main road. "Not a church, but there's an old stone house up here from an old farm. It has a window in the attic and stained glass in the door, so maybe it looks like a church."

Amanda eyed the orange line dubiously. It was so thin, it was nearly invisible. "What kind of road is that?"

"A very bad one." Sylvie laughed. "I remember that house from hunting with my father. It's got an old sugar shack, too. It was deserted and so dark inside that us kids used to call it … what's the word?"

"Haunted?" Amanda said.

"*C'est ça.* It was barely a road even back then. What's this about?"

Amanda took a deep breath to brace herself. "I got a call from Luc. He wants to meet me there."

Sylvie's eyes widened. "Is he all right? Lost?"

Amanda chose her words carefully. "He sounded fine but he wants help. Can I get to this road by truck?"

Sylvie shook her head. "You will need a snowmobile off this main road. But you can't go! It's too dangerous, and what about your students?"

"Could you go with them?"

"To Montreal? *Non, non!* Zidane did not even want me on this trip. I am not having responsibility for his students. Call the police!"

"Luc doesn't want police."

"Of course he doesn't! Because he's a terrorist!"

"No, I think he is trying to help Yasmina. He wants me to get her away safely. That's all I want to do, Sylvie. Go there and bring them back. She's been manipulated, and she's going to be used, either as a warrior's wife or a sex slave."

"Then call the police."

"And they will arrest her as a terrorist."

"If she's not, the courts will find out."

"Do you really believe that?" Amanda asked. In the current hysteria over terrorism, she wasn't sure reason would prevail. The court case would likely be top-secret, with a dreaded security certificate invoked and evidence withheld in the name of national security.

Sylvie stared her down. Her dark eyes were hard.

"I can take the students to Montreal," her husband said quietly.

Sylvie didn't budge.

"Thank you, Sebastien," Amanda said. "Now I need a truck and a snowmobile."

"Have you got a trail permit?" Sylvie snapped.

"No, but I can get one."

"Do you even know how to drive a snowmobile?"

"I've driven motorcycles all over the world," Amanda said.

"It is much more dangerous. You don't know the trails, how to read the snow and the ice on the lakes. And no one should travel those trails alone."

"Maybe someone from the village …"

Sylvie swore softly. Snatching up the map, she rolled it into its plastic tube. "It's madness, but I am mad."

"No, Sylvie. I may be mad, but I'm not putting you in danger too."

"You can't borrow my truck or my snowmobile. It's me, or nothing."

Sebastien looked alarmed, but he seemed to know it was pointless to argue. "You will need emergency supplies, warm clothes, food …"

"The most important thing we will need is a gun," Sylvie replied. "Can you shoot a gun?"

Amanda shuddered. Memories crowded her mind of the heavy, cold barrel against her arm and the trigger beneath her finger. Of the rifle slamming back against her shoulder, deafening her. Of the blood, and the screams. Newfoundland blurring with Nigeria.

"I can if I have to."

CHAPTER SEVENTEEN

After fleeing the Plaza Côte-des-Neiges, Matthew was halfway back to his apartment before he had his nerves under control. His call to Chris Tymko had gone unanswered. Goddamn cellphones anyway. He assumed Chris was on the case, doing something useful, but he had no idea where. He was pretty sure he wasn't just sitting in a classroom memorizing the conjugation of French verbs. Chris always took the bit between his teeth, rules and expectations be damned, and despite the twinges of jealousy, Matthew loved him for it.

Once he'd recovered from his fright, however, Matthew began to think about his own next moves. Chris wasn't the only one fond of the bit between his teeth. He would accomplish nothing by retreating to his apartment. There were a dozen questions to be answered, and time was of the essence. What was the name of the older brother with Faisel? What did people know about him? Had he attended the Collège de La Salle, and had he known Yasmina, Abdul, or Luc Prevost there? Were there any rumours about the two brothers being radicalized?

The obvious place to start was at the college itself. But if he was going to ask anyone about the al-Karim brothers, he had to do it fast before the brothers warned them off. He deftly steered his little car east toward the campus. After parking on a side street, he ducked behind snow banks to stay out of sight as he skirted around the campus toward the science building. No point in being kicked off campus before he'd even started. Faisel, he recalled, was taking a course load heavy in science and tech.

He found a predictable cluster of students shivering by the back door of the building, smoking and thumbing their phones. Although alarmed at being discovered, they were even more alarmed to be asked about Faisel al-Karim. We don't know him, they said. He sticks to himself. As for a brother, never heard of any.

Just then the bell rang and more students began to spill out the door. The buzz of laughter, conversation, and stomping boots swirled around him. He craned his neck, trying to identify Middle Eastern-looking students who might move in Faisel's circles. Why were kids today all so tall? Soon he resorted to stopping students at random and asking about Faisel al-Karim. Most looked at him as if he were an alien and pushed impatiently past him.

"Not here today," one of them finally volunteered. "Been sick all week."

"All week?" Matthew repeated. "With what?"

The young man shrugged his ignorance.

"Is he sick often?"

Belatedly, suspicion clouded the youth's face and he pushed past, leaving Matthew to consider the meaning of Faisel's long absence. Was he up to something? Matthew turned toward Zidane's building, trying to decide how to approach the man. Would he have known the older al-Karim brother? Would he cover for him? How much information should Matthew reveal, given that he wasn't sure where Zidane's allegiances lay? What excuse could he, Matthew, possibly dream up for inquiring about the al-Karims without giving away his suspicions?

He was just marshalling his questions when he spotted the college custodian rushing out of the maintenance shed on the far side of the property. He slipped and scrambled in headlong flight, his coat flapping and his mouth agape. Matthew hustled across the grounds to intercept him. At the last minute the custodian saw him and veered over. As he drew closer, Matthew could see the whites of his eyes and the flecks of froth on his lips.

"*Il est mort. Mon Dieu, il est mort!*" He lapsed into some incomprehensible dialect.

Matthew grabbed the man. "*Qui? Qui?* Who is dead?"

By way of answer, the custodian tore free and turned back toward the shed. "*Venez!* In here."

He stumbled back along the icy path toward the shed, the side door of which was ajar. In his rush for answers, Matthew plunged headlong into the gloom, narrowly missing the blades of a snow blower. The interior was packed with the tools and machines of landscape maintenance. As Matthew strained to decipher the dark, the silence was broken by the sobbing gasps of the custodian, who hung back in the doorway, refusing to enter.

"*Monsieur,*" he kept saying, and as Matthew followed his shaking finger, he spotted a bloody pruning knife lying on the floor and what looked like a body, half-stuffed into a dark corner behind the tractor mower. Its limbs were twisted like a pretzel.

It was impossible to tell how long it had been there, but there was no smell of decay. Only the sweet metallic tang of blood and urine.

Matthew forced himself to approach for a closer look at the waxy, pale face and felt the bile of horror and fear rise in his throat. This whole case had just become a lot more dangerous, for the dead man was Zidane.

Within half an hour, the campus was awash in cops. All the students had been sent home with the advisory that the police might need to question them and the request to contact the police liaison officer if they had any information, however tangential, to the case. Counsellors had also been lined up to help any students personally affected by Zidane's death.

The police had cordoned off the entire grounds around the shed as they tried to determine where, how, and when Zidane had been killed. From his brief glimpse of the body before being ousted by the first officers on the scene, Matthew had a pretty good idea of all three. The *how* was an expert slash across the throat that severed his carotid artery and nearly half his neck. The *where* was exactly where he lay, judging from the arterial spray drenching the walls and the blood pooled on the concrete floor beneath him.

The *when* was the trickiest. Matthew was not a forensic expert, but he'd seen a few bodies in his time. Judging from the coagulated blood and the cool skin of his neck when Matthew made a futile but automatic check of his vital signs, Zidane had died at least an hour before the custodian found him.

In those few minutes after he'd made the 911 call and before the custodian was whisked away to an EMS van, Matthew had managed to pry little information out of the poor man. Perhaps haunted by his past, or perhaps simply afraid he'd be accused, the man was nearly incoherent. He shook all over, tears streaming down his face and his eyes rolling back in his head. He'd seen no one, he insisted, not going into the shed or running away.

It appeared the killer had slipped in and out without being seen and melted into the adjacent streets.

The custodian kept muttering that he'd been working all morning, as he always did, on the other side of campus and had only returned to the shed because he had run out of salt for the main walkway. Perhaps the killer was familiar with his routine and had been counting on the body not being discovered for a couple more hours. With an hour or two's grace, he could have been far, far away.

While the Montreal police secured and evaluated the scene, Matthew was stuck in the back of a police cruiser under watch. He was desperate to phone Amanda or Chris but didn't want to give the police anything to think about beyond what they had. Blame it on an age-old mutual distrust between press and authority, born in the dark corners of the world he had covered. More importantly, he didn't want them to confiscate his phone, with its photos of the al-Karims, their car, and Zidane's body.

After a couple of hours, they took his statement and his contact information, warned him not to talk to anyone or publish any details, and sent him on his way. By that time a string of official vehicles including the forensics van, an ambulance, and a mobile command trailer was blocking access to the entire street. Matthew was tempted to blend into the crowd that strained against the crime scene cordon, hoping to pry more information from the officers scurrying back and forth.

But he had more important things to do. Amanda and the students would be arriving back at the college any minute, and she needed to be warned. He was itching to get on his computer to research Zidane. He knew little about the man, whom he'd thought peripheral to the case. Clearly he'd been wrong. But before all else, Chris had to be brought up to date. The whole case was spiralling out of control. Best to let Chris be the one to handle liaison between the Montreal cops, the RCMP, and INSET. On their own, the Montreal cops might not make the connection between Luc's disappearance and Zidane's death for hours, perhaps even days, especially if it required them to call in the feds.

As soon as he was driving home and out of sight of the police, he began his calls. To his dismay, Amanda's cellphone went straight to voicemail. She had either turned it off or was out of range. He left her a brief message telling her of Zidane's murder and urging her to phone him ASAP.

He had more luck with Chris, who answered his phone on the second ring.

"Where are you?" he asked.

"On my way back from Mont-Laurier, after what has mostly been a waste of time, except for learning the feds have clamped a lid on the entire investigation."

"Zidane is dead."

"*What?*"

"Throat slit on the college campus this morning." Bile rose in his throat and he fought for control.

"Holy fuck! What the hell happened?"

"The Montreal police are investigating. I was going to see him, to ask about the al-Karims—"

"Wait, wait. Who?"

"The kid who didn't go on the trip. I think he's the link. Not him directly, but he's got an older brother, and the two of them are up to something." Matthew barely missed a car turning left in front of him. The traffic felt unreal, his actions like a robot. "I think the older brother may be Abu Osama."

"Jesus, Matthew! What have you been up to?"

Matthew gave him the abridged version of all that he'd learned from Yasmina's family and from trailing the al-Karims.

"Jesus H.! I did some digging myself. CSIS and the RCMP have been trying to identify Abu Osama for months, and you just waltz in ..."

"It's a guess, that's all. I'm following my nose, and it seems to be leading me to them. It also tells me Zidane is involved somehow.

Either he knew something, asked the wrong questions, or he was considered an expendable liability to the operation at this point."

"What operation?"

"I have no idea. But the brothers were going somewhere this morning with some supplies in several large duffel bags. It looked like the older brother was hiding out and the kid Faisel was acting as the go-between."

There was silence on the phone for a minute. When Chris spoke, he sounded calmer. Like a cop following a lead. "Did anyone know you were going to see Zidane this morning? Did you tell anyone?"

An icy chill crept over Matthew. He did a quick check of the vehicles around him. "No, but … it's possible the brothers noticed me. The younger one, Faisel, would recognize me."

"Fuck, Matthew!"

Matthew banished the chill. "Look, it's Amanda I'm worried about right now. She's on the bus bringing the kids back to Montreal, but I can't reach her to warn her."

"Does she know any of this? About the al-Karim brothers? About Abu Osama?"

"No."

"Well, at least that's good. She won't be asking any questions that could get her into trouble."

Matthew almost smiled. How well the guy knew Amanda! "What's the next step?"

"I'll see if I can reach Amanda from where I am, and if not, I'll try Sebastien and Sylvie. And I'll pass this stuff on to my RCMP contact, who seems to have her finger on all this."

Belatedly, Matthew remembered his phone. *Boy, you're not firing on all cylinders, Goderich!* "I've got photos of the two brothers, a pretty clear one of the older brother, and some of the SUV they drove off in. I'll send them to you right now."

Steering with one hand, he thumbed through the photos on his phone. Looking at them now, he noticed that the SUV was covered in dirt, just like every other car in Montreal in February, when salt, sand, and slush coated everything. But the licence plate of the SUV was almost completely obscured. *Damn it,* he thought and an instant later wondered whether that was deliberate.

He sent the photos off just as he was approaching a parking space outside his apartment. At the last minute, he drove around the corner and parked on the busy main street instead. As he sneaked toward his apartment, he scanned the crowds, feeling like a spy in a bad Cold War movie.

The hall was empty and serene, with no sign of knife-wielding killers lurking in the shadows. An odd smell of musk or perfume lingered in the air. He climbed the stairs, huffing as he reached the top, and at the last instant, with his key already in the lock, he froze. His heart slammed his chest. The door was unlocked.

His first impulse was to flee, to run all the way back to his car and phone the police. But instead he stood stock-still, barely breathing, and listened. Beyond the pounding of blood in his ears, he heard nothing. He twisted the knob. Poked open the door an inch.

Nothing.

He pushed it again, and when it drifted open harmlessly, he stuck his head inside. The little apartment was empty. Even the bathroom, visible through its open door, was empty. Unless the guy was under the bed or in the closet....

It took him a moment to register. The room looked the same as always. The clutter was still piled on the bed, the small kitchen table was strewn with papers, his laptops were open.

But Luc's little computer was gone.

CHAPTER EIGHTEEN

Amanda stood by the truck, chafing with frustration as she waited for Sylvie. She was so hot in her snowmobile suit that she barely noticed the sharp north wind. She had watched patiently while the woman packed up their gear and loaded it onto the snowmobile trailer, grateful for her foresight and knowledge of wilderness survival. A hot tent, four sleeping bags, dehydrated food, and warm changes of clothes — not just for the two of them but for Luc and Yasmina — were expertly stowed in the back of the truck.

Amanda had still been patient while Sylvie checked and cleaned the shotgun, and printed off more maps, but just when they seemed all ready to go, Sylvie had disappeared back inside. At that point, at nearly one o'clock, Amanda's patience finally ran out. The day was slipping away. The van carrying Sebastien and the students had left over an hour ago.

What the hell was the woman doing? Was she deliberately trying to sabotage the trip, hoping Amanda's second sober thought would kick in? Or had she notified the police behind her back and was buying time until they could get their own officers in place?

Throughout the last hour Amanda had noticed helicopters and several small planes flying overhead. Not unusual, Sylvie had reassured her, because the small planes airport was just on the other side of the river, and this was the end of a busy ski weekend.

But what if it was more than that? Amanda was about to march back inside when Sylvie emerged with her helmet under her arm. She yanked her truck door open with a loud squawk. Within minutes they were heading toward the main highway, the snowmobile trailer bumping along behind them and the shocks of the old truck jolting over every pothole. Amanda had seen many old jalopies held together with string and chewing gun in the developing world, and this truck ranked among the best.

They wove their way on backcountry roads up through the village of L'Annonciation, which was dominated by a large regional hospital perched on a hill, and continued north toward the more remote village of L'Ascension. Amanda recalled passing through La Conception farther south and wondered idly whether the early settlers, having run out of saints' names, had moved on to the story of Christ's life.

Beyond L'Ascension, the road became little more than an icy, rutted track. Kaylee balanced on the console between them, her tongue lolling and her eyes shining at the prospect of a wilderness adventure. As the truck rattled over the ruts, Amanda steadied herself on the dash and glanced uneasily at Sylvie.

"Is this truck going to make it?"

Sylvie laughed. Oddly, she seemed to be enjoying herself. "*Bien sûr!* I keep this truck in perfect shape!"

In the sky overhead, Amanda saw another plane. Her uneasiness grew. Just as her spine was begging for mercy, they came across an opening on their left, marking a snow-covered track into the scrubby bush. Sylvie pulled over and unrolled her map. After a moment of study, she rolled it back up.

"*Bon! C'est ça!*" She climbed out, and they peered down the track, which curved out of sight in the distance.

"Probably an old logging or sugarbush road," Sylvie said. "This land is full of them. It's here that we need the snowmobile."

Kaylee leaped out of the truck and bounced in excited circles while they manoeuvred the snowmobile and toboggan off the trailer. After tossing a stick for her, Amanda walked over to study the beginning of the trail. It had not snowed in nearly four days, and there were clear signs of traffic on the trail, not only snowmobile tracks but also snowshoes.

"Who uses these trails?"

"This is private land, but often the owners give permission to locals to pass. Sometimes the owners are not here anyway."

Kaylee bounded back with the stick. Distractedly, Amanda threw it again. "Where would they be?"

Looking up from the toboggan, Sylvie shrugged. "Florida? Working in Montreal? What are they going to do up here in the winter?" Having secured the load, she pulled on her helmet and climbed on the snowmobile. "Let's go."

Amanda climbed behind Sylvie, gathered Kaylee in her lap, and held on tight as Sylvie gunned the big machine forward. As they bounced and lurched over the snow, the roar of the engine precluded any conversation, so Amanda used the time to study her surroundings. The area was scrubbier than the wildlife reserve they had been in. They passed through a swath of what had probably once been pasture, now reclaimed by brush and poplars.

A short distance later they entered a hilly area of tall maples, grey and skeletal against the sky, and Amanda saw the remnants of piping in the trees from an old sugarbush. Was it still in use, or had it been abandoned?

Up ahead she glimpsed a roofline through the trees, and as they approached, the outline of a tall, thin house emerged. Amanda signalled to Sylvie to stop. Once the engine sputtered to a stop, Amanda tugged off her helmet and studied the house cautiously. It stood in a clearing, looking remarkably like a church with its high, peaked roof and the broken stained glass window in the door. Soot streaked the stone walls. At the edge of the clearing were two wooden shacks, one completely collapsed, the other sagging precariously. There was no sign of movement in any of the buildings. She sniffed the air. Besides the stink of gasoline from the snowmobile, she detected a hint of wood smoke.

Relieved to escape the machine, Kaylee headed off, nose to the ground in search of a new stick.

"I think we should approach the rest of the way on foot," Amanda said.

Sylvie snorted. "If anyone is there, they will have heard us a mile away."

"I know, but I don't want to disturb the tracks."

Behind her, Sylvie unpacked the shotgun and nestled it in the crook of her arm. Trying not to think about it, Amanda led the way forward. The snow was trampled by snowshoes and boots. How many people had been here?

Her pulse was pounding in her ears as she approached the silent house. The front door hung ajar, and Amanda peered through it. The house had been gutted. The upper floor had largely collapsed, leaving a gaping hole with charred edges, as if fire had ravaged it years ago. Holes in the roof had allowed rain and snow inside, so that little was left of the interior but a solid stone fireplace against one wall. Judging from the size of the saplings growing inside, the house had been abandoned decades ago.

Yet now, as her eyes took in the details, there were signs of recent habitation — a small pile of ash in the fireplace and a bed of flattened fir boughs on the floor by the fire. She felt the ash and jerked her hand away from the warmth.

"They're gone," Sylvie said.

Amanda glanced through the window. "Luc sounded scared. They may have heard our engine, and they're hiding in the bush to see who it is."

In the distance, Kaylee began to bark. Amanda rushed outside. The last thing she needed was for the dog to take on a porcupine. When she called her, Kaylee came back from the wooden shack slowly, snuffling the snow.

"She smells something," Amanda said.

"What?"

"I don't know. Could be anything." Skunk, deer, wolf … or person. Putting the dog on a leash to keep her out of trouble, she walked over to investigate. One shack was full of old spigots, empty fuel cans, and plastic piping, while the larger one housed a rusted-out stove and vat, along with stacks of old firewood. She recognized the paraphernalia of a sugar shack, long fallen into disuse.

There were footprints everywhere. She stood outside, listening. Nothing but the distant drone of an airplane and the wind raking through the trees. She scanned the surrounding bush for movement. The flicker of a squirrel jumping from one branch to another, but nothing more. Where the hell were they?

Strapping on snowshoes, she walked around the perimeter in a broad arc, looking for tracks leading away from the house. She saw deer tracks, wolf tracks, and two sets of snowshoes. She felt a surge of excitement, for the webbing pattern was identical to the snowshoes they had used on the trip. Luc and Yasmina had been here!

Kaylee strained on the leash, her nose high in the air as she pulled Amanda forward. Up ahead, the snow was trampled and the bushes snapped and broken. In the midst of the melee, traces of red splashed the snow.

Dread shot through her. She looked around and called Luc's name. No response. She studied the blood again. It was spreading into the surrounding snow but looked fresh. How much had been spilled? A small wound, or life-threatening? Maybe it was just an animal kill. A deer or a rabbit, brought down by the wolves. Even though there was no sign of fur or bones, Amanda latched on to that hope.

Kaylee was still tugging at the leash. Was she just after a stick, or had she caught the scent of something else? After a moment's hesitation, Amanda unleashed her. It was a risk, but if the dog found Luc or Yasmina, worth it.

"Go find it!" she cried, giving Kaylee the command to find whatever the dog was so intent on. Kaylee headed into the forest, her nose to the ground. Turning her attention back to the snowshoe tracks, Amanda tried to determine where they had gone after the apparent fight. She found snowshoe tracks leading diagonally away from the house and out into the bush. Where on earth were they heading?

She made her way back to Sylvie, who was standing watch by the snowmobile, her shotgun at the ready. "Can I look at the map?"

Sylvie unfurled the map on the seat of the snowmobile, and they both bent over it. Sylvie quickly found their location, and Amanda studied the surrounding countryside. According to the map, it was all bush.

"Who owns this land?"

Sylvie shrugged. "No idea. It used to be sugarbush, but whoever owns it hasn't done anything with it in years."

"Someone has been hurt. There's blood back there."

"How much?"

"Just a few drops, but heavy clothing might have absorbed much of it. And there are snowshoe tracks leading off in that direction." Amanda scrutinized the map farther north. "What's up there? Isn't that where that farmer's body was found?"

Sylvie stepped back from the map and gazed around, frowning. "I think this may be his land. His old farmhouse and sugarbush."

At that moment Kaylee came bounded back through the deep snow, her eyes shining. She was carrying what looked like a stick in her mouth, but when she dropped it at Amanda's feet, the two women gasped in unison. It wasn't a stick but a hunting knife, and its blade was blood red.

Matthew cleared out of his apartment in less than five minutes. He threw fistfuls of clothes into his overnight bag, stuffed his notes, laptops, and camera into his shoulder bag and scuttled out, barely pausing to lock the door.

Outside, he drove in random, half-panicked circles for half an hour before pulling up to a budget hotel on Sherbrooke Street and signing in as Peter MacKay from Leeds, U.K. He'd first used that ID overseas as a joke when prominent Conservative Member of Parliament Peter MacKay was minister of foreign affairs. He hadn't used it in over a year, not since his dangerous days in war zones in Africa, but he could still affect a passable North English accent. At least enough to fool the French Canadian girl at the front desk.

Once inside his modest room, he threw his bags on the bed, picked up the hotel phone, and started to phone Chris. Halfway through, he froze. He had to think this through. Before he made another move, he needed to know where the danger lay. Someone had broken into his apartment to steal Luc's computer. His first assumption had been one of the al-Karim boys or their associates, anxious to prevent any leaks about their jihadi network. He was pretty sure he'd been recognized at the coffee shop that morning, and although they wouldn't have been able to follow him back to his apartment, his address was hardly a secret. Several people involved in the Laurentian Extreme Adventure might have known it, including possibly the al-Karims and certainly Zidane.

Zidane. His mouth went dry at the memory of him. *This is way out of control*, he'd told Chris, and at the time he hadn't known the half of it!

But there was another party interested in getting their hands on Luc's computer. Perhaps even more interested. The RCMP. They had barged into Luc's father's house with a search warrant, and when the computer failed to turn up, they would almost certainly have gone to Luc's mother. Ghyslaine didn't have the computer, but she knew who did. The question was, would the fiercely protective mother give up Matthew's name to the cops and risk her beloved son going back to jail?

The raid on Matthew's apartment had been almost surgical. Nothing had been disturbed. Either the intruders had put everything neatly back in its place, or they had gone straight for what they wanted and that was all. If the RCMP had done it, either they had been unable to get a warrant, or they hadn't wanted Matthew to know.

Before he called Chris, he needed to know whether it was Chris's own people who had the computer, or whether the jihadists were now in possession of all Luc's contacts. Matthew had no idea what other secrets were on that computer, because in the whirlwind of the past two days, he'd forgotten to copy the hard drive. Now the chance had slipped through his fingers. He cursed himself for that stupidity.

Thankfully, Ghyslaine snatched up her phone before the second ring, suggesting she'd been hovering near it. She sounded disappointed and angry to hear him at the other end of the line.

"Have you news on Luc?"

He hesitated only briefly before deciding not to mention Zidane's death. No point in pushing the woman farther over the edge. "Ghyslaine," he replied, dispensing with any attempt to soften her up. "Did the cops visit you looking for his computer?"

"Yes! National Security, they called themselves. Very unfriendly people, asked me all sorts of questions about Luc."

"What sort of questions?"

"About his friends, his activities, his late-night meetings. They accused him ..." Her voice broke and a strangled cry rose in her throat. "They searched everything in his room! All his school notes, books, clothes, even his old computer. They were very angry and demanded where the other computer was."

"What did you tell them?"

"Nothing! I'm not going to tell those bastards anything! They accuse my son — they want to say those awful lies about my son, they can prove them by themselves!"

He cut through her rage. "Ghyslaine, what did they accuse him of?"

"That he is a terrorist! That he is going to Iraq to fight."

He dropped his voice and chose his words carefully. "You suspected that already, didn't you? That's why you didn't want to report him missing to the police. That's why you didn't want me to have his computer."

She said nothing, but from her ragged breathing, he suspected she was fighting for control. "I cracked the password, you know," he said softly. "It was Yasmina. Is she a good friend of his?"

"It is all her fault! It is for her that he converted to that awful religion and began to go to prayer meetings. But he wasn't good enough for her. Poor Luc, always the loser. I think she was after bigger fish."

Like Abu Osama, he thought. "Did Luc ever mention a man named Abu Osama?"

"Who's that? A Muslim?"

Distaste dripped from her tone, but he ignored it. "Did you ever see him with a young man with a thick beard and black hair in a bun?"

"I never met any of those friends. He made sure of that."

"What about Faisel al-Karim? Does that name ring a bell?"

"No." Her voice grew uncertain. "I saw something once … a note in his book. Not Faisel, but al-Karim. Ta — Talid? Tawhid? Something like that."

Matthew tamped down his excitement with an effort. Could this be the name he was looking for? "What was it in connection to?"

"A meeting. I asked Luc about it, and he got angry that I looked in his book. He said I didn't trust him. I do, I do! My son is not a terrorist. That's crazy. He detests violence; he doesn't even kill spiders. One time he hit a squirrel with his bike, and he didn't eat for a day. He said I have to trust him. Don't pay attention to any stories the police tell about me, he said."

Matthew frowned. "When did he say this?"

"When I ask him about this man, Tawhid. He says things are not what they seem."

CHAPTER NINETEEN

The sky was leaden and threatening snow by the time Matthew reached Yasmina's house. All week the meteorologists had been gleefully predicting a blizzard beginning late in the afternoon and intensifying overnight. But forecasters were notorious for their prophesies of doom, and Montrealers generally just rolled their eyes. More than likely it would be five centimetres of snow, over and done with by morning.

However, the threat lent a feeling of urgency to Matthew's search for answers. He had a name now — Tawhid or Talid — and a few minutes of ferreting around on the Internet at Starbucks had confirmed that there was indeed a twenty-two-year-old al-Karim brother named Tawhid. It struck Matthew as ironic that the name meant belief in the oneness of Allah, which was the most fundamental principle of Islam but was being used by jihadists, along with their one-fingered salute, as a rallying cry for their violent cause.

When Matthew had stared at the familiar, darkly handsome face on Tawhid's Facebook profile, a chill crawled through him. It was the same man Faisel had met that morning. On a hunch, he'd run a Google search on Yasmina's brother, Abdul, also twenty-two. The two men would have been at Collège de La Salle together. He recalled how Abdul had almost panicked at the mention of the al-Karims the evening before and had all but ordered his mother not to speak.

Abdul knew something. This time Matthew was not going to take no for an answer.

It was a shot in the dark, turning up at Yasmina's house in the middle of the afternoon when the whole family was probably at work, school, or searching for Yasmina, so he was surprised when Leila opened the door. She looked grey with fatigue, as if she hadn't slept since her daughter's disappearance, but she still insisted on bringing tea and a platter of dates and cheese.

"I don't know where Abdul is. When I came downstairs this morning, he was gone. I heard the phone ring. Perhaps it was about Monsieur Zidane."

Matthew seized the opening. "Did he know Zidane?"

"At the college, yes. To the students, at least the Muslim ones, Zidane was like an uncle. A very stern but helpful uncle. Such terrible news. Who would do such a thing?"

"Did he make enemies among some of the students when he disapproved of their behaviour?"

"Their behaviour?"

"I mean ..." Sensing her wariness, Matthew searched for the vaguest of allusions. "You know that age. So much freedom, so much to explore."

She studied her hands quietly. She had many rings on her fingers, and she examined them each in turn. "It's difficult to believe it was one of the students, but as a counsellor, he did learn a lot of secrets."

Cautiously, Matthew ventured further. "Last night, Abdul seemed upset when you mentioned the al-Karim family. Why?"

She looked at him obliquely and leaned forward to offer him more dates, although she hadn't touched a single morsel of food herself. "It's a long story. Perhaps not mine to tell."

"But with your daughter missing ..."

Still she said nothing.

He took a date. "I'm not the police," he said gently. "But I am very protective of my good friend Amanda Doucette. I need some answers."

That seemed to reach her. He had not told any of the students or their families about Amanda's past, but it was still there, in all its raw horror, all over the Internet at the click of a mouse.

"You are right," she said. "Abdul is worried about the al-Karim family. He blames them for leading Yasmina into ... for making her devout. They talked a lot about the Quebec Charter of Values, which made her feel like an outsider. The al-Karims were so proud and certain of their faith." She smiled wanly. "We are not so certain, you see. We see religion as the creation of man, not God. But uncertainty makes us seem weak in Yasmina's eyes. Our doubt is the work of the devil. Their passion and certainty was like a magnet for her. They were like ..." She raised her gaze to the ceiling as if for inspiration. "Bigger than ordinary men."

"Who? Faisel?"

She paused.

"Or Tawhid?"

She shot him a surprised glance.

"Are Tawhid and Abdul friends? Is that why he is so upset?"

"*Were* friends, yes. Close friends, years ago. But they had a disagreement."

"Over religion?"

"No." She twisted her rings and then gestured to offer him more tea. This time he shook his head, not wanting to break the mood. "Over Yasmina," she finally said.

"What happened?"

"When they were boys, Tawhid was often at our house. He and Abdul used to play music together and video games on the Internet. I think those things were not allowed at Tawhid's house. He was an exciting young man, full of life and teasing. Yasmina was young and a friend of Faisel, so we were not paying attention. We thought she was with Faisel. But secretly, it was Tawhid she wanted, and recently Abdul found out."

"How?"

"Monsieur Zidane told him. He knew many things. Abdul always said he has eyes all over campus."

Matthew felt a quiver of excitement. "When was this?"

"About two months ago, when Tawhid came back from the Middle East." She sighed. "We have been blind to so many things. When Yasmina first started exploring her religion, she asked to go to the Islamic summer school in Cairo. We didn't want to discourage her. We sent Abdul with her. That was our first mistake. It turned out Tawhid and Faisel were there too. We should have seen the signs. Even before then, Tawhid had stopped coming to our house, stopped playing music and video games with Abdul. On his last visit, he refused to have dinner with us because we were having wine. He said we were all going to hell, and he left. When Yasmina came back from Cairo, she started to say the same things. We humoured her. We stopped having wine and music." She looked up at him bleakly. "We were wrong."

"Did she continue to see Tawhid?"

She shook her head. "Tawhid stayed overseas. But they stayed in touch secretly on Skype and email. She went out a lot, studying with Faisel and classmates, she said. We were worried —Abdul was very worried — but we wanted to trust her."

The front door opened, and Abdul burst into the room. He stopped short at the sight of Matthew, but his mother pre-empted any objection by barking something at him in Arabic. It was a question but sounded more like an accusation. His eyes darted to Matthew as he gathered his reply.

"I tried to fly up north," he said in English, "to check on the search."

Leila half rose from her chair. "Any news?"

He shrugged off his parka. "The cops have it all blocked off. I couldn't even hire a plane." He jerked his head toward Matthew. "What's he doing here?"

"We are talking about Tawhid al-Karim," Matthew said before his mother could divert the subject.

"You *told* him?"

"Abdul, there is no fooling around here," Matthew said. "Two men are dead, and some kind of terror plot is in the works. You can't shield Tawhid just because he's a friend."

"I'm not shielding him! But I'm not helping you either."

"Is Tawhid Abu Osama?"

Abdul's mouth gaped open. He stared at his mother. "Did you tell him that?"

The colour had drained from Leila's face. "We didn't even talk about that. But … but it makes sense."

"Mother!"

Her eyes flashed. "Enough, Abdul! You must tell what you know. This has gone far enough. Do you want bombs here in Canada, like the ones in France? In Brussels? In the U.S.? Do you want Canadians turning against us? This country has given us sanctuary, and this is how we repay them? By our children planting bombs?"

"Mother—"

"No! You must choose! The time for protecting is over. Millions of refugees are risking their lives to get to safety from these killers. They are putting their babies on rafts. What about protecting them? Or do you not care about them? About us? About Canadians?"

Abdul was shaking his head angrily. "Mother, he's a journalist! It will be in all the papers. Our story. Our shame."

"Is that all that matters? Is that more important than your sister's life? She has been tricked, Abdul. He has filled her head with fantasies."

Matthew had been carefully watching Abdul. The young man had flinched at every accusation his mother hurled at him, but Matthew sensed something deeper and more powerful than shame. The man was mortally afraid. Zidane's death had sent a message.

He held up his hand to stop Leila's barrage and reached into his pocket for his card. He scribbled a name and number on the back. "This is my friend. He's an RCMP officer, but more importantly a good friend of Amanda Doucette. If you don't want to talk to me, at least call him. He'll know what to do, and he'll keep your name out of it."

Sebastien and Sylvie's farmhouse looked ominously quiet, but Chris brushed aside a small twinge of concern. It was barely three o'clock in the afternoon, too early for Amanda to be back from Montreal. Sebastien and Sylvie's truck was gone, but they were probably off replenishing supplies in town. Even when he phoned Amanda's cellphone and got no reply, he told himself that cellphone coverage in the mountains between here and Montreal was probably unreliable.

The clouds pressed in and the temperature was dropping. The wind was picking up, and a couple of snowflakes stung his cheeks. It would be a night for curling up with Amanda in front of a blazing fire. Maybe on a bearskin rug.... The thought brought a thrum of desire. He hoped she would arrive back before she got caught navigating that twisty Macaza road in a snowstorm.

He tried the front door and found it unlocked. How like the country. The interior of the house was chilly, and he was just heading toward the back to fire up the woodstove when he caught sight of a big square of white paper thumbtacked to the wall by the door. *Chris*, it said in big letters.

A note from Amanda? A change of plans? He pulled it off the wall and unfolded it. The note was scrawled and barely legible, as if dashed off in a hurry.

A. and I gone meet Luc take Yasmina to safety. Abandoned stone house off road north L'Ascension. Marked on map on desk. Need snowmobile. Sylvie.

Chris raced into the office to examine the map. Goddamn her. *God damn her!* Had the woman learned nothing from her past brushes with death? He found the thin, squiggly road and the hastily drawn X, which appeared to be in the middle of nowhere. He suspected the backcountry roads would have no signs. Possibly not even names. He grabbed the phone to call the SQ detachment commander in Mont-Laurier. Hopefully the man could mobilize his officers to search. Darkness was coming fast and with it, snow, which would complicate search and rescue efforts.

But no one answered at the SQ detachment. Had everyone gone home already? When voicemail kicked in with an emergency number to call, he hung up in frustration. If the local SQ was spread as thin as most rural detachments he'd worked for, there wouldn't be enough officers within a hundred kilometres to mount a decent search anyway. It would be faster to do his own search.

Calmer now that he had a plan, he ran through the outfitter's store packing up emergency supplies: a warm change of clothes, sleeping bag and camp stove, emergency food bars, and first aid. Piling everything into his truck, he set off into the village, hoping that the little *dépanneur* cum gas station was still open. Jeanne Marie was sweeping up and looked glad for the diversion. Her brow furrowed when he explained his request.

"Old stone house?"

"Yes, north of L'Ascension somewhere."

She shook her head, still baffled.

"Is there anyone in town here who knows that area? Or who would know the old farms?"

"My dad." Her eyes lit up. "Or Gaetan. He used to hunt up there."

Gaetan — the Montreal Canadiens hockey fan with the sharp memory for history. "Where can I find Gaetan?"

She glanced at the antique clock on the wall, which miraculously still kept accurate time. Its hands were inching toward three thirty. Chris chafed with frustration. Two hours of daylight left! "Probably he will be at his house. Across the bridge, to the left. Red roof." She smiled. "There is a big sign for firewood. *Bois de chauffage.*"

Chris thanked her, bought some chocolate bars and an extra-large coffee, and raced back to his truck. Fortunately, he found Gaetan's house on his first pass and spotted the man outside, splitting logs. Gaetan turned off his log splitter with relief at the sight of Chris, but his big grin of recognition turned to concern when Chris posed his question. He bent over Chris's map, and his whole face furrowed with concentration as he traced his finger over the roads.

"Do you know where this stone house is?"

Gaetan nodded slowly. "I think yes. At L'Ascension here, you take this road to left and you go north maybe … twenty-thirty minute … and you have to turn to left again, but—" He shot a glance at Chris's truck. "Not in that. In a *motoneige*. You 'ave one?"

Chris hesitated as he eyed the two snowmobiles sitting under tarps in Gaetan's side yard. The man was a trained SAR volunteer, which would be a great asset, but the police had already deemed it too dangerous to put civilians at risk. While he was vacillating, his phone rang. Hoping it was Amanda, he snatched it up.

"Corporal Tymko?" a vaguely familiar voice barked. "Sergeant Sechrest here. Where are you?"

Chris scrambled to put a face to the name. The RCMP officer he'd spoken to in Montreal about Luc's jihadi connections. He searched for as vague and neutral a reply as possible. With the snow intensifying and darkness nearing, he hadn't time for a long argument about what he was up to. While he hunted for words, she chuckled.

"I happen to know you're not in French class, so we can skip to the chase. You're up in Tremblant, sticking your nose in."

"I'm concerned about a friend up here in the area," Chris said. "I'm not interfering with any investigation."

"You're a blind bull in a china shop, Tymko. You're asking questions that shouldn't be asked."

Chris thought of Amanda, who was blundering right into the middle of a jihadi conspiracy. In that split second, he realized maybe this was the help he needed.

"A lot has happened since I last talked to you," he said, "and I'm extremely worried about my friend's safety." Aware of Gaetan's curious stare, he turned away and took a deep breath. In a rush he told her about Zidane's murder, about the al-Karim brothers, and about the elusive Abu Osama, who might have left Montreal that morning with several duffel bags full of supplies.

Sandy Sechrest had been listening without comment, but at this news she came alive. She quizzed him on the duffel bags and the vehicle he'd driven. "Have you an ID on this Abu Osama?"

"My source thinks he's an older brother in the al-Karim family. I don't have an address, but my source texted me a photo of him and of the vehicle, which—"

"What are you doing sitting on this stuff, Tymko!"

He didn't have an answer for that. In truth, he'd been so focused on finding Amanda that he'd forgotten about the photos.

"Send them to me ASAP, and then stay the hell out of the way!"

"But there's more."

"Of course there's more! There's a whole lot more, but you don't know what the hell you're looking at—"

"My friend Amanda Doucette has gone off into the bush to meet this Luc guy and a young woman named Yasmina."

"*What?*" Her voice reached the stratosphere before she reined herself in enough to listen while he spilled out the story of Yasmina's disappearance, Luc's call for help, and the stone house rendezvous. Sechrest interrupted only long enough to clarify the location.

"It's real bush country," he said, "about twenty kilometres north of L'Ascension."

"Leave it to us. We'll handle it."

"But I'm not far away. It will be dark soon, so there's no time to waste. I can be there in an hour, but I'd appreciate any reinforcements—"

"I said, let us handle it, Tymko."

"Where are you?" he countered.

She hesitated. "Mont-Laurier."

She's on the case herself! he thought with astonishment, once again wondering just who the hell Sechrest was and how she was mixed up in this. "I'm going. Period. But if you can get up to L'Ascension in forty minutes, I'll meet you at the crossroads."

"Chris—"

"I'll take the flak later, Sergeant, but right now I don't give a fuck about the rest of the investigation!"

A pause. A soft curse. "See you in L'Ascension. And Tymko, don't forget those photos."

CHAPTER TWENTY

Freaked out by the bloody knife and the clear evidence of danger, Sylvie wanted to go back to town immediately, but Amanda persuaded her to let her assess the situation first. After wrapping the knife in a scarf for safekeeping, she put Kaylee on a leash and examined the bloodstained snow.

Among the trampled footprints, she found more blood kicked under in the scuffle, creating pink washes in the snow. It looked as if a fight had taken place, but the area was so churned up that it was difficult to say how many people were involved. However, on the periphery, a single set of snowshoes led away northward into the bush.

Kaylee was straining at the leash, trying to pull her along the lone snowshoe trail. Amanda followed carefully, studying the ground. At first there was nothing, but about twenty feet out, another small pink wash marred the snow. Then more, larger and more frequent. The heavy clothing must have absorbed the blood at first, but now it was leaking out faster.

Her adrenaline spiked. It was what she feared. This lone snowshoer was injured and had fled into the bush, perhaps without a plan or a direction in mind.

Yet no one had pursued him. Was the person still here, watching her and Sylvie from the cover of the forest? Her heart in her throat, she pulled out her cellphone and punched in the number Luc had used. No signal. She returned to Sylvie. "Let me use your sat phone."

"We have to call the police!"

"First I want to check with Luc. I want to know whether he's the one who's hurt."

The call to Luc's number went directly to voicemail, as if the phone was turned off or out of range. Glaring at her, Sylvie snatched the phone back. "I am calling the police."

"Which police?"

"The SQ."

"They are not the ones in charge of this investigation. Probably the RCMP."

Sylvie rolled her eyes. "The RCMP has no presence here in the country."

Amanda tried to remember what Chris and Matthew had told her. The search had become a national security investigation involving multiple agencies. There would be secrecy and tight control. She wanted to make sure the information got into the right hands as soon as possible.

"Let me phone my RCMP friend, Chris. He's up to speed on the details, and he'll know who to contact."

Sylvie handed the sat phone back without argument. The phone rang and rang before Chris's voice came over the line, muffled by the rumble of an engine. When she identified herself, he shouted aloud.

"Thank God! Where are you?"

"I'm in the bush north of L'Ascension."

"Are you at the stone house?"

She paused, suddenly aware of Sylvie's evasive gaze. "Sylvie called you."

"Left a note. I'm on my way with backup. Are you all right?"

"Yes, Sylvie and I are, but someone has been hurt."

"Who?"

"I don't know. There's no one here, but there's a bloody snowshoe trail leading into the bush, and Luc is not answering his phone." She found she was trembling. Adrenaline or a delayed fear reaction now that help was on the way?

"Okay, I'll relay that to the others."

Amanda pulled herself together. "We'll need EMS, maybe even a helicopter medevac."

"On it." His voice was crisp and sure. She felt a rush of warmth. How she wanted to hug him! "And you stay put. I'm probably forty-five minutes away. Are you in a safe place?"

Amanda looked around her at the silent, sinister woods. The stone house was abandoned but had clearly been used that day. Where was the second person involved in the fight? "I think so, but ..." She trailed off, not trusting her own fear.

"Go back out to the main road so I can find you."

"What main road?" She laughed, the absurdity bubbling up. "It's an icy, rutted stretch of mud."

"My best kind of road," he replied. "Go there and wait."

She was silent as she eyed the trail leading into the woods. The grey sky was darkening, and snow-laden clouds swirled snowflakes into the tracks.

"Amanda? Promise me?"

"Come soon," she said. "I'm really worried."

After he hung up, she handed the phone back to Sylvie. "He wants us to wait back on the road. It will be warm in the truck."

"*Bon!*" Sylvie turned to go but Amanda hung back, tugged by the need to do more than just wait. Chris would be furious with her, but she hoped he'd understand. The temperature was dropping as the wind picked up. Soon it would be dark, and the snow would obliterate the trail. Someone was out there all alone, bleeding and running for their life. Possibly they had already collapsed and now lay dying of hypothermia mere metres away.

"You go ahead," she said. "I want to follow the trail for a bit while it's still light."

"No way! We wait for your friend."

"I won't go far, but the person may be less than a mile away. Every moment counts."

"Not enough to risk your own life! The person could be a killer!"

Amanda turned to head back to the snowmobile. "Sylvie, I'm not arguing! I'm going! I'll grab a few emergency supplies, a flashlight, and a thermal blanket in case I find them. If I'm not back when Chris gets here, you guys follow as fast as you can."

When they reached the snowmobile, Amanda began to throw some supplies into her daypack. She took the map and compass, but seeing the fury on Sylvie's face, she did not ask for the sat phone.

Sylvie watched as she hefted the small pack onto her back. Only then did she break her stony stare. "Fine. But you take the gun."

Amanda stared at the horrid, alien thing that Sylvie held out. Once again the two stared each other down, and this time Amanda relented. Without a word, she reached out.

Amanda kept Kaylee on a leash in front of her so that she could watch her ears and nose. The dog's finely honed senses would pick up trouble far earlier than hers.

At first the silence of the woods seemed absolute, save for their own breathing and the pounding of her heart, but as her ears gradually attuned to nuances, other sounds filtered through. The swish of wind, the moan of tree boughs, and the distant drone of engines. Whether they were airplanes, snowmobiles, or chainsaws, the alien intrusions travelled miles across the frozen, empty land.

The snowshoe trail was wavering and uneven, as if the person were stumbling and stopping frequently to rest. At times it meandered off course around deadfall, dense trees, or steep rocky outcrops, but according to her compass it maintained a vaguely consistent direction north, despite the twisty, undulating terrain where every snow-shrouded tree and rock looked the same and where it was possible to get turned around in a minute.

This suggested that they had a specific destination in mind. And more importantly, they still had their wits about them.

After trudging through the deep snow for a few minutes, Amanda heard the roar of a snowmobile behind her as it revved to life and drove away. Sylvie was heading back to the road. The whine grew quieter until it stopped altogether, leaving only the whisper of the trees. As she strained her ears to listen, another sound, this time the throaty rumble of a truck. Sylvie, starting the truck to warm herself? Or Chris arriving with his reinforcements?

She stood in the woods debating what to do. She could go back to meet them, she could wait for them to catch up, or she could carry on. She peered at the trail disappearing into the brush ahead. Where was the person going, and how far away were they? Snow was sifting through the trees onto the trail, blurring the tracks. Through the blur, she spotted a line in the snow. Something dragged along by the side of the trail? A stick, perhaps used for support as the person's strength waned?

Kaylee stood on the trail, looking at her expectantly. Nothing in the dog's behaviour signalled alarm. Amanda took a closer look at the mark and realized it was an arrow traced deep into the snow with its tip pointing straight ahead.

A message! Her mind cartwheeled. Was it Luc, trying to tell her where to go? Or was the message intended for someone else? By someone else?

Of all the possibilities tumbling through her mind, two stood out. First, that the snowshoer wanted someone to follow them, and second, that the message would soon be obliterated and all chance to follow would be gone.

She cursed her decision to leave the phone with Sylvie. She would have to improvise her own message of sorts in the snow and hope that Chris and his pals found it. She rummaged in her backpack for something she could leave behind, opting in the end for the bright red sack that held her first aid kit. She hung it from a branch at waist level and for good measure traced her own big arrow in the snow.

Then she put on her headlamp and unfolded her map to get her bearings. It felt as if she'd been trudging for miles, but she had probably travelled less than a kilometre from the stone house, almost due north. She traced her finger farther north. Why was the snowshoer so hell-bent on going there? What was up there? Barely anything. A thin wisp of road leading to a lake and …

Her pulse surged. Three tiny black squares were marked on the map at the end of the road. Houses? Could it be a farm or a collection of summer cottages? Was that where the snowshoer was heading?

Chris drove as fast as he dared, dodging the potholes he could and thudding over those he couldn't. He was heading into the back of beyond, without backup and unsure what lay ahead. He had waited in the parking lot of L'Ascension's only auto shop for ten minutes with no sign of Sechrest. Nor had she answered her phone.

He couldn't believe she'd managed to jump through all the procedural hoops and mobilize a backup team so quickly that she'd beat him to the rendezvous spot. More likely, she was still gathering gear and manpower. At the ten-minute mark, his phone had rung. He snatched it up. Any news from either Amanda or Sechrest would be a relief.

It was Sylvie. "Are you almost here?" Her tone sounded tense. Even accusatory.

"In L'Ascension. Any news up there?"

"She's gone. In the woods to follow the trail."

Chris felt a spike of anger. He didn't need to ask why, or why she hadn't waited. This was Amanda, responding to someone in need and used to handling things herself. He hoped at least this time she was prepared. "Does she have supplies?"

"Yes, some. And she has a gun."

Chris's anger had dissolved into alarm. Amanda hated guns, but in a crisis, with the memories of trauma crowding all around her, she just might be capable of anything. "Where are you?"

"At the stone house, but I'm going out to the road. I'll be waiting in the truck."

Chris gave one last look at the road behind. Not a single car had driven past, let alone a convoy of reinforcements. With a final curse, he'd thrown the truck into gear. "Stay in the truck, I'll be there soon!"

He hung up and accelerated onto the little road north out of town. A few kilometres past the village, the pavement turned to gravel and then to an icy, one-lane track. As he jolted over the ruts, he was grateful for his years navigating what passed for roads in the Northwest Territories. The rural houses strung along the sides of the road gradually petered out until there was nothing but scraggly bush pressing in on either side. The terrain rose and fell as the road twisted along the Rouge River valley.

Twice he was forced to stop to consult his map at a fork in the road. He should be getting close, but there was still no sign of Sylvie's truck. Nothing but endless, bleak, snow-covered bush. After about twenty minutes he spotted a snowmobile and trailer in a clearing on the left. He skidded to a stop and got out for a closer look. The smell of gasoline and diesel hung in the air, and when he laid his hand on the hood of the snowmobile, it was still warm. The keys dangled in the ignition.

But there was no truck. "Sylvie?" he called.

Nothing. Where had the woman gone? Why hadn't she waited for him? He swore long and loud. She was as bad as Amanda, going off half-cocked after some crazy idea.

He studied the road ahead. Fresh tire tracks were visible through the falling snow, but it was impossible to tell whether they were Sylvie's truck. He considered his choices — check out the stone house or continue up the road. Best to rule out the house before going off on a possible wild goose chase.

The trail leading to the house looked well travelled but cer tainly not navigable by even the best off-road truck. He started the snowmobile and followed the trail into the maple grove until he reached the house. He scanned it quickly. Barely a house anymore, more like a shell.

"Sylvie? Amanda?"

Nothing. He quickly searched the inside, noting the fresh ash and the flattened evergreen boughs. But no Sylvie. When he headed back outside, he noticed two fresh, deep gouges in the snow leading toward a shed. Fighting a quiver of foreboding, he hurried across the compound. The sugar shack was dark, with only a faint light coming through a hole in the roof, but it was enough to make out the tracks on the ground and something in the corner. Boots, poking out from behind a rusted cauldron.

Oh no! *No, no!* He shoved aside the cauldron to reveal the rest of the body, stuffed like a rag doll into the small space by the wall. Blood streaked her face and plastered her hair.

Sylvie. He flung himself down at her side to check her pulse. Weak and rapid, but she was alive! He checked her airways. Breathing soft and shallow but not laboured. He peeled back her jacket to check for bleeding or evidence of trauma beyond the head wound. Nothing. It looked as if someone had hit her on the head, dragged her into the shed, and left her to die.

He yanked off his parka, wrapped her in it, and gently placed his fleece under her head. The head wound had stopped bleeding, but her pallor was alarming. As he hurried back to the snowmobile, he was already phoning Sechrest to see whether she had dispatched an EMS team. Still no fucking answer.

He phoned 911, praying that there was service to this back of beyond, and was relieved to get an immediate answer. The dispatcher proved knowledgeable, and even more importantly, bilingual, as she led him expertly through an assessment of the situation.

"L'Ascension has a first responder service," she said. "I will send them up to assess and administer first aid until the ambulance can get there."

"How long will that be?"

"For the ambulance? Because of the distance, normally half an hour to an hour. But because of the snow, we have some road accidents. And a few skiers injured on Mont Tremblant. So it may be longer. Keep her warm and tell me any change in her condition, but don't try to move her."

She must have read my mind, Chris thought as he signed off and rechecked Sylvie's pulse. Same rapid rate but a little weaker. Her breathing seemed weaker too. She had lost some blood, but the greater danger was the head injury. If she was bleeding inside the brain, she could go downhill fast. The EMS, even if they got here in half an hour, would waste precious time transferring her to and from the snowmobile.

There was no way he was going to stand by uselessly and watch the life ebb from her. He checked for broken bones as carefully as he could through her bulky clothing. There was a possibility of neck injury due to the blow to the head, but that was a chance he would have to take. He dragged the snowmobile toboggan into the shack and gingerly manoeuvred her onto it, using a piece of handy two-by-four to stabilize her head and shoulders. Using some plastic piping from the sugar shack, he lashed her onto the toboggan and pulled it out to the snowmobile.

There, he paused to figure out how to proceed. Darkness had fallen, so he turned on the snowmobile headlights and put on his headlamp. Snow swirled in the haloes of light as he hitched the toboggan to the snowmobile and towed it back to the truck. Standing by the road, he listened for the rumble of an engine and stared into the snowy darkness for the headlights of the approaching EMS van. Nothing. *Damn it!* Sylvie's vitals were weakening, her system shutting down bit by bit. Should he get her into the bed of the truck and go down to meet the ambulance en route? The potholes might kill her, but doing nothing might be worse.

And what about Amanda? She was alone out there somewhere in the darkness, and God only knew what danger she was in. She was expecting his help, she was expecting RCMP backup, but she was getting neither. He needed to deliver Sylvie safely into the hands of experts as quickly as possible so he could turn his attention back to Amanda before the snowstorm made the road impassable.

Thus galvanized, he lowered his truck tailgate and prepared to hoist the toboggan on board.

CHAPTER TWENTY-ONE

Amanda burrowed into the snow and tried to make herself and Kaylee as warm as possible during the blizzard. The lean-to of dense evergreen boughs kept off most of the snow, and the thermal blanket combined with every stitch of clothing in her possession should have been enough, especially with Kaylee snuggled inside the cocoon with her. But despite it all, she shivered herself awake frequently during the night.

By the time she'd sought refuge for the night, weary and blinded by the blizzard, she figured she'd covered most of the distance to the little black specks on the map. She decided to complete the remaining kilometre or so in the morning while still under cover of the predawn darkness. She didn't know what she would find but suspected it wouldn't be good.

Well before dawn, she was melting snow for tea and sharing a power bar with Kaylee. She felt a pang as she thought of Chris, no doubt furious and frantic in equal measure. She hoped he had found her trail. But as she lashed on her snowshoes, her headlamp played over the snow ahead and her heart sank. The trail was obliterated, and she found herself guessing the path from the faint undulations in the fluffy surface. Judging from the fresh tracks that crisscrossed the snow, wolves, deer, rabbits, and tiny scurrying creatures had been busy during the night. Mercifully, the snow had stopped, but it clung to the branches and drifted down in fine clouds with each gust of wind. The greying horizon gave no hint of sunrise.

Kaylee strained at the leash, her ears pricked forward and her nose twitching to catch the smallest molecule of scent. Amanda could see and hear nothing through the gloom, but she kept a tight grip on the leash. Something was ahead.

Finally, she caught a wisp of wood smoke, so faint it could have been her imagination. But the scent grew stronger, travelling on the wind that also brought snatches of sound. Tree boughs moaning? The distant drone of a snowmobile? Or the rumble of airplanes?

She was almost upon the clearing before she saw it. She crouched down and crept forward before literally stumbling into a long, narrow open field. She squinted through the dark. It was a paler patch roughly five metres by thirty, contrasting with the dark border of trees and swept almost clean by the wind. Even with the recent snow she could see the tracks of dozens of boots.

She stepped forward cautiously and felt something hard beneath her moccasin. She brushed the snow away with her snowshoe, and in the faint light of the emerging dawn she saw the glint of metal. She picked it up. A shell casing. She brushed away more snow, revealing multiple glints of metal sprinkled like shards over the snow.

Her throat went dry. She dropped to a crouch and pulled Kaylee close, aware that they were dark shadows on the expanse of pale grey. She imagined a dozen eyes upon her. She backtracked into the woods and worked her way along the edge of the clearing. Up ahead, dark shadows took shape, lined up like silent sentinels in the snow. As she drew close, she could see the crude outline of a human shape painted on each. Closer still, she ran her trembling fingers over the pockmarked spray of a hundred bullet holes. Most were wildly off the mark, but some had blown holes in the dead centre of the chest. It was a shooting range.

Fuck.

For a crazy moment, she tried to rationalize it as a practice range for hunters. But the shapes were human, not deer. She floundered back into the woods and ducked behind a fallen tree to weigh her options. The camp, if it was a camp, was silent. But surely it was almost time for predawn prayers. Soon the campers would begin their morning ablutions. Had Chris found his way here with his police backup? Were they lying in wait for first light?

She slid her backpack to the ground and pulled out the shotgun. One gun in her inexpert, reluctant hands against dozens. Kaylee was scratching at the ground around the tree and soon uncovered a frozen chunk of red. She was happy to present her prize to Amanda, who shuddered as she recognized it. A blood-soaked mitten. She studied the ground and saw what she'd missed in her blundering haste to get off the shooting range. Someone else had hidden here. The snow was trampled, and a meandering snowshoe trail skirted the bottom of the clearing. She peered into the distance at what looked like the outline of a roof, partly screened by trees. Too small to be a house or barn. Possibly a shed of some sort.

The sensible course of action would be to stay where she was, hidden and hopefully safe until backup arrived. She didn't know whom she'd been following or what lurked ahead. As the darkness lifted, more silhouettes began to emerge against the pale backdrop of snow, and the outlines of several vehicles glinted darkly in the yard. One trundled across the yard toward the shed, and its door opened with a familiar squawk. Amanda peered at it through the gloom and caught her breath. What the hell?

Clutching her gun in one hand and Kaylee's leash in the other, she crept closer, poised to abort the mission at the first hint of trouble. She circled the end of the shooting range and hugged the trees as she skirted around the back of the shed, where she stopped dead, barely able to believe her eyes.

It was Sylvie's truck.

Chris's eyes were heavy with grit. He was so exhausted, he could barely keep his head up, yet he was desperate to keep going. It was nearly dawn, and he had lost so much time already!

In an effort to avoid jolting Sylvie on the potholes, he'd been forced to drive the road back to L'Ascension at a snail's pace, hoping to encounter the ambulance coming the other way. But he'd been well past the village and halfway to the hospital in L'Annonciation by the time he spotted the flashing lights coming up the highway toward him. The paramedic crew was apologetic — cars off the road and skiers with hypothermia — and took a long time to assess, stabilize, and transfer Sylvie to the warmth of their ambulance. Minutes crawled by as Chris paced, his back to the vicious snow. The bumpy, frigid trip had not been kind to Sylvie, and the paramedics were already muttering darkly about airlifting her to Montreal for more advanced treatment of her head trauma.

While he'd waited, it had fallen to Chris to notify Sebastien, answer his frantic questions, and give him the number of the emergency room in L'Annonciation. It was past midnight by the time he'd got back on the road toward l'Ascension and nearly one in the morning when he'd reached the stone house turn-off. By then the snowstorm was in full force, the snow lashing his windshield in slanting sheets. He'd parked and climbed down to take stock. The snow was rapidly filling in the snowmobile tracks leading to the house, and he realized that any chance of following the trail Amanda had taken through the bush was lost.

Snow was even blanketing the road itself. His truck headlights lit the ridges of multiple tracks, all heading farther into the hinterland. Was one of them Sylvie's truck? Had the person who hit her over the head stolen her truck and carried on up the road?

Toward what? What was up there? He climbed back in his truck and used the cabin light to study the map Sylvie had left him. He traced the barely visible road as it twisted and looped up to a small cluster of dots by a lake. That had to be it. It was all he had to go by, so it had damn well better be it. Determined anger took hold. He grabbed a chocolate bar, drained the last of his coffee, now stone-cold, and set off.

Even with his wipers working full speed, snow kept coming at him and ice built up on the windshield. His headlights caught the blinding swirl of snowflakes, and he could barely see the road beyond. The tire tracks faded quickly, and the road blended with the whiteness of the bush. Clutching his steering wheel, he crawled along as fast as he dared, up and down hills and around blind bends, praying that he stayed on the road. The rush of snow hurtling at him was mesmerizing. After a while, he felt his mind blurring. Eyes closing.

Then with a gentle bump, he found himself off the road, branches raking the door of his truck as the truck lurched into the ditch. He spun the wheel, felt the tires slip and spin uselessly. He climbed out and used his headlamp to survey the problem: a big rock lodged in front of the tire. It took him nearly an hour to pry the rock loose, dig around the tires, and spread salt and sand on the track. Despite the icy wind, he was soaked with sweat by the time he managed to get the truck back on the road. He leaned his head on the steering wheel, exhausted.

Enough, he thought. *I need to grab some sleep, or I'll end up in the ditch again.* Ten minutes, that was all he needed. If Amanda was still out in this, he hoped she'd taken refuge too. He'd be no use to her if he ended up wrapped around a tree somewhere in this back of beyond.

He found a small turn-off just up the road, likely part of an old logging road, and pulled in so that he was out of the way. He didn't think anyone would be fool enough to attempt this road in the dead of night, but if they were, they wouldn't be expecting a truck parked in the middle of it. He'd left his thermal blanket and extra parka with Sylvie, an oversight he now cursed, so he was forced to leave the truck running while he napped. Ten minutes max, he told himself before his eyes closed.

He awoke with a start three hours later, just as a faint sheen of light was creeping into the sky. The snow had tapered off.

Furious at himself, he rummaged in his food pack for an energy bar and water and slammed the truck back onto the road. What the hell? He'd expected he'd have to drive through several more inches of unbroken snow, but the road was already rutted by multiple sets of tracks. Who the fuck used this road on a night like this, and where were they going?

None of the possible answers were any comfort to him. There were killers on the loose, and possibly terrorists too. As a precaution, he turned off his lights and drove down the middle of the road as fast as he dared. His gaze raked the unbroken bush around him. There was not a single vehicle to be seen.

Up ahead, the bush gradually thinned to reveal pastures and side lanes with no markers. One by one, the tire tracks turned off and disappeared into the bush. Perhaps he was nearing the cluster of houses. He hesitated. He had no idea what he was blundering into, and even with the headlights off, he was a sitting duck in his big, rumbling, black truck. Against the backdrop of white snow, there was enough light in the predawn sky to see it for miles.

He pulled off the road into one of the lanes and tucked the truck under cover of an overhanging fir. Hugging the side of the road, he set off on snowshoe. Up ahead, he could see the landscape opening up into broad swaths of pasture, and in the distance, behind a wind barrier of evergreens, a vague outline of roofs. The cluster of buildings he'd seen on the map! Sensing he was close, he slipped into the trees to circle around the property out of sight. There were no signs of movement except for the wisps of smoke coming from the farmhouse chimney, but he had a sense of a thousand eyes. Silent, watchful, waiting … as if the whole place were holding its breath.

Ridiculous, Tymko! He shook himself. Took a cautious step forward out from behind a tree, and—

A rush of movement, a violent shove, and he hit the ground face down in the snow. A knee in his back, a cold gun pressing his cheek, and hot breath whispering in his ear.

"Don't even breathe, you fucker!"

Sylvie's truck. What the hell? For a moment Amanda felt as if she'd gone down the rabbit hole. Had the woman driven up here for some reason or had someone else taken it? Amanda quailed at the thought. Crouching out of sight, she circled to the back of the truck in search of clues. A low growl bubbled in Kaylee's throat, warning of an imminent bark, and Amanda lunged forward to clamp her hand over the dog's muzzle. Kaylee was staring toward the distant edge of the woods. Amanda strained to see through the pale, blurry light. What had the dog seen?

Another muffled growl, and a flit of movement at the edge of the trees. Amanda dived to the ground in the shelter of the truck, dragging Kaylee down with her. She thought fast. The shed door was only five feet away, partially ajar. She crawled across the open space and pressed herself against the wall. No sound from within. She peered through the narrow opening, her eyes adjusting slowly to the gloom. The shed was empty.

A false and temporary reprieve, she suspected, but she took it. Inside, the little room smelled of must, chemicals, and gasoline. It was stacked with bags and containers, but a quick inspection revealed no people. She kicked off her snowshoes and hunkered down behind the bags, her hand still firmly around Kaylee's muzzle. *Now is not the time to play watchdog, princess.*

The bag labels in front of her were clearly visible. Ammonium nitrate fertilizer. Piles and piles of it. She tried to calm herself. This had once been a farm, after all. Yet the white plastic bags looked brand new.

She crept over to the other wall, where boxes of plastic containers were stacked. Diesel fuel. Again, normal farm supplies. Yet the combination of ammonium nitrate fertilizer and diesel oil pointed to something far more sinister.

Double fuck.

Any delusional hope that the shooting range was intended for deer hunters to hone their skills vanished. She had walked right into the middle of a bomb-making factory, with no phone, a single shotgun, and unknown assailants hiding in the trees.

Footsteps crunched across the snow outside, drawing near. Kaylee fought to get free, and Amanda held on tight as they cowered behind the bags. The shed door swung open cautiously, and a small figure stood silhouetted in the doorway. Kaylee renewed her wiggling, and it took Amanda a moment to realize she was wagging her tail. Thump, thump against the ground.

The figure crossed the room quickly. Amanda raised her shotgun the best she could one-handed and pointed it as the figure peeked over the bags.

Their eyes met with a shock of recognition.

"Amanda! What are you doing here?"

Kaylee broke free and rushed to greet her. Recoiling, Yasmina quickly shut the door before kneeling at Amanda's side. "You shouldn't be here! There is danger."

Amanda lowered the gun, her thoughts racing. Yasmina didn't appear injured; she had moved without pain, and her voice, even in an urgent whisper, sounded firm and strong. Nevertheless, Amanda gripped her arm. "Are you all right?"

"Yes, yes. But they must not see you here."

"Who?"

"It doesn't matter. You shouldn't have come."

Amanda thought fast. Yasmina's eyes were wide with concern, and there was no threat in her tone. What part did she play in this, and more importantly, where was Luc? She decided to play along.

"I have been trying to find Luc, and I ..." She gestured helplessly. "I have no idea where I am. How do I get out of here? And you, how can I get you out of here?"

"You can't get me out," Yasmina said flatly. She glanced toward the door. "You said you were looking for Luc?"

"Have you seen him?"

"Why do you think he's here?"

Yasmina sounded genuinely puzzled, but Amanda kept her guard up. Until she knew the dangers, she was not going to give anything away. "No reason," she said, "I just want to get away from here. I'm exhausted and cold, and I must have taken a wrong turn."

"Does anybody know you're here?"

What was the safer answer? "I don't know," she answered. At least that much was true. "But they will be looking, so the sooner I get away, the better. What about that truck outside? Can I take it?"

Yasmina was frowning, and Amanda could almost see her weighing her options. "Wait here," she said, picking up the gun. "You are safe in here. I will see what I can arrange."

Then with a swish of her long skirts, she turned on the threshold. She looked apologetic. "For your own safety," she said as she locked the door.

The interior of the shed was so dark that Amanda had to grope around with her hand to find Kaylee. The stink of old manure clung to the air, overlaid with oil and chemicals. She felt her way around the walls of the small enclosure but could find no way out, but through the flimsy walls she heard murmuring and the sounds of doors opening and closing nearby. The truck?

Only a few minutes passed before the shed door cracked open and Yasmina slipped back in. "Come!" she whispered. "Quickly. They must not see you."

Tugging Amanda's sleeve, she drew her outside and around the front of the truck to the driver's door. Amanda peeked over the roof, straining to make out the distant farmhouse.

Yasmina yanked her arm. "Keep your head down!"

Dawn was already a dark coral smudge on the horizon behind the trees, and there was enough light for Amanda to see Yasmina's face. She looked pale and tense as she crouched by the truck door.

"The keys are inside, but don't start the engine yet! There's a back lane at the bottom of this hill. Follow it all the way around the lake, and it will take you to the main road again."

"But Yasmina—"

"Go now! Before it gets light!"

"Come with me!"

Yasmina shook her head and eased open the door as quietly as she could. "Drive straight to CSIS in Ottawa." She thrust a small leather portfolio into Amanda's hands. "Take this! Give it to the director of the Canadian Security Intelligence Service—"

"I have an RCMP contact."

"No! They have spies everywhere. It must be Director Blair at CSIS headquarters on Ogilvy Road. Do you know it?"

Amanda didn't, but she nodded. She could find it. When she glanced into the truck, she recoiled in shock. Slumped against the passenger door was Luc. His eyes were closed, his lips were blue, and he was shivered violently

"He's alive!" Yasmina said hastily. "He's lost blood, but I took good care of him. You can take him to hospital in Ottawa after you deliver the notebook."

Kaylee leaped happily into the truck and Amanda followed. She leaned over and shook Luc gently. "Luc?"

His eyelids fluttered, but he didn't reply.

"Go, go!" Yasmina hissed as she eased the door shut. "Don't turn on your lights, and don't stop for anything! You have to get that to Blair right away. There's food and water in the truck."

Amanda turned the auxiliary power on, released the handbrake, and allowed the truck to drift down the hill, keeping one eye on the rear-view mirror and the other on the darkness ahead. Rocks and trees loomed in her path, forcing her to spin the wheel hard. She saw no one coming after her, but the old truck rattled so loudly that she was sure the whole terrorist army would be on her. Blood pounded in her ears, and sweat slicked her hands despite the chill.

For what seemed an eternity she bumped down the hill before she drifted to a stop at the base. Up ahead, she could just make out a pale ribbon of road disappearing into the shadowy bush. It was little more than a track through the snow, packed down by snowmobiles and ATVs. She started the truck, cringing as the engine coughed to life. Her gaze flicked to the mirror. Nothing. Nothing ahead either. She turned the heater up high and pressed the gas gingerly. The truck sputtered and lurched forward, its tires growling as they caught the snow. She crawled along, barely daring to breathe, her hands gripping the wheel in anticipation of every dip and rut. Beside her, Luc didn't stir.

Soon the trees swallowed them up. Through their lacy boughs, she caught glimpses of a frozen lake. The stillness and silence felt eerie. Where *were* they?

Slowly, heat spread through the cabin. It felt like hours before the nose of the truck finally poked through the dense bush onto the main road. Utterly empty. Only then did she draw a full breath. *Turn right*, she told herself, picturing the topographical map in her head. It should be a clear route all the way down to the main highway.

The road was marginally better than the ATV track she'd been following, so she gave the truck more gas and used her teeth to tear the packaging off one of the granola bars on the console beside her. She fed some to Kaylee before popping the rest into her mouth. Luc hadn't stirred, but when she waved a granola bar under his nose, he moaned. Given his blood loss, he probably needed water more than food. At least his lips were no longer blue. Studying him out of the corner of her eye, she could see caked blood on his parka, but nothing fresh. Still wrestling the steering wheel with one hand, she groped for his pulse. Weak but regular. His breathing too sounded regular. She debating stopping to check him over more thoroughly but decided getting him to hospital was more important.

Now that she had time to think, she tried to make sense of what was going on. She examined the small notebook, which was zippered shut with a small combination padlock. She explored it with her fingers. It was surprisingly heavy, with what felt like a thick file folder inside. Secret files? Yasmina had emphasized the urgency and had also insisted she only hand it over to the head of CSIS. She even knew his name. There were traitors everywhere, she'd said, but her urgency suggested a more imminent threat. Were the terrorists in the compound on the verge of an attack? Was that what the file warned of?

Amanda had assumed the compound was a training camp to prepare ISIS recruits for battle overseas. From the tickets on Yasmina's computer, everyone had assumed the group was going to the Middle East in a week's time to join ISIS. But what if the target were closer to home, and the tickets were for the escape afterward? She thought of the stacks of fertilizer and diesel oil in the shed. As ISIS lost key ground in the Middle East in recent months, they were focusing more on taking the war to the West. What if they were planning an attack here, now? A bomb, or a series of coordinated bombs carried in backpacks or cars, as in the Brussels and Paris attacks?

As she made the turn at l'Ascension, she noticed a dark car in the distance behind her. Her pulse spiked. When had that appeared? Was it someone from the village, or had it been behind her all along?

Her nerves thrummed and her hands tightened on the wheel. Carefully she sped up and watched the car drop back. Taking a deep breath of relief, she tried to think. Luc needed medical care, and the authorities had to be alerted to a possible attack. She had no phone, but if she stopped in L'Annonciation to drop Luc at the hospital, she could make a quick phone call to Chris from a pay phone before continuing on to CSIS. He was not a traitor, and surely he would know whom to notify.

She was just beginning to relax when, on the road far behind her, sunlight flashed off metal.

CHAPTER TWENTY-TWO

"What the *fuck?* Tymko!"

Although he could see nothing but the combat-style boots planted in front of him, Chris recognized the voice.

"Get him up!" the woman snapped.

The knee eased off his back, and the arms pressing him flat to the ground grabbed him by the collar instead. The man gave him a shake for good measure before hauling him to his feet. Chris looked around at the tense, angry circle. Five men and one woman, dressed in full combat regalia, protected from their steel-toed boots to their helmets. He didn't recognize the outfit, which was nonregulation white camo, but he recognized the firepower. RCMP C8 assault rifles.

And he recognized the furious glare of the woman who appeared to be in charge. Sergeant Sandy Sechrest. She looked close to levitating with rage. "What in sweet Jesus are you doing here, Tymko?"

"You didn't meet me. You didn't wait for me." He knew he sounded like a whiny kid left out of the game, but he was still trying to process the shock and the implications.

"Because I didn't want you fucking up the operation, you moron! Which you may well have done if they spotted you."

"Who?"

She glanced at her precision watch and then at the streak of deep red smudging the horizon. "I don't have time for this," she said. "I don't have time for you! Sweet Jesus H., Tymko, if you've screwed this up ..."

"It's a raid!" he exclaimed. "You've known all along where Luc and Yasmina were going!"

"No, we didn't know the precise location until you told me about the stone house. But yes, it's a raid, months in the planning, with multiple agencies, cyber intercepts, undercover intel, and—"

"Ma'am," one of her men said, "we have to move."

Sechrest broke off, her lips in a tight line. "What am I going to do with you? Gag you and tie you to a tree?"

"Take me with you," Chris said.

"Absolutely not! You're not trained, you're not equipped...." She flicked a hand at his hunting rifle. "You think you're going to scare the terrorists with that?"

"I'll stick right behind you." He tried for his most boyish, crinkly grin. "It's the safest way to keep track of me."

Boyish didn't work on her. "No, this is a precision operation which we've been planning for weeks. These cockroaches are deadly. Just look at who they've already executed for getting in their way. This is not some group of silly schoolboys playing at being warriors. Their leader has been on the ISIS front lines in Iraq. You'll be a liability to us, and you might just get yourself killed."

Chris went cold. His grin vanished. "Amanda Doucette is in there."

"*What?*" Sechrest shrieked before remembering the need for stealth. She clamped her hand to her mouth. "Sweet Jesus H. What else do you know?"

"She went looking for Luc and Yasmina. Bushwhacking on snowshoe following their trail."

"Of all the goddamn, motherfucking—"

"Ma'am!" The officers were readying themselves.

She managed a few more swear words before she turned to go. "You stick with me like a tick on a dog, Tymko. And if you get in the way or in my line of fire, I just might ..." Shaking her head, she spun around and gave the signal to proceed. GPSs in hand, the six officers fanned out in pairs to follow their assigned paths. Tymko tramped through the snow in Sechrest's footsteps.

She gave him a disgusted look. "Jesus H., try to keep low. You stick out like a bug on a bedsheet."

He suppressed a smile. The woman sure liked her bugs. But anxious to stay alive and be an asset rather than a liability, he crouched low behind her. "Are we the only team?" he murmured.

"Sure. An operation months in the planning and involving hundreds of agents, and we put just six guys on it. Emergency Response is in charge. We've got this camp surrounded, Tymko, and we're coming in from all sides. So if you move wrong, you're just as likely to get your head blown off by one of ours as by a terrorist."

He absorbed this, ducking under a branch as he struggled to keep up with her. The woman was in shape! "Can you tell the other teams that Amanda is in there? To be careful?"

"I can't be held accountable for civilians who barge into the middle of an active operation."

"But—"

"The woman's a fool! Ever wonder why she's always walking into the middle of danger? She looks for it! Thrives on it! So no, I'm not deviating from our plan."

Chris was silent as he tried to keep up. Was she right about Amanda? Had all those years working in dangerous corners of the world turned her into an adrenaline junkie? He remembered her face as she'd stared down the barrel of the rifle in Newfoundland. The fury, the focus.

The triumph.

He was panting, and sweat trickled down his back, but still he felt a chill. Up ahead, the trees opened up into a clearing scattered with buildings, in the centre of which stood a farmhouse. Tall white pines would offer some concealment from air searches, but on the ground, visibility was good. Sechrest paused to scan the scene with binoculars.

"You know they pray before dawn," he said. "They will be up."

She nodded and consulted her watch before continuing. "But they pray again at the moment of sunrise. The times are very precise. They will be all together, and otherwise occupied."

Chris winced. He couldn't fault the strategy, which terror groups themselves used with great success the world over, but that didn't make it moral. She swung around to stare him down, as if reading his mind.

"Now shut up," she whispered. "It's zero hour."

The red streak along the horizon had lightened to peach. Without warning, Sechrest took off and sprinted across the open space toward another clump of trees. Chris raced to keep up. Out of the corner of his eye, he saw flashes of movement as white camo-clad figures advanced in short bursts from all sides. One by one the teams reached the cabins, the barns, and the vehicles, and secured each of them. There was not a single twitch of movement from the farmhouse.

Chris saw several figures wearing gas masks emerge from the cover of a trailer and race toward the back of the house. Halfway across that open space, war erupted. Automatic gunfire strafed the ground and a grenade burst near the trailer, spewing clouds of snow into the air. Someone had obviously not been praying. Instead, their quarry had been watching them, biding their time.

Chris and Sechrest dove for cover behind a nearby truck. In the clearing, a couple of officers were down, and almost immediately tear gas and smoke bombs shattered the windows on the first and second storeys, filling the farmhouse with toxic gases. While officers raced out to drag the wounded to safety, a second wave of the tactical team took advantage of the chaos to rush toward the farmhouse. Because of fears of booby traps inside, they stood clear of the exits to capture those coming outside.

To Chris, it seemed like pandemonium. He had taken part in attack simulations over the years, but the real thing was up several notches. Bloody, deafening, and filled with confusion and shouts. Like the others, Chris waited for the jihadists to come pouring out the door.

But none did.

Beside him, Sechrest uttered her favourite epithet. "Sweet Jesus H. The cockroaches have gas masks too. We may be in for a long siege." She looked around and nodded to a nearby log cabin. "That's the target we're supposed to secure. It may not protect us from a bullet or a grenade, but it's better than this truck."

She made a run for the cabin, forcing Chris to hustle. He could feel the giant bull's eye on his back as he ran, but to his surprise, no one shot at them. Sechrest burst the door open, C8 at the ready, and froze so abruptly that Chris crashed into her. His heart slammed as an image leaped into his mind. The flash of an explosion, eardrums blown out, body parts flying …

Instead, standing in front of them in the gloom with a shotgun aimed at them and a look of horror in her eyes, was a young woman.

"Police!" Sechrest shouted. "Lay down your weapon!"

The young woman didn't move. Didn't blink. Behind her was a spartan room with a bunk-bed and a dresser. She was clad in a long, flowing black skirt, pink parka, and black hijab, but Chris could see she was still a teenager. This cause grew them up so fast!

Sechrest waved her gun barrel. "Down. Now!"

"Yasmina?" Chris ventured.

The girl's concentration broke for just a second, and her gaze flickered.

"We're not here to hurt you," Chris said. "If you lay down that gun, you will be safe."

The girl seemed to be weighing her odds, and in the silence, Chris took a half-step toward her. Beside him, he heard Sechrest's muffled curse.

"You can't get out of this," Sechrest said. "The camp is surrounded. No matter what happens, you will all be captured."

"Or dead," Yasmina said.

Chris was reminded of Osama bin Laden's famous saying, *We love death more than you love life.* Because death brought the glory of paradise. Chris had dealt with suicidal people before, but they were usually seeking an end to extreme pain and despair. It was a route of last resort, and if you could give them hope, you had a chance of saving them. That was stressful enough to handle. He'd never faced someone who saw death not as an end to pain but as a path to paradise.

Sechrest too seemed to recognize the stakes. "But what's the point of dying this way?" she said. "This is not a warrior's death. This is just a common criminal's death in the backwoods of Quebec. A drug raid gone bad."

Yasmina's grip on the shotgun tightened. "Not if I can kill two enemies before I die."

"You won't even get one round off before I splatter you against that back wall."

"Yasmina," Chris pleaded. "You were studying to go into law. You care about injustice. I understand that. You can have so much more time to fight for that. To do some good."

"From the inside of a prison cell?"

"Even from the inside of a prison cell. And you're a minor, you won't be in long." He took another half-step, aware of Sechrest's finger on the trigger beside him. Reached out his hand. "You have lots of time to do good."

Yasmina looked about to back away. She shifted her gaze from his face to his hand, and in that instant he lunged for her, slammed the shotgun sideways, and tackled her to the ground. The shotgun went off, deafening him, but miraculously Sechrest didn't fire. Instead she whipped out her pistol and aimed it at Yasmina's head. An instant later, the girl was handcuffed hands and feet to the steel frame of the bunk. Sechrest positioned herself by the cabin door, pistol still raised, and peered out through a crack.

"Now," she said to Yasmina, "you're alive because this idiotic young officer thought your life was worth saving. So we're going to wait out this battle until all your friends surrender. Or die."

In the dim light of the cabin, Yasmina looked from one to the other. Chris's scalp prickled. The expression on her face was difficult to read, but if he could pinpoint one emotion, it would not be anger or fear or defiance.

It would be triumph.

CHAPTER TWENTY-THREE

Matthew awoke at the crack of dawn. In truth, he hadn't slept much. Images of Zidane's gaping throat kept tumbling behind his eyes. He forced himself to think of other details of the case but inexorably found himself running back to that shed and taking his first peek inside. How many Scotch-filled nights would it take to wipe out that memory?

And when he wasn't picturing the bloody body, he was worrying about Amanda, who'd blundered full-tilt into the middle of a deadly plot. In the kaleidoscope of his dreams, she was beheaded, hung on a cross, raped, or abducted to Syria to be paraded in ISIS videos.

The update he'd received from Chris just before he went to bed had only made things worse. Sylvie had been attacked, and Chris had lost precious time taking her to hospital before continuing his search for Amanda.

Lying awake, Matthew tried to distract himself from all these fears by focusing on what he could do, and by dawn he'd come up with a plan. He was not a warrior. Even twenty years younger and forty pounds lighter, he'd never been a warrior. Rushing up north to join the fray would not help the cause and might only get him killed. His skill was intelligence-gathering. The intent and target of the terrorist cell, the identity of the leaders, especially Abu Osama, and the role Zidane played in it — these were all questions he could ask.

The police, of course, would be asking the same questions, but they were hampered by rules and by their own jackbooted authority. He could slip in, oblique and innocuous in his sneakers and battered fedora, and encourage people to talk. The place to start, if he could get past the police barricade, was the Collège de La Salle itself. Someone there, either Zidane's colleagues or friends of the al-Karims, had to know something.

While he downed a quick coffee to sharpen his fuzzy brain, he scanned various websites for information on Zidane's death and possible terrorist links. Zidane himself had a website in English, French, and Arabic. The English name was reachingacross.com, and it seemed to be aimed at helping young Muslims navigate Western culture, peer pressure, and conflicts with their parents. Some of the articles were heavy on religion, with quotes from the Qur'an and Hadith, whereas others were more practical. Interfaith dating, managing prayer in a secular milieu, and the equality of women.

From the content, it seemed unlikely Zidane was a terrorist sympathizer unless he was operating as a kind of Trojan horse. He urged caution, consensus, and respect. According to his bio, he was born in Algeria, but his family was forced to flee during the Algerian unrest of the 1980s. He had spent much of his youth in a refugee camp, but rather than hardening him, the experience seemed to have heightened his sensitivity to suffering and his abhorrence of war.

The blog on his website offered commentary on current affairs, and in recent posts he had pulled no punches when it came to Islamic extremism. Fanatics live among us, he announced, seducing young minds and twisting the noble principles of Islam. As a community and as defenders of our faith, we have a special responsibility to root them out, to counter the vitriol, and to win back the hearts of the young and the searching.

Was this what had got him killed? Had he learned of the terror camp and tried to dissuade the young people involved? Maybe even going so far as to confront the al-Karims?

Matthew scrolled through news sources in search of answers, but the authorities had clamped the lid down tight. About the investigation itself, there were almost no details. However, he was dismayed to learn that all college classes were cancelled due to a potential ongoing security threat. Which meant Zidane's killer, or his accomplices, had not yet been caught.

He phoned Rolly Gendron, his contact at the Montreal Police, with the excuse that he was not interested in breaking the story but was worried about his good friend Amanda Doucette, who was in the thick of it. Nobody here knows anything either, was Rolly's reply. Not even rumours? Matthew asked. Our Chief of Detectives is handling the case personally, Rolly offered, and he spent all day yesterday with the feds, so you figure it out.

All of which told Matthew little except that the police had already made the link between Zidane and national security. He was curious to know whether they'd already zeroed in on the al-Karims or Yasmina's family, but if he wanted to get ahead of the police crackdown on information, he had to get to the college staff first.

The morning was clear and sunny but frigid. His car grumbled and shook as he coaxed it to life. The overnight snow had reduced traffic to a crawl. It took him over half an hour to get across the mountain to the college, and he spotted a half dozen official-looking vehicles already in the parking lot, including a cruiser outside the administration building. So much for casual chats with college staff. A crime scene cordon still roped off the grounds around the shed, and as Matthew debated his next move, he spotted the custodian at the far side of the parking lot, fiddling with a snow blower.

Olu was only too grateful for the break and climbed into Matthew's warm car with relief. "Eleven years in Canada, and I can't get used to this!"

Matthew left the car running and let the windows fog up so the police would have trouble seeing inside. He waited while the man rubbed his hands in front of the heater and eased into the topic by asking how he was.

Olu shook his head dolefully. "The sight of blood. I never get used to that either."

"Have the police arrested anyone? Questioned anyone else at the college?"

"Many, many students. All yesterday, in the principal's office. But no arrest."

"Did the students tell you anything? Or talk about who did it?"

"They never talk to me."

"What about the staff? They must have been concerned about you."

Olu shrugged. "The principal want to give me the day off, but with all this snow, better not wait."

Matthew probed as much as he could, but the man seemed to know nothing about anything, at least that he was prepared to share. Matthew shifted gears. "Remember you told me Zidane asked you to keep an eye on Luc Prevost? Were there any others that he asked you to watch out for?"

Olu nodded and rattled off a few names Matthew didn't recognize. Most of them sounded Arab or North African, although there were a few native Quebeckers like Luc in the mix.

"Faisel al-Karim?" Matthew suggested.

Olu's nostrils flared. "All them. Faisel, his brother ..."

Matthew's hopes spiked. "You knew Tawhid?"

"Tawhid, yes. Not a nice boy."

"How not nice?"

"Bad temper, and I see him steal sometimes, when others not see. Him and other friend get in much trouble."

Matthew took a wild guess. "Abdul?"

The man's face lit with memory. "Abdul! Brother of Yasmina. They ..." At a loss for the English word, he mimed puffing out his chest. "Walk around like big men."

Matthew filed these observations away. It looked as if the two had been fast friends in college and had engaged in some intimidation and theft. Petty stuff, but revealing a casual contempt for the rights and feelings of others. Perhaps even a pleasure in hurting them.

"Did they ever get in trouble with the police?"

"Not police but parents, yes. Many meetings with parents. Monsieur Zidane ask me all the time about them. Who they meeting."

"Was he counselling them?"

"He try, but they not listen. After they graduate, parents send to school in Egypt, maybe to fix them."

"And did it?"

Olu shifted uneasily but said nothing. Something about the boys seemed to unnerve him.

"Did they come back more religious?"

Olu gave a barely perceptible shrug. "Tawhid not come back. Stay to study. But Faisel and Yasmina, I think so."

Through the foggy windshield, Matthew could see a police officer suspiciously studying his car. Time was running out. He leaned in. "Olu, I'm sure you've thought about this. Who do you think killed Zidane?"

The whites of the man's eyes flashed. "I tell the police I know nothing."

Matthew nodded his sympathy and leaned even closer. Olu was proving himself to be more astute than during the first meeting, and Matthew suspected his bumbling English and hapless ignorance were practised survival tactics. "But I am worried about my friend Amanda. She is with these boys. Luc, Faisel, maybe even Tawhid. Do you know what happened to Zidane?"

Silence.

"Did you see *anything?*"

The man stared at his grease-blackened hands. "Monsieur Zidane arrive when school open. He go in his office, he come out with his book. He is talking on his phone, looking around like this—" He swivelled his head as if scanning the grounds. "When he get to the shed, he sound angry."

"What language was he speaking?"

"Arabic. He go in the shed. I have to finish my work, so I go away, but I think very strange. Monsieur Zidane meet me in the shed sometimes, so I think maybe he meet someone. When I go to see, he is … like that." Olu drew his finger across his neck.

Matthew forced his thoughts away from that dreadful image. "Before you went to the shed, did you see anyone nearby?"

"The principal arrive, and some professors."

"What about near the shed?"

"One man, near the street, walking away."

Matthew sucked in his breath. "Who?"

The man reached for the door handle. "I must go now."

Matthew caught his arm. "You knew him, didn't you? If I say some names, just nod. Abdul, Faisel, Tawhid …"

At each name, Olu trembled beneath his touch but betrayed no answer. He jerked his arm away and opened the door.

A second officer had joined the first, and they began to approach. "Okay, okay," Matthew said. "I'm sorry to scare you. This book — did the police find it?"

"No."

"So the killer took it?"

The man hesitated, one foot out the door. "Zidane hide it."

"So it's still there!"

Silence.

"*You* took it?"

"It's the book Monsieur Zidane write in about the students. The things I tell him."

Matthew's mind raced. Zidane had kept a record of his concerns about the students, including Olu's observations and possibly his own suspicions about their illegal activities. Olu was probably terrified that if the police got hold of it and used it as evidence, the terrorists would trace the material back to him. He'd be labelled a spy and face a fate like Zidane's. Matthew scrambled for a solution.

"I can keep it safe, Olu. I'm a journalist, I learn secrets all the time, and I never reveal where I got them. You can't keep the book here. The police will find it, and by law they will have to tell the lawyers for the bad guys what's in it and where it came from."

Olu blinked rapidly. "I can burn it."

"But then the evidence is lost. Everything Zidane worked so hard for — what he died for — will be gone. The bad guys will win!"

Icy wind swept across the parking lot and billowed into the car. Olu stood shivering, searching the grounds for danger. He saw the two officers crossing the lot, their hands resting on their holsters.

"Take me to it, Olu. Please."

With a slight hand gesture, the man invited him out of the car.

The wheels of Matthew's little car slithered and spun on the slushy streets as he raced back to his hotel. Once again he took the long way, ducking and weaving through back streets in an effort to lose any tail. The thin book was tucked under the passenger seat, out of sight but easy to find if the thugs caught up with him. He'd been so anxious to get away from the campus before the cops closed in that he'd not even glanced at it.

Finally, in the privacy and relative safety of his budget hotel room, he opened it. It was a hardcover student notebook frayed by use and crammed full of handwritten notes. Barely legible French was interspersed with utterly illegible Arabic. All Matthew could decipher at first glance were the dates that preceded each entry like a diary of sorts. The first entry was last September, the last on the day before the camping trip.

There were other books from previous years, Olu had said, but he didn't know where they were. Presumably found by the police in their search of Zidane's office, Matthew thought, but he kept quiet. Olu had enough to worry about.

He paged slowly through the book again, hoping to find something he could read, but his deciphering skills and his French weren't much up to the task. He recognized the names of Luc, Faisel, Abdul, Yasmina and many other Arabic-looking names, including several Tawhids. Since only first names and occasional initials were used, he had to guess that Faisel and Tawhid referred to the al-Karim brothers.

He focused on the latest page of entries. There had been a flurry of notations in the two weeks before the camping trip. Earlier notes had been neat, but these were hastily scrawled and peppered with underlining and exclamation points, as if Zidane was agitated. Matthew laboured over the translation. *Visit from Abdul, checking on Yasmina. Asked me to watch. She is practising snowshoes. She says study, but A. suspicious! How far is training camp?*

Matthew paused as the implication struck him. Zidane had known! He'd known Yasmina was up to something and might be planning an escape. He'd known about the camp. Yet he kept it all to himself.

Faisel quit group! Excuse of female guide is lie. He has female teachers and students, never object. A week before the camping trip, this entry: *What is the plan? Is there a plan? Kids not talking. Afraid? Protecting?* Some Arabic writing, followed by a new entry two days before the trip. *Olu saw Luc get in car with two strangers, not students. Planning? Yasmina followed, made phone call!* More Arabic, another date. *Who should I tell?*

That final sentence spoke volumes. After writing it, Zidane had gone camping with the group. However, his final actions were telling. He had left the camping group early on the pretence of handling the fallout from Yasmina's disappearance, but instead he'd rushed to hide this book in the custodian's shed, and a few minutes later, he was dead.

Matthew seethed with frustration. Why had Zidane not told anyone, or at least confided his suspicions? Had he known he might be killed? Or had he confided in the wrong person?

Matthew knew there might be more clues in the Arabic sections, but he was not sure whom to trust with translation. He had no Arab contacts in Montreal. He knew he had to hand it over to the police, but the journalist in him wanted to know the contents first. Damn, how he wished Chris were in town! He would know how to get it into the right hands, but as it was, the man wasn't even answering his phone. After a couple of futile attempts, Matthew photocopied each page of the notebook at the hotel and placed his second call of the day to his police contact.

Half an hour later, feeling like an inept spy in a John le Carré novel, he joined Sergeant Roland Gendron in a downtown

Starbucks and slid a large manila envelope across the table. Gendron, he noticed, looked stone sober, but it was early in the day.

"It belongs to Zidane," he said. "It might contain information about his killer or about extremist activities at Collège de La Salle."

Gendron slid the notebook out onto the table and flicked it open with a knife. John le Carré meets *CSI*. "You touched it?"

Matthew nodded, choosing not to mention that he'd also rubbed off all previous prints. Gendron shot him a look of disgust. He scanned a couple of pages. "Where did you get this?"

"It fell into my hands."

Gendron held his gaze. Expressionless. "Did you read it?"

"You'll need a translator."

Gendron flipped it shut and eased it back into the envelope. "*Bon!*" he said, standing up. "This isn't the end of it. Don't leave town."

Matthew watched him stalk out of the café with the envelope tucked under his arm and his collar turned up against the wind. *No way I'm leaving*, Matthew thought. *I've got places to go and people to see*. Starting with another visit to Olu. Because he had just realized that even without the notebook, Zidane's killer might know that Olu was feeding Zidane information. With this crowd, even if it was just the smallest suspicion, Olu was as good as dead.

"But I know nothing!" Olu exclaimed. By luck, Matthew had intercepted him waiting for the bus outside the college and had hustled him into his car. He drove away rapidly, keeping one eye on his rear-view mirror and the other on the tangle of traffic he was deking through.

"You don't know what you might know," he said. "You saw things, you overheard things. And you told Zidane."

"He was asking about drugs! About sex. Not terrorists!"

Matthew snatched up the photocopied notes and brandished them under his nose. "But you understand Arabic, don't you. That's why he asked you."

"A little. But I never speak it."

"Which makes you the perfect spy."

Olu deflated. "Monsieur Zidane is not like that. He care about his students."

"Maybe he did. But maybe one of them killed him."

Olu shrank in his seat. "Are you taking me to the police?"

"No, I'm taking you someplace safe. And then I want you to talk to me."

Matthew was driving north along Boulevard Saint-Laurent, and once he reached the chaotic Metropolitan expressway, which streamed east-west through the northern suburbs, he was forced to devote all his attention to navigating its ever-changing lanes, frequent construction delays, and kamikaze drivers. By a miracle and a prayer, he managed the right exit to the tunnel which took them under the St. Lawrence River to the working-class South Shore, as far from immigrant Muslim enclaves, student radicals, and nosy police investigators as he could imagine.

He'd checked out of his hotel that morning and drove now through the spaghetti tangle of overpasses, ramps, and expressways until he found a surprisingly upscale hotel in the bleak industrial wasteland of Longueuil. He checked them into adjoining rooms and ordered coffee and sandwiches from room service. While devouring the sandwich, he checked his phone. Still no message from Chris. He suppressed a twinge of worry as he entered Olu's room to find the man staring out the window in dismay at the blighted commercial landscape below.

"I can't stay here. My wife will worry."

Wife. Shit. "Kids?"

Olu shook his head, looking regretful. *Thank God for that small mercy*, Matthew thought. But how dangerous were these bastards? Would they take out an innocent woman who had nothing to do with anything?

Why am I even asking that question?

"I'll go get your wife," he found himself saying. "Can you read Arabic?"

Olu shrugged. "A long time ago, in school, I study."

"Can you write English?"

Olu drew himself up, looking affronted. "I study English in university."

University! The man was full of surprises. "What did you study?"

"Law. But I never finish before I have to leave."

Four languages and half a law degree. No wonder Zidane had enlisted his help. Another grossly underemployed, underestimated immigrant, Matthew thought ruefully. Maybe someday the man would be able to return to his studies, but for now he had to concentrate on staying alive. ISIS killed for far smaller transgressions than his.

Matthew took some blank printer paper from his bag and handed it over, along with the photocopies. "Write your wife a note so she won't think I'm abducting her. While I'm gone, I want you to translate as much of this as you can, starting with the most recent. Write both the French and Arabic parts, and where you can, put down full names instead of initials."

He left Olu hunched over the notes, and when he returned nearly two hours later with his wife, the man was still at it. His wife proved to be a practical, unflappable woman with good command of English, who seemed relieved that her husband was out of the line of fire.

"I didn't want him helping Monsieur Zidane in the first place," she said in her musical Haitian accent. "It didn't seem right to spy on kids. But Olu is too kind-hearted for his own good, and he didn't want to upset Monsieur Zidane."

Although neither had mentioned it, Matthew supposed the money had been useful, too. While she unpacked their few belongings, Olu finished the final pages. Excitedly, Matthew flipped through them. Unlike Zidane, Olu's handwriting was neat and formal, as if the lost art of penmanship had been important at his school.

Much of the material meant nothing to Matthew and read like one day in the life of your typical teens. Remarks about who had been seen talking to whom, drug deals in the back corridors, girls taking off their hijabs in the washrooms, kids sneaking off campus together, arguments between and about boys, brothers spying on their sisters. Most of the students were Muslim, but not all. Some, like Luc and a kid called Michel, hung around on the fringes of the Muslim group, intrigued by Islam and fired up by the conflict in the Middle East. Zidane expressed occasional worry about what he called their obsession with religion, but he seemed more concerned about coercion and bullying, especially of the girls.

In the more recent entries, however, Zidane began to note the development of secretive cliques who met up with non-students or former students just off campus, and who shunned outsiders and skipped out on classes. Faisel al-Karim was at the centre of such a clique, along with the student named Michel, whose name cropped up frequently. Michel, it seemed, was from a large French Canadian family, and the only red flags Zidane noted were two recent deaths in the family — his mother from breast cancer and his older brother from suicide.

As Matthew continued reading, his blood chilled at the flurry of notes. *Tawhid al-Karim on campus? Back from Iraq?*

Meeting with Yasmina! Zidane exclaimed with harsh pen. *Too friendly!* Later. *Abdul looking for Yasmina, shouting with Tawhid. Luc watching from bushes.*

And the last entry, dated the evening before the group left on the camping trip. *Tawhid here again today, looking for Luc. I'm very afraid they are planning something big!*

Matthew paged back through the notes with mounting frustration. They felt like fragments of some invisible whole that shifted and shimmered just out of focus. The central player appeared to be Tawhid, back from Iraq and trying to build up connections on campus. Yasmina seemed involved with him over her brother's objections, and poor Luc, always on the fringes, was drawn to her. Why had Tawhid been looking for Luc that last day? Had he found him? Had they set up a place and time to meet in the wilderness? Was Luc committed to jihad or just eager to get into Yasmina's pants? Radicalism had been fuelled by less, as Matthew knew from his own embarrassing foray into student radicalism years earlier.

He turned back to Olu. "Were Luc and Tawhid al-Karim friends? Have you seen them together?"

Olu looked doubtful. "In the beginning, maybe. But they fight. Tawhid like Yasmina too."

"But Tawhid was looking for Luc that last day."

"I remember that was strange. It was evening, maybe seven o'clock, he drive in parking lot. He parks at end and stays in car. Faisel comes to the car. I try to hear, because this is my kids and Tawhid is bad. They talk about Luc. Where is he? Tawhid is mad that Faisel not know. He shouts in Arabic. He talk about a traitor, he says you were supposed to watch him. We're too close now, he said. Then they grow quiet, maybe they see me."

You were supposed to watch him, Matthew thought. *What the hell does that mean? Protecting Yasmina? And who was the traitor?*

He faced Olu squarely. "Olu, talk to me. The man you saw walking away from the shed after Zidane was killed — was that Tawhid?"

Olu met his gaze, inscrutable. "The man's face was hidden. He wear long coat like a woman. He was tall like Tawhid, but I cannot say."

The man's words said one thing, but his eyes another. He was smart enough to know that if he implicated Tawhid on the basis of a vague glimpse at night, the defence lawyers would demolish his evidence in seconds, leaving him open to a jihadi bullet in the back.

But the eyes were enough for Matthew. Tawhid al-Karim had been on the run when he met his brother in the coffee shop on the morning of Zidane's death. Faisel had packed up his things and given him a car to get out of town. By now, Tawhid was either back in Iraq, or even more frightening, up at the terrorist camp planning something big.

Nodding his understanding, Matthew leaned closer. "And is he Abu Osama?"

"Abu Osama is a lie, Monsieur Zidane said. A fiction."

CHAPTER TWENTY-FOUR

The little cabin felt claustrophobic, and as the siege continued, Sechrest grew restless. She wasn't a trained tactical unit officer, Chris realized, but an intelligence officer used to operating in the shadows, making connections and following her nose. Probably because of that, she had argued that she be allowed to keep Yasmina with her for the duration of the operation, in the hopes of getting information out of her. So far without success. Sporadic exchanges of gunfire echoed across the clearing, more posturing than serious war. The jihadists were going nowhere, Yasmina wasn't talking, and a standoff of sorts had settled over the compound.

Chris, who was used to hours — indeed, days — of nothing much happening in his rural outposts, was trying to be patient, but fears kept buzzing around in his head. Where was Amanda? Was she safe, or was she strapped to a booby-trapped bomb somewhere inside the farmhouse?

Sechrest's radio crackled. It was the tactical commander requesting a briefing out back of the barn in five minutes. Sechrest signed off and looked from Yasmina to Chris and his pathetic deer rifle.

"Are you trained on a C8?"

"Absolutely," he lied. "In my previous posting up north, we didn't have any resources but ourselves." That much at least was true.

"I'll get you one. You watch the prisoner while I get new orders."

She disappeared out the door and returned a minute later with the carbine. Chris cradled it in his arms as he'd seen in the training videos, hoping that the mere presence of the menacing weapon would be enough to dissuade Yasmina from any thought of rebellion. Once Sechrest went back outside, Yasmina sized him up from her perch on the bottom bunk. Did she have to look so damn calm, he wondered, as if she were holding all the cards?

"Yasmina, where's Amanda?" he asked gently. "Where's Luc?"

She didn't answer. Her very silence was a challenge.

"Whatever fight you have, whatever grievances you have, Amanda is not part of them. You know that. Amanda is one of the good guys."

"Good guys die all the time," she countered. "Look at Syria. Iraq. Hospitals bombed, school children killed."

He knew he wouldn't win on her turf, so he tried to keep the focus on Amanda. "Amanda has been working all her life to help the innocent. She never got involved in any wars, no matter who was fighting who; she just tried to help the children. We need people like her in the world." He almost added *We have enough warriors*, but he stopped himself.

"You think she's an angel?" Yasmina said. "Meddling in other people's lives — other people's countries — instead of fixing her own?"

"That's what she's doing right now. Working with young people, the hope of our future, reaching out to build bridges among you."

"Nine kids, while millions are suffering in Iraq and Syria from Western bombs."

"It's a start. It's what she can do."

"It's what she *wants* to do. It makes her feel good, like donating a hundred dollars to the Red Cross while your government sends bombs to kill us."

He knew he was being sucked into her battle despite his efforts. "Amanda was trying to help you," he said lamely.

"Do we need her help? Us poor little immigrant children? Can we not think for ourselves?"

His anger sparked. "You could have refused to go."

"Amanda gets off on helping us," she snapped. "Don't fool yourself. It makes her feel important. Needed. In control. She does it for herself, not us, because she can't face going back to Africa, but she needs to feel that power again. She's not alive without it. She has no purpose without it."

He groped for a response. In his silence, she read weakness and leaned forward. "You know I'm right. She told me herself, she has nothing else. Deep down, her life is empty. She moves from place to place with no place to call home. She doesn't talk to her parents; she has no one to love and who loves her. She *needs* us. Everyone needs to belong somewhere, and everyone needs a purpose. She does these good deeds to give her life meaning. We all find our own meaning. Why are you a cop?"

He tried to let her words wash over him. He knew he should stop her or divert her, but perhaps as long as she was talking, she might give away something useful. "I don't disagree," he said.

"Being a cop makes you feel powerful," she said as if he hadn't spoken. "Useful. You're solving the world's problems and keeping people safe. But have you got a place to call home? Have you got someone to love?"

He thought of his childhood home back in hardscrabble rural Saskatchewan, where he and his sisters had lived by the rhythm of nature. Spring planting, summer watering, fall harvesting. Long, hard days with searing sun, relentless wind, and constant dust. Squabbling and laughing and gathering around the table for food at the end of the day.

The farm was gone, sold when all the children had rejected the hardscrabble life for greater opportunities elsewhere and his parents had moved to a condo in the city. During his twelve years in the RCMP, he'd moved from posting to posting, never buying a home or putting down roots, making friends only to leave them. Occasionally finding lovers, only to leave them too. Promises to stay in touch fading as time and distance grew.

She broke the silence. "Where is your family?"

"All over." He cleared his throat. "Regina, Vancouver, New York."

"You see, that's wrong. Being a cop — helping people, doing these little activities — that's just a band-aid. We're all the same. We need a place to belong and a way to live that is fulfilling. And that's what's wrong with Western society. No one belongs. People buy bigger and fancier houses, trying to get into the best neighbourhoods, but they are not homes. They are not roots. And their jobs — chasing promotions and sales and new clients — they are meaningless. The West has lost its way. Its soul."

The argument was not new to him, nor to the social scientists he'd studied at university, but sitting in the cabin in the semidarkness, with a battle of world views going on just outside the door, it felt intensely personal for the first time. He *was* lonely. He did know he'd lost his roots. He tried to make up for that loss by being the best damn cop he could be and by keeping in touch with old friends like Liam McIntyre, but on dark nights, sometimes it was not enough. He thought about Amanda — about the spark that had ignited between them six months ago, vibrant and hopeful and scary as hell — and how they had both let it fade. A dozen times on those dark nights, he'd thought of picking up the phone, but instead he'd stayed wrapped in his familiar, solitary cocoon. Was Amanda the same? Safe in her loneliness? Afraid to shed it and risk losing all?

In the gloom, he saw Yasmina's eyes upon him, quiet and gentle. He didn't want to leave her the last word, nor debate how very wrong it was, but he sensed it would be pointless to argue. Beneath her façade of sympathy and perceptiveness, the woman was a fanatic. She had an answer to this existential crisis, and it was rooted in a return to an ancient, brutal tyranny. A single path to fulfillment, or death.

Instead, he stepped toward the door and opened it a crack to see outside. The sun was on the rise, flooding the clearing and casting the trees in long shadows. The acrid smell of gunpowder filled his nostrils. What was the Emergency Response Team planning? What were the jihadists holed up in the farmhouse planning? He should have been grilling Yasmina about that instead of being sucked into her philosophy of life.

As he contemplated the stone farmhouse and the little log cabins scattered around the perimeter, fragments of information fell into place. The local farmer, Yves Stremski, his farm up north, and his failed attempt to build a hunting and fishing lodge. The brutal attack that had left him dead.

"Who owns this place?" he asked her. When she didn't answer, he pressed on. "It was the dead farmer, wasn't it? Killed because he knew too much."

She shrugged. "The innocent die all the time."

"Who killed him?"

"Who isn't important. We are one."

Fucking riddles, he thought. "How many are in the farmhouse?"

"It doesn't matter. Numbers don't matter."

"A dozen? Two dozen?"

"Eight."

"What are they waiting for?"

Unexpectedly, she hesitated. "You will see."

"Are they waiting for us to attack? The longer they wait, the more firepower we bring in. They can't win, you know. Even if they kill a couple of us, they will be captured or killed in the end."

"There are different ways of winning."

Anger flared within him. She sounded so calm and sure of herself, as if death was a mere stepping stone. But Amanda might be in there, and he was damned if he were going to let them kill her too because they all wanted a martyr's death.

He peered around the clearing. It looked empty, but he knew the ERT teams were hidden, waiting for orders to move in. They knew Amanda could be in there, but would that be enough to restrain them? Belatedly, he remembered his sat phone in his jacket pocket. He'd silenced it earlier in the interests of stealth but now realized perhaps Amanda had been trying to reach him. Perhaps she was safe and trying to tell him crucial information.

He turned it on and scanned the full screen of alerts. None from Amanda but half a dozen missed calls from Matthew Goderich.

Almost instantly, Matthew picked up. "Yeah?"

"It's me," Chris said.

"Chris! About fucking time! Where are you?"

"North."

Silence. "Oh. Can you talk?"

"No."

"Okay, just listen. All hell is breaking loose."

A burst of gunfire spat up the snow nearby. Chris ducked back inside the cabin. *No kidding*, he thought.

In a rush, Matthew told him about the college custodian, the notebook Zidane had kept, and the students he'd been spying on. Chris glanced at Yasmina, who was watching him intently.

"Who were they?"

"Yasmina, the al-Karim brothers, Luc, Hassan, and some others who are just first names."

"You have it?"

There was a silence, as if Matthew were deciphering the request. "No, I gave it to my friend in the Montreal police. It will go up the line, because the feds are running the Zidane murder investigation."

"Good."

"But there's more. Zidane knew about the camp up north and about something big being planned. Unfortunately no details, but I think the attack is in Canada rather than overseas. And soon."

Chris thought back to the date of Yasmina's airline ticket, now only a week away. Was it the escape route after the attack? "What else?"

"The terrorists are not one big happy family. They are fighting among themselves. Tawhid doesn't trust Luc, and Yasmina has been avoiding him." Matthew chuckled. "Not very martyr like of them, but I'm not sure it's just plain, old-fashioned jealousy. They seem suspicious there's a traitor in their ranks."

Chris tightened his grip on the phone and glanced at Yasmina. He was tempted to repeat the word aloud to rattle her but decided to bide his time. "Who?"

"Again, no details. But there is one last piece of intel. My custodian contact said something interesting. He said Zidane claimed that Abu Osama was a lie."

"What the hell does that mean?"

"No clue. *Fiction* is the word Zidane used. But it raises interesting possibilities, doesn't it?"

A fiction! Chris turned the word over in his mind. As in not a real person? Or someone who is not what they appear to be? A trick?

"That's very interesting," he said aloud, turning back to give Yasmina a challenging look. Signing off, he walked toward her and sat on a stool nearby, keeping his rifle ready and a wary eye out for sudden movement.

"The police in Montreal, Yasmina. They know many things, including the big attack you have planned."

"*Plus ça change,*" she replied with a shrug.

"They also know that Abu Osama is a lie." He let the word float, hoping her reaction would shed further light.

"He is not a lie."

"People can pretend to be all kinds of things on the Internet," he said. "Pedophiles can pretend to be twelve-year-old girls, married men can be suitors. People are forming a relationship with a lie."

"What matters is the relationship."

"Have you ever met him in person?"

She smiled. "There can be power in mystery. Abu Osama is the unity of the group. He connects us. He understands how confused and powerless and unappreciated we feel." Her eyes glinted in the darkness, and her voice shook. "He gives us hope. He shows us the path out of the darkness."

Chris felt a flare of frustration. She was spouting indoctrinated bullshit. "Not everyone," he said. "There is a traitor in your midst."

She blinked. A spasm of surprise passed over her face before she could stop it, but she said nothing.

"Someone doesn't believe your dream of jihad. Someone is working against you. Right this moment they could be inside the farmhouse, setting a trap. Helping the police." As the words left his lips, a random phrase Sechrest had mentioned tumbled into place. She had been rattling off all the research and planning that had gone into this raid. Cyber intelligence, surveillance …

And undercover intel. The RCMP had someone on the inside! An undercover operative or an informant.

He studied Yasmina through new eyes. She was calm and collected. A smart, educated, and until recently, westernized young woman who'd been dreaming of a career in international human rights law. Had she truly been converted to jihad? Could she really believe the ISIS propaganda that her divine calling was to be a warrior's wife? Could she ever accept that role?

He leaned forward and lowered his voice. "I don't need to know everything," he said. "But where's Amanda? Is she safe, or is she in the farmhouse?"

Yasmina's expression didn't flicker.

"You know the way this will end. With everyone arrested or blown up. Either way, their big plan is over. So you can tell me. We're alone. Is Amanda safe?"

She smoothed her skirt in an infuriating gesture of nonchalance. What would it take to move this woman!

"The plan is unfolding as it should."

CHAPTER TWENTY-FIVE

Amanda drove as fast as she dared, yet the occasional flash in the distance told her the vehicle was still behind her. Black, she thought. A minivan or a large SUV with tinted windows. She couldn't make out the shapes inside. Who were they? Why were they tailing her? Biding their time for the right moment to attack or making sure she did as she was told? *Don't stop for anything!* Yasmina had said. What would they do to her if she stopped at the hospital in L'Annonciation?

As she neared the village, she slewed around a corner too quickly, slamming Luc against the truck door. He moaned and stirred. She glanced at him and touched his arm. "Sorry."

His eyes fluttered open, and he ran his tongue over his lips. She reached for her water bottle, and, with one hand wrestling the steering wheel, she tilted the bottle to his lips. Most of it dribbled down his chin, but he managed a few sips. A faint nod of thanks.

The hospital appeared up ahead on the right. She glanced in her mirror. The road behind her shimmered golden in the dawning sun, and in the distance, a windshield caught the light. *Bastards!* Luc didn't seem as bad as she'd first feared, and if he was reviving, it might be safer to continue on to Ottawa as ordered.

The hospital blurred by. She passed through town and took the entrance ramp onto the main highway to Mont Tremblant, all the while offering Luc small sips of water. He seemed to sleep between drinks, but she sensed some strength returning. She slipped her fingers around his wrist. His pulse was stronger too. At her touch, he opened his eyes and blinked at the road ahead.

"What's going on?"

"We're on the highway on our way to Ottawa."

Kaylee nuzzled his elbow, and he looked at her in surprise. He raised his eyes, which were bleary but focused.

"Amanda?"

Relief flooded her. "Do you know who you are?"

He nodded. "What happened?"

"I followed you to the training camp. Yasmina put us in the truck and told me to take you to hospital in Ottawa."

"Yasmina did that?"

She heard the surprise in his voice. "Yes. Why?"

He shrugged, but the movement made him gasp in pain. "I just … don't … understand."

"What happened, Luc? Who stabbed you?"

He was silent. When his eyes drifted closed, she thought she had lost him again, until he spoke. "I tried to talk her out of it. I wanted her safe. I told her it wasn't going to end well. She got very upset. She said I was a traitor, and she couldn't let me ruin everything."

"Ruin what? What are they planning? Were they making bombs?"

He nodded, looking profoundly sad and weary. "For February twentieth."

"What's on February twentieth?"

"It doesn't matter. Yasmina said I betrayed them, so they had to change their plans."

She felt a chill. "To what?"

"I don't know." He lapsed into sleep. She coaxed more water into him and then fed some chocolate-covered raisins into his mouth. He needed an energy boost. When had he last had any food?

He roused enough to chew the raisins slowly. "They wanted a big bang on the first big celebration of Canada's one hundred and fiftieth birthday."

Her thoughts raced. This year was the 150th anniversary of Canadian Confederation, and she knew most of the country was planning huge pageants and parties throughout the year. Most would be in the more hospitable spring and summer months, culminating in big birthday bashes on July 1st, but surely the terrorists wouldn't begin training in February for an attack in July. February 20th made sense, perhaps during a winter carnival of some sort.

"Where?" she snapped. He drifted again. She was so freaked out that she almost missed the exit for the highway to Ottawa and had to wrench the wheel sharply. Tires squealed, and Luc cried out in pain.

"Luc, where?" she repeated. As she passed the sign on the new highway, dread shot through her. "Ottawa?" He nodded. "I heard them make a joke when they thought I was unconscious. It'll be a St. Valentine's Day massacre, they said."

St. Valentine's Day. February 14th. She counted the days. "That's today!"

"Too late," he murmured.

"But where in Ottawa? And when?"

Tears leaked out his eyes. "I don't know. I don't know. I never wanted any of this. I'm just a kid. I just wanted to be a kid."

"How did you even get involved in this, Luc? What were you thinking!"

"Our society is so fucked-up. We worship empty-headed, narcissistic celebrities. We pay guys millions of dollars just to hit a puck while people starve in the streets. I just wanted something better."

"But this is no answer, Luc. It's a con. They'll use you for propaganda videos and cannon fodder on the front lines. That's what they do with naïve, untrained recruits."

He just hung his head. She backed off, for now was not the time to climb on her soapbox about manipulative cults. She trained her eye on her rear-view mirror. There was a steady stream of cars in the other direction on the two-lane highway, but traffic headed south was light because there was nothing but small villages, farms, and forest between here and Ottawa.

A light winked behind her. There it was, far in the distance, hanging back behind curves. The same fucking car! She was now pretty sure it was an SUV, mud-covered, and, in her imagination, radiating menace. She entered the small village of Saint-Émile-de-Suffolk, rounded a curve, and slowed to a crawl. With any luck, it would look as if she was merely obeying the speed limit.

As she hoped, the SUV was almost upon her before it came around the curve and spotted her. It dropped back, but not before she caught a glimpse through the tinted windows of two figures in the front seat. She floored the gas.

"What is it?" Luc asked, jolted awake.

"We're being followed. Do you recognize that black SUV?"

He peered in his side mirror. "Looks like a Ford."

"We have to alert the cops, Luc. If you're right about the bombing plans, we're running out of time." A thought occurred to her. In her experience, big black SUVs with tinted windows were either drug dealers or cops. She had alerted Chris at the stone house. Could the cops have mobilized that fast? "Could that be the cops tailing us?"

"Maybe. But it could be *them*, following us."

"I have to get to a phone."

"No! If it's them and we stop, they'll kill us."

She fed the truck more gas and watched the speedometer needle climb. Sylvie's old truck rocketed down the highway, its suspension swaying dangerously.

"We can't outrun them!" Luc cried, clinging to the overhead strap. "Not in this junk heap."

"I'm not trying to outrun them, although that would be a bonus. I'm trying to get a speeding ticket."

"Are you kidding? They'll blow the whole lot of us up! Cop car and all."

"How, Luc? How can they blow us up?"

"I don't know. Rocket-launched grenade or something? These guys were practising with some serious shit."

"Well, then," she said, picking up the notebook beside her, "we'd better get our asses to Ottawa before time runs out. See if you can open this up. It's supposed to go to the head of CSIS, but if it contains the where and how of the attack …"

Luc turned the notebook over and examined the small padlock. "Where did you get this?"

"Yasmina gave it to me."

"Yasmina?" He frowned. "I don't understand. Was she …? Could she have listened to me after all? I've never seen her so angry. She tried to *kill* me!"

Amanda glanced at the notebook, which Luc was just beginning to pry open. A final piece of the puzzle fell into place. Why them? And why Director Blair? "Fuck!" she cried, snatching the notebook away. "Don't!"

Luc jerked his hand back as if burned. She laid the notebook gingerly in her lap. "This is a set-up. We're nothing but a human bomb. It's a classic terrorist tactic! This notebook is rigged to blow up somehow — maybe when it's opened, maybe on a timer or a remote control — but you can bet it was meant to destroy not only us but the head of CSIS and possibly half the communications hub at CSIS headquarters."

Luc's eyes bulged. "But it's ... minuscule!"

She slowed to go through another village, which lay peaceful and sleepy in the sunshine, oblivious to the danger. "I'm not an explosives expert, but there are lots of high-powered explosives on the black market. The plastic explosive Semtex, for example, can be bought if you have the money, which ISIS does. But a competent chemist can also make a bomb from stuff you buy at the local store, like hydrogen peroxide and acetone, boiled to make TATP, which is all the rage in jihadi circles. Do you think your group has the know-how to make a bomb like that?"

He nodded. He was the colour of paste, and he was beginning to shake. Part of her felt sorry for the eighteen-year-old kid who'd wandered in way over his head, but part of her felt cold rage.

"There's these two guys from the University of Montreal. One's in chemical engineering, the other's in electrical. Abu Osama worked hard to sign them up." He swallowed. "I thought ... I thought they were working on remote-controlled car bombs."

Amanda remembered the bags of fertilizer and diesel oil in the shed. It took a large quantity to make an effective bomb, but a car packed with the stuff could work wonders, and it wasn't as likely as TATP to blow up in your hands. The challenge was to detonate it at precisely the right instant.

Her next thought stopped her cold. A car bomb. The two of them were already a human bomb intended for CSIS, but what if there was a backup in case that failed? Yasmina had told her not to stop for anything. Amanda had assumed it was because of the urgency of the message, but what if it was to make sure she went directly to Blair? And if she didn't — if she somehow figured out it was a trap — the whole truck could be blown up somewhere in downtown Ottawa, where the carnage would be spectacular.

She lowered the rear-view mirror to see into the truck bed but could make out nothing but the tops of boxes. Had the truck been empty when she and Sylvie left it, or had it still been full of supplies? Damn it, she couldn't remember!

"Luc, can you turn around to see what's in the back of the truck?"

With grunts of pain, he twisted around and struggled to rise in his seat. Sweat broke out on his face, and the panic in his eyes told her he grasped the implication. "It's a bunch of plastic bins, like workers hold their tools and shit in."

Her blood ran cold. There had been no plastic bins in Sylvie's truck, only duffel bags, food barrels, and camping supplies. Luc read her silence. "We're sitting on a bomb, aren't we?" He quavered.

"I think so, and I think those guys behind us are keeping us on track."

"Two bombs. Fuck! We're dead!"

She readjusted her mirror to study the road behind. The buggers were still there, not even bothering to hide now. "Somehow …" She fought to keep her voice calm. "We have to get out of this truck."

"How?"

She glanced around at the countryside of scattered farms interspersed with clumps of forest that could provide cover. She knew that soon they would be turning onto the major controlled-access highway from Montreal, making it almost impossible to slip onto a small side road. "We'll take one of these little roads as soon as we get out of sight. Then we jump out of the truck. Are you up to that?"

"We can't! The minute we turn off, they'll blow us up!"

"Not if we're fast enough."

"And even if we do escape, where are we going to hide? They'll find us in minutes, and they've got AK-47s!"

"That's a chance we'll have to take. We've got no choice!"

"We do. We could keep going, the way they want us to. Maybe lose them in the city."

"I'm not driving a truck full of explosives into the middle of Ottawa, Luc. We'd kill hundreds."

"But maybe we can signal ..."

They passed a little road on the right, and she felt her anger spike. "Which side are you on, anyway?"

"Yours! Yours!" The word came out as a sob.

"I'm going to do my damnedest to keep us alive, so pay attention. Open your window. The moment I see the opportunity, I'm going to take the truck off the road and you're going to throw that thing out the window. When I yell jump, get the hell out and get as far away as you can to find cover. Got it?"

He bobbed his head, struggling to stem his tears. She had no time for panic or tears. She had a job to do. "Do up your jacket and put on your hat and mitts. We don't know how long we'll be outside. I will try to slow the truck as much as I can, but hit the ground rolling. The snow should cushion your fall."

She pulled on her own gloves and snapped on Kaylee's leash. For a couple of tense miles, they drove through open country, and she began to slow the truck almost imperceptibly. Behind her, the black menace dropped back. Up ahead, the road entered a hilly forest and disappeared around a bend. She prayed there was a road, even a little overgrown lane, beyond that bend. Her heart hammered, and her hands grew slick from gripping the wheel.

"Be ready."

The road curved. The trees swallowed them from view. And miraculously up ahead, a roadside mailbox marked a lane that dropped down a steep wooded slope. She jerked the wheel and the truck slewed sideways, broadsiding the mailbox and rocking wildly. She fought to stay on the road.

"Throw it!"

Luc tossed the notebook like a Frisbee, aiming for the road behind them. It arced far into the air, but she had no time to wonder where it landed. They had mere seconds to get the truck out of sight and themselves out of the truck. Bracing herself for an explosion, she floored the accelerator. Spitting snow and gravel, the truck plunged down the slope and around a hairpin turn.

"Jump!"

His hand on the door handle, Luc froze. She reached across him and thrust open his door. Without a moment's hesitation, she shoved him out with her foot. He gave a little cry as he disappeared from view. The truck was picking up speed. Spinning around, she grabbed Kaylee's leash, slammed open her door, and hurled them both out. Praying the truck would carry on. Praying that Kaylee wouldn't get caught under the wheels.

She hit the snow with a head-splitting thud. Pain shot through her side, and she couldn't catch a breath. She lay a moment, feeling the icy chill seep through her clothes and knowing she had to get up. To run.

A warm nose nuzzled her cheek and a wagging tail thumped against her arm. Relief flooded her as she sank her hands into the silky red fur. She raised her head to look for Luc just as two explosions ripped through the silence. A blast of wind flattened her, snow swirled, and the earth shook beneath her. Smoke and flying bits of trees, truck, and slush flew through the air. And all around her, the roar of fires igniting.

I didn't think about fires, she thought, staggering to her feet. Luckily, the smoke and debris provided cover as she scrambled in search of Luc. If the bad guys were looking for them, that would slow them down. Her eyes burned and streamed with tears, her lungs screamed with pain. Coughing, she pulled her scarf over her nose. No use. No use. Where was he? She squinted through the smoke. No sign of their pursuers either, and the roar of the fires obliterated all shouts for help. The heat was melting the snow, churning up mud and slush.

It was Kaylee who found him lying at the bottom of a gully, face down in the slush. She slithered down to his side and eased him onto his back. So silent and still! But breathing! As she probed his body for injuries, he opened his eyes.

"I'm alive," he mumbled, "but I think I'm bleeding again."

The fires were slowly dying down, extinguished by the melting snow and the sodden trees. Amanda was just rigging up a stretcher from broken pine boughs when, over the hiss and sputter of the flames, she hear the distant roar of an engine. Panic gripped her until she registered that it was a different kind of engine and coming from the opposite direction.

"*Allô?*" a deep voice bellowed. "*Y'a quelqu'un?*"

Leaving Luc's side, she stumbled toward the sound, shouting as loud as her raw, scorched lungs could. A moment later a snowmobile emerged through the haze, and a small, wiry old man leaped off. He was missing several front teeth and all of his hair, and Amanda stifled a giddy laugh when he opened his mouth to speak in the most indecipherable colloquial French she'd ever heard. Nothing had ever sounded as sweet.

He introduced himself as Paul Ménard, and she was able to make out that he lived on the farm next door, and the explosions had even knocked the dishes off his shelf. He had already phoned 911, and the cops and firefighters were on their way. But then, he shrugged with Gallic skepticism, it might be a while. It's not Montreal here, he said. I will take the boy back to my house.

Amanda could hear other people shouting and other engines rumbling, and through the smoky haze, she could see shapes and movement in the distance. Other helpful neighbours, or killers? She suppressed her fear as they wrestled Luc onto the back of the snowmobile, and then Paul Ménard bellowed, "*Par icite!*" This way.

"Sh-h!" Amanda whispered. "Don't yell! There are bad guys after us. They blew up my truck. We have to get out of here fast!"

Paul recoiled. "Bad guys?"

"I'll explain later, once the cops come. But for now ..." She gestured to Luc. "Please help him."

The man took no more persuading. Revving his snowmobile, he lurched forward around rocks and shattered tree stumps. Amanda limped along in his wake, suddenly aware of every bruise and gash on her body. His clapboard farmhouse sat on the top of a gentle rise, surrounded by rolling fields, its steeply pitched roof silhouetted against the grey sky. Like the barn and outbuildings that clustered around it, nature and time had worn it down.

By the time Amanda finally reached it, Paul had settled Luc on the sofa, wrapped him in a warm blanket, and a neighbour was brewing tea. Seconds later, the first of the emergency responders was screaming down the lane, a baby-faced kid from the local Sûreté du Québec who knew Paul and his neighbours well. Everyone spoke in rapid, animated French. Amanda had grown used to all kinds of regional dialects in her years overseas, but this rural *Joual* was nearly impenetrable. She could tell only that they were describing the explosion, the fires, and their rescue.

Amanda watched the young officer's floundering response. *The poor kid is way out of his depth*, she thought. Within less than a minute he was radioing for backup. From the crackling radio response, Amanda determined that an ambulance and volunteer fire crews from two neighbouring villages were on their way, but that additional police backup might take a while. The dispatcher appeared to be telling the young man to take statements.

Amanda gestured to the radio. "I need to talk to her. The explosions were terrorist bombs, and they are planning a bombing in Ottawa."

The officer stared at her in disbelief. He had already signed off and immediately fell back on his training. *Establish calm, obtain identification....*

Amanda supplied her name and address. "I have no ID because ..." She broke off. Where the hell was her wallet anyway? "My wallet is missing."

"You were driving the truck without documents, madame?"

"Yes, but that's not important. This is an emergency."

"Was it your truck?"

"No, but—"

He gestured to Luc. "His?"

"No!" Amanda breathed in. She knew she must look like a madwoman — wide-eyed and soot-covered, her jacket shredded and her face bloodied. She marshalled her thoughts. "I know it sounds crazy, but it's a national security emergency. You must let me speak to your top boss! I rescued this young man from a terrorist camp and we were on our way to see Director Blair at CSIS headquarters when our truck blew up, and ..." Her voice trailed off. It sounded ludicrous, even to her, and the officer had taken a step backward, as if afraid she might erupt into madness any second. He blinked and glanced over at Luc, who nodded weakly.

The neighbours added their own sharp urgency, and the young officer edged toward the door. "One moment. I will make the call from my vehicle." With those words, he scurried out the door. No doubt he'd be checking her name and her police record, as well as Luc's, and perhaps any corroboration of terrorist activity, but she hoped he would at least relay her story up the line. Even with the notorious turf guarding, surely some agents in the higher echelons of the SQ, the RCMP, and the security services were talking to each other.

When he returned, however, he was even more tight-lipped and cryptic than ever. "I am going to speak to the firefighters. Two more officers will be here in five minutes, and they will take your full statement."

"But did you speak—"

"Be patient, madame. Paul, perhaps a little brandy?"

He disappeared back out the door. *Brandy, my ass*, Amanda fumed. Squinting out the window at the trucks parked willy-nilly in the yard, she spotted one advertising Ménard snow removal and landscaping in peeling French letters on the door. It was old and rusty but possibly in drivable shape. She swung on the hapless farmer, who looked sympathetic but wary. No wonder. He'd seen the bomb devastation, but he'd also heard her crazy story.

"May I borrow your truck? Luc can give them our statement, but I—"

Paul was shaking his head wildly. A laugh bubbled up in her throat. Adrenaline was still pumping through her, tipping her toward the brink of hysteria. "I won't blow it up. And I'll stay in communication. Do you have a cellphone I can borrow?"

Still he shook his head.

"Amanda, no." Luc spoke up, his voice hoarse from smoke.

"Luc, you'll be safe here. We've notified the authorities, but it may not be soon enough. There's no time to waste. There was a black Ford chasing us, and if it didn't stop to check on us, it will be in Ottawa within an hour! If I have to drive onto Parliament Hill itself, at least I will alert the RCMP!"

It was, she realized, the first semirational argument she had given. Without another word, Paul picked up a cellphone from the table in the hall, plucked a jacket from a peg, and held both out to her.

"The keys are in the truck."

CHAPTER TWENTY-SIX

Chris's toes were turning numb with cold. Shifting the C8 to his other shoulder, he stamped his feet. This endless waiting was killing him. At least Sechrest got to move around when she went outside to confer with other team leaders. As the morning wore on, the clearing outside was warming in the sun, but the cabin remained damp and dark. Yasmina was shivering, and despite the threadbare blanket he'd wrapped around her, she kept rubbing her hands and feet. He wondered whether the cuffs were too right.

Peering through the half-open cabin door, Chris could see no signs of activity, but from the constant growl of heavy machinery and the thump of helicopters overhead, he knew plans were afoot. At one point he spotted a tiny surveillance drone flying low over the farmhouse.

At ten o'clock Sechrest reappeared. "Any change in the prisoner?"

Since Chris's earlier, unsettling conversation with her, Yasmina had remained steadfastly silent. "No, but she's cold," he said.

"Tough titty."

Still hoping to reach Yasmina and soften her up, Chris pressed the point. "I think the cuffs may be cutting off her circulation. Can we take off the ankle cuffs so she can move around?"

Sechrest seemed to weigh the idea. "Do what you want. We wouldn't want the media accusing us of cruel and unusual punishment."

Without a word of thanks, Yasmina paced the small space, stamping her feet.

"Maybe a heater?" Chris added.

Sechrest blew out a puff of air in dismissal. Frustrated, Chris drew her over toward the door. "What's happening? What's the holdup?"

"Nothing. We're waiting them out."

"But all this air power and what sounds like tanks. Are we preparing for war?"

"ERT brought in a couple of LAVs as a precaution. But until something changes, it's a waiting game. It's not worth putting officers at risk."

"But Amanda Doucette might be in there!"

"All the more reason to bide our time, if we want her out alive." Sechrest glanced at Yasmina and drew Chris outside. "One of our guys is monitoring Twitter. These bastards love the spotlight, so if they had Amanda, they'd probably have plastered her photo all over social media by now."

Chris shuddered. Like everyone, he'd seen the brutal photos of ISIS hostages. He also knew how shattering any threat or assault would be to Amanda's fragile psyche. Rage rose in his throat. If they did anything to harm a single hair on her head, he'd storm the farmhouse personally.

"Can the drone detect anything?"

Sechrest gestured to the farmhouse, which was solid stone with a metal roof. Tendrils of smoke from the firefight still drifted around it, but it looked serene in the sunlight. "I doubt it. Nothing goes through walls like that. We need eyes inside, and it's not worth disturbing the status quo."

"Can our mics pick up any conversation?"

Sechrest nodded. "The walls are two-foot-thick stone, so we only get snippets. A jumble of English, French, and Arabic. These kids are mostly Canadian-born, raised in Montreal. When they're not arguing about the Qur'an, they spend most of their time on social media. They seem to be waiting for something."

"What?"

"Word. Orders. Who knows? They've posted a couple of warnings about how our time is coming. They're also tracking news of this operation, which, thanks to the lid we have on it, is minimal. They're not too happy about that. Good propaganda potential going to waste."

Chris mulled over the information. "I don't like the sound of it. It feels like we're waiting for the other shoe to drop. *They're* waiting."

"I agree. We're all waiting. But they probably know we're listening in, so they're just feeding us what they want us to know. Nothing about their actual plans. Nothing about booby traps or suicide vests in the farmhouse either."

Chris sent out a probe. "I think this camp belongs to that local farmer who was killed."

Sechrest remained poker-faced. "Did the prisoner tell you that?"

"Not outright, but in so many words. She implied he was expendable."

Sechrest glanced at the closed cabin door and raised her voice marginally, as if intending Yasmina to hear. "The Montreal lab got DNA from his fingernail scrapings. The analysis is top priority, so we'll know soon enough who killed him. We've also connected him to the al-Karims. He did some construction work for al-Karim Senior in Montreal last summer. All above board, but his bank shows an additional large paycheque in September. Six thousand, much more than his wages as a roofer." She grimaced. "Poor bugger sold himself cheap. He probably didn't know what he was getting himself into."

When Chris marched back inside, he found Yasmina listening by the door, as Sechrest had hoped. She gave him an amused smile. "That farmer liked the idea of blowing up a few *têtes carrées*, as he called the English."

"Was that your plan?" he asked. "This brave army of eight? To blow up some English?"

She didn't answer. Instead, she looked through the doorway into the clearing. "You will not defeat us with airplanes and tanks and a hundred men."

"Ultimately we will. We have all the time in the world."

"So do we. Another lifetime."

"Maybe your friends are not so sure of that as you. Maybe they are afraid of death."

Yasmina shrugged. "It is but a stop on the journey. We welcome it."

"It's not so easy when death stares you in the face, Yasmina. Believe me, I know. It's programmed in our very DNA to fight for our life."

From behind him, Sechrest pitched in. "These are Canadian kids, Yasmina, not hardened by war and loss. We've got their mothers and their girlfriends and their imams coming up here to talk to them. You think they'll hold fast?"

Yasmina rolled her eyes. "They know their families have lost their way, and the imams have been corrupted. They know there is glory, not shame or defeat, in death. That's why you won't defeat them."

Sechrest's voice grew hard. "Then why are they cowering inside, hiding from the enemy instead of coming out to face us?"

"You are too late, all of you, with your war toys and your tricks. None of it matters."

The cabin door opened behind them, shooting a shaft of sunlight into the room. Yasmina flinched. It was the ERT commander, who gestured to Sechrest. "We've got an SQ officer on the line. He says there's a guy named Luc who wants to speak to you."

Paul Ménard's truck was worse than Sylvie's. The steering had a mind of its own, threatening to toss her into the ditch at every turn, and the shocks bottomed out on every pothole. Black smoke spewed from its exhaust. When Amanda tried to push it above eighty kilometres an hour, it shook like an old man with palsy, and she was afraid every bolt would fall off.

Once she hit the main highway, she forced it to its limit. She didn't care if it fell apart on her completely, as long as it got her to Ottawa first. She'd happily spring for a new truck for the bewildered farmer in exchange for saving countless lives. Sylvie was already getting a new truck. She giggled at the thought of striking a deal for two trucks. Maybe three. Maybe she'd get herself one as well, to complement her motorcycle.

From the moment she'd left the Ménard farm, she'd tried to think of whom to call. She hadn't much faith in the clumsy bureaucracy of police forces, and although she assumed the SQ would eventually get her concerns to the right people, it might be too late. Chris was the only one she trusted to connect the dots and mobilize the right people quickly, but she didn't know his sat phone number. In fact, there were almost no numbers she knew by heart.

Except one.

As soon as she was on the straighter, smoother main highway and no longer had to devote both hands and all her wits to keeping the truck on the road, she fished out Paul Ménard's ancient flip phone. No bells, no whistles, but it worked! Matthew's familiar smoke and whisky-ravaged voice answered after the first ring.

"Amanda!" he shrieked the instant he heard her voice. "Holy fuck! Where the hell are you?"

She suppressed a giggle of relief. She really needed food and maybe a decent sleep. "I'm on my way to Ottawa, in a truck worthy of our days in Cambodia. Matthew, you have to help me. Do you have Chris's number?"

"Yes, why?"

"I think the terrorists are about to blow up a location in Ottawa, and I need someone to take it seriously. The SQ thinks I'm Looney Tunes."

"Wait, wait, you mean our merry band of terrorists from Montreal?"

"Yes."

"Well, the cops have them all pinned down in their camp in the Laurentians."

"Not all of them. At least two of them tried to blow up Luc and me in a truck an hour ago—"

"Holy jumpin' fuck!"

She hit a bump and fought the truck back into line. "Matthew, listen! Luc says their target is somewhere in Ottawa. They've got sophisticated bombs, which could be in a backpack, purse, or even something as small as a book."

"What's the target?"

"I don't know, Matthew! I'm on the highway in the middle of nowhere in a death trap of a truck, with no Internet and nothing but a ten-year-old flip phone! I need the RCMP, the military, the fucking CIA, I don't care!"

"Okay, okay. Let me handle it. What exactly did Luc say?"

She sucked in a deep, calming breath. "He said his group had been planning something big for February twentieth — a bomb that would hit at the heart of the nation on its one hundred and fiftieth anniversary — but when they thought he was an informant—"

"*What?*"

"Never mind! I don't know if it's true, but it doesn't matter. They changed their plans. Bumped the date up to Valentine's Day. Today."

"February twentieth," Matthew was muttering. "Celebration in Ottawa."

"What are you doing?"

"Googling it. Fucking miracle, this Google." There was a pause, and she forced herself to be calm. To wait. Around her, the midday traffic was light but steady, and impatient Quebec drivers piled up behind her rattling truck.

"Oh my God," Matthew exclaimed. "February twentieth is the final day of Winterlude — that's Ottawa's big winter festival. The prime minister is scheduled to speak at noon, along with other big shots, a live band ..."

Amanda had been to plenty of Winterlude festivities during her childhood. Her family had lived in the trendy downtown neighbourhood of the Glebe, a short walk to the famous Rideau Canal skating rink, and she had grown up skating its seven-kilometre length, eating the delectable BeaverTail pastries, and marvelling at the intricate ice sculptures in the park. "That's it! That's the big bang. Where is the prime minister supposed to speak?"

"At Confederation Park, where the ice sculptures are. Hang on, I'm Google-mapping it. It's right downtown on the edge of the canal, opposite City Hall and between the two main downtown bridges over the canal."

"Bridges!" Fear shot down her spine. "If they blow those up, they paralyze downtown and kill everyone gathered in Confederation Park, as well as everyone skating on the canal underneath."

"Do they have a bomb big enough?"

"Multiple bombs, Matthew! Hidden in everyday places like backpacks. It's as easy as leaving a backpack propped against the base of the bridge." She glanced at her watch. It was an hour before noon. "Even today there will be people skating on that canal, enjoying their lunch hour, families with their kids, people looking at the ice sculptures. I have to tell Chris!"

"I will tell Chris," Matthew said. "You concentrate on getting yourself safe."

"But—"

"Amanda, let me do this. I've got the Internet search and mapping capability. You said there were two men?"

"I think so. I only got a glimpse, but they're driving a big black SUV."

A brief silence. "What make?"

"Luc said it was a Ford."

"Licence plate?"

"It must be Quebec, no front licence plate. But the truck's covered in mud."

"It's the al-Karim brothers."

"Al-Karim? The kid who dropped out of my group?"

"And a lot more," Matthew said. "I've got photos of them. I'll contact Chris right away and tell him you're out of harm's way."

"I have to keep going, Matthew. I have to get to Ottawa and warn anyone and everyone about the danger."

"Amanda ..."

"I'll grab the first Mountie I see, I promise, but I'm not stopping until I'm sure the fucking bastards have been stopped."

Yasmina sat still. Unnaturally still, Chris thought as he paced the small cabin, waiting for Sechrest to return. He did try once to draw her out by asking if she knew anything about Luc's whereabouts. He was met with stony silence.

Sechrest burst back into the cabin fifteen minutes later, with a bounce in her step and a glint of triumph in her eye. "Well, well, well. It's over, young lady. Luc is safe, Amanda is safe, and the two bombs you planted on them have just blown a few dozen trees into the next province."

Yasmina had obviously steeled herself for this news, for she merely smiled. But relief slammed Chris with a force that nearly knocked him off his feet. He shouted aloud. "Where is she? They, I mean!"

"They were en route to Ottawa. Luc is now headed to hospital in Gatineau, and he didn't say where Amanda was. But Luc was able to supply a lot of intel on the group's plans." She glanced pointedly at Yasmina. "And the ERT Commander is on the phone to Ottawa as we speak, mounting a response."

"What plans?" Chris asked.

"Do you want to tell him, darling, or shall I?"

Yasmina said nothing, as pale and icy as marble.

"Never mind, it's all in hand," Sechrest said, beckoning Chris toward the door. Outside, her triumphant act vanished and tension tightened her voice. "We don't actually know the details. The cockroaches had targeted the Winterlude closing ceremonies on February twentieth, but they must have discovered, at least suspected, that Luc was an informant …"

Chris managed to hide his astonishment with an effort. For an intelligence officer, Sechrest was being remarkably chatty, and he wanted to keep it that way. "I heard you might have a man inside," he said. "I thought it was Yasmina, since Luc wanted her out of the way. But the way she's been acting …"

"Oh no, she has all the boys wrapped around her little finger. She's deadly, that one. But Luc's behaviour tipped her off, and the silly boy was captured the moment he arrived at the camp. Then the group moved their plans up. The only thing he heard of the discussions was a lot of arguing and the phrase 'St. Valentine's Day massacre.' That's all we've got to go on."

Chris's phone rang. After glancing at it, he sent it to voicemail. Matthew's news might be important, but Sechrest's took priority.

"But Valentine's Day is today."

His phone rang again. With a curse, he picked up.

"Don't hang up on me again!" Matthew cried. "Amanda called. I've got news!"

Chris listened as Matthew summarized his conversation with Amanda and the results of his Google searches. "It's the al-Karim boys! In that black SUV! The ones I sent you the photos of. They're headed to Ottawa. I'm guessing same time and place as their original February twentieth plan."

"Why?"

"Well, I'm not a spook, but it makes sense. They've got no time to make new plans and scout new locations. This plan will still bring a lot of destruction to the downtown core and to the festival, even without the PM."

"Okay, let me pass this on and get those photos out to the field. Give me Amanda's number so we can talk to her directly."

"Well, that's the other thing. She's going to Ottawa. She's determined to stop this, even if it means going into the belly of the beast."

"Oh, for fuck's sake, Matthew!" Fury crashed over him on a wave of fear. "Goddamn the woman! Is she trying to get herself killed?"

"I don't know, Chris."

His tone, so quiet and sober, stopped Chris's fury in its tracks. Was there an element of desperation in Amanda? Not a wish to die, but an urge to stare death defiantly in the eye, over and over, as if to confirm that she could beat it? Did she need that adrenaline rush to soothe the restless drive inside?

"What's her number?" he demanded. "This is bigger than her goddamn need to fix the world. Hundreds of lives are at stake!"

Chris repeated the number aloud several times as he hung up and began to search his phone. Sechrest had been standing at his side, her expression tense and expectant. "Hang on," he said to her. "I'll give you the whole story in a minute, but we have an ID on the suspects. I'm sending you photos of them and their vehicle."

He located the photos and forwarded them to Sechrest's phone. "The suspects are Tawhid and Faisel al-Karim. Matthew Goderich has done some background checking, and he thinks they'll use the same target and time as in the original plan. Two downtown Ottawa bridges at noon. It's a good guess."

Sechrest was already moving away, so focused on her phone that she didn't even react to Matthew's name. "I'll pass this on. Keep an eye on our black widow there."

Chris stepped back inside the cabin. Yasmina hadn't moved, but he thought she looked even paler. *It's crumbling all around you, sweetheart*, he thought, shifting his rifle so he could use his phone. He was about to punch in the number he had memorized when the phone rang. He picked up, praying it was Amanda.

The stranger's voice was barely audible. "Corporal Tymko?"

"Who's this?"

Hesitation. "Abdul."

"Abdul?" Chris frowned as he rifled through his memory.

"Yasmina's brother. Mr. Goderich gave me this number. You're the police?"

The memory fell into place. Matthew thought Yasmina's brother might know more about the al-Karim brothers and the identity of Abu Osama than he let on. "I'm Corporal Tymko. Are you calling about the al-Karims?"

"No." A pause. "About Abu Osama."

"What about Abu Osama?" He glanced at Yasmina. Her eyes were wide and her lips curled back.

"It's her." Abdul spoke as if dragging the words from the bottom of his soul. "Yasmina is Abu Osama."

Without warning, Yasmina leaped to her feet and charged him, slamming him and his rifle aside as she rushed outside. Her black robes swirled and her voice rose in an unearthly scream. Before he could regain his footing and run outside, he heard shouts and a burst of gunfire.

Shit, he thought, as he watched the stain of red spread across the snow.

The thirty seconds of shouting and gunfire lasted an eternity. A volley from the farmhouse and a staccato burst of return fire from the police as three officers rushed into the clearing to drag the crumpled black form to safety. It had taken all of Chris's self-control not to run out there himself. From the cabin, he watched with a sick, heavy heart as they wrapped her in a blanket and carried her off to the first aid tent.

Minutes later, Sechrest burst through the cabin door. "What the fuck did you do?" she shrieked. "I told you to guard her!"

He had no answer. No excuse. Except that he had let his guard down. He'd thought of her as a young woman — misguided, but full of ideals and passion — and he'd forgotten she was one of the bad guys.

Sechrest waited exactly two seconds for the answer he couldn't find before she unleashed her next volley. "Now she's part of their propaganda war! They're already posting photos of her all over fucking Twitter! There will be a video next."

"Is she dead?"

"Yes, she's dead. She's got half a dozen bullet holes in her." Sechrest paced. "Goddamn! The CO is madder than a swarm of hornets. We don't even know who pulled the trigger — one of ours who got too eager, or one of theirs who saw the chance for a propaganda coup. Either way, they're blaming us and calling for all-out war against Canada. Goddamn it, Tymko! We were making some headway on de-escalating the situation, and with one stupid move, you've blown it all to hell."

"I know," he said quietly. He'd finally found an answer, half-assed but all he had. "I was distracted by a phone call from her brother. He told me she was Abu Osama."

"She was *what?*"

"The recruiter who probably got most of these kids into the cell."

"Ridiculous. Abu Osama is an ISIS warrior from Iraq."

"Have you got confirmation on that?"

She paused and shook her head as if to banish the idea. "A woman would never hold that kind of position."

"But what if they didn't know she was a woman? She only communicated over the Internet. You can be anybody on the Internet."

She scowled. "She'd have to be damn good."

He thought of his earlier conversation with Yasmina. Of her soft, persuasive voice and her uncanny feel for the heart of his need. He felt a heavy sadness. The girl could have accomplished great things. "She was. Do you think Luc knew?"

"That's one of the questions I'll be asking the stupid kid when I lay my hands on him. But meanwhile, thanks to you, we've got a real mess to clean up!"

CHAPTER TWENTY-SEVEN

The traffic picked up as Amanda neared the city of Gatineau, and she jockeyed to get into the proper lane for the bridge across the river to Ottawa. But long before the exit ramp, she spotted a huge backup of cars and flashing lights in the distance. Hemmed in on all sides, she crawled along toward the lights. The truck's radio was long dead, and the cellphone had no Internet capability, but she was eventually able to see what the holdup was. The bridge access was blocked off, and a cranky, reluctant line of cars was being funnelled into one lane toward downtown Gatineau.

As she passed the blockade, she craned her neck south for a glimpse of the bridge. There was no traffic on the Ottawa-bound side except for a scattering of police vehicles, but a steady stream of cars poured across the bridge out of the capital. She heaved a sigh of relief and for the first time relaxed her death grip on the steering wheel. Her warnings had been heeded. The downtown core of Ottawa was being blocked off and evacuated.

The detour eventually dumped her onto Maisonneuve Boulevard, where more cops were scrambling into position to keep the flow moving. She wanted to get as close to the river as possible to see what was happening on the Ottawa side.

Ducking left at the first cross street, she hit another traffic jam as the police blocked the second bridge ahead. A no-nonsense cop directed her left onto Laurier Street. The striking curves and pale glistening stone of the Canadian Museum of History loomed ahead. A stunning architectural jewel designed by renowned Canadian architect Douglas Cardinal, it was set amid acres of parkland that sloped down to the river. Perched on top of a high bluff across the river were the lacy Gothic spires of Parliament Hill. Overhead, the sky was filled with the thrum of helicopters, but the iconic structure looked deceptively peaceful in the brittle winter sun.

As part of the general evacuation of the waterfront, museum patrons were being herded out the front door and across the street. The noisy crowds provided good cover, so with a quick check in her rear-view mirror, Amanda pulled the truck off onto what appeared to be a service road that skirted behind the museum. From that vantage point she should have a view down the slope to the water's edge and across the river to Ottawa.

As she drove around behind the museum, craning her neck to study the shoreline, she glimpsed the nose of a vehicle tucked under the interprovincial bridge. She slammed on the brakes. She'd seen that menacing grill before! She jumped out of the truck to alert a police officer, but they were all busy directing traffic and arguing with angry motorists. Taking Kaylee, she slithered down the slope to the base of the bridge. As the whole vehicle came into view, tucked against the steel girders, she lost all doubt. It was the same muddy black hood and the same tinted windows, now streaked with soot.

She approached cautiously and laid her hand on the hood. Despite the cold temperature, it was still warm. She looked inside. Empty. She walked around it, wiping off the soot and cupping her hands to see in the back. Rectangular shapes. She peered closer. Plastic bins exactly like those in Sylvie's truck.

She recoiled, her heart in her throat, and then raced back up the slope to find a Gatineau police officer inspecting her truck.

"There's a car bomb!" she cried, grabbing his arm. "Down under the bridge. They're going to blow up the bridge!"

The officer froze. His hand shot to his holster. "Step away, madame. Is this your truck?"

Amanda backed up, realizing how she and Kaylee must look. Soot-covered, scratched, and desperate. "Yes. I mean no. I'm Amanda Doucette, the woman who first alerted you to this attack. That's their truck down there."

The officer dropped his hand, looking bewildered. "Some identification, Madame Doucette?"

"I'm sorry, I have none. Please believe me! Call your supervisor."

"First, show me this vehicle."

She knew they were wasting precious time, but fortunately, as soon as the officer saw the SUV and checked it against his alerts, he immediately radioed in a report. Within minutes the grounds were swarming with cops rushing to establish a wide perimeter and bring in the experts.

In all the drama, Amanda was forgotten. She stood on the riverbank, trying to think what the al-Karim brothers were up to. Once they found their bridge access to Ottawa blocked, the brothers had probably improvised. She doubted the car bomb would bring down the entire bridge, but it would create a spectacular distraction and keep the cops busy while the brothers worked on a Plan B.

Luc had said they would have backpacks or suicide vests, and she doubted they'd hesitate to detonate them once they found a worthy target. Or if anyone tried to stop them.

Where would they go? What would be a worthy target? The Canadian Museum of History was one possibility. It was a jewel in Canada's crown, a symbol of the nation's achievements.

But on the bluff across the river stood the worthiest target of all. Parliament Hill. Even if casualties were few, the propaganda value of destroying the heart of Canada would be irresistible.

But the brothers were on foot, and the bridges were all blocked. To reach it, they would have to cross the Ottawa River, wide and deep at this point, and even in February, a torrent of frigid, fast-moving water. To attempt a crossing would be suicidal.

Yet their whole mission was suicidal. For them, success might be worth the risk of dying.

Below the museum, a windswept parkland of trees and open space sloped down to the water's edge. It was snow-covered, but she could make out a shore path heading west. Kaylee was standing at attention, her head up and her gaze focused down the path. Behind them, Amanda could hear the shouts and crackling radios of the officers as they fanned out to search the museum grounds. She wondered whether they had called in snipers or tracking dogs, but the manpower and equipment looked pretty sparse. The police had had so little time to mount a response, and their containment and evacuation of downtown Ottawa would have required masses of personnel.

No one stopped them as she and Kaylee walked along the deserted riverbank trail. She scanned the rushing water and the shoreline opposite, where a thin ribbon of pathway ran alongside the river beneath the nearly vertical limestone cliffs of Parliament Hill. Trees clung miraculously to the cliffside, providing some camouflage, but surely no one could climb far without being seen.

Kaylee tugged on the leash, her ears pricked and a soft whine bubbling in her throat. Amanda followed her gaze. Farther upstream, the river narrowed and an island sat in the middle, slicing the river into two channels. Amanda squinted. The island was mostly snow and trees, but the gaping remnants of an old stone mill occupied the middle, and a tall totem pole commanded the tip.

On this side of the river, an imposing cliff loomed over the water up ahead. Two figures stood on the top of the cliff, silhouetted black against the snow as they peered across at the island. Her breath caught. She looked around for the police. None. Should she go for help? Call 911? While she groped for her phone, the figures disappeared into the trees on the other side of the bluff. She scrambled to close the gap, leaving the path and fighting through the steep brush down toward the riverbank.

When she emerged from the trees, she was almost upon them. She yanked Kaylee back behind the cover of a pine tree. The two men were dressed like typical Canadians, with parkas, toques, backpacks, and skates over their shoulders, but beneath the toque and scarf she recognized Faisel's young, pinched face. She had met him once during an orientation session — a thin, wan-looking boy — and had thought a week in Canada's wilderness would bring some colour to his cheeks. The memory gave her a pang of sorrow.

The two were standing on the bank, staring across at the island. Ice formed delicate crystalline sculptures along the shoreline and out into the channel. The distance across was deceptively short, perhaps a hundred metres, but in the middle the water churned cold and fast.

They put one foot on the ice and jumped back in a comic dance of uncertainty. Their voices clashed in argument, Faisel afraid, Tawhid determined. They looked up and down the bank in search of better options, and their gaze locked on her. She shrank back, her fingers fumbling for 911. About fifty metres lay between them, and she didn't like her chances if they chose to detonate their backpack bombs.

Faisel's eyes widened in recognition. He whispered to his brother. For a long moment, no one moved. Behind her, she heard shouts and sirens, the whap-whap-whap of helicopter blades, but down here on the river, it felt almost disconnected. Serene.

The brothers turned toward the river and stepped cautiously back out onto the ice. The ice held, emboldening them.

Amanda watched in horrified fascination. It was possible, with a well-placed foot, strong swimming skills, and a great deal of luck, for them to make it to the island. And with even more luck, from the island to the other side. To Parliament Hill.

Instead she watched, mesmerized, as they took one step and then another. The fools stuck together, holding on to each other, concentrating their weight on the fragile pieces of ice under their feet. The ice teetered, and one foot sank through to the ankle. They lurched the other way, scrambling for balance, dancing over the crumbling ice in an increasingly manic effort to stay upright.

They were halfway to the island when the ice gave way, plunging them into the frigid current. Amanda gasped as if the shock of the cold water had hit her too. They began to swim, flailing their arms inexpertly toward the island's shore. So tantalizingly close and yet impossibly far.

From above she heard shouts and looked up to see the dark shapes of police officers racing down to the shore. They skidded to a stop at the water's edge, bellowing into their radios, helpless to do more. The al-Karims thrashed about, inching closer to the island. They didn't call for help or scream in panic. The cold had taken their breath away.

Paul Ménard's phone rang in her hand, jarring her so much she nearly dropped it.

"Amanda! Thank God!" Chris's shriek nearly broke her eardrum when she answered it. "Where the hell are you?"

"In Gatineau."

"Are you all right?"

"Everything is under control. The city is in lockdown."

"Yasmina is dead. We don't yet know who shot her, although they are blaming us. They've blasted a photo of her body all over Twitter, demanding revenge. She's fodder for their propaganda war now."

Yasmina, that bright, passionate chimera of a girl framed against the sunset, seemed very far away. Amanda watched as one of the brothers slipped beneath the surface. He bobbed back up, thrashing, only to sink again. The current was carrying them both beyond the tip of the island.

"What are you doing?" Chris asked.

"I'm watching the al-Karim brothers drown in the Ottawa River in an ill-advised attempt to swim across to Parliament Hill."

"Jesus." Silence on the line. Then a cautious "Amanda? Are you all right?"

The second brother, Tawhid, she thought, tried to reach for a chunk of ice, only to have his arms fall uselessly short. She knew she should feel horror, even sorrow, at the sight of young lives snuffed out. She knew she should feel something.

"I'm all right," she said. "Kaylee and I are safe on shore. I know a thing or two the al-Karim brothers don't about the power of a Canadian winter."

CHAPTER TWENTY-EIGHT

By the time Amanda had been checked out by paramedics and answered all the endless police questions, she wanted nothing more than to crash in a hotel and sleep for a week. But Matthew had driven up from Montreal with a bag of take-out curry, a bottle of Scotch, and an offer to take her back to her aunt's cottage. The thought of her cozy retreat, far from the news cameras and suspicious police eyes, sounded like heaven.

Darkness had fallen by the time they arrived at the cottage. They fed a ravenous Kaylee, lit a fire, and curled up in front of the flickering flames to enjoy their meal.

Matthew looked drawn and exhausted. He had stripped down to his undershirt, but his bald head was shiny with sweat. She knew it was getting too hot in the cottage, thanks to the logs she kept piling into the woodstove, but she couldn't seem to get warm. She felt as if she'd been cold for days, and she couldn't shake the image of the icy Ottawa River from her mind.

"I would have been there earlier," he said, "but I had to make sure the college custodian and his wife were safe. We don't know how many more of these radicalized bastards are hiding in the woodwork, and he knows too many secrets for his own good. They got Zidane; they'd get him too."

"Who killed Zidane?"

"My money's on Tawhid al-Karim. He was spotted lurking near Zidane's office shortly before the murder. He was arguing on his cellphone, and my custodian friend said Zidane was also arguing on his phone just before he went into the shed where he was killed."

She picked at her food. "I didn't actually like the guy, but his heart was in the right place. The cops said he was working on deradicalization, so I hope they can cobble together enough evidence to identify the killer. Although it doesn't sound as if Tawhid was calling the shots, at least not alone."

"Yasmina?"

She nodded. "God, I run halfway around the world to escape these fanatics, only to find them in my own backyard. In the most innocent of guises."

Matthew studied her. She knew he was worried about her state of mind. "I'm okay, Matthew."

He nodded. "I also wanted to talk to Abdul and his family."

"Poor Abdul. I'm sure this wasn't easy for him."

"That doesn't begin to describe it. His parents are furious with him. They think if he hadn't kept so much from them, they could have helped her and changed her mind."

"I'm sure he thought he could stop her himself," she said, "but this was far bigger than him. Her whole world view had shifted, and he had become the other."

"Tawhid al-Karim was his friend. Yasmina was his sister. He blames himself for them getting together in the first place. He thought it was an innocent attraction between two intelligent people. While they were all taking this religion course in Cairo, they naturally hung out together, and Abdul didn't realize until too late what a radical turn they had taken. At first he even thought Tawhid might make a good brother-in-law someday. Tawhid was always very respectful of Yasmina; he talked about the purity and holiness of their love. When they started talking about fulfilling their divine purpose, Abdul says he should have seen what lay behind their words — a fanatical, single-minded obsession that would lead directly to jihad. Once he realized it, he brought her back to Canada, hoping the obsession would fade, but it was too late. With the Internet, distance means nothing. Tawhid went on to train with ISIS in Iraq, and Yasmina carried out her part to get recruits for the global jihad."

"How did Abdul learn about Abu Osama?"

"She was trying to recruit some of his engineering friends at the university, and one of them warned him. So he started following her and breaking into her computer. At first he thought Tawhid was Abu Osama and she was under his spell. It was a shock to discover it was the other way around. *She* was the recruiter, and her web was far larger than just Tawhid. She played the dual identity masterfully. Even Abdul could barely believe she was the charismatic warrior who promised a glorious new Islamic world. To him, part of her will always be his little sister, whom he couldn't save."

"So the woman exerts her control even from the grave." Amanda leaned back, profoundly weary from her ordeal. Every muscle and joint ached, despite the double dose of painkillers she'd been prescribed. "Their poor families. Not just Abdul, but his mother and father, and the whole Muslim community. More prejudice, more distrust, just when they're trying to build a new life over here. They live with enough stigma over here as it is." Sorrow washed over her. "Losing their daughter will be bad enough, but everything they worked for …"

"And the al-Karims lost two sons," Matthew said. "I wonder how they will handle it. Will it moderate their own views?"

"Maybe, but I wouldn't count on it," she said bitterly. "Father will likely frame their deaths as martyrdom. Easier than changing his whole understanding of the world."

Matthew merely grunted, and they lapsed into silence. It felt as if they'd been going around and around in circles. The cottage was a sauna, the take-out cartons lay discarded, and the Scotch bottle was almost empty. Kaylee was curled at Amanda's feet, fast asleep.

After a while, Amanda voiced the question that had been on her mind all along. "Why hasn't Chris called?"

"Probably delayed up at the camp. It's been a helluva day up there, and he probably has to repeat his story to every new bigwig who arrives. He's in deep shit over Yasmina."

"He wasn't the only one who let his guard down with her. I did. Luc did. She had a way."

"I know, but I doubt that makes him feel any better. Have you spoken to Luc since he went to hospital?"

She shook her head and tilted it to let the Scotch slide down her throat. "They won't let me anywhere near him yet, so I'll give it a couple of days. But he's going to be okay, as is Sylvie, so at least some good came out of this disastrous day."

"You mean besides Parliament not getting blown up?"

She chuckled. "I hope we have enough funds in our bank account to cover two new trucks. Some people went above and beyond all call of duty to help me."

"We're floating in money. Although if word gets around about what happens on your adventure tours ..."

She didn't smile. Instead, she stood up, gripped by sudden anger, and began to clear the clutter of dishes and empty food containers. The RCMP had used her to get an informant close to the action, and in the process not only ruined the experience she was trying to give, but also put the kids' lives at risk.

"It's outrageous that the RCMP recruited Luc in the first place," she said. "What the hell were they thinking! The kid's barely eighteen years old!"

"As were most of the kids in the terrorist cell," Matthew added. "That was the point. Luc was in place, he already knew many of them, and he was flirting with their ideology. The RCMP saw their chance."

"To what? Make him an offer he couldn't refuse?"

Matthew inclined his head. "I talked briefly to his mother. She thinks they coerced him. Either work with us, or we'll lay charges. He'd already been to jail, and he couldn't face that again. A sensitive, geeky kid like him in with tough guys and wannabe Al Capones?"

Amanda thought back to Luc's tearful lament in the truck. "I think he didn't want any part of it. I think he just wanted to be a kid again."

He cocked his head in thought. "I bet that's why he begged his father for the five thousand dollars. He wanted out, and he probably tried to take Yasmina with him. That may be what tipped her off. Poor kid didn't know that five thousand would barely cover a month in some jungle in South America, let alone a lifetime."

Headlights played across the interior of the cottage, and Kaylee leaped to her feet, ready to guard the homestead. A moment later a car door slammed, boots crunched over snow, and then silence. Amanda had rushed toward the door, but now she frowned. She opened the door cautiously to find Chris propped against the doorframe as if that were all that was holding him up.

She took him into her arms, pressed against his chest, and breathed in the scent of him. Relief and longing spread through her. After a moment, aware of Kaylee clamouring for attention and Matthew watching, she detached herself.

"I needed that," she murmured.

"Did you?"

She blinked. "You look done in. We saved you some curry."

"I'd rather have some of that Scotch."

Seconds later he was ensconced in the chair nearest the fire, his boots and jacket off and the last of the Scotch in his hand.

"Are you allowed to talk about it?" Amanda asked. "Can you tell us what happened at the camp today?"

"I don't give a fuck if I'm allowed to talk about it or not. I've been dicked around by the security forces more than I care to think. Sechrest used me. She was running Luc, and when things started to go south, she signed up for my French course just so she could keep tabs. She knew we were all friends. And Luc's computer? I never told them Matthew had it, but she guessed."

"So it was the RCMP who stole it?" Matthew asked.

Chris nodded. "They're the ones who gave it to him, for his jihadi communications. They had to get it back before you compromised the whole operation. All part of National Security's fucking paranoia." He took a deep breath. "So you'll hear this official statement tomorrow. Due to the skill and patience of the Integrated National Security Enforcement Team, a cell of homegrown terrorists was dismantled with only two losses of life. One was a young woman who died in the crossfire — and we're awaiting autopsy and forensics results to determine whose weapon caused the fatal injury — and the other was a young man who took his own life upon witnessing the death of the young woman. The remaining six subsequently surrendered to police without incident."

Amanda smiled at him sympathetically. "That's a victory of sorts, Chris."

"You could say that." Chris sighed. "Although Yasmina's death was preventable, as was the young man who shot himself in the farmhouse. Michel Roy, just a lonely French-Canadian kid from Rivière du Loup who'd never been to the Middle East in his life. Barely heard of the Qur'an before Abu Osama started crooning in his ear." He drank his Scotch. "Two young lives."

Amanda leaned forward to touch his hand. "That's a choice they made. Yasmina chose to run into the line of fire."

He nodded. "I know. In fact, I think she welcomed it. As her small part in the glorious war. I think she hoped her martyrdom would inspire the others to take up the fight. It could have been the start of something ugly if the al-Karims had succeeded in their mission. As it was, their deaths — not in a hail of enemy bullets but from drowning in the river — took all the fight out of the group."

"They knew about the drownings? So quickly?"

For the first time, a ghost of a smile softened Chris's face. "On Twitter. As Sandy Sechrest said, two can play this Twitter game."

She watched him a moment as the firelight played over his dark curls, his crinkly eyes, and his comical ski-jump nose. He looked done in, bitter and betrayed. "What a day we've had," she murmured.

He met her gaze. The silence lengthened. Matthew roused himself and staggered to his feet. "I'll get some more firewood," he muttered, grabbing his jacket off the chair.

Watching him leave, Amanda forced a smile. "Matthew Goderich going out to chop wood? Stop the presses!"

"I think he knows we need to talk."

"Do we?"

"I almost didn't come."

She dropped her gaze, dreading what was coming.

"I don't know if I can do this," he said. "Amanda, why do you do these things?"

"I don't choose these things. They choose me."

"But you charge ahead, blind and deaf to caution, when you could get yourself killed!"

"What would you prefer me to do, Chris? Not help people when they're in trouble? Not try to stop something bad from happening?"

"But even once the police were notified and were responding, you still charged ahead, as if no one but you could possibly save the day."

She jerked back, stung by his words. "But I didn't know the police were on top of it, and in fact they weren't! If I hadn't spotted that SUV under the bridge—"

"But it's a pattern, Amanda. It's like you always have to prove something to yourself."

"Prove what, Chris? What do you think I have to prove?"

He gave a weak gesture, as if apologizing in advance. "That you can beat death? That death is your own personal enemy?"

She sat back, astounded at the thought. She knew she felt guilty for surviving when the Nigerian school children in her care had not. A year of therapy had taught her that. She knew she felt a need for atonement and redemption, and she knew this charity tour was partly that. But death as her own personal enemy?

She groped her way through her thoughts. "If … you're reading this as some kind of leftover from Africa, as some sort of post-traumatic saviour complex because of that ordeal, you're wrong. I've always cared about people and tried to help. That's why I went into international aid work in the first place. And if I seem driven to take on death and don't seem to worry much about risking my own life in the process … maybe it's because in the places I've worked, life is cheap and death too often wins." She paused. A profound weariness stole over her. How often had she had this conversation with the men in her life? Men who couldn't handle her passion, her commitment, and her refusal to play it safe. How she'd hoped Chris would be different.

"I'll always give my all, Chris. It's who I am."

"I know," he said, but his voice was sad. He twirled his empty Scotch glass. "But the rest of us, who have to stand on the sidelines and watch … I just don't know if I can do that."

As she fought a flash of anger, she heard footsteps on the front porch. *Bad timing, Goderich!* "Chris," she said urgently. "You're a cop. You charge into life and death situations every day. Don't ask any less of me. Don't give up on me either. At least not until you've had a good meal and a week of sleep. If you still think I'm crazy and impossible after that, then maybe …" She fought a tightness in her throat. "Maybe you're right."

CHAPTER TWENTY-NINE

Amanda was relieved to find a police guard outside Luc's private hospital room and even more relieved when he double-checked his list before letting her in. The youth's face lit up at the sight of her. Three days later, he still bore the scars of his ordeal, from his bruised face to his singed hair, but his colour was good and his gaze clear.

When she embraced him with a careful hug, he returned it fiercely. "Thank you," he murmured. "Thank you."

All her anger and accusations of the past three days evaporated, but she still had a dozen questions to ask. A dozen puzzle pieces to find. "My trip didn't go quite as I intended," was all she said, softening her words with a light smile.

His smile wavered. "I'm sorry about that. It wasn't the plan."

"What *was* the plan, Luc?"

"I'm not allowed to talk about it."

A spark of anger returned. "Then who is?"

"Probably no one." He hesitated, then straightened his shoulders as if gathering his nerve. "Fuck it. What more can they do to me? I was supposed to be sticking with Yasmina, that's all, and feeding back information. Something big was in the air. My RCMP contact — handler — never said what, just that they thought the training camp would make contact with her. They wanted its location, which they knew was up north somewhere, so when Yasmina joined your camping trip, they told me to go too. I was just supposed to watch and listen and report anything I learned."

"So what changed?"

"Yasmina. I heard her talking on the phone that first night at the outfitters' place, arranging a pickup for her and me. When I called my handler, she told me to go along with it. That freaked me out. I'd never done anything but pass along information. My handler promised they'd be tracking me every step of the way."

Amanda thought back to the mysterious snowshoe tracks at the camp. "That first night, that was you who went out into the woods?"

"To make the call. I had to climb the hill to get a signal."

"And Yasmina and you were both supposed to go?"

"Yes, but I thought she was being manipulated, and I didn't want her caught or killed. So I sneaked off to the rendezvous alone."

Amanda remembered Yasmina's outburst the morning after Luc disappeared. It hadn't been fear for his safety, as Amanda had assumed, but outrage at being left behind.

"How did you keep her from going with you?"

"I slipped a roofie into her tea the night before, while we were cleaning up." He gave a sheepish grin. "I still had a few, so I brought them along, just in case. I think Hassan saw me, because he got really mad, and when I sneaked out that night, he thought I was going to see her. I told him I was just going to the can."

That was the argument the Haitian youth Jean-Charles had overheard. "Who did you meet on the trail that night, Luc? One of the al-Karim brothers?"

He dropped his head into his hands and shook it slowly. "So many dead. What a mess. It was that farmer, Yves. He met me on an ATV. He said he was supposed to take Yasmina and me to the meeting point, that old stone church—"

"It was his old farmhouse."

"He said someone from the training camp would come to pick me up. He was upset Yasmina wasn't with me, scared he'd be in trouble, so he left me some supplies and took off again. Maybe he was ordered to go back to get Yasmina."

"Well, he never made it."

"Faisel al-Karim killed him. Sechrest just told me they fast-tracked the analysis, and his DNA was found under the poor guy's fingernails."

So both brothers had committed murder. Amanda tried to fit the last pieces of the puzzle into place. Still too many missing! "How did you meet up with Yasmina later?"

"I waited at the stone church for two nights before Yasmina suddenly showed up by herself on snowshoes."

That's a long way to travel by snowshoe, Amanda thought. "Someone must have helped her."

He sighed wearily. "Probably Tawhid al-Karim. It was always Tawhid. She must have phoned him."

"Did she have a sat phone?"

"Zidane had one. Maybe she borrowed it."

Amanda thought about the day Yasmina had begged to stay in camp, claiming a sore ankle. Zidane had insisted on staying with her. At the time Amanda had been suspicious of his motives, but now she realized he must have been suspicious of hers. Had she stolen his sat phone, or had she used her wiles to persuade him to lend it? A frisson of horror crept over her. Was that the final straw that got him killed? Yasmina, tidying up all the loose ends that might trip her up?

If so, it was a final, secret betrayal she would take to her grave.

Luc was lost in his own memories of betrayal. "She could have gotten Tawhid to kill me too, but she wanted to do it herself. She'd brought the traitor into the group, she said, so it was personal. She pretended we were going to the training camp, she let me lead, and then she stabbed me in the back. She was checking to see if I was dead when we heard a snowmobile."

"That was probably Sylvie and me."

He looked profoundly sad. "I thought it was her contact, because she took off back to the stone house."

With a sinking heart, Amanda remembered Kaylee barking at something in the shed. If only she'd heeded her dog's warning, Yasmina, and the others, might still be alive.

His eyes filled. "I didn't know what to do. My phone, my GPS, she took them all. I knew the RCMP couldn't track me, and I was the only one who knew where the training camp was. The only one who could stop them. But I knew you were coming, and I hoped you'd know what to do. Get your cop friend, maybe. So I laid a trail."

She laid a gentle hand on his arm. "It was very brave of you, Luc. But the RCMP should never, ever, have put you in that position."

He smiled wanly. "I put myself in that position. I bought their whole lie about how they were making a better world. When I realized where it was headed — to terrorism and ISIS — I reported it to the cops. I got dragged down to the station, held for questioning, released, dragged down again, accused of being part of it. It was a nightmare. Then finally Sechrest showed up. She said if I was a good Canadian, I'd want to help. I said I was scared, and she said they'd protect me. All I had to do was stay in the group and report back. And so it started. And from there ..." He gave a helpless shrug.

"Luc, did they force you?"

He looked her straight in the eye. "Just hints. Like I had to prove my loyalty if I wanted to stay off the watch lists. But the stuff I told you in the Vietnamese restaurant was true. I *did* want to prove myself."

Voices outside distracted her, but Luc seemed oblivious. He was unloading grief and guilt and anger that had been secret for months. "But these were my *friends*. They believed in their cause. And Yasmina, I thought we ..."

The door was flung open, and a large, florid man burst into the room. On his heels, the alarmed guard was unholstering his gun.

"Dad!" Luc exclaimed.

"Luc, my boy!" And to the officer, "Oh for fuck's sake, put that thing away!" Luc's father crossed the room in two strides and enveloped his son. "What a sight for sore eyes!"

The officer retreated outside to radio for advice. Rising to better meet the man eye to eye, Amanda held out her hand. "Mr. MacLean, I'm Amanda Doucette."

He crushed her hand. "Brad MacLean. Pleased to meet you, Amanda. Good work you're doing. Luc, pack your toothbrush. You're out of here."

"But I'm not going home 'til tomorrow. The cops want to make sure I'm safe."

"And I'm not relying on those morons for that. I've bought us a nice little villa in Costa Rica, under a company name so those ISIS nutjobs can't ever find you."

"Us?" Luc looked terrified.

"You and me. I sold that oversized dump in Westmount—"

"But what about Mum?"

"She's fine with it. Not happy, but fine. Anything to keep you safe. I told her she can visit, and I bought her and the wife nice little condos in downtown Montreal. Almost next door to each other." He roared with laughter.

"But … Dad … why?"

"Any kid of mine with the balls to take on ISIS deserves a second chance." He paused, and for a nanosecond, Amanda thought he might be going to apologize, but then he hefted a suitcase onto the bed. "That's all I'm going to say on the matter. Now let's see if these new clothes fit."

"I'm not sure how long that will last," Amanda said wryly to Chris. She had a lot more worries about Luc buzzing around in her head and a thousand more rants to make against the RCMP, but she knew she had to let it go. She couldn't fix everything.

He had invited her out to La Forge, an exquisite restaurant in the Alpine village at the foot of Mont Tremblant. Their table was nestled between the floor-to-ceiling stone fireplace and the picture window that opened onto a stunning view of the mountain with its floodlit runs cascading down like streamers against the night sky.

Knowing that their relationship was on fragile ground, she had dressed in her only alluring outfit, a cream silk blouse and midnight blue skirt. She had let her hair loose down her back. But sitting opposite him with the tea light shimmering between them and a half-empty bottle of New Zealand Sauvignon Blanc in a bucket beside them, she had yet to face the unspoken question between them. Instead she babbled on about Luc, his recovery, and his unexpected rapprochement with his father.

"Fathers and sons," Chris said, repositioning his knife and fork on his napkin. "It's complicated."

As are all relationships worth working for, she thought, wondering whether she dared voice it. He was strangely distant, sitting in his white, open-collared shirt and sports jacket, devoid of his usual jokes or teasing. She knew he was still wrestling with his own guilt over Yasmina, because as a cop, if he'd maintained his objectivity, Yasmina would still be alive. In fact, the whole standoff might have been defused without a single loss of life. He'd face disciplinary action for that, but she knew that wasn't what troubled him.

The dinner held an aura of farewell. It had been his idea, but she fought desperately against her sense of foreboding.

"Matthew has already started organizing the next Fun for Families trip," she said gaily. "That's his reaction to this debacle. Summer this time. Warm, peaceful, cottage country summer."

"Where?"

"I'm thinking of kayaking in Georgian Bay. Deserted little islands, shimmering bays, sunsets over the Great Lakes."

"Sounds lovely. I've never seen the Great Lakes."

She hesitated. Was that a simple statement of fact, or were there layers of meaning folded into those words? An expression of hope, the beginnings of an offer? She barely breathed as she ventured her own small response. "You're welcome to join us. Matthew would never set foot in a kayak."

"Wise man. They tip easily."

"But in the right hands ..." She met his gaze. Wordless. Then she lifted her glass and tilted it toward his ever so slightly. "Will you think about it?"

He grinned — his full, wide, crinkly grin — and tilted his own glass back at hers. "That much I can do."

ACKNOWLEDGEMENTS

Writers are often advised to write what they know, which in my case, after a couple of semi-autobiographical, navel-gazing novels mining the themes of my life, would lead to very dull fiction indeed. Instead, I choose to write about themes that excite me, disturb me, and raise a hundred questions in my mind. For me, writing is a process of exploration and discovery, which I hope will capture the reader as much as it does me. *The Trickster's Lullaby* took me on a journey far into the psychological unknown. I am indebted to the many journalists, scholars, historians, and social scientists who have tackled this compelling topic in books, newspapers, and online, among them Stewart Bell, Mark Bourrie, Farhad Khosrokhavar, Michael Weiss, Hassan Hassan, Dounia Bouzar, and others.

Where possible, I took my research on the road as well, and I would like to thank my long-time friend Elizabeth Paquette and her husband Marc for lending me their condo while I explored the roads and countryside around Mont Tremblant. A special thanks also to Dave and Kielyn Marrone of The Lure of the North wilderness tours for their expert guidance and to my friend Patricia Filteau for being crazy enough to accompany me on their winter camping snowshoe trip in the middle of February.

Once the research is done and the story written, the polishing and editing begins. As always, I am grateful for my wonderful writing friends; Linda Wiken, Mary Jane Maffini, Sue Pike, and Joan Boswell all came through with thoughtful, expert critiques, and the astute suggestions and encouragement of my editor Allister Thompson provided the final touches. I'd also like to thank Laura Boyle, who designed the spectacular cover, as well as Kirk Howard, Beth Bruder, Michelle Melski, and all the staff at Dundurn Press for continuing to support my work and that of Canadian writers.

Most of all, a huge thank-you to the booksellers, librarians, and readers everywhere for their inspiration and support.

dundurn.com
@dundurnpress
dundurnpress
dundurnpress
dundurnpress
info@dundurn.com
FIND US ON NETGALLEY & GOODREADS TOO!
DUNDURN